THE IRISH RETRIBUTION

BRUCE COOKE

BALBOA.PRESS

A DIVISION OF HAY HOUSE

Balboa Press books may be ordered through booksellers or by contacting:

Balboa Press
A Division of Hay House
1663 Liberty Drive
Bloomington, IN 47403
www.balboapress.com.au
AU TFN: 1 800 844 925 (Toll Free inside Australia)
AU Local: 0283 107 086 (+61 2 8310 7086 from outside Australia)

Print information available on the last page.

ISBN: 978-1-9822-9012-2 (sc)
ISBN: 978-1-9822-9013-9 (e)

Balboa Press rev. date: 04/01/2021

Chapter One

Belfast 1996

Sean Flynn sat in the back of the taxi twiddling with the safety catch of the Sten gun lying across his lap. He wasn't nervous as he had done this many times before, it was because he was bored waiting for his victim to appear. This one was going to give him much satisfaction as Inspector Hugh Grayson had sent many an Irishman to their grave in carrying out his so called duty. He'd been a thorn in the side of the IRA for over thirty years and now he had decided to retire. There had been notices in the newspapers and invitations had gone out to many police agencies asking them to send a representative at the retirement dinner being held in the Belfast Reception Centre. O'Rourke had given the order and he had much pleasure in carrying it out. The smell of blood always made him excited and he sat patiently in the car waiting for the evening to end. At last guests began to emerge from the entrance to the centre and Sean nodded to Michael Flannery to start the motor.

Grayson and his wife emerged and stood on the pavement accepting the well wishes of leaving guests. Sean could see some of them shake his hand and one slapped him on the back before leaving. Now alone with his wife, Grayson raised his hand for a taxi as even retiring police inspectors weren't allowed to drink and drive. Flannery eased forward and pulled up as Grayson reached for the door. Sean smiled at the look of astonishment on Grayson's face when he saw the Sten gun pointed at him.

"Congratulations and have a happy retirement Inspector," said Sean and pulled the trigger. Both Grayson and his wife staggered back as the hail of bullets cut into them. Blood and tissue flew into the air as both fell to the ground. A pool of blood quickly began to gather and started to run into the gutter as the car took off at high speed.

"Get to the changeover car as quick as you can Michael, then drive normally to the farm."

"You're telling a chicken how to lay an egg?" Flannery grinned as he turned around the corner. An hour later they pulled up outside the farmhouse and reported to O'Rourke.

"No problems?" asked O'Rourke as Sean sat down at the table.

"Smooth as a bottle of Johnny Walker. No traffic at one in the morning," said Flynn pouring himself a drink.

"Good. Now pass over the photos and I'll send them off," said O'Rourke.

Sean did as he said and watched as O'Rourke addressed the envelope.

"This should get to Australia in a week and then we might be able to take care of the remaining problem." He handed the sealed envelope back to Sean.

"First thing tomorrow take this into Belfast and post it. We should get a result soon."

* * *

Sydney. 1996

They call it Murphy's Law. If something can go wrong it will. Why they called it after an Irishman Carrie Sanderson had no idea. If she thought it had been a crappy day she had no idea of what was to come. Her fingers felt like she had calluses forming after three hours in front of the computer. Her editor Richard Harding had been at his bulldog best, yelling at her how the Sydney Tribune never missed a deadline. Then the copy boy spilt his coffee all over her computer sending the screen blank.

Who said journalism was easy? Her bloody father, that's who but it was before she announced her career choice.

"Tully Sanderson's daughter better shape up or else." Richard's bark frightened most reporters but Carrie knew that though he insisted on high standards, he had a soft spot for her. She hated it when he compared her with Tully, despite his retirement from the media world.

2

"Tully Sanderson was a legend as far as foreign correspondents are concerned," said Richard often enough. It was her cross to bear, but Jesus, bearing Tully's famous name would break anyone's shoulders.

Finally she typed the last sentence of the third story and hit the print button. Richard said she was born with skates on but even skates needed oiling after a grueling day.

At last it was time to go home. She covered her computer, looked at her watch and saw she had seven minutes to catch her train at Wynyard Station. Hurrying out of the office as fast as her long legs would carry her she dashed to the elevator. Impatiently she glanced at the numbers lighting up as it stopped on almost each floor. As she ran out onto the street, she almost slipped then looked down to see the cause of her stumble.

"Bloody hell," she muttered when she saw the dog droppings spread over her good shoes. They may have been man's best friend but there was a time and place for everything. There was a seat on the footpath and a rubbish bin nearby. Carrie found a screwed up paper bag, wiped her shoe clean, dropped the bag in the bin then continued her pursuit of the five thirty-six train. Maybe the smell would get her a seat, maybe not. Trying to force herself down the steps through the tide of people coming up she groaned as her train pulled out of the station leaving her stranded.

"The bastards won't wait for anyone will they?"

She turned to see a disgusting looking man with a cigarette hanging from his lip giving her the eye. His pot belly was overhanging the tight belt holding up his trousers and she wondered who smelt the worst, her with her shoes or him with his stained clothes and dirty face. She figured he won the contest and moved away.

The empty platform soon filled in the fifteen minutes for the next train.

While she waited, her reporter's mind was at work, always looking for a headline story. As usual it was the humdrum crowd she studied daily. She sighed; nothing extraordinary ever came her way. Carrie tried to pass the time by scanning the many faces of Sydney's commuters. A girl with green and ginger hair and a ring through her nostril stood beside a boy with spiked hair giving Carrie the impression he had been electrocuted. She giggled softly. He wore a sleeveless leather jacket and had a large tattoo on each arm. His left ear supported a brass ear- ring large enough to hang Carrie's handbag on.

At the other extreme some men wore snappy business suits carrying leather briefcases and several women looked as though they'd stepped off the cover of a magazine. Late shoppers struggled with parcels all eager to get on the train. When her train finally arrived, the disembarking passengers hurried off and the mad scramble to alight began. Surprisingly, the boy stood back allowing Carrie to board before him. She smiled, thanked him, and then found the last empty seat, settling down for the twenty-minute journey.

An elderly woman struggled to maintain her balance trying to juggle her parcels. Carrie immediately rose to offer her the seat. No sooner had she vacated it a young businessman rushed in and sat himself down.

"I got up to give this lady a seat," she said angrily.

"When there's a vacant seat it's first in," he said and started doing the crossword in the paper.

"Pig," said Carrie. "I'm sorry, Ma'am, I tried," she said apologetically to the woman.

"Its okay, love. I'm only going one stop," the lady said with a thankful smile for Carrie. She gave a disgusting glance at the young man and moved toward the exit.

Carrie fumed all the way home. The incident had not added to her already dark mood caused by the harrowing day she left behind. All she wanted was to take off her shoes, relieve her aching feet and collapse into a hot bath.

Wearily she opened the gate and hurried toward the front door of her house, her home on and off for the last six years. It was just as well she shared or the rent would have sent her to the poor house. Her share mate Stephanie Farmer took care of the garden duties, as Carrie had to admit a green thumb she didn't have. Steph on the other hand had the place looking like a picture. Fortunately there was little lawn but Steph had the pansies bursting out in a blaze of color. It was Stephanie's favorite past time and gave her immense pleasure and a little ammunition to throw at her friend when Carrie became stroppy.

The living room faced the front and had a marvelous view of the garden. The room was comfortable, cozy and again it was Stephanie's taste, which made the place very livable. Throwing her bag on the table, Carrie kicked off her shoes and gave an audible sigh. Sometimes taking your shoes off is better than sex she thought collapsing in an overstuffed the armchair.

"How was your day, Steph?" she said watching her mannerisms.

From her body language, it was obvious Stephanie had something on her mind. It was the way she kept touching the tips of her fingers together before she spoke.

It was marvelous what living for six years with a person told you about them. They were not all that alike.

Sometimes Carrie felt she was talking down to the top of Steph's head for she was at least four inches taller. What Steph lost in height was compensated by her loving caring nature. The way she flashed her brown eyes to the side without moving her head was a dead give away when she had a problem. Carrie was always jealous of her petite figure and elf like face although Carrie herself had not missed out in the feminine things that attracted men.

Carrie waited. Steph always went the roundabout route before telling her bad news. You'd think being a schoolteacher would enable her to control her habit, she thought. Steph could see the tired look on Carrie's face made worse by her disheveled long black hair

"I'm fine. You look like a bus has hit you. Hard day?"

"Sort of."

"I had some wonderful news. I've received a promotion but it's still at the same school. The staff all clapped when I was told at the staff meeting. Looks like I'll be teaching grade three next year."

"That's great, Steph. Congratulations," said Carrie enthusiastically still waiting for whatever it was that made Steph nervous.

"There's something else," Steph said.

"If you tell me the hot water's cold I'll kill you. What is it, Steph?" Carrie didn't feel like playing mind games.

"I've some news you won't like," she stated watching the expression in Carrie's blue eyes. Her eyes always reflected her feelings. They were like the sea, always changing hues.

"The water IS cold."

"No, I'm moving in with Greg. If everything works out we'll get married."

"That's not bad news, Steph. I'm happy for you."

"It means you'll be alone."

"Steph, I'm out of the country more than I'm in it. Foreign correspondents are always alone. When are you moving?" Carrie asked, her mind quickly working figures if she could afford the place by herself.

"Next week if it suits you. You're sure it's all right?"

"Of course it is. I'm a pain in the butt lately."

"It's just we've been together since University. I have a guilty conscience about leaving you alone."

"You think we'll be old maids? I know you love Greg deeply. It's a great idea."

"I made a special steak and kidney pie to sweeten you up."

"Thanks, you know by now what a lousy cook I am."

"Coffee?"

"Thanks, Steph, it's just what I need.

Carrie was halfway through her second coffee when the musical sound of the doorbell announced a visitor.

"Perhaps it's Greg," said Carrie. "You open the door."

"No, it can't be. He said he would call me tonight."

Wearily Carrie walked to the door to answer it. A young man in a uniform, a broad smile on his face, greeted her.

"Afternoon, are you Carrie Sanderson?"

"Yes," she answered wondering what he wanted.

"Special delivery. I have a letter for you. Sign here please." Thrusting a sheet of paper at her he handed her a pencil.

"What is it?"

"Dunno, lady, I just deliver the stuff."

"Where are you from?"

"Same day delivery service," he answered cheerfully shifting his wad of chewing gum from one cheek to the other as he spoke.

She glanced at the lad with distaste. He was about eighteen with long hair and a bad case of acne. The cap thrust back on his head gave him a larrikin appearance. Beanpole was her first impression. Carrie wondered how many times he hit his head on the doorframe when he walked through.

"Who sent this?"

Looking at the sheet he grinned. "Mr. John Smith. People bring things to us all the time for quick delivery. We guarantee prompt service," he said while handing her a card.

"Thanks," said Carrie and began to close the door. The boy's hand stayed extended.

"Don't I get a tip?"

"Just a minute," said Carrie while thinking about her empty wallet. She hurried to the living room. "Steph, lend me a dollar."

"Grab it out of my change jar." Stephanie looked up from her task of setting the table.

Carrie quickly gathered enough change to make a dollar and hurried back to the front door. She handed the lad the change.

"Thanks, lady, I don't suppose you'd be interested in dinner tonight?" he said with a grin followed by a huge bubble of gum.

When Carrie raised her eyebrow he tipped his hat.

"Have a good day."

While walking back into the living room and plopping into her chair, Carrie studied the envelope.

"More work?" asked Stephanie noting the frown on her friend's forehead.

"Don't know. There's a return address in Belfast on the envelope. The Shamrock Hotel."

"Who do you know in Belfast?"

"Nobody as far as I know." She turned the envelope over again.

"Only one way to find out," said Stephanie and threw the letter opener to Carrie.

Carrie slit the envelope. Someone she didn't know wanted to tell her something. Four photos fell onto the coffee table. A note was attached to the top photo.

Her interest now peaked; Carrie leaned forward and studied the contents carefully. Of the several photos, three of them were black and white and one was colored. One of a beautiful young woman, not unlike Carrie herself. She had long dark hair, finely arched eyebrows, and a soft tender face.

Her strong jaw showed a determined character but the highlight of this lovely face were her dark piercing eyes. The sort of eyes you could lose yourself in.

To her surprise the second and third photos showed her father with his arm around the woman. Of course, she would be just Tully's type. Carrie studied the couple carefully. Apparently neither of them were aware of the photographer.

Carrie picked up the envelope and turned it over to check the sender's address. Nothing but Shamrock Hotel.

Who the hell had sent me these pictures?

Carrie felt joy looking at the two pictures. The woman and a younger version of her father looked like young lovers on a leisurely stroll. They had broad smiles and were looking deeply into each other's eyes. They were obviously in love.

The pictures had an English look about them. Was that Westminster Abbey in the background? The picture evoked the romantic poems she had read about England. It looked idyllic. The woman appeared to be pregnant and happy to have Tully's arm around her. Carrie involuntarily put her hand across her belly. She realized she was the swell in the woman's womb.

The last picture shocked her. In full color she could clearly see Tully kneeling beside the woman holding her head, a head covered in blood. The side of her face and her neck were crimson with the stain flowing from a head wound.

The woman's shirt was torn and bloody and a horrible wound had almost torn her in two. Carrie shuddered. A deep feeling of doom invaded her.

What appeared to be the girl's entrails were hanging out and Tully's hands were covered in blood as he tried to push them back into the gaping wound.

Only high-powered bullets from army issue were able to cause such wounds. She'd seen similar wounds in Bosnia after snipers hit people. Tully's clothes were spattered and his face was racked with anguish. Never had she seen his face mirror so much pain.

Carrie's eyes scanned the note, it was short and to the point.

Photo one is of your mother in Belfast. Photo two and three are of your father and mother in London after the bastard made her pregnant.

Photo four was taken moments before he killed her. Her name was Briony O'Rourke and she was just nineteen years old. My name is Kevin O'Rourke. I'm your uncle and its time you knew the truth.

Carrie dropped the photo and note in disbelief as if it scalded her fingers. She couldn't believe her eyes.

He'd done some questionable things in his life but to have killed her mother was beyond comprehension. It had to be a mistake. Her training as a reporter told her the accusation as unproved information and therefore false but she had to know. She had to find out the mystery behind this sudden communication from an uncle she'd never even heard of. Why had he sent her this terrible picture?

Her mother's life was a complete mystery. Tully never spoke about her, even when Carrie questioned him, plagued him for answers; he remained stubbornly silent as if her mother never existed. All he ever told her was that her mother was Irish and had died after Carrie was born. Sometimes she wondered and ached to know more about Briony. Who was her mother? What did she look like? What caused her death? Now it was time to find out the truth but before confronting Tully, she wanted to meet and talk to the man who claimed to be her uncle. She needed answers.

For moments she studied the other pictures again. Her throat felt tight, as she looked at the face so much like her own. Finally she had something precious she'd longed for all her life. A picture of her mother. The happiness written all over Tully's and Briony's faces caused waves of emotion. She swallowed hard as tears burned to break free. It was the fourth picture that brought pain. She closed her eyes and sank slowly back against the rear of the chair

Stephanie was disturbed by the anguish painted on Carries face.

"Are you all right?"

Carrie opened her eyes and looked at her best friend.

"Oh God," she cried handing the photos to Stephanie.

When Stephanie looked at the last picture, her face was a study of revulsion.

"Steph, this can't be true. I don't believe Dad would do such a thing. I know he's a bastard but to do this. It can't be right."

Stephanie, noting Carrie's chalky face, stood up and quickly walked to the bar. She poured some brandy into a glass.

"Take this and steady yourself," she said and handed Carrie the glass. To see Carrie so upset disturbed her deeply. In all the time they'd been friends, nothing had ever daunted Carrie. But that picture would have shocked anyone. Who could be so cruel?

Carrie's hand shook. The brandy splashed over the glass as she brought it to her lips and sipped it. Slowly the burning liquid calmed her.

"Please, Steph, will you call Jason? I have to talk to him."

"You've become very fond of my cousin since Bosnia haven't you?"

Carrie nodded, tears filling her eyes. "Yes, but not as you think. After he saved my life, we bonded and formed a strong attachment. He has his girlfriends and I have my boyfriends."

"I'll ring the hospital. He should have finished his shift by now."

Stephanie went into the other room and rang her cousin. The phone rang for a long time. Stephanie wondered why it would take a hospital receptionist so long to answer. What if it was an emergency? At last she got some response.

"Can I speak to Doctor Armatige please? It's important."

Seconds later Jason answered.

"Jason, it's me Steph. Can you get here now? Carrie's had some bad news, she's a mess."

"Hell, did someone die?"

"You could say that but it was a long time ago. She just received some disgusting photos and is distressed. She asked for you. It's a bit of an emergency."

"Give her a glass of brandy. I've just finished my shift. Should be there in fifteen minutes."

"I already ha . . ." But he had hung up.

As soon as Jason burst through the front door Carrie broke into tears.

"Hey, it's all right, Snoopy. Let's talk."

He was beside her in seconds and pulled her into his arms. Steph thoughtfully left the living room so the two of them could be alone. Carrie buried her face in his chest. The familiar scent of his cologne and his comforting brotherly arms as they hugged her close, calmed her. She felt his large hand stroke her hair as if she were still a child.

"You're a good doctor, Jason, you make me feel better already," she said in a trembling voice.

"You thought I was a dork when we first met," he joked trying to put her in a lighter mood. Carrie thought how much he was like his mother. Same color hair, same color green eyes, same skin texture. He reminded her of someone but she couldn't quite place. Good looking and over six foot tall, he had a body one would expect from a manual laborer instead of a doctor but then he was always on the go.

It seemed jogging was his passion. He said it helped him wash away all the stresses doctor's seemed to be under.

Carrie moved out of the circle of his arms and plopped back into the chair.

"You were sixteen and shy when you helped Steph and me move into the house all those years ago."

"And now I'm clever and handsome," he laughed while pulling some tissues from a nearby box and handing them to her.

"With tickets on yourself," she added sniffing loudly. "You'd better look at the pictures."

He studied them as if viewing a x-ray.

"You're mother was very beautiful, Carrie. I always wondered where you got your good looks."

"She died shortly after I was born. Tully never told me anything about her."

"Those are terrible wounds. She must have been in agony."

"The note says Dad killed her."

"He looks very upset. If he killed her, would he show such pain?"

"Hard to tell. What should I do?"

"Tully has always been closed about his private life. I don't really know him all that well. But he doesn't come across as a murderer. You and I have seen enough killers to know the difference. Better talk to him about it."

"I can't, not without evidence. Pictures can be faked."

"You and Tully don't get along very well, right?"

She sent him a cynical look then gazed into space, for moments lost in thoughts about the picture.

"How do you feel about your father, Carrie?"

"Are you trying to spoil my day?"

"You must have some feelings for him."

"How can I have feelings for someone who deserted me when I was still very young?"

"Maybe he had good reasons?"

"He always had a reason. It was the lure of an important story that pulled him away. I saw him about twice a year when I was young. Seems he didn't want to be with me anyway."

"It was his job for Christ sake. You of all people should know that now. He provided for you didn't he? Don't you believe he loves you?"

"Ha. He thinks money will buy his love. Most people would feel proud of his achievements. I just wanted him to be with me. He didn't give a shit."

"What about when you became a journalist?"

"He was jealous. Why else would he want to keep me away from the places where all the action was happening? He didn't even show up for my graduation. Sorry, busy in Bosnia. Congratulations. That was all there was on the card. I ripped it to shreds and threw it in the wastepaper basket."

"Maybe he wanted you to be safe. From experience you know the dangers involved in your type of work."

"Maybe he was afraid I'd upstage him."

"Do you ever think you'll be friends?"

"Not unless he changes, but we both know he never will. And now --- after seeing this picture…".her voice trailed off

"Why don't you tell him how you feel?"

"What's the point? He has his life and I have mine."

"Think about it. He is your father."

"Maybe. Perhaps one day."

"What about your mother? Aren't you interested in the truth about her? Tully is the only one who can help you and give you the answers."

"Perhaps I'm afraid of the truth. He's a womanizing drunk and it's better I don't know about her."

"You think she might have been a one night stand?"

"Yes---no, I hope not. I would like to know but he won't talk about her. I guess he was fond of her. She gave him this zodiac necklace I'm wearing. On those pictures they look very much in love."

"I know. Is there anyone else who might have a clue?"

"Pat Scanlon. He worked with Dad in Ireland when I was born."

"Then talk to Pat. It could make things better between you."

12

"He's pretty loyal to Dad. He was an Interpol officer in Ireland when it happened."

"Do you know where he is now?"

"Sure. I see him every now and then. He's the police inspector in charge of the Goulburn region."

"Then ring him."

"I can't let this slide, Jason. I have to know the truth."

"Perhaps Pat can fill you in."

"I didn't become a good reporter by listening to hearsay. I'll talk to Pat but I'm going to Ireland to find out the truth. If he did kill my mother then he has to be punished."

As she said the words, the thought of Tully killing her mother was unthinkable and caused her flesh to pucker. Though they were estranged and she felt little love for the man, she could not bear to think of him as a murderer.

"I'd come with you but I've used up all my holidays. The hospital wouldn't let me go."

"Maybe my boss won't either but I'm going, regardless of what he says."

"Do you have enough money?"

"You're a sweetie, Jason. I've got my savings. I'll get by."

"Sure?"

"Jason, I'm well paid, I have a good salary, I have a car I can't drive in Sydney because of the traffic and I have a weekender in Bateman's Bay. I'm not rich however money's not the problem."

"Okay, if you need anything then call me. Feeling better?"

"Yes, and thanks for being there for me."

"Any time. Be careful over there. It's a dangerous place."

"More dangerous than Bosnia?"

"Look at the picture again."

She stood up and kissed him on the cheek. "Thanks for caring."

"We're friends, Carrie. Our time in Bosnia together formed a lasting bond. When we're both married with families I hope we'll always be friends."

A sudden thought occurred to him. Carrie noticed the expression on his face. "What are you thinking, Jason?"

"Just a thought. Why don't you have a week at Mum's place before making any decision? You've been there often enough and I know she'd welcome you."

"Kate's done enough for me as it is. She was a great help when I was injured and she soothed my pain away when I was really pissed off with Dad. How come you've got such a great parent and I've got Tully?"

He laughed. "Just lucky."

"Don't tell her about the pictures, Jason. She'll come rushing up from Moruya wanting to mother me. I don't want to put this off."

"Okay, it was just a thought."

"I'd better think about what I'm going to tell Richard. Then I'll ring Pat."

"Good luck."

Stephanie heard the front door slam and hurried into the living room.

"You look better. Thank goodness for Jason."

"I feel better, Steph. I've decided to go to Ireland. I need to get to the bottom of this."

"Are you nuts?" Stephanie asked in shock disbelief.

"No. Perfectly sane. You know me. I never let a story pass. I guess we'll have to give up the house altogether because I doubt if Richard will agree to let me go.

Maybe I'll take unpaid leave---and then I can't afford the rent while I'm gone. I have no idea how long this investigation will take."

Stephanie shook her head. "Carrie, the thought of you in Ireland scares the shit out of me."

"It's a mess I know. I have to do this, Steph."

"Carrie Sanderson, you're the most stubborn creature I've known. Just like your father."

"Don't compare me to Tully please. I suppose I'd better think how I'm going to confront Richard."

"You do that while I throw something together to go with the pie. But I'm still not in agreement with this whole plan of yours. Just had an idea. How about we keep the place for a month? If it only takes a short time you'll have somewhere to come home to."

"What about Greg?"

"He can move in while you're gone. Then we can get a place of our own."

"Makes sense, Steph. Thanks."

After Stephanie left for the kitchen, Carrie sat at the dinning room table, the pictures spread out before her. Ireland! She'd always planned to visit the country of her birth but not quite this way.

Chapter Two

A poor night's sleep saw fury replace the shock and dismay Carrie felt after seeing the photos. Anger simmered within her like a festering sore, at her father, at the secrets he'd kept from her all these years and at this distant uncle whom she never met. Fury at how Tully had escaped punishment for what he may have done. Why now? Why after all those years? What happened twenty six years ago to keep this secret tightly locked away?

From the tone of the letter there was no love lost between Kevin O'Rourke and Tully. How come her name was Sanderson and not O'Rourke? Tully was never married. She liked to check then double check before she filed a story. No one was going to say Tully Sanderson's daughter fucked up.

When Carrie was after a story, she was like a tenacious fox terrier chasing a rat. Not big enough to take it by the scruff of the neck but determined to worry it until it gave up in frustration. In most cases it did.

The trip to work seemed to take only half the time. Maybe it was because she had her mind on other things.

*   *   *

The Tribune's office building was close to the station on busy York Street. It was an old building as far as architecture was concerned but the inside was as modern as any newspaper office in the country.

The doorman nodded his usual morning greeting and was surprised when Carrie failed to acknowledge him. Usually she was bright and cheerful but today she had a face like she'd swallowed lemon juice.

Carrie pushed her way into the crowded elevator and pressed her floor button four times. Other passengers glanced at her body language. Hell it was only eight thirty in the morning and here was a walking time bomb.

Walking through the copy room she saw some of her colleagues were already hard at it. A few sent her a smile then attended to their work. Others were already drinking their morning fix of coffee, nodded then settled down to begin their daily task.

"Morning Carr...." one started but continued working when he saw the look on her face. She ploughed toward Richard's office like some pedestrian doing a power walk.

She drew in a deep breath, rapped on his door and walked in without invitation.

Richard was on the phone; he glanced at her frown, indicating his annoyance at the interruption, but gestured for her to sit. Carrie closed the door behind her and waited until he finished. He completed his conversation. Immediately after he hung up the phone, he picked up a pen and began writing.

"Richard, I have to talk to you."

"Shut up, Carrie, for Christ sake. Wait until I finish this." He continued writing knowing she was getting more irritated by the second. Carrie sat tapping one finger on his desk.

"All right, what's the problem?" He completely threw her off and all her neatly prepared speech vanished from her mind.

There was no way but to blurt it out. "I want you to send me to Belfast for a while. There's something I have to follow up."

"Like what? Officially it's still a war zone but it's been pretty quiet for the last few months except for the murder of that copper."

"It's just something that's come up."

"We already have Bernie Young over there. We don't need anyone else."

She bit her lip knowing sympathy was not going to get her anywhere. Another tact was needed.

"It's personal business."

"Personal? This is not a bloody charity organization."

"It's important to me, Richard."

"I don't think I can spare you."

"Please, Richard. I was going to use threats but how about bribery?"

"Bribery? What sort?"

"You can use my weekender at Bateman's Bay free of charge to take your wife away for a dirty weekend."

"I already do that twice a year."

"Oh yes. So you do."

He studied her grim face; she was just like her father. Neither would bend. She was going to nag him until he agreed.

"If it's so important take a month's leave of absence. We can get by for a while."

"Without pay?"

"You said it was important."

"And here's me thinking you were a generous boss."

"Told to you by Tully no doubt."

"Don't mention his name. Thanks, Richard. It may not take that long."

"Take a bloody coat. Even a brass monkey would suffer over there."

"I won't have that problem." She leaned across and kissed him on the cheek. "See you soon." Just before she left the office she turned and frowned at him. "I thought you said you couldn't spare me."

"I lied."

"One more favor."

"Bloody hell, do you want me to go and see you off?"

"No. Can I book the plane fare on the paper's account just like when I'm working, then have you take it out of my wages."

"Jesus."

"If I use the paper's name I may be able to get on a plane immediately."

"There better be a story in this."

"You're an angel, Richard."

Carrie tidied up her desk and attended to a small amount of unfinished work. When she was done she rang the paper's regular travel agent.

"Hi, Carol, its Carrie Sanderson."

"Hi, Carrie, I presume you didn't just call for chit chat by the sound of your voice. Are you off on a hot lead?"

"To Belfast, how soon can you book me?"

There was a silence for a few seconds while Carol looked at her monitor.

"There's a British Airways plane leaving at six. Plenty of room at this time of the year. That soon enough?"

"Thanks, Carol. Book me on it. I'll pick up the tickets at the airport."

"You're on flight 662. Do you want hotel accommodation?"

"The cheapest you can find."

Again silence, then, "Wanderer's Arms hotel on Donavan Street. Cheap, but clean. I've got you in for a week. Have a good trip.

Carrie left for home in a better mood than when she boarded the train that morning. The house was quiet when she arrived. She'd already said her good-bye's to Steph that morning. Before she began packing there still was one more thing to do.

Quickly, she picked up the phone and dialed the number of the Goulburn Police Station.

"Goulburn Police, constable Timmins speaking."

"Could I talk to Inspector Scanlon please?"

"Your name please?"

"Tell him it is Carrie Sanderson. It's important."

A few seconds later Pat answered.

"Carrie, it's great to hear from you. Must be six months since we've seen each other."

"Yes, Pat. I'm after some information."

"If I can help?"

"Remember when you were with Interpol investigating the kidnapping of that English industrialist."

"Lord Ashley! Good heavens, that was before you were born."

"I know but I'm trying to find a man possibly named O'Rourke. Have you ever heard of him?"

There was an eerie silence for a few seconds and Carrie thought she'd been cut off.

"Hello, Pat. Are you still there?"

"Why do you need to find him, Carrie?" Pat's voice had changed to a soft monotone.

"It's important to me. I can't explain why just yet. Did you know him?"

"I knew him. So did your father."

"His name is Kevin isn't it?"

"Carrie, you would do well to leave it alone. He's bad news."

"Please, Pat. I have to find him."

"Carrie, he's a bloody IRA terrorist. My advice is to keep away from him."

"Why don't you want me to talk to him? I've spoken to terrorists before. What's different about this one?"

"He hates your father. He might harm you if he finds out who you are."

"Why does he hate Tully? What did Tully do to him?"

Again silence for what seemed an eternity. Carrie raised one eyebrow waiting for an answer.

"You don't want to know."

"Cut the crap, Pat, this call is costing me money."

"All right. He's your Uncle. He and your father didn't get along."

"Why?"

"That's something you'll have to ask Tully."

"I see. What can you tell me about him?"

"I know he did three years for carrying a gun. There were other charges but nothing was ever proven. He's a killer, Carrie. Stay well clear of him."

"I have to talk with him. I have an address that says The Shamrock Hotel. Know anything about it?"

"It's a well known hangout for the IRA. I believe it's on Glean Street. Be careful. The place is bad news."

"I will, Pat. Thanks." Carrie hung up wondering what the implications would be when she found Kevin O'Rourke.

With the phone call out of the way she began to think about packing. What do I take? Richard was right, Belfast would be cold at this time of the year. Most times she wore slacks that covered her long legs. Fashion was not foremost on her mind. When she was on the road or traveling, it was comfort she sought. One suitcase was all she ever required when moving fast so her choice wasn't great. It could take three weeks or three days, she had no idea.

Some suitable warm clothes, a few changes of underwear, night apparel, another pair of slacks, some warm tops and of course her toiletries. As a last thought she threw in her warmest coat. No telling what the weather would do over there. Snow one-day rain the next.

* * *

On arriving at Mascot airport, she booked herself in. Her ticket was handed to her and she watched her suitcase begin its slow journey on the conveyer belt taking it to the plane to be picked up.

She walked to the waiting lounge usually reserved for special customers. As the newspaper often used the airline she encountered no problem. After a two-hour wait she boarded the Boeing 747 for Heathrow to make the exchange for Belfast. A last look from the jumbo's window at Sydney's sunny weather as it disappeared slowly and turned into a miniature town, then she finally settled down for the long journey. Carol had been right; the plane was only half full so comfort was no problem. After a few drinks giving her nerves a chance to settle, she began to think about finding Kevin O'Rourke.

The stopover in Singapore annoyed her. Speed was the main thing on her mind. It was another two-hour wait before the plane took off again for Heathrow. She watched a movie but couldn't concentrate, then decided to get some shuteye. Because there was plenty of room, Carrie had no trouble in stretching out. She had a full row to herself so sleep came easily. Sleeping on a plane was always difficult but this time she surprised herself. She woke with a shock when breakfast was brought around with only an hour and a half from Heathrow.

The pilot's announcement made her groan.

"Well be at Heathrow in seventeen minutes ladies and gentlemen. The sky is clear and the outside temperature on arriving will be minus two degrees. I hope you had a comfortable journey and thank you for traveling with British Airways."

The washrooms were busy. Impatiently she waited her turn. When one of the doors opened, she scooted into the small cubicle, freshened up and she was ready to change planes for Belfast.

*   *   *

Heathrow was filled with people. Not unusual for one of the busiest airports in the world. Because she was still in transit, she didn't have to follow the embarking passengers making England their destination. Just as well, she thought watching people leaving for several of the busy exit ports from planes arriving from all over the world. Still in customs, she was directed to terminal two for the flight to Belfast. As she had another hour delay, Carrie filled in some of the time browsing through the duty free shops. At last the call came for Belfast and she hurried for the last part of her journey.

The Air Lingus flight took only an hour and landed through heavy cloud. After a quick customs check she was free to gather her luggage. Her solitary case looked lonely as passenger luggage came down the belt. Most people had two big suitcases. They made her suitcase look quite small in comparison. Belfast airport was quiet. A few people waited for an outgoing flight, and a couple of women were there to greet arriving family and friends.

Compared to Heathrow it looked like a country airport. Perhaps two dozen shops; not many doing much business however the Hertz hire desk was busy.

Carrie looked for a money exchange and soon felt solvent again. It's a lousy feeling being in a strange country with no money in your pocket.

She easily found a taxi and began the journey into Belfast. The driver was full of conversation but Carrie preferred to look at the streets and landmarks new to her. Small streets, buildings put up in terraces, no gardens, and dreary looking shops.

Maybe they would look better in bright sunshine if such a thing existed in Ireland. The traffic was light, not like busy Sydney and the journey to her hotel uneventful. Before she knew it she was at her accommodation.

It was cheap but clean. At least it was better than some places she'd overnighted. Cairo, Beirut and Sarajevo came to mind. She glanced at the small room with a single bed. No en-suite and just the basics. A shared bathroom was down the hall and Carrie hurried there to have a shower. Instead she found only a bath. At least the water was hot. Getting onto Belfast time was a problem. It was nine in the morning but jetlag told her she had to get at least a few more hours sleep. By three that afternoon she was ready to try and find this mysterious uncle of hers and hopefully get a few answers.

Chapter Three

A greasy meal of Irish stew was consumed at the hotel. She thought the dish would be the country's favorite but when she looked at the fatty liquid encircling the small pieces of meat and potato she had her doubts. Bar meals were always handy when working. It saved precious time looking for a restaurant. The quality sometimes left a lot to be desired but it was cheap and quick. Carrie wanted to wait until at least eight o'clock before seeking out the Shamrock Hotel. Nothing happened until late anyway and she figured this would be a good time to start.

The minutes seemed to drag and she looked at her watch constantly as if urging the hands to speed up. The television in her room was playing neighbors giving her a feeling for home, even if it was three years behind. At last it was time and she stepped outside to hail a taxi. This was definitely not like London. There, taxi's seemed more prevalent than private cars but Belfast was entirely different. It was at least half an hour before one came by. It was definitely not the tourist season.

"Where to my, dear?" asked the driver when she sat down.

"Do you know the Shamrock hotel in Glean Street?"

"I can take you to better pubs than that if you're looking for a night out."

"No, I'm meeting someone there," she said settling back.

"Have you there in ten minutes. You Australian?"

"My accent?"

"Yes, we get lots of Australians here in the summer."

"Just a quick holiday." She didn't want to have to explain her business to a taxi driver. The rest of the trip was in silence.

As soon as she saw the quaint, typically Irish pub with a huge sign in the shape of a shamrock, Carrie knew she was at the right place. Suspended over the door by a chain the sign clanked in the evening breeze. The whole place looked as though it hadn't had a coat of paint in years.

Carrie winced as she entered. The loud music hit her ears and the noise was actually painful. Men and women were drinking at small tables; some stood at the bar while a large group was singing around a piano with everyone depressingly out of tune.

She blinked rapidly with a stinging sensation in her eyes from the air filled with tobacco fumes. Through the dim smoky atmosphere she made her way to the bar. The fat balding barman with the cheery smile reminded her of a used car salesman. His grin seemingly cemented to his face displayed yellow teeth. He took her order.

"A small brandy thanks," she said. "And maybe a little information."

He poured her drink then looked at her.

"Information? What sort of information would a Colleen like you be after?"

"I'm looking for a man named Kevin O'Rourke. I believe he used to drink here."

The barman's mood changed instantly as he looked suspiciously at her. "Who are you and what do you want him for?" She was glad she already had her drink. He gave the impression he would like to fill it with rat poison.

"I think maybe I might be a relative. Thought I'd look him up while I was here."

"You're not English are you?" The word English came out like an insult directed to a poor referee at a soccer match.

"Australian."

"Thought so. It's not hard to pick by your accent."

'That's nice. Do you know Mr O'Rourke?"

"Maybe. Haven't seen him around for a while. He's a bit shy these days."

"I'd be most grateful if you can help me." Carrie looked hopefully at him widening her eyes in what she hoped was a helpless gesture.

Hesitating for a second he turned her request over in his mind. "I could make a phone call. What's your name?"

"Carrie Sanderson. I'm from Sydney."

"Find yourself a seat, Carrie. I'll get back to you shortly."

Carrie picked up her glass and found her way to a small table away from the piano. On the table stains were still prevalent where the previous customers had spilt their drinks. She moved across to the dry area and waited.

The fumes still got to her as she tried to open a window behind her. Suddenly she was aware of warm breath close to her ear and the smell of alcohol in her nostrils. Turning sharply she was confronted by a sandy hair, pale faced young man almost on her lap.

"Shall I help you with the window?" Looking as if he wouldn't take no for an answer, his brogue was hard to understand.

Carrie looked up not wanting to converse with him. The last thing she wanted was a Romeo. "No thanks. I'm waiting for my husband."

Raising his eyebrow the man was persistent. "Perhaps I could keep you company while you wait."

"If you're game," said Carrie.

"If I'm game?" The man was puzzled.

"Yes. My husband is Mick Malone, the heavy weight boxer. He's very possessive."

"Well I'll leave you to enjoy your drink," he said and quickly walked back to the singers. Carrie noticed a few sniggers aimed at the man. She sat alone and finished her drink, the atmosphere still jovial. The stories about the friendly Irish and the pubs seemed to confirm that piece of information. A few minutes later the barman signaled her.

"Yes?" She jumped up anxiously.

"Walk south slowly. A man will contact you," he said and turned his back on her resuming his duties. She knew she had been dismissed.

Carrie left the pub at once walking south as instructed. The street was dark and almost deserted. There was a chill in the air and a light mist was beginning to fall. Ahead she could see a man some distance away walking towards her. Almost a ghostly apparition, his footsteps echoed in the night air but he appeared to be in no hurry.

Her heart beat stronger as she peered through the gloom trying to see his face. Still he made no sign of recognition.

When he reached her he kept on walking leaving Carrie with a wave of disappointment as he began to move further away. Suddenly a car appeared out of nowhere pulling up with a screech of tires.

Startled, she only had time to look towards it when two men leapt out and bundled her into the back seat. Both wore balaclavas over their faces, their eyes being the only recognizable feature. A wave of concern overtook her as the car sped off quickly.

When one produced a hood to slip over her head, she began to protest until the other pressed a gun to her head. Carrie feeling cold metal against her temple knew it was not a time to argue.

"Shut up and don't say a word." His Irish brogue was strong and she was scared. She allowed them to cover her head. They then tied her hands behind her. Carrie tried to make herself familiar with sounds, anything, like a train going by or a ship leaving port but the night was silent except for the hum of the engine. She lost the feeling of time but was sure they drove for at least half an hour before they stopped. The distinct smell of hay tingled her nostrils and she knew they were at a farm a long way from anywhere.

Grabbing her by the arms Carrie felt them almost carry her into the house. The hood was removed quickly. Blinking her eyes she tried to focus as the light of a kerosene lamp hit her. It gave a pallid appearance to the room and she wondered why they didn't use the electric lights. Maybe they thought it might help keep their identity a secret. The room was drab, the floor bare of any covering. The walls needed a good paint, and Carrie could see wallpaper hanging down in one corner.

"Untie her." A soft voice came from the corner and she followed the direction of the sound. It reminded her of the hiss of a tiger snake about to strike. A man around fifty was seated at a table. She noted he wore a faded shirt with a tattered blue vest, his legs tucked under the chair and his hands resting in his lap.

Not bad looking for a man of his age. Carrie couldn't help but wonder if his gray hair made him look older than he really was. She noted a 45 pistol lying on the table alongside him, well within reach. Its surface reflecting flickers of light from the lamp like a warning beacon.

When the ropes where removed Carrie rubbed her wrists to regain circulation. Without expression the men watched her flex her fingers.

"I had always heard the Irish were friendly," she said trying to evoke some humor to hide her nervousness.

"We can be very friendly when the occasion calls. Especially with young women." It was chillingly direct. Carrie felt like a cannibal's victim about to be devoured.

"Are you Kevin O'Rourke?"

"I ask the questions here. First tell me who you are and no lies or we may have to slit your throat."

Carrie tried to stop her hand from shaking. He gave the impression he was deadly serious. Maybe it was a bad idea coming here.

"My name is Carrie Sanderson. I'm an Australian journalist. I'm looking for Kevin O'Rourke."

"And what would a pretty young thing like you want with Kevin?" The man was mocking her.

"That's for me to know and you to find out," she said sharply. No sense in letting them think she was scared, even if her knees were knocking. Sandersons never took a backward step.

"Don't give me any of your shit, girlie. Why do you want Kevin?" He hadn't moved a muscle, just stared at her giving no indication of his thoughts. It was very intimidating. She'd never seen pure evil before but this could be the first time.

Carrie bit her lip then answered. "I think he's my uncle. Someone sent me some photos and I want to know if it was him and if the photos were real."

"Did they now? How many photos?"

"Four. One of a beautiful young woman. Three of my father with the woman. One of them looked like she was badly hurt."

"Anything else?"

"There was a note saying my father killed her. It said she was my mother."

"And how old did it say she was?"

"Nineteen. You are Kevin O'Rourke aren't you?"

"I am. I sent you the photos. You're very beautiful just like your mother. She was my sister and I'm your Uncle Kevin."

Carrie stared anxiously at him. "Why would you send me something so horrible?"

"I thought it was about time you knew the truth about your family and about the bastard who killed your mother."

"Why now? You could have sent me this information years ago."

"You wouldn't have believed me then. You're grown up now and a well-known journalist. You know about life and what goes on and you know how to ferret out the truth. I can't reach him while he's in Australia but you can."

"What do you mean?" Carrie began to fidget uneasily.

"I want you to kill him for me."

Carrie jumped up horrified. "Are you mad? He's my father."

Carrie watched him as he took up the gun and opened the breech. Six bullets were standing upright on the table like tiny harpoon missiles. O'Rourke slid one into an empty chamber.

"You're going to kill me?"

"No, this is a symbolic gesture to show you why he has to die. Six chambers of retribution. The first bullet represents his interference with the political frustration of Ireland."

"He was only a journalist reporting the events."

O'Rourke ignored her comment. He inserted the second bullet then addressed Carrie again. "This one represents his intruding into the O'Rourke family. He was never invited and wouldn't take warnings to leave us alone."

"He loved my mother." Carrie was actually defending him. She couldn't remember when she had done that before.

"The third bullet is for seducing Briony. He let his carnal urges destroy Briony's faith to the cause."

Carrie remained silent as he continued to load. He was taking his time allowing her to absorb the words he was giving her.

"The fourth bullet was for taking her away from the land she loved. The city chosen was the land of our enemies."

"London?"

"London. The next was for making her pregnant without the blessing of the Holy Church."

"They must have been in love for God's sake."

"You obviously think that's an excuse for illicit sex. The last is for the greatest crime of all. For killing your mother. All these crimes are punishable by death that's why you must comply.

"Crimes invented by you."

"He killed your mother. He deserves to die. You're the only one who can do it."

Carrie sat down again. "I don't believe he killed my mother. The pictures prove nothing."

"There's another picture. I wanted you to come and see yourself so I didn't send it."

"I was told you were an IRA terrorist. How can I believe anything you say?"

O'Rourke's laughter unnerved her. "Undoubtedly told by the English or an English sympathizer. It's true I am a loyal member of the IRA sworn not to give up until the invaders are driven from our country."

"Then it's true, you have killed people."

"Of course. Let me put this to you. If you were alive in the Second World War years and the Japanese invaded Australia, wouldn't you fight them until the death?"

"Maybe but I wouldn't go around killing innocent women and children."

"Contrary to what you might have heard, neither do we."

Carrie laughed cynically.

"It's true some innocents always get hurt in war. As a correspondent you must know that."

"You know bombs don't worry about who happens to be walking by," said Carrie realizing he was looking for excuses.

"If you mean the English, they're the enemy. One day they'll understand the only way to stop it is to leave Ireland."

"I'm sure you didn't bring me here to argue the pros and cons of war. What do you want to tell me about my father?"

"You're right. Would you like a drink and I'll tell you a little story?"

"Perhaps a cup of tea if that's possible."

O'Rourke nodded to one of the men who left the room and returned some minutes later with a tray. Nothing was said until he returned. Carrie noted O'Rourke's cold eyes staring at her. She had never felt so intimidated before. He poured them both a cup and Carrie waited expectantly.

O'Rourke said nothing at first as he continued studying her. They weren't undressing eyes but she felt he was trying to look deep into her soul.

"Let me see now, it happened about twenty seven years ago but it seems like yesterday." He sat back in his chair. He definitely had her attention.

"A crowd of people, Briony amongst them was running panic stricken down the main street of Belfast. There had been a bomb blast quite near them. People were hysterical and anxious to escape from danger when your father's car pulled up and he tried to pick up Briony."

Carrie leaned forward, all ears.

"At first she was suspicious thinking he was English but as soon as he spoke she knew her first impression was wrong. He did have a sort of charm about him and as she was frightened, she accepted."

"Sounds like him," said Carrie knowing this was Tully's style.

"Instead of taking her home he took her to a pub for a drink to settle her nerves. They ended up having quite a few drinks together. He was charming and she felt at ease so he asked her for a date. Being young and gullible, she accepted."

O'Rourke paused to let the information sink in.

"Biscuit?" He offered the tray.

"No."

"When he came the next night to pick her up, I was suspicious of him having learned from Briony he was a journalist. I gave him a friendly warning about taking care of my little sister. He was brash and arrogant and more or less told me to mind my own business."

Carrie had forgotten about her tea as she strained to listen further.

"He hasn't changed much." It confirmed O'Rourke's words.

"I asked him how long he was staying in Belfast. He told me he was going to be there for quite a while as his job was to cover the war between the English and us.

I waited up until Briony returned home and asked what she knew about him. She told me he was covering Interpol who was investigating a kidnapping."

"He's like a dog with a bone," said Carrie. "He hates to give up a story."

Carrie wished she had a tape recorder with her but she let O'Rourke carry on.

"Seems he had this friend in Interpol who he had known back in Australia. I warned Briony to drop him as his mate was probably using him through her to get to us."

"Pat Scanlan."

"That's him. The two of them were like brothers. Good drinking mates as you Australians say."

"Pat's a good friend. I've known him all my life."

"He's an English sympathizer who put a few good Irishmen in jail."

"Arguing about that will get us nowhere."

"Agreed. Sanderson began seeing Briony as often as they could in fact he was becoming an embarrassment with some of our soldiers. None of them trusted him and there was talk of eliminating him. It was almost agreed until we learned the British were going to arrest Briony to get to me."

"Surely they couldn't jail her just because she was your sister." Carrie wasn't naive enough to believe English justice would work that way.

O'Rourke laughed loudly. "The English are past masters at cruelty and deceit. Some Irish women have been tortured and raped by those pigs. Then they're fished out of the harbor; some of them covered with cigarette burns all over their bodies. The English then blame us for some sort of payback to the women for informing on us. They know we don't let informers get away."

"I've heard about knee capping."

"Only on traitors to the cause. We respect our women."

"What happened then?"

"Your father heard about Briony's imminent arrest and took her away before it could happen."

"He must have cared about her to risk that. He took her to London?"

"The only thing he cared about was whether he could extract information out of her about the IRA. Yes he took her to where they set up a flat and lived together. She became pregnant and had you."

"I was born in London?"

"Yes. Then Briony heard I'd been arrested on a trumped up charge of carrying a gun. As she was no longer in danger of being arrested, she wanted to return to Belfast to help me. The English had jailed me some years earlier on the same charge. I spent three years in one of their prisons and Briony didn't want it to happen to me again."

"And so they came back?"

He nodded. "Yes but Sanderson was still working with his mate. They wanted to pin the murder of the Englishman on me. He told her the English were setting up an ambush on a quiet road and after I was shot, they were going to plant weapons on my body and fill my car with bombs. All neat and tidy."

Carrie ignored her tea now cold.

"He wanted to take you and her to Australia after I was dead. Briony was horrified and rushed to warn me. Sanderson followed and got there just as the English opened fire on my car."

"What happened?"

O'Rourke looked grim, the memory still painful to him but continued.

"Briony rushed to my car and pulled me free but was hit by English bullets. She yelled for me to get away. I escaped in Briony's car."

"You left her to die?"

"The cause is greater than the individual. Scanlan was furious I got away and wanted to arrest Briony. Sanderson said he could get the information without embarrassing the police. Scanlan agreed and let Sanderson drive her back to the farmhouse."

"This farm house?"

"Yes."

"How do you know this?"

"Our people are everywhere. We use cameras to positively identify people we're suspicious of. That's how we had the photos of your father and Briony in London."

"What happened then?" She felt like a parrot repeating the same question. Carrie was trying not to believe this man but her resolve was weakening.

"When they arrived back Sanderson pulled her from the car. She lay on the ground unable to stand from her wounds, he then demanded to know where I was. He said if she didn't tell him he would kill her."

"That's bullshit," said Carrie angrily. "He might be a bastard but he's not a killer." She surprised herself. Here she was defending Tully against her uncle. Usually she was fighting with him.

"She was in a lot of pain but wouldn't give me away. He kicked his boot into her and she screamed in agony. He told her he was only using her to get a story about me and said he didn't care if she lived or died."

Carrie felt his story was incredulous.

"She could hardly speak from pain and beckoned him to come closer. He leaned down to hear what she had to say and she spat in his face. He went insane and took out a gun then shot her in a fit of anger. Before we could get to him, he picked up you and his few belongings and took you back to Australia."

"I still don't believe you." Carrie was horrified by the story. "My father wouldn't do that."

"Remember I mentioned another photo."

Carrie nodded as O'Rourke reached into a drawer under the table and handed her another photograph. Her eyes widened. Like the fourth photo is was in full color.

"Oh God," she said looking at the image.

It was a picture of Tully standing over her mother with the gun pointing at her. Smoke was rising from the barrel and the woman was obviously dead. It was the final proof. It was true, he had killed her. He'd killed her own mother and let her grow up without telling her the truth. He was the monster O'Rourke had said he was. Fury was the only emotion she felt and revenge was the only answer she wanted.

"Perhaps you will believe me now," said O'Rourke watching closely at the anger in her eyes.

"It's true. I didn't believe he would do such a thing. He actually killed my mother."

"Even Scanlon was disgusted. I heard he resigned and went home."

"He's a police inspector now in a large country town."

"You can see why I want you to kill him. He's a vile person with no scruples. He killed my sister; your mother and he must die. Only you can do it."

Carrie stared ahead blankly and then looked down at the photo again.

"I can't let him get away with this. He murdered my mother. I agree, he has to be punished."

"Punished in the way all traitors are. Then it's up to you, lass. We'll take you back to your hotel and you can return to Australia tomorrow. Send me a message when it's done."

"To where?"

"Care of the Shamrock pub. Just say the sun has set."

"I don't have a gun. I don't think I can kill my own father, no matter what he's done."

"You're going to let him get away with this?"

Carrie thought about what O'Rourke had said. Maybe she could frighten him into confessing his crime. Then it would be up to the police to handle it. She hated guns but it might just work.

"I can't take a gun back into Australia."

"When you get home you'll find a package waiting for you. Wipe it clean and throw it into the harbor when it's done. Remember that your mother was only nineteen years old when he killed her. You're quite beautiful. You know you look exactly like her? When it's done send the message."

Sadly Carrie gathered up the photo and was escorted to the car. When she was safely out of the way O'Rourke called to one of his soldiers.

"Get my wheelchair, Sean."

Sean entered the next room and wheeled in the chair, then helped Kevin into it lifting his useless legs into position, one after the other.

"Do you think she believed you?" he asked.

"Yes. The circumstances of her mother's death were news to her. She's very beautiful, just like Briony."

"But will she kill him?"

"We'll have to wait and see won't we? If she doesn't she'll at least make a lot of trouble for him. Twenty years in jail would satisfy me."

Carrie stared at the picture of her mother as they drove her back to her hotel. This man who was her father had done her a terrible injustice. All the money he'd sent for her upbringing was now irrelevant. Nothing could forgive him for taking her away.

Of course he would deny it but she'd seen the proof. O'Rourke had admitted he was IRA but his fight with the British was not her fight.

She could see why he wanted revenge. Briony was his only sister and so young. Now she also hungered for revenge and revenge was what she was going to get.

Chapter Four

Before she left Ireland Carrie felt compelled to do one last thing. Aided by directions from the hotel staff she found the Belfast cemetery and the Catholic section.

Among the rows of a mixture of ancient and modern headstones stood a small simple cross. The black Gothic style print read. Briony O'Rourke. June 10th 1951-September 29th 1970. Dearly loved friend, sister, mother. Rest in Peace. Slowly she knelt and placed her small bouquet against the headstone. So this is where she now lay.

Carrie wanted to throw herself across the hard stone slab and cry. Her eyes filled with tears and her heart with a longing for the mother she never knew. Why did she feel so close and connected toward this person she'd never met? She almost expected ghostly hands to rise up and embrace her.

Struggling with her emotions she offered a silent prayer for her soul. What sort of a woman was my mother? Was she like Kevin? Was she really dedicated to the cause as he said she was? Did she truly love Tully or just stay with him for my sake? What would Briony want her to do? Would she really want Kevin's wishes carried out? Was justice the normal expectation of the Irish? No such revelation came forth and Carrie turned with tears in her eyes and walked away not looking back.

* * *

Carrie gathered her hand luggage as soon as her plane touched down at Mascot airport. Collecting her one suitcase from the turntable, she picked up her car from the long term car park, then went directly to her home. The bumper to bumper traffic mixed with the usual honk of car horns reminded her she was back home. As usual she caught every red light, but at last her street loomed up and she turned gratefully into her drive.

It had been a long trip and she needed to get herself back on Australian time. A few hours in her bed looked good. Steph was at work and it was obvious by the lack of men's things Greg had not yet moved in. It looked as though they would now find their own place seeing she was back so soon.

Checking the mailbox she found some bills. On the table was her unopened mail where Steph had neatly tied them together with a rubber band. Dropping her suitcase on the floor, then throwing the bills on the table she headed for the bedroom. After undressing and slipping on a robe Carrie hurried to the bathroom and turned on the water in the shower.

The needle points of the hot shower on her body was heaven making her feel a little more refreshed. Closing the blind and wearily pulling back the covers she fell into bed. It was six hours before she woke.

"Shit," she said and looked at the clock. Her stomach told her it was time to eat. The thought of how many people having breakfast at three o'clock in the afternoon amused her. The events of the past couple of days were still turning over in her mind. Ireland now seemed so far away but the reason for going there still fresh in her memory.

It was halfway through her second cup of coffee when the doorbell rang. The same young man in the uniform smiling broadly greeted her.

"Afternoon. Carrie Sanderson again. Right?"

"Yes, what can I do for you this time?"

"Have another package for you. Can you sign here please?" He thrust a sheet of paper in front of her and handed her a pencil extracted from behind his ear. Tentatively she took it in her fingers eyeing the end with teeth marks all over it.

Carrie studied the parcel. It was small, about half the size of a shoe box and wrapped in plain brown paper.

"It's not a bomb is it?"

He laughed loudly. "Hope not. I just deliver them."

"I guess you want another tip?'

"It all helps," he answered cheerfully.

"I suppose you don't know who sent this?" she asked but received a shrug in reply.

"Not a clue."

He stayed with his hand out looking expectantly again.

"I don't suppose you've changed your mind about dinner?"

"I like a determined man," she said reaching into her purse.

Carrie found another dollar then closed the door and took the parcel to the table, quickly unwrapping it. Hell she thought in surprise. Encased in a clear plastic bag buried in polystyrene balls was a black evil looking revolver and a box of ammunition. She gingerly took it out and handled it carefully.

It wasn't the first time she'd held a gun in her hand. She hated the things because of the horrible injuries she'd seen inflicted by them.

A typed note with it simply said, "The sun has set." O'Rourke meant what he said. All she had to do now was find her father. The sooner the better. She had to know his version of the truth.

Nothing had been heard from him but she knew he was like the proverbial bad penny. There was no hurry to do what she had to do. When Steph arrived home she was ecstatic.

"I was so worried for you, Carrie. Is everything okay now?"

"Not until I speak with Dad. What happened about Greg?"

"He said to put it off for a week or so until you came home. He's a Darling."

"Well I suppose you'll be looking for another place."

"We already have. It's nice and fairly reasonable. Greg's already there and I'll move in soon now you're home."

"Looks like I'll have to learn to cook properly," she said giving Steph a hug.

"You're invited over whenever you feel like it."

It was a week later when Steph left. Carrie helped the lovers shift Steph's things to the new apartment only fifteen minutes away. She liked Greg from the moment she met him back in Uni. and thought he and Steph were well suited.

Maybe it was going to be good having some time to herself. It was not something she could tell Steph about. Better to leave it as it was.

Nothing happened until a fortnight later. A call came from Pat Scanlon.

"Pat. This is a surprise."

"Glad to see you got home safe and sound," he said cheerfully. "Did you get to meet O'Rourke?"

"I did and I must say you were right, he is IRA."

"Why the hell did you want to see him?"

"He wanted to fill me in on what a bastard my father is."

He gave a chuckle. "I can imagine. O'Rourke wasn't one of your father's favorite people."

"He told me a lot of things I found hard to accept."

"Don't believe half of it, Carrie. He delves in half truths and leaves the rest to your imagination."

"He wasn't very sympathetic to you either."

"Yeah, like I'm a Pommy sympathizer who hates the Irish. Did he tell you he killed the English Lord Ashley?"

"No but I thought he might have been involved."

"He was in it up to his neck but we couldn't prove anything."

Carrie paused. "He also told me things about my mother, about how she died."

Pat retorted back quickly. "His side of the truth I imagine."

"He said you were going to arrest her but she was killed."

"Not me but that part was true. I'm sure it didn't happen as he said."

"He also told me who killed her. Would you like to tell me your version?"

"I would but I think I'd better let Tully explain it. You deserve to know but you may not like it."

"Oh, I intend to discuss the matter with him in length if I can ever find him."

"Actually that's the reason I called. He's in the hospital."

"What happened?" She gasped. It was perverse. She wanted to perhaps see him punished but was alarmed he was hurt.

"The usual. Women and booze. Got involved in a brawl and was set upon by three thugs. Seems one of them was the boyfriend of the woman he was with."

"And they beat him up."

"Afraid so."

"Was he hurt badly?"

"Cuts, bruises and a small fracture in his wrist. His face is even uglier and he's sporting a big black eye. They kept him in overnight for observation. He gets out today. I thought you might like to go and get him."

"I know what I'd like to do to him," she said cynically.

"Look, Carrie. He pretends he doesn't need anyone but he's doing it badly at the moment. You don't know half of what he's been through. Why don't you entice him to tell you it all? Maybe confession will help you both see things in a different light."

"You always were soft as far as he was concerned, Pat."

"Not always but I know him better than anyone. Sometimes I fear for him."

That puzzled her. "Fear for him? What's that supposed to mean?"

"He's a lonely man. If you knew the whole story you'd have some sympathy for him."

Carrie stifled a laugh. "I doubt it. What hospital is he in?"

"St. Mary's. They're throwing him out at midday."

"What am I supposed to do with him?" she said unimpressed.

"Take him down the coast to that cabin you own. A bit of salt air will do wonders for him."

"Why should I care about him? He never cared about me." The bitterness was in her tone.

"You couldn't be more wrong. You're one of the few things in life to keep him going."

"Bullshit. I only ever saw him once every six months when I was a child. All he did was send money and thought it was enough. When I made it as a correspondent he did his best to bring me down."

"No. He did his best to keep you safe. Talk to him, Carrie. Get him to unload or he's going to self destruct."

"All right. I'll go and get him. It's time we spoke openly. Thanks, Pat."

"Take care of him. He needs you."

"Yeah, sure," she said and hung up. It could be her only chance to get him alone.

Now is as good a time as any, she thought and placed the gun in her shoulder bag, then headed to the hospital. She still had doubts about killing him. She was sure she couldn't do that. He could give her his side of the story when they reached the coast. If she got it all on tape then that might be enough to see justice done.

* * *

39

The drive to the hospital was a drag. Sydney traffic was always a nightmare and today was no different. St. Mary's was situated in Bondi, a good three quarters of an hour from her place. Finding a parking spot in the parking area, she went up the steps to the front desk for information about Tully. People were walking in and out but finally she had the attendant's attention. There was a nurse standing alongside the attendant looking at a clipboard.

"Which room is Mr Sanderson in please?" she asked. Rather pretty thought Carrie when the nurse looked sharply at her. Nice figure and blonde hair. She expected her to look on a sheet for the information but it didn't happen.

"I hope to God you're here to take him away." The nurse seemed pleased by Carrie's arrival.

"He's been giving you trouble?"

"Most of our patients are usually friendly and respectful. Every time I walk past, Mr Sanderson asks me to pull the curtain and jump into bed with him."

"He must be feeling better." Carrie stifled a smile.

"Are you Mrs. Sanderson?"

"I'm his daughter. Is he ready to go?"

"As soon as he's dressed. I'll take you down. Get him to sign his release papers when he leaves."

Carrie followed her to the ward where she found Tully sitting up in bed. The room had four other beds in it but only three were occupied. She grimaced when she saw his face. Pat was right, he had taken a beating but he tried to smile when he saw her.

"Hot shot," he exclaimed and she gritted her teeth. Every time he called her hot shot she felt like it was a sarcastic put down. The more she complained the more he did it.

"I see you've been up to your usual tricks." She stared at his battered face.

"Just a little misunderstanding. Nothing serious. You almost missed me, I was about to leave."

"Pat rang me. He wants me to take care of you."

"Christ. What am I, a child? Tully Sanderson doesn't need anyone to take care of him."

"So I see," she said cynically. "I only came because Pat insisted."

"He should have been a mother," he said laughing. She watched him writhe in pain. It was obvious he also had a broken rib.

"Something wrong?"

"Must have hurt my ribs. I'll be right in a moment, just don't make me laugh."

"Laugh! Get dressed. I'm taking you down to the cabin for a few days. There's something I want to talk to you about."

"Not another lecture? You're worse than any wife."

"No, not a lecture. Just a frank discussion about the past."

"Shit. Maybe a few days by the ocean might help. We'd better pick up some grog on the way."

"I'll wait outside." Carrie left him to dress. He walked very slowly stooping over and met her outside the room. She could see he was still in pain.

"I'll stop at my place and pick up a few clothes," he said giving her a lopsided grin.

"Take my arm." He ignored her arm and tried to stand up straight.

"I'll be fine in a few seconds. Let's go." Pausing, he then walked slowly again.

"Bye bye, Nursie. You should have taken me up on my offer," he said to the nurse as they walked past.

"You really look like you're ready for a night of passion." She then winked at Carrie who shook her head.

Within an hour they collected some clothes and a few provisions from their respective homes and were soon heading south towards the coastal town of Bateman's Bay. Tully insisted she stop at a bottle shop where he bought a slab. Carrie wound her way through the traffic and concentrated on her directions ignoring her father for a while. Finally glancing at him she saw he was fast asleep. Her radio was softly playing and she drove the three hours just humming to herself, trying not to let her mind wander to her mother's death. On arriving Carrie helped him from the car into the cabin. Not big, but comfortable with two bedrooms and a great patio area overlooking the ocean where she liked to sit and read.

"This is where you take your men for a dirty weekend? I like it."

"This is where I come when I'm stressed."

41

"Are you saying I stress you out?"

"Let's keep my stress and sex life out of this."

"Hey, I'm broad minded."

"Just get inside, Dad while I get the luggage."

Coming back with the bags, she noted Tully was already sipping from a can and stretched out on a lounge chair.

"Want one?" he asked taking a sip.

"No thanks," she said looking at him with disgust.

"Don't know what you're missing." He flashed his cheeky grin once again.

"I'll get some supper on and we can talk after dinner."

"Whatever," he said with little interest.

Carrie prepared some vegetables she brought with her and took some fish from the freezer. If you liked seafood, Bateman's Bay was the place to come. Tully ate like he'd been starving for a week.

"I thought you were a lousy cook?"

"I get by. Time to do the dishes."

It was after eight before Carrie had finally washed up. She sat down opposite him and studied him with a blank look on her face.

"You look like you're down to your last dollar. What's up?"

"There's something I have to talk to you about and I want some straight answers."

He could see she was serious and frowned. "I figured there must be something you wanted, otherwise you would have left me to rot in the hospital."

She ignored his comment knowing he was right. He blinked when she put her recorder on the table and pressed the button.

"What's this, the third degree?"

"Maybe but what I want to ask you is important. So important you may not get out of here alive."

"I'll drink to that," he said opening another can.

She realized he didn't think she was serious and pulled the revolver from her bag, pointing it at him. Maybe it was just the thing to scare him into telling her the truth.

"Jesus, is that real?" he said unperturbed.

"Very real." Her voice was soft and low.

"Then for Christ sake keep it steady. It will take you ten shots to hit me waving it around like that."

"You're not scared?"

"No. You won't shoot but maybe it would be a good thing if you did. I've thought about it a lot lately."

"I can understand why after what I've learned."

"Yeah? And just what the hell are you talking about?"

"I've just come back from Belfast."

"So. Nothing's happening there at the moment. The IRA have been very quiet."

"I've been to see my Uncle Kevin."

"Oh shit," said Tully viciously. "Is that prick still alive?"

"Very much so. He sends his regards."

"I can imagine. How come you went there?"

"He sent me some photos of my mother and told me the truth about her."

"And you believed him?" Tully drained the can and reached for another. "He couldn't tell the truth if you hit him between the eyes with a bit of four by three."

"He told me he was a member of the IRA. Would you like to see the photos?"

"I suppose you're going to show them to me anyway."

Carrie handed them to him one at a time. First the lone photo of her mother. Tully looked at it for long seconds his eyes filling with moisture. "Yeah, that's her, that's your mother. Beautiful wasn't she?"

"Very."

She then handed him the other two of Tully with her in London.

"Those bastards would follow you into the toilet if they could. We were pretty happy then."

"I can see from the photos." She then handed him the fourth with him kneeling beside her with his hand under her head.

"Oh, Jesus," he said his face turning white. "How did they get that?"

"Compliments of Uncle Kevin. There's one more." She handed him the last photo showing him pointing the gun at her body. "He said you killed her. Is it true?"

His face became tense. "You don't want to know the truth, love. Let your mother lay in peace."

"Is it true? Did you kill her?"

Tears were running down his cheeks, something she had never seen before and then he nodded. "Yes, I did kill her. Maybe it's time you knew the whole story."

"You, bastard," she screamed trying to hold her hand steady as she pointed the gun straight at his head. He did nothing. He just sat staring at her, unafraid but with the saddest expression Carrie had ever seen. Nothing was said as he waited for her to pull the trigger. Hell, she thought. He didn't care.

With eyes staring at him she was trying to decide what to do. Her hand was shaking uncontrollably, the gun waving from side to side. Her eyes were so filled with tears she could hardly see. She didn't know if she meant to but the roar of the gun discharging filled the room as the trigger was pulled. The bullet went past his head and thudded into the wall behind him. Tully turned his head to look at the hole in the plaster.

"Christ, I told you to keep it steady. Hold it in both hands and try again."

After what seemed like an eternity she dropped it and put her hands to her face sobbing loudly.

"Come here, love," he said. "It's time you and I talked."

She sat beside him and he put his arm around her holding her tightly. At last the sobbing stopped and he lifted her face.

"I guess there's more to tell you about your stupid father. It's not just Belfast, there's more, much more. Fill up the kettle, let's have a drink, this is going to take a while."

"You want coffee or tea?" She blew her nose on the tissue he had handed her from the box on the sideboard.

"I need a clear head to tell you this. I'd better have strong coffee. I'll tell you all, from Belfast until now, then if you want to shoot me you have my permission."

Carrie sniffed loudly and wiped her nose again, then made them both a pot of strong coffee and sat down to listen.

Chapter Five

Belfast 1969

Struggling into his top coat he joined the other new arrivals in the Belfast airport; all waiting for their luggage to appear on the slow moving turntable. He was young and brash but held an air of self confidence that got him there in the first place. The trip had been long and tedious but Tully Sanderson felt his first foreign assignment for the Sydney Tribune more than compensated for it.

Vietnam was his first choice, but when the boss says to cover the violence in Northern Ireland, then that's what you did, especially when you were new to the game.

Twenty-one years old was considered young for the responsibility entailed with a foreign assignment, but he had the talent and he knew how to use it. Three years apprenticeship on the Tribune had only whetted his appetite and he was eager to see the world and its troubled hotspots. Being brought up in the Sydney suburb of Balmain, Tully was aware of the need to be tough and he knew how to take care of himself. Physically he was well built. Just over six-foot tall with good body strength developed from his days as a rugby player. His sultry good looks attracted many a female.

There was something about his dark hair and cool blue eyes that held some sort of magnetism for women. It was an attraction he always took full advantage of. Tully was never without a bed partner when he wanted one but his interest in journalism was his prime motivation.

"Get your arse over to Belfast," Richard Harding his boss had said when Lord Ashley, the English industrialist was kidnapped.

"You're throwing me in the deep end?" he said happily.

"You want to be a foreign correspondent or what?"

"Can I kiss you?"

"If you do you're fired. Stay and cover the violence and show me what you're made of."

"If there's no news I'll make it up."

"Get out of here, Tully---and take care. It's too much trouble to replace you."

"I knew you cared, boss." He needed no further urging and packed immediately.

If Richard was giving him this chance he wasn't going to stuff up, not Tully Sanderson.

It was the first time he'd been out of Australia and he was excited about it. He resolved he was going to make the most out of it. Half the staff was pleased to see him go.

This upstart had scooped quite a few of them in chasing stories. His name was beginning to be monotonously prevalent on the bylines appearing daily in the newspaper.

"Tully, keep your nose clean and for Christ sake don't get yourself blown up," said Richard after he gave him the orders.

As Vietnam was the talk of the world the more experienced journalists were happy to leave Belfast to the inexperienced Tully.

Inexperienced he may have been but naive he was not. He saw it as the start of his career to become one of the best foreign correspondents in Australia. His expectations of a busy terminal were wrong. Maybe it was the time of the year before the tourists arrived as he had no trouble picking up his luggage. He figured he was going to have to get used to airport terminals in his business.

He always traveled with only just one suitcase, standard for travelling journalists and was soon on his way out of the terminal looking for a taxi. The last thing he expected was to be mugged in the airport. He felt a hard object thrust into his back and heard chilling words whispered into his ear.

"Make one move and you're dead."

A sly grin spread across his face as he turned around.

"Jesus, Pat. If you're going to do Irish impersonations then you'd better work on your accent."

Pat Scanlon stood grinning like a school kid and returned his pen back to his pocket, then thrust out his big hand. "G'day, mate, welcome to Belfast."

"How the hell did you know I was coming?"

Pat raised a finger to his lips as if whispering a state secret. "Interpol knows everything, even the color of your underwear."

"You always made a good spy, even at Uni. I hear you're in charge of the kidnapping. Not bad for a twenty four year old idiot from Balmain."

"Talent is like cream, it always comes to the top," he said confidently.

"And so modest too," said Tully shaking his hand. "Thanks for meeting me. Can you recommend a cheap hotel somewhere?"

"Of course. Let's go. I have a car." He led Tully to the car-park where a black Bentley was waiting.

"Shit, this can't be yours on your wages."

"One of the perks of the job. It's bullet proof too."

As Tully settled down alongside Pat he started with the questions. "There's a few things I wanted to ask you."

"Like what progress are we making and do we have any suspects?" said Pat expectantly.

"Christ! I can find that out later. What I wanted to know was where to find the gorgeous women and the best drinking holes."

"I see nothings changed." Pat shook his head and laughed. "How come they sent a smart arse like you over here?"

"As you said, mate, they recognize talent, besides, everyone else wanted Vietnam."

"Last choice hey? Believe me, this place can be just as dangerous as Vietnam. For Christ sake tell everyone you're Australian and not English. You might last longer."

"I'm sure they'll know when I open my mouth. What's happening?"

"Anything I tell you can't be printed without my say so. Understood?"

Tully looked at him with disgust. "Shit, it's going to be like that is it?"

"Yes. Things are delicate here and we don't want any mistakes."

Tully wasn't happy about it but conceded. "All right. If I want to send something then I'll show it to you first. Agreed?"

"Right. Here's where we are. The main suspect is a bloke named Kevin O'Rourke. He's already done time for a gun charge but he's a smart cookie, smart enough to hide any evidence. This English Lord has been missing for a week now and a ransom of five hundred thousand pounds has been asked for."

"This O'Rourke is IRA?" asked Tully thoughtfully.

"The worst kind. We know at least five murders he's been responsible for but he has an excellent intelligence network to cover him. Two months ago he blew up a police car carrying three men. Two died and the other poor bastard will never work again."

"Why didn't you arrest him?"

"We did but he had twenty men swearing he was attending a meeting fifty miles away."

"Is the ransom going to be paid? Wouldn't that be a chance to nab the crooks?"

"Ashley's family have agreed to pay but it's to be a bank transfer to an anonymous account in Switzerland. Impossible to trace."

"What's the chances of seeing the Pom alive again?"

"About the same as Balmain winning the grand final this year."

"Shit, that bad," said Tully grinning. "Any tidbits for me?'

"One or two. I'll fill you in when I get you settled."

Tully took in the streets of Belfast as the car moved through the traffic. "Just something to keep the boss happy. How's the chances of getting a car like this?"

Pat looked at him as if he were mad. "Buy an old one. It's cheaper than using taxis or hire cars if you're going to be here for long."

"Thanks, mate. Where do I find you?"

Pat handed him a card with his office address. "Call me anytime."

"Won't the English press be pissed off if they hear you're giving me information?"

"They get info. too. All I'm interested in at the moment is getting this Lord back."

"Don't like your chances. Got time for a drink tonight?"

He glanced at his wristwatch. "Maybe. Give me a ring about six."

Pat pulled up outside a hotel and Tully stepped out. It looked run down and dirty.

"Is this the Hilton?"

"It's all you can afford. See you later." He drove off leaving Tully standing on the footpath with his suitcase beside him.

Tully made arrangements for a two-week stay at the hotel and then went looking for a cheap car. It wasn't much but it would do the job. A darned sight better than paying for taxis every time he wanted to move around.

At six he rang Pat and they met at a nearby pub. Most of the evening was spent catching up on what was happening back in Australia. Then they began reminiscing about the old days of chasing women and trying to drink each other under the table. At least he had Pat for company if it became too boring.

*   *   *

The heavy morning rain had eased off to soft drizzle, then stopped by late afternoon. The evening was depressingly dark.

There was no breeze, just a gray pall of low cloud, which enveloped Belfast like a funeral shroud. Kevin O'Rourke looked at his watch, then at his teenage sister Briony.

"It's time. Just drive up normally, set the timer, post the letter and walk away slowly." O'Rourke got a buzz every time he thought about an attack on the English.

"Do I have to do this, Kevin?" Briony could feel her stomach turning over and her heart seemed to beat like a drum in her chest. Violence was not a part of her makeup.

"We all need to show our loyalty, Briony. You know that."

"But this is not right. There could be innocent people walking by."

"At this time of night? All the shops are shut and the only people likely to be around will be English soldiers."

"But what if there are others?" Briony's fears were probing her conscience.

"Where were others when they took our father out into the country and shot him like a dog? You can't remember that?" A heavy scowl creased O'Rourke's face showing intense hatred for the English and the Orange men of Ireland. In his opinion, any fear, any damage inflicted was certainly worth the effort.

Briony bit her lip. She remembered only too clearly when as a fourteen year old, the police came to tell them of the murder of her father and her uncle. Both had been taken into the country and executed with a single shot to the back of the head. It was the worst moment of her life as her father was the person she loved more than anyone.

Kevin broke her thoughts and gained her attention. "All true Irish men and women must fight until Ireland is free. This is a small part you can play."

"Why me?" Briony wanted no part of killing just to make a point.

"A man leaving a car in front of the Post Office and walking away would be suspicious. A young girl innocently posting a letter would be ignored. Once you press the trigger you have three minutes to get clear. Don't run, just walk quickly."

Briony nodded and took the car keys offered, resigned to her fate realizing her brother was adamant.

"You'd better take this too." O'Rourke handed her a heavy army issue colt 45 revolver. "In case they try to take you."

She stared at it with distaste. Briony put it into her bag quickly. She hated guns but knew the soldiers would shoot her if she were cornered.

O'Rourke watched her eyes knowing she would do it albeit reluctantly. She had her mother's compassion, which he didn't like but he was sure he could drive it from her in time. Only the cause mattered.

The drive to the Post Office filled her eyes with tears. Terrorist or patriot, she had seen the words often in the newspapers. Now she was about to cross the line and reminded herself these were the people who murdered her father. Only a few people were in the area and she was relieved to think, maybe no one would be hurt. Looking around carefully she parked the car.

Satisfied no one was close by she pressed the timer switch under the dash and posted her letter. Her stomach was churning over, her legs feeling like jelly. With pounding heart she began to walk away.

The fear the car bomb would explode prematurely took over. She walked quickly, then trotted until finally she broke out into a run.

She didn't want to do it but Kevin was right. Her father's honor was at stake. She was a hundred yards away when it exploded but she didn't falter. Her legs found new strength.

She broke into a sprint, one hand on her bag, the other pumping up and down as she ran. The sky behind her was red and she could hear shouting from soldiers suddenly on the scene. When the car came screeching to a halt she panicked. Sure it was the police, her fingers fumbled, then closed and tightened around the gun. As the door flew open she pointed it at the driver and was surprised when she saw a young man smiling at her. He had a strange accent which further adding to her confusion.

*   *   *

Carrie O'Rourke died when Briony was seven and Brian O'Rourke had taken care of his children like any devoted father could. It was he who took her to dancing lessons, it was he who attended the school play, and it was he who consoled her when she fluffed her lines. She remembered the laughs and wanted to run away, but it was Brian who took her in his arms and wiped away the tears.

"They're all jealous my little angel and I don't blame them. You are the most beautiful girl in the whole school. Show them you're a true O'Rourke and keep your head high."

He was always there when she needed him, a person she could rely on. He filled the void of her now dead mother more than anyone would have expected. When the Protestants took him away she wanted to die herself. Devoted to his children to the end, Brian O'Rourke tried to make up for the loss of their mother in the only way he knew how.

Even though they were poor, he always tried to take them away at least once a year. The farm they lived on was in a quiet area and Briony and Kevin worked hard to grow their own vegetables. While Kevin hated milking the only cow, Briony was contented to take over the chore. They were both happy children despite losing their mother at an early age, and both did their best to assist their father.

Briony never missed Mass and often prayed for her mother's soul, wishing for the violence to end but it never did. At least they were isolated to some extent but surrounded by Protestant farmers. It was the rule practiced by both sides you never played with the children of people not of your religion. Briony could never understand why. When her father was murdered Kevin changed dramatically. No longer an innocent, he joined the active cell of the IRA and was soon into murder. He took Briony into

Belfast where they rented a house in the Catholic area and she was alarmed at the hate he now expressed to all Protestants. She knew by tradition she was bound irrevocably to the cause with the thousands of other Catholics, and there was not much she could do about it.

*   *   *

It was just after nine when Tully left Pat on his fourth night in Belfast. For someone who lived in sunshine and good weather Tully found the place depressing. At least the Irish beer was palatable but he resigned himself to get used to his new living arrangements.

As he drove back towards the hotel Tully couldn't help but see the soldiers in full combat gear, and rifles at ready patrolling the streets. It was a strange feeling

Growing up in Australia he always felt safe at night on any street, even when some of the local gangs were at war.

There were a few people walking along the footpath and a small amount of traffic around when he noticed a girl ahead running as if to catch a bus.

Long legs flashing, and dark hair flowing; his attention was gathered for he knew attractive women when he saw them. Her build was slim; she was dressed in a plain dress, a turtleneck pullover and was definitely in a hurry.

Taller than most girls he knew but then he liked tall girls. They made better bed partners as far as he was concerned. As he drove nearer, a huge explosion suddenly shattered the stillness of the night. A car disintegrated half a block back. The dark sky lit up like daylight and every window in the street shattered as shrapnel sprayed the area.

A soldier was thrown across the street while another lay a bloody mess on the road.

Whistles blew, people screamed and more soldiers came running with guns held high as they came face to face with the carnage. The Post Office was now a heap of rubble, bricks piled on top of each other in a disjointed way. Wooden trusses were pointing to the sky like a devil's trident and the road covered in debris.

People in the street were running and confusion was rife as flames leapt higher and higher. Tully sped up and overtook the girl who was still running.

He threw on the brakes bringing the car to a screeching halt and opened the passenger side door. The girl's eyes widened when she saw him, fear clearly etched on her face. She reached into her bag and produced a gun pointing it straight at Tully.

"Shit, love. I was just going to offer you a lift. A simple no thanks will do."

She hesitated when he spoke. "You're not police?"

"Do I look like a copper? I think there's some soldiers coming down the street and they don't look pleased. The offer is still open if you like."

She glanced back quickly and saw what he said was true.

"Last chance," said Tully noting the anxiety in her face.

She slipped the gun into her bag and jumped into the car. Tully sped off leaving the destruction behind.

"I'm Tully Sanderson, an Australian journalist. What's your name?"

"Briony. If you could drop me at the bus station I'd be pleased."

Tully noticed she was shaking and she kept glancing behind.

"I've got a better idea. How about if we go to a pub somewhere and have a drink. It will settle your nerves."

Briony eyed him suspiciously but then abruptly agreed. "There's a pub called the Shamrock about a mile away in Glean Street. I have friends there."

"On one condition," said Tully good-humoredly.

"And what's that?"

"You keep the gun in your bag. I've never been shot taking a girl to a pub before. Mind you some fathers had definitely thought about it."

Briony laughed easily, the tension she felt calmed.

Several men greeted her enthusiastically as they walked into the Shamrock. Tully brought one or two glances but chose to ignore them as they sat at a table.

The usual tobacco smoke filled the air but Tully tried to ignore it. He liked beer but smoking had been off his list since rugby days.

"What would you like?" He searched his pockets for Irish money.

She seemed amused as he looked at the coins. "A brandy please if you have enough cash. Maybe I can lend you some."

"No worries there, it just takes some working out." He ambled away counting out an assortment of unfamiliar coins.

An elderly man rugged up walked past Briony with a pipe protruding from his mouth. "Nice evening," he said tipping his hat.

"Now that the sun has set," replied Briony as Tully returned with the drinks.

"A friend?" he asked looking at the man.

"Just a friendly patron." She took the drink and didn't give the man another glance. Tully studied her face now they were in brighter light. She was quite beautiful, no more than eighteen years old, very self-assured and confident. She smiled back at him sipping her drink.

"Thanks for picking me up. The bomb frightened me. When it went off I didn't know what to do."

"You know you Irish are amazing."

"What do you mean?"

"Not many people run from a bomb before it goes off, especially if they don't know it's there."

"I was running for a bus."

"Of course. Were you going to hold up the bus for the ride home?"

"Belfast is a dangerous place at night. A girl has to take care of herself."

"If all the girls carry a gun like that then I'm going to remain celibate."

Briony laughed so much she nearly choked on her drink.

"Well it was just a thought." He watched her closely thinking her amused expression made her even prettier.

They talked for an hour as Tully told her all about life in Australia and how he had become a journalist. Briony told him a little about herself and how she wished the English would pack up and go home. He could see she was republican through and through but didn't press the issue. When they were all talked out he gave her his best smile.

"As a stranger here I'm unfamiliar with the best restaurants, so where should I take you to dinner tomorrow night?"

"You fancy yourself don't you?" said Briony definitely attracted to this easy going Australian.

"No, but I certainly fancy you. Do you want me to go down on one knee and beg?" He slid to the floor and put both hands together.

She looked around quickly. "Get up, you're embarrassing me."

"Then it's a date," he said springing to his feet.

"It's a date. Now I think you'd better drive me home."

"My pleasure, ma'am." Holding her hand he led her to the car.

Briony was relaxed until they turned a corner. As he drove following her directions they were halted at a checkpoint.

Three soldiers in full combat gear surrounded the car. Tully wound down the window as a soldier peered into the interior of the car.

"Good evening, sir. We're checking all cars just as a precaution after tonight's disturbance. Do you mind releasing the boot?" he said as he clasped his rifle.

"No worries, mate." Tully stepped out of the car and opened the boot. "What's happened?"

"A terrorist explosion earlier, sir and we're just making a spot check. Do you have some identification?"

"Sure," said Tully and handed him his press card.

The soldier inspected it and curtly handed it back.

"And the young lady?' He bent to face Briony.

"I have nothing with me," said Briony holding her bag tightly, not wanting the soldier to search it.

"Your name, miss?"

"Briony. Briony O'Rourke."

"Did you say O'Rourke. Are you related to Kevin O'Rourke?"

"He's my brother. I haven't done anything wrong."

"She's been with me, mate. We're just on our way home after dinner."

"Would you mind stepping out of the car, miss?"

"I can vouch for her. She's been with me all night."

"And who can vouch for you?" The soldier eyed him suspiciously.

"Captain Pat Scanlon of Interpol. Give him a call and I'll talk to him."

Briony was very nervous and tried to slip her bag under the seat. The soldier stepped aside and spoke on his radio. Tully could hear the crackling reply.

"Captain Scanlon here. What's the trouble?"

"I have a man and a woman here, sir who may be suspicious. He says he's a friend of yours."

"What's his name, soldier?"

"Says he's Tully Sanderson, sir."

"Put him on," said Pat and the soldier handed Tully the radio.

"Is that you, Tully?"

"Yeah, mate. This is not a very friendly place."

"Where are you?"

Tully looked at the soldier appealingly.

"Quinn Street. I'm just taking a young lady home after a very pleasant evening and we've been pulled up."

"Christ, it didn't take you long did it?"

"Can't let the grass grow under your feet, mate. You should see her. She's stunning." He looked at Briony and winked.

"Put the soldier back on."

Tully handed back the radio. The soldier listened, nodded a few times then put down the receiver.

"Sorry to detain you, sir. You can go now. Have a pleasant evening."

"Yeah thanks, same to you."

He gave the soldier a wave and drove off.

"Where's the gun?" said Tully as the car moved away.

"Under the seat. Thank you."

"It was you who set off the bomb wasn't it?"

She didn't answer, just stared straight ahead.

"You have friends in Interpol?" she said at last.

"Close friend actually. We went to Uni together and have been mates ever since. Don't worry. My job is to report the news not dob in the IRA."

"Dob in?"

"Inform on. Relax now it's all over, why not start thinking about the delicious meal I'm going to shout you tomorrow night."

"You Australians use a strange language. Shout! Dob! I wonder I can understand you at all."

"Sometime you don't have to say much to understand a person."

"That's true. Pull up there, it's the red brick house."

Tully studied it. The front door was on the street and the place was hard to distinguish from the dozen or so others all joined together. All the houses were doubled story with an upstairs window overlooking the street below. Some houses had been rendered and painted but Briony's was still a red bricked place. The bricks being hand made and old.

"May I come in?"

"Maybe tomorrow night. Pick me up at seven if that suits you."

She reached for the door handle but Tully grabbed her hand and pulled her close.

"This is an old Australian custom." He kissed her gently and she softened and went with him not pulling away.

"That's funny. It's an old Irish custom too," she said when they broke free. "Goodnight, Tully."

He watched those lovely long slim legs carry her to the front door step.

She reached for the door latch with one hand while the other touched her lips and then waved him a kiss. He watched until she closed the door, then with a very contented feeling he started the engine and drove to his hotel.

Chapter Six

Tully called by Pat's office the next morning to be met by a stony faced friend with raised eyebrows. He looked mad but then Tully knew his friend couldn't stay mad at him for long.

"Shit, Tully. Here five minutes and into trouble with the army. Will you ever change?" Pat leaned back in his chair with his hands behind his head. The feigned anger soon disappeared.

"Do you have a bar fridge?"

Pat pointed to a small fridge in the office corner. It seems he was going to be at home where ever he was.

"Does the army always interfere with a person's sex life in this country?" Tully gave him a lopsided grin and appealed with both hands outstretched. Then he popped a can.

"I guess you can't really blame them," said Pat. "The IRA blew up a post office last night. It was a damn car bomb. Two soldiers were badly hurt so they had orders to stop everyone. Who was the girl you picked up?"

"You won't believe me when I tell you."

"Oh." Pat's interest was suddenly raised.

"Yeah. I dropped into a pub for a drink and saw this stunning girl. Absolutely gorgeous. Tall, dark hair, dark eyes and a figure to make you drool. Of course I couldn't resist her and asked her to join me."

"The old charm still working is it?" asked Pat.

"Is that jealousy I detect? Anyway I bought her a drink and she told me her name was Briony."

"Now there's a good Irish name."

"Actually it was Briony O'Rourke. She's the sister of the terrorist you were talking about."

"What?" Pat was now very interested.

"I thought that might get your attention. I made a date for tonight."

"Was she anywhere near the post office last night?"

"I told you, she was in the pub," lied Tully.

"You've stepped right into a hornet's nest here, mate. Dally with O'Rourke's sister and he'll have your balls cut off."

"I haven't met him yet. Maybe tonight I'll get lucky."

"If you want some advice, drop her now. It's bloody dangerous mixing with the IRA."

"Look. It's my job to report the news; it's yours to clean up the criminals. Who I see shouldn't upset anyone."

"You don't know who you're dealing with here. O'Rourke is a killer with no qualms about stepping on anyone who gets in his way."

"I'll try not to antagonize him." Tully was not going to be deterred.

"If you find out anything about O'Rourke then I'd appreciate a tip." Pat scratched his chin in deep thought. Maybe this had possibilities.

"I'm strictly neutral as far as Briony is concerned. I won't use her to get to O'Rourke."

"Have you considered she might be a terrorist too?"

"No way. She's only eighteen. Just because her brother is an IRA soldier doesn't automatically make her one."

"Look, this is a war. The republicans hate the English and will do anything to get them out of Ireland. Men, women, children. They're all the same when it comes to fighting. Be bloody careful and for Christ sake watch O'Rourke. If he even suspects you know me he'll eliminate you quick smart."

Tully recalled how he had told Briony of his connection to Pat. He only hoped she didn't mention it to her brother.

"Your point is noted. Now, how about some details on the bomb explosion? I have a story to send back home to help pay my wages."

Pat gave him the same information he had given the English press but with one or two extra details. Tully jotted down the info. as it was told to him.

"Thanks for that, mate. I'd better go and get it typed up."

"Have a nice night and if you get into trouble ring me if you can," said Pat, as he was about to leave.

"Since when did I need help seducing a beautiful girl."

"Not what I meant," said Pat.

Tully grinned as he left. "I know."

Tully took extra care making himself presentable for his date. Usually it was take me as you find me but Briony O'Rourke ignited a passion in him he hadn't experienced before. A hot bath, a close shave, a patter of after-shave, his best shirt and he was ready.

With Pat's warning and instructions ringing in his ears, Tully rang the doorbell with bated breath. A man not much older than he was opened it. It was not hard to see he was Briony's brother. Same dark eyes, same complexion, same jaw line. The only thing missing was Briony's friendly attitude. He scowled, then looked up and down the street.

"Do you want something?"

"Actually I came to get Briony. We have a date tonight." Tully returned the cold stare starkly aware of the hostility emanating from the man.

"You are?"

"Tully Sanderson."

"You're Australian."

"Now how did you guess that?" Tully's voice was full of sarcasm.

He just glared at Tully for a few seconds, then opened the door wider.

"You better come in. Briony said you're a journalist."

"Foreign correspondent for the Sydney Tribune. And you are?"

"Kevin O'Rourke. I'm Briony's brother."

Tully offered his hand but O'Rourke ignored it.

"Briony said you saved her from the soldiers last night."

"It was just a routine check. Nothing serious." Tully was anxious to hear just how much Briony had told her brother.

"You're only taking Briony out. Any attempt to learn information from her about me or our cause will result in retribution."

"Like you said, I'm here to take Briony out to dinner, and it's nice to meet you too."

O'Rourke scowled fiercely at him but Tully ignored him. He obviously regarded Tully as a smart arse. The dislike was mutual.

"Also any mistreatment of Briony will further anger me."

"It would anger me too if I heard she suffered by going out with me."

"Just so we understand each other," said O'Rourke. The conversation ended abruptly when Briony stepped into the room. Tully's heart raced. A vision of loveliness took his breath away. Her white dress was in stark contrast to her dark features.

"Wow. You look stunning."

"Thank you." She was delighted by his reaction; the time she spent getting ready was well worth it. Normally a girl for jeans and tops, Briony had carefully laundered and pressed her one good dress. This was one occasion she wished she had a greater range to choose from. "I see you've met Kevin. Shall we go?"

"Sure." Tully offered her his arm.

"See you later, Kevin," said Briony sweetly and they left him with a deep scowl on his face.

"Yeah, see you later, Kevin." Tully couldn't help himself.

"I gather you didn't tell him I had friends at Interpol." Tully looked dubiously at her as he held the car door open.

"You'd be dead now if I had."

"That's what I figured. Well stuff the police and stuff your brother. We're going to have a nice dinner and enjoy each other's company."

"He's very nervous about me going out with a journalist."

"I'll make a bargain with you. I won't ask you about your brother and you don't ask me about my friend."

"I couldn't have put it better myself," she said laughing.

*   *   *

Briony selected the restaurant and as Tully knew little about Belfast, he was pleasantly surprised. It was a quiet place, tastefully decorated with a warm homely atmosphere and not very crowded. Even better, not very expensive. There was a wide selection of food and a three-piece band was playing soft music. They danced between courses, which gave Tully a chance to get his arms around her slim waist.

"If I'd known all Irish girls were like you I'd have come here sooner."

"I thought blarney was exclusively Irish."

"Maybe I have some Irish blood way back."

61

She laughed delightfully at his tales about Australia and his antics at Uni. She in turn told him about her strict Catholic upbringing and living with the constant violence around her.

"And how come a gorgeous girl like you bombs post offices for amusement?" he said light heartedly

Her mood changed immediately. "I don't enjoy violence of any sort," she said seriously. "The English have murdered many a good Irishman and we just want them out of our country."

"Have you lost any family in the war?"

"My father and uncle were both taken out into the country and shot like dogs by the Protestants under the protection of the English. They were guilty of nothing but being Catholic. It is the duty of all Irish people to drive the soldiers out."

"You know at the other side of the world, we all think the Irish are crazy fighting each other. When Irish people immigrate to Australia, whether they're Catholic or Protestant, they talk to each other just like the rest of the population. There's never any trouble."

"That's because they're no longer a part of Ireland. When you live here your heritage is important."

"What happens if a Catholic girl falls in love with a Protestant boy?"

"Then they're both in trouble. If that happens then it's time to leave."

"Boy, I'm glad I'm not Irish then." He pulled her closer and rested his head against hers as they danced slowly to the music.

From then on politics was put aside and they were just a man and woman enjoying each other's company for the rest of the night. It was nearly two a.m. when Tully took her home.

"Looks like big brother is waiting up." He pointed to Kevin's shadow against the blind.

Tully leaned across and took her in his arms. They stared at each other deeply before Briony brought her lips to his and kissed him softly at first, then with a deep passion. He responded eagerly and they stayed locked together, neither wanting the evening to end.

Tully stroked her face gently almost hypnotized by her clear shining eyes. It was a feeling he had never encountered before with a woman. Sure he had made love to many girls in his younger years but never had he encountered the emotions he was feeling now.

"Tomorrow night?" he asked tentatively.

"Same time is fine with me."

He opened the car door and stood on the footpath until she went inside and closed the door. He was about to leave when he heard raised voices. There was a slamming of a door, then silence. When a light went on in an upstairs window he drove off.

They met again the following night, then the night after. It seemed they couldn't see enough of each other. Briony took him on sightseeing tours of Northern Ireland during the weekends. Tully had to admit, except for the weather Ireland really was a beautiful country. By the end of the month they were both hopelessly in love, much to the disgust of Kevin O'Rourke.

Over the next couple of months, there were four more murders. The IRA killed a policeman in his home and wounded his wife, then two Catholic men, a father and son were walking home from work when a car pulled up and both were sprayed with sub machine guns in retaliation. Then shots were fired into a pub frequented by Protestants where another man was killed.

The madness only made Tully shake his head in disbelief.

He covered these stories and sent them back home much to his boss's pleasure. It made good copy and always took the near front page. He was sleeping late after a night of booze with some journalist mates when the jangling of the phone disturbed him.

"Tully, it's Pat. We just pulled Lord Ashley's body out of the harbor. He's been shot in the back of the head."

"Bastards. Has the ransom been paid?"

"Yes. The funds were transferred three days ago. The body has been in the water since yesterday."

"Can you give me any further details?" asked Tully, his pen poised.

Pat proceeded to fill him in and warned him the news would hit the media within the hour. Tully had the story on its way before the English press knew about it.

He picked up Briony that night very subdued.

"Something wrong, Tully?" She was not used to him being so quiet.

"Ask your brother. Lord Ashley has been executed after the ransom was paid. If this is your idea of war against the English then it stinks."

She hung her head in silence. "Tully, I know it's hard for you to understand but these things happen. I'm not saying Kevin was involved but if he was then he was doing it for Ireland."

"Fighting soldiers is one thing, murdering civilians is another? If you condone this then I feel sorry for you."

"Let's not argue. I don't want to go out tonight. Let's go back to your place. Try and put all this behind us."

Tully nodded not wanting to fight with her. He bought a bottle of French wine and together they drank half of it while they were sitting on his sofa with their arms around each other.

She looked up at him and smiled. "Make love to me, Tully. I need you to make love to me."

He placed down his glass and kissed her tenderly. She put both arms around his neck and responded, then rose to her feet and took his hand, leading him to the bedroom. He watched as she removed her clothes slowly. She stood in her underwear and undid his shirt and let it slip to the floor.

He needed no further urging and hastily removed the rest of his clothes, then hers before lowering her onto the bed.

He had enough experience with women to suspect it was her first introduction to sex so he took things slowly enjoying the pleasure he was giving her.

"I haven't done this before. It's my first time," she said smiling at him.

"Then I'll see that you always remember it," and he proceeded to caress her body in all the right places.

His expert fingers fondled every inch of her body. Her skin tingled at his touch and she thrilled at the sensation. He kissed her all over, in all the secret places, which brought her excitement and heightened her passion.

She wasn't sure how to please him and her inexperienced fingers tentatively smoothed across his face, then his neck and chest. Gradually she gained courage to slide her hand down toward his groin. He moaned softly and his manhood hardened further under her soft caress. His fingers found her hot moist opening and he probed and touched until she thought she would scream.

"Please, Tully, please," she begged. As he slid into her, she raised her hips from the mattress to meet his entry. They moved in unison, slowly, gently, and firmly. She had never known such sensation. She moaned and writhed and begged for more. Their passion heightened and their movements quickened.

"Oh God, Tully, Tully." She rode the crest of the wave and his crest peaked with hers and together they drifted as if in heaven. Finally together they subsided and slowly returned to reality.

"I love you, Tully," she whispered in his ear.

"I love you too. It's never happened to me before. You mean everything to me, Briony. You're in my thoughts constantly. I have trouble doing my job, as I can't stop thinking about you. You're my whole world."

"I think we could be in trouble you know. You realize I'm a Catholic and you're not."

"I think it's okay because I'm not Irish," he teased

"I'll have to think that logic through," She turned towards him and entwined her arms and legs around him. "Are you rested enough to try this again?"

As he reached for her delicious delights, he wondered what Kevin O'Rourke would think of the situation and how Pat would react. He was sure he knew what both answers would be.

Chapter Seven

Tully sat deep in thought about his situation. The consequences of falling in love with Briony O'Rourke were great. She was not only a devout Irish Catholic but having a brother, a high-ranking member of the IRA presented further complications. He wanted to marry her and take her back to Australia but knew she wouldn't leave Ireland. It was obvious the strong attachment for her brother and for the cause meant she wouldn't leave until the war was won.

He also knew Pat would be horrified at the thought of him being the brother-in-law of a known IRA terrorist. Their friendship had endured years and was strong, but no doubt would be sorely tested by this announcement. Pat was convinced O'Rourke was the instigator of the Ashley kidnapping and murder but proving it was another thing entirely.

Pat's role had been to investigate the kidnapping; the terrorist attacks were the responsibility of the police and army. Unless he solved the case quickly then he would be on his way to another port of call where Interpol's involvement was needed.

When they met in the pub for an evening drink, Pat could see he was troubled.

"I know the beer is not cold like at home, mate but it's not that bad."

"I wish that's all it was. I've got troubles," said Tully at last.

"Haven't we all. What's yours?"

"You won't believe me but I've fallen in love."

Pat nearly choked in his beer. "Shit, not Briony O'Rourke."

"Yeah. Stupid isn't it."

"Bloody hell. What does O'Rourke think about this?"

"Stuffed if I know. Briony hasn't told him yet."

"You're kidding me right. Tully Sanderson in love,--- with an Irish terrorist," he added.

"Why do you think she's a terrorist?"

"By simple association. You can't tell me she's an innocent Irish girl who knows nothing about her brother's activities. I told you, men women and children are all part of their army."

"What the hell am I going to do?"

"Are you sure you love her?"

"Head over heels. I think about her every minute of the day."

"Then you'll just have to sit down and talk it through with her. If she feels the same then you'll work something out. If O'Rourke finds out he may solve the problem. He'll blow your stupid head off."

"I feel the same about him," said Tully. "We'll have to talk tonight."

"Good luck, mate. If I pin this murder on O'Rourke then we may never be able to be friends again, not if you're with Briony."

Kevin O'Rourke was livid when Briony told him.

"You must be mad, girl. Not only is he a Protestant but he's a bloody foreigner."

"I know, Kevin but I love him dearly."

"I also happen to know he meets regularly with a policeman named Scanlon. I had him followed."

"Scanlon is an Interpol Officer investigating the kidnapping and murder of the Englishman."

"You knew and you didn't tell me," shouted O'Rourke.

"Tully has always remained neutral. He doesn't ask me about you and I don't ask about his friend."

"I don't trust the bastard. You want to see me behind bars again?"

"Of course not. Tully will only report the news. He won't make it."

"It's a police trap for you to tell him about our operations." Briony could see the venom in his eyes. She was fearful for Tully's safety.

"Did you kill the Englishman, Kevin?"

"You think we were going to let him go? Grow up, Briony. He had to go and I think Sanderson has to go too."

"You touch one hair of his head, Kevin and I swear I'll tell his friend all about you."

"Don't threaten me, girl. That's treacherous talk and it has its consequences."

"I've always been loyal to the cause and I expect the cause to be loyal to me, but I'd never forgive you if he's harmed."

Kevin scowled at her then his mood changed. "All right. I will give you a test for your loyalty."

"What?" she was anxious to change the subject from Tully.

"We have plans to rob a bank and you can be the driver. That should help prove your loyalty."

"I thought blowing up the post office did that."

"That was a small test. This robbery will bring in a profit for the cause. We need money to buy guns and explosives."

"You're determined to turn me into a criminal aren't you?"

"It's not a crime to fight the Brits. You're either with us or against us. The consequences of rejecting us could be bad for Sanderson."

Briony hesitated briefly then agreed. His meaning was clear enough. If she was going to keep Tully safe then she was going to have to compromise.

"All right but Tully is not to be harmed."

"If he says nothing to the police then I'll think about it, but first I want to see which way your loyalty lies."

"When is the robbery to be?"

"Today just before they close. There'll be four of us including you. Casey has been arrested and you're the replacement. You only have to wait in the car with the engine running. You better take this." He handed her a revolver.

"No. The last time I had one of these I was nearly caught. If it hadn't been for Tully I'd be in prison now."

"Suit yourself. We'll be carrying machine pistols. Make sure you're ready on time."

Reluctantly Briony agreed and spent a restless few hours thinking about her Irish heritage, her brother, the cause and her love for Tully. By mid-afternoon her mind was a muddled turmoil, but promptly on time a car pulled up outside and there was no further time for any musings.

Michael Flannery handed Briony the keys. "Got it this morning. The owner won't want it anymore."

"What did you do to him?" asked Briony annoyed.

"You don't want to know. Are we ready, Kevin?" He was quite ebullient.

"Let's go," said Kevin picking up the weapons.

* * *

Briony's fingers had a death grip on the steering wheel as they drove towards the bank. To refuse to go would have meant a death sentence for Tully. She had no doubt what her brother and his friends would do. As much as she wanted no part in it she was resigned to the fact there was no escape.

It was two minutes to closing time when they pulled up outside the bank. There were only a few people in the street but Kevin ignored them. It was one of the newer banks in the town. The big glass windows showed only a few customers, mostly women. Kevin, Michael Flannery, and Sean Flynn pulled on their masks and rushed into the bank with their guns raised, while Briony stayed outside in the car with the motor running.

The staff was anxious to get home and was annoyed at first when they burst in. The annoyance turned to fear when they saw the guns and masks. The women screamed but offered no resistance as O'Rourke leapt the counter, snatched up the money from the tills and stuffed it into a bag

The manager hurried from his office to see why people were shouting and before he could even open his mouth, O'Rourke shot him straight between the eyes. His head seemed to explode as brain matter splashed across the wall as his body fell to the floor. A woman screamed and fell sobbing.

O'Rourke then fired a burst into the ceiling causing everyone to follow the woman's lead and fall flat to the floor. The safe door was open and he filled his bags with as much cash as he could find. With the bags full they rushed out of the bank and into the car. A lone policeman hearing the shots came running, leaned into the car and pulled Briony's balaclava from her face. Flannery shot him with a quick burst and Briony took off at high speed.

"Slow down, just drive normally once you're around the corner. We don't need to attract unnecessary attention."

"That policeman saw me," said Briony ashamed at what had happened.

"Michael took care of that little problem," said O'Rourke grinning. "At the end of the street there's another car waiting. There, the blue one." He pointed to the car standing apart from others in the street. The four quickly transferred to the next car and headed for home.

A police car rushed past but the occupants took no notice of the small sedan as Briony tried to hold the wheel steady on the trip home. When they arrived O'Rourke handed Flannery the money and weapons. "You know what to do?"

Flannery nodded and drove off leaving Briony and O'Rourke standing on the footpath.

"We've been here all day, understand, Briony?"

"Of course," she said quietly. "You won't hurt Tully will you,---please, Kevin?"

"We'll see my girl, we'll see."

*   *   *

Inspector Hugh Grayson of the police stormed into Pat's office. "There's been a civilian killed and a policeman badly wounded during a bank hold-up over on Tara Street."

"O'Rourke's IRA?" asked Pat.

"We think so. The policeman managed to tell us he snatched a balaclava from one of them. He said it was a girl. His description was vague due to his injuries but it sounds like it may have been Briony O'Rourke, Kevin O'Rourke's sister."

"Can you question him again?"

"No. He lapsed into unconsciousness and was undergoing surgery."

"What are you going to do?" Pat was concerned for Tully with his feelings for O'Rourke's sister.

"Arrest her. If we question her she might just crack and implicate her brother."

"You really have no substantial evidence, only a fleeting glance. A solicitor would tear that apart."

"I'm all too aware of that but if we hold her for a couple of hours and give her some attention then she might crack."

"You mean torture."

"Obviously Australians have different methods from us, Scanlon. I'm just paying you the courtesy of knowing what's happening."

"You work like that?"

"When it's necessary. You'd be surprised at the results we get sometimes."

"Like the girl fished out of the harbor a month or so ago."

Grayson gave him a sickly smirk. "Never heard about that one. Must go and attend to Miss O'Rourke." He closed the door leaving Pat with a decidedly uneasy feeling.

"Shit," said Pat reaching for his phone. "Come on, answer the bloody thing, Tully." It almost rang out before Tully reached it.

"Yeah, mate," said Tully cheerfully.

"I'll only say this once. Get Briony out of Belfast now. Not in an hour, now. The police are on the way to arrest her and it won't be pleasant for her."

"Why?"

"Details later. You only have fifteen minutes at most." He had slammed down the phone before he even considered the consequences of what he had done. If the Irish police were going to flout the law then he was going to do his small part to assist his old friend. He knew what she would be in for if she were picked up.

Tully never hesitated. He ran from his room, leapt into his car and rushed to Briony's home pounding on the door with both fists, with enough venom to alarm even O'Rourke. O'Rourke snatched it open about two feet keeping his body half hidden.

"What the hell do you want, Sanderson? You're not welcome here."

Tully put his shoulder to the door and pushed pass him. He noticed O'Rourke silently slip a gun back into his pocket.

"Shut up, O'Rourke. The police will be here in a minute to arrest Briony. She has to come with me now."

"She'll be safe here."

"She bloody won't. I know for a fact, now where is she?" Briony rushed down the stairs at the sound of raised voices.

"Tully, --- what are...?" Her eyes widened in surprise.

"We have to go right now. The police will be here in a few minutes."

"I'll pack some things."

"You haven't got time. I mean now. Tell your stupid brother to let you go."

O'Rourke looked at Tully, then at Briony.

"You want her to be fished out of the harbor?" Tully was almost shouting.

"All right." He removed a card from his wallet, which he handed to Briony. "Go to the harbor and find this man. He'll take you to England on his boat without asking questions." Tully almost dragged her to the car and drove off just as the police came around the corner.

"Jesus, that was close," he said when he was sure they were safe. "What the hell did you do?"

"Kevin said he would kill you unless I helped him rob a bank. I drove the car but a policeman saw my face. Flannery shot him. I thought he was dead."

"I'll be dead if I keep seeing you. You and I will have to spend some time in London until things cool off. We can get a flat and keep ourselves indoors."

"That sounds nice," she said moving closer to him. He gave her a grin and she moved even closer kissing him lightly on the cheek.

"That'll do for starters," he said speeding up.

O'Rourke raised the linoleum, lifted a floorboard and put the gun in the opening.

The police surrounded the house and were hammering on the door, O'Rourke picked up a half full cup of tea taking his time answering. He faced three police all holding sub machine guns.

"Well, Inspector Grayson. This is a surprise. What can I do for you?"

Grayson pushed past him and stormed inside. "Your sister. Where is she?"

"You mean Briony. The dear girl is in Dublin looking after a sick aunt. Compassion was always one of her strong points."

"When did she leave?" Grayson was furious.

"The day before yesterday. Is something wrong?"

"Search the place," Grayson ordered and men streamed into every room looking for Briony.

"Can I get you a cup of tea?" O'Rourke gave him a sickly grin, a grin Rayson wanted to wipe from his face with his pistol.

"Nothing here, sir," reported his sergeant. "No girl, no weapons."

"Will you English never stop persecuting us poor Irish? Why don't you just go home?" O'Rourke knew he had them beaten this time.

"We'll get you one day, O'Rourke," snarled Grayson. "Then we'll see who's grinning." They left empty-handed much to O'Rourke's amusement. He had no illusions about what the English would have done to Briony. At least Sanderson had saved her that but still O'Rourke didn't trust him.

*   *   *

It was near midnight when Tully and Briony landed in England. The wind was freezing and Briony was thankful she had the presence of mind to grab her coat. She huddled close to Tully and he put his arm protectively around her.

"We'll find a hotel for the night and take the train to London tomorrow."

They roused a sleepy eyed man from his bed and took a room where they booked in as Mr. and Mrs.Green.

"Newly weds are you?" he said handing Tully the key.

"Just married today," said Tully. "Please don't call us early for breakfast."

"Don't worry, Mr, Green. I was young once too."

Tully slipped him a pound note and took Briony to the room. The man said nothing about them not having luggage.

"Seems we'll have to sleep in the all together," he said turning down the blankets.

"Mother would never approve." She smiled as she climbed out of her slacks and sweater. She opened her arms and beckoned Tully toward her.

Chapter Eight

On reaching London, Tully went straight to see some media acquaintances he thought might help them. He managed to get the key to an apartment some journo had just vacated. Then scrounged a loan of a few pounds until he could retrieve his bankbook. It was just a short bus trip to Lambeth and Briony was like a schoolgirl on the journey

"Tully, there's Big Ben. Isn't that the Tower Bridge? This must be the Thames." Everything was new to her.

"You haven't been to London before?"

"No. I always wanted to. Is that St. Paul's Dome?"

"No, but I'll take you to all sorts of places once we're settled."

They were just two young lovers on a holiday. Tully was enthralled at Briony's excitement.

"This will do fine for a while," Tully said surveying their new home. "You'll be all right here for a couple of days. We'll go and buy some food to stock up."

"Where are you going?" Alarm registered on her face. She hadn't expected him to leave her.

"I have to go back to Belfast. I need to collect my clothes and equipment and I better let Pat know where I am. You'll need some clothes too so make a list I can give your brother?"

"You will come back won't you?" Her voice trembled.

"Mrs. Green. Would I leave my wife stranded in a strange city?" His grin was comforting. "I'll leave you some money. It will get you by until I return."

Her face reflected her relief. "Can I borrow your pen?"

Tully watched her sit down and make a list of her requirements. The next day he returned to Belfast.

On reaching Belfast the first thing he did was phone Pat. "Thanks, mate. I owe you one."

"I work within the law, Tully. What the police had in mind for her was not legal. I still think she's involved but I'm no butcher. Is she safe?"

"Yeah. Out of the country."

"Don't tell me where. I don't want to know."

"Okay. I'll be leaving Belfast for a while. Just have to pick up a few things."

"It wouldn't be smart for a certain person to come back in the near future."

"Yeah, I know. I'll keep in contact."

"Good luck, mate. See you around."

"Thanks again, Pat."

Arriving at O'Rourke's house, Tully found he was his usual friendly self.

"Where is she?" O'Rourke's voice was sharp but his eyes looked relieved.

"We've got a flat in London. It's better no one knows. She'll ring you whenever she can."

"You'd better look after her, Sanderson or you're dead."

Tully ignored his words and handed him Briony's list. "She'll need these things. Can you pack them in a suitcase? I'm in a hurry."

O'Rourke snatched the list from his hand. "Wait here," he said snarling and left Tully standing on the doorstep returning ten minutes later with the suitcase. "There's money in there for her use."

"I'll see she gets it. We may have to stay away for some time."

"The Irish are used to making sacrifices. Just look after her or else." With that he slammed the door in Tully's face. Wasting no time Tully collected his own things.

He unloaded the car for a hefty loss where he bought it. At least he had extra money in his pocket.

Soon he was on the first flight he could get back to London. In less than twenty-four hours he was back in their love nest, much to Briony's pleasure.

"How was it?" she asked.

"Your brother was his usual friendly best but he did put some money in the case for you. Apart from that there was no trouble. I didn't give him our address. It's better no one knows where we live. You can ring him whenever, but keep our address secret for the time being."

"Why?"

"Because they might ask you to blow up Buckingham bloody Palace or Parliament House. You're going to be a law-biding citizen from now on?"

"Then I guess I'll have to start looking for a job."

It turned out to be the happiest time of Tully's life. Briony found a job in a women's clothing store while Tully settled down as the paper's London correspondent. He kept in touch with Pat and even made one or two trips back to Belfast in his capacity as a journalist. Three months after they moved to London, Briony told him she was pregnant.

"Tully, do you think this flat is big enough for three?"

"You're pregnant. When?" he asked excitedly.

"Two days after my nineteenth birthday. June 10th."

"That's wonderful Briony. Let's get married."

"Not yet, Tully. Marriage will mean you'll want me to go to Australia but I'm not ready for that yet."

"Just as long as we're together. I love you, Briony."

Tears formed in her eyes. "I love you too, Tully Sanderson. More than you'll ever know."

Kevin O'Rourke was far from pleased when Briony rang him with the news. "You're going to desert me and our cause now aren't you?"

"I'll have a baby to think about, Kevin. After it's born we'll discuss it."

O'Rourke cursed over the phone. "That bastard has caused nothing but trouble ever since he arrived."

"I love him, Kevin. You have to make peace with him."

"Never," he said defiantly. "He's no better than the English."

"He's going to be your brother-in-law one day."

"If he lasts. He's only using you, Briony to get to me."

"That's not true. He hasn't mentioned you once since we've been together."

"Trust no-one, Briony. Especially not him."

*   *   *

Briony did her best to make a home for Tully. Money was short but she always tried to keep herself nice. The house was always clean and she proved herself to be a good cook with tempting meals for him. Sometimes she bought him odd little surprises.

"What's this?" he asked when she gave him a small present wrapped in cellophane.

"You'd better like it. I tramped all over London looking for it."

She was amused when he laughed loudly as he unwrapped a jar of Australian Vegemite.

"Want to try some? He spread it on fresh bread and glanced in her direction.

"It's the devils brew. Who would want to eat that?"

Another time she managed to find a copy of his favorite rugby league magazine. Even if it was just a chocolate bar she seemed to always manage to delight him with her ideas. One night he dragged himself up the stairs feeling very tired after having had a pretty hectic day.

He pushed the door open to be greeted by a delicious aroma filling the small first floor flat.

The table was set with a clean white bed sheet, ironed and starched to look like a linen table cloth. There was an empty bottle in the center with a yellow candle and yellow paper serviettes at each setting. She had bathed and her hair shone like black silk. Her best dress was in contrast to her normal clothes she wore while at the store.

"What's the occasion?" He looked around impressed at the sight. He always thought she was an angel but she was exceedingly beautiful tonight.

"Well now, Tully Sanderson, a man who forgets his own birthday must be scared of growing old."

"God, it is the twenty fifth already."

She folded her arms around him and kissed him with a fever betraying her feelings.

"What a great birthday present."

"That's not your present. Here's your present." She handed him a tiny box.

His eyes glowed with love and pleasure as he eagerly tore away the wrapping, revealing a gold zodiac medallion and chain. He gasped. Engraved on the back was *To Tully, with all my love, Briony.*

"It's not real gold," she apologized.

"It couldn't be more special if it was 24 carat. I love it and I love you too. Come here while I thank you."

Briony kept working until the seventh month of her pregnancy. As June approached Tully became nervous for Briony on the imminent birth. Nothing seemed to worry her and she kept good health. Her birthday came and the prospective father was getting impatient, then four days later her labor started.

"Jesus, we have to get you to the hospital."

"I suppose," she said calmly.

Tully wanted to hurl the taxi driver from his seat and take over himself, but Briony sat back smiling at his antics. They reached the hospital in plenty of time.

He paced the hospital corridors like all expectant fathers. The sterile white walls and the hard chairs gave him little comfort. He must have read every magazine in the rack, along with the other expectant fathers. Nurses came and went without news. The hospital coffee tasted awful and he walked up and down worrying about the love of his life. When a nurse approached him to give him the good news six hours later, he was more than relieved.

"Congratulation, Mr. Sanderson. You have a beautiful baby girl. Both mother and child are doing well. You can see them now."

Tully rushed past her anxious to be with the two women in his life. Briony was propped up on a pillow looking tired but radiant. She was smiling proudly.

"Oh, Tully, isn't she beautiful?"

His eyes blurred with happiness as he reached out to touch the tiny creature their love had created.

"Beautiful, just like her mother. "What are we going to call her?"

"I'd like to call her after my mother. Her name was Carrie."

"Then Carrie it is," he said happily. "Come to your father, Carrie Sanderson." He took her in his arms, his chest swelling with pride. The love he felt for this woman and child couldn't be put into words.

"I'll always take care of you, Briony and I'll always take care of Carrie. I swear."

"I know you will, Tully. I'm so happy." She squeezed his hand lovingly.

* * *

He had not spoken to Pat for three months. Of course he'd rung to tell him of the birth but had heard nothing since. With some time on his hands, he put through a social call.

"How's the family man, mate?" asked Pat pleased to hear from him.

"Things couldn't be better. What about things in your part of the world. Solve your case yet?"

"Could be. We've arrested Kevin O'Rourke in Londonderry. One of his IRA cronies has agreed to turn states evidence if we can guarantee him safe passage to a foreign port. Says O'Rourke was the brain behind the kidnapping. We're going to bring him back to Belfast next week."

"Briony will be upset."

"She can come back now we've got her brother. She's quite safe."

"I'll tell her. What else is news?" They made small talk for a while and both agreed to ring more often, which of course they always said but never got around to doing

I have to tell Briony but how will this affect her? The thought didn't sit well. Maybe once O'Rourke was behind bars she would go to Australia. There was no point in staying in Ireland while he did twenty years in Maze prison.

Tully took a deep breath before he confronted her.

"Something's wrong, Tully. I can tell by your face." He could hide nothing from her.

"Sort of. I've been talking to Pat. They've arrested your brother in Londonderry for the murder of Lord Ashley. They're taking him back to Belfast next week."

"Oh, Mary, Mother of God. Poor Kevin. I have to go to him. He'll need his family for support." She crossed herself and bit her lip.

"I was afraid you'd say that. Pat said if you insist, it was safe for you to return."

"Then I must go. You can stay here if you like."

"I think he's a murdering bastard but he is your brother and I won't let you go alone. I suppose we'd better pack."

Her eyes were filled with compassion for this man. "I love you, Tully."

"You'd better. I wouldn't go back there for just anyone." He wasted no time in arranging tickets and the next day they were in Belfast.

"Well we have to find somewhere to stay." Tully was deep in thought as he picked up the suitcases. "There's no way I can stay in your brother's house."

"There's an old farm house about thirty minutes out of Belfast. It used to belong to my father. We lived there when we were children. It's a bit primitive but it will do for a while. It hasn't been used for some time."

"Sounds fine. I'll hire a car while you wait with the baby and luggage."

The car was no problem. Tully took it for a week and safely deposited his family into the back. Half an hour later they were at the farm.

It was not as bad as Tully had expected. Most of the furniture had been covered with sheets and after a couple of hours they had the place livable. The water was supplied by tank but Ireland's weather meant it would never run out.

As there was no phone and they needed provisions, Tully left Briony to finish her unpacking and returned to Belfast. He rang Pat to let him know they were back and in turn was told O'Rourke was being returned to Belfast tomorrow.

Briony was settling Carrie in a make shift bed of pillows when she heard a car. Thinking Tully had forgotten something; she hurried onto the veranda and was dismayed to see Sean Flynn drive up.

"Sean. How did you know we were here?"

"We know everything, Briony. You're aware of that."

"Tully will be back soon. He mustn't find you here."

"He'll be gone for quite a while. I've been watching the place."

"What do you want?"

"Kevin is being brought back to Belfast tomorrow. We intend to set up an ambush and release him."

"I'll not be part of it," she said defiantly.

"Our information is he'll be brought back through Killead. We need you to dress as a farmer's wife and pretend to clear hay from the road after we stage a road block."

"I said I'll not be part of it."

"You'll do what you're bloody told. How can you refuse to help your brother?"

"I have a baby to consider now and Tully wouldn't like it."

"If your Australian friend wasn't here then there would be no problem. A bullet in the head should take care of it."

Briony's blood froze. Sean was just as callous as Kevin and would think nothing of shooting Tully.

"Please, Sean. Just leave us alone."

He gave her a sadistic smile. "That's you choice then is it?"

Briony knew he would kill Tully without giving it a second thought. It seemed they were never going to get peace while the IRA were active.

"All right. As long as you promise not to hurt Tully."

"Fine. The security van will arrive about four p.m. Michael will pick you up at two. Send Sanderson into Belfast on some message to get him out of the way."

"What about my baby?"

"I'm sure her father can mind her for a couple of hours. You better take this." He pulled out a fully loaded revolver, which he placed on the veranda step.

"Remember, Michael will be here at two."

Briony nodded as if in a trance, then scooped up the gun slipping it into her apron pocket. Michael Flannery was of the same mould of Kevin and Sean. Killing was a way of life with him. As Tully returned he passed Flynn on the farm road and frowned. It was obvious he'd been to the farm. He wondered who he was and what he was doing on their road.

"I just passed a car. Did we have a visitor while I was gone?" he asked Briony.

"No. No one," she said quickly, too quickly. She looked away and Tully knew she was lying. He expected the IRA would try to contact her but said nothing.

Next day Briony seemed edgy all morning. Her mind began to wander. Tully had to ask her several times about things that she wanted done. By one thirty she suddenly had a bad headache.

"Something wrong, love?"

"I have a bad migraine, do you think you could go into Belfast and get me some tablets. Take the baby so I can get some rest."

What about the tablets we bought before we left London? he thought. She obviously wanted him out of the way.

"Sure, no trouble. You better put warm clothes on Carrie. The wind is chilly."

She dressed Carrie and he headed for Belfast as if nothing worried him, but parked his car behind some bushes some distance from the house. Some time later Michael Flannery drove up. A smallish man but with shoulders like a weight lifter. He was more solid than either Kevin or Sean.

Briony watched him swaggering to the house; her heart beating as it had on the night of the Post Office bombing.

"Did you get rid of lover boy?"

She nodded. "He went into Belfast to buy something."

"Good."

He opened the door and Briony jumped in knowing Tully and Carrie were safely away. From his observation point Tully watched them leave. He followed at a discreet distance wondering where they were going. They turned left toward Killead, a small village only fifteen minutes from the farm.

On the edge of the village, they met two more cars and a dray loaded with hay. Briony tied a scarf over her head and covered her jeans and jumper with a work apron. She and Flannery drove the dray out of the village toward Londonderry.

A short distance out they began emptying the hay onto the road. Tully knew immediately what they were planning. Racing back to the village he rang Pat.

"Tully. How are you, mate?" His familiar voice warm and friendly.

"Not too bloody good. Am I right in surmising O'Rourke is being brought to Belfast today via Killead?"

"How the hell did you know that?"

"Some of O'Rourke's IRA cronies have Briony. They thought I'd left for Belfast but I followed them. They're setting up an ambush. I think they're going to try and free the bastard."

"And Briony's with them?"

"Yes."

"Shit. You have to get her out of there. The security van is being tailed by a truckload of SAS soldiers. They'll shoot first and ask questions after."

"Christ. I have to go." He dropped the phone and ran to the car. Tully broke all records driving toward the ambush point. Coming to the top of a hill overlooking the valley he could see he was already too late.

There was the security van coming around the bend and five IRA soldiers waiting with automatic weapons crouching behind a stone wall. Five hundred yards behind but round the bend and out of sight of the ambush was the truck containing the SAS soldiers. Panic gripping him, he sped down the hill knowing he couldn't get there in time.

As the truck slowed, blocked by the dray the five IRA assassins jumped up from behind the wall opening fire spraying the cabin. The driver and front guard died before they knew what had happened. Flynn banged on the door of the truck.

"Open up or you're dead men."

"You'll shoot us anyway." A voice from inside sounded less than confident.

"All we want is Kevin O'Rourke. You have five seconds to open the door."

Slowly the door opened and O'Rourke bounded toward his men. He grabbed Flynn's automatic weapon and turned toward the two guards.

"You said we'd be safe if we opened the door," one said.

"They did but I didn't." He then cut them both down with a quick hail of bullets.

Briony couldn't believe how Kevin had callously killed the guards.

"Kevin, you've killed those men in cold blood," she said horrified.

"They're the enemy, Briony. They show us no compassion. Why should we show any to them?"

Just as they were congratulating themselves on a good job, the SAS truck rounded the bend surprising them all. English soldiers jumped out firing toward the group. Bullets sprayed the dray, dirt and hay flying into the air. Tully could hear the clatter as the bullets struck the back of the armored truck used to move O'Rourke.

A body was hurled backwards and Tully was horrified to see it was Briony clutching her side.

"Briony." His voice rose to a wild pitch and Flannery let go a burst in his direction.

"It's that bloody Australian," yelled O'Rourke as Tully ducked behind his car. They ignored Tully and fired at the soldiers who had also taken cover. Tully crawled forward to Briony's inert body. Blood was seeping in a huge crimson stain across her body. He could see her entrails hanging from a terrible wound in her stomach area. One arm was totally shattered and blood was streaming from a head wound. Her eyes were staring and she was making small sobbing noises.

"Fuck you, Sanderson," yelled O'Rourke. "Get her out of here."

Tully gathering her in his arms ran for his car, bullets zipping past his head like bush flies at a picnic.

Laying her in the back of the car as gently as he could he sped toward the farm leaving the battle raging behind him? On reaching the farm he lay her on the ground, rushed into the house and snatched up clean linen and blankets. Placing a pillow under her head he tried to tend her wounds. One high velocity bullet can wreak terrible injuries to the human body. Several bullets made it a hopeless task.

"Briony," he sobbed as he tried to push her entrails back into her gaping wound. They kept sliding out like eels escaping from a container. He was vaguely aware of Carrie crying in the car but her mother's needs were far more urgent. The bullets had ripped her open revealing her torn and bleeding organs. It was a miracle she was still alive. Blood was trickling from her mouth and running down her chin. He wiped it away with the back of his hand.

Her voice was weak, barely audible. "I can't move my legs, Tully."

Tears poured down his face. He knew she had only a short time left.

"The baby," she whispered.

He knelt closer to hear what she was trying to say.

"Take care of Carrie, Tully. She needs you more than ever now."

"You'll be all right, Briony. You will. I'll get help for you."

"Don't leave me. I'm dying. We both know that. Take her away to somewhere safe. To Australia. She'd like that."

"I love you, Briony," he said sobbing uncontrollably. "You can't die. We need you."

"And I love you. Forgive me, Tully. They were going to kill you unless I helped them."

"I would have taken the risk?"

Her eyes closed and he thought she was gone. He went to gather her in his arms and she screamed at the movement.

"Its agony, Tully, please don't try to move me. I feel cold, hold my hand."

Stroking her hand softly, his heart was breaking with every breath she struggled to take. Blood was still trickling from her mouth. The head wound sent the red stain over her face and down her neck. She was going to die; this woman he loved with every fiber of his being was going to die.

"I don't want you to leave me, Briony," he sobbed.

"I want you to do something for me, Tully." Her voice was now soft and her eyes glazed.

"Anything, Briony. Anything."

"In my pocket there's a gun. Can you take it out?"

He removed the fully loaded revolver Flynn had given her thinking she was lying on it. She winced at his movement.

"I have it. What am I supposed to do with it?"

"I want you to kill me."

"What?" he gasped.

"Kill me. Please, Tully, I can't take the pain."

"Briony. I can't."

"You want me to suffer?"

"Of course not, but I can't kill you. I love you."

"I can't stand it, Tully. How long do you think it will take me to bleed to death? I can't recover and I'm not scared of dying. If you go for help I'll be dead when you get back. I don't want to die alone. If you stay any longer Kevin will find you and kill you." Her words laboring, every breath agony. "You must go and keep Carrie safe."

He had never felt so helpless in his life. He would have done anything to take this pain from her. What she said was true. She wasn't going to recover.

"Briony," he sobbed.

"You can do it, Tully. You can. Please stop this pain. I'd do it for you. If you don't go both you and Carrie will die. Save Carrie if not yourself."

He knew she was right. His hand wavered as he turned the gun toward her body.

"In the heart, Tully, it will be quick. Kiss Carrie for me."

*　　*　　*

O'Rourke grabbed Flannery's arm as the battle raged. "Let's get out of here. We'll take the first car while Sean takes the other. He can lead them away once they break through."

"What about the other two?"

"They can hold off the English until we're gone."

O'Rourke and Flannery took off leaving the battle still raging behind them. Sure they had gotten clean away, they headed for the farm. Hidden there were guns, money and clothes.

It would only take them a few minutes to gather their goods, and then they would cross the border into Eire. Here they could lay low for a while and make further plans. After a furious drive they came to the farm.

"Stop," yelled O'Rourke. From the end of the road they could see Tully holding Briony's head in his hands.

"Have you still got your camera?" he asked Flannery.

"Complete with telescopic lens."

"Then take me some photos," said O'Rourke pointing toward Tully and Briony.

"If she's still alive we can use it as a lever to make Sanderson follow our instructions. It's evidence he was involved in the breakout."

Tully tried to hold the gun steady but his hand shook uncontrollably.

"Press it into my chest, Tully. Hurry."

He did but still couldn't pull the trigger. Briony whispered to him once again.

"Now, Tully now. Do it for me, do it for Carrie."

She heard him sob involuntarily, his body shaking with grief. He turned his head and pulled the trigger. Briony's body gave a jerk and then lay still, her agonizing pain was over.

"You bastard, Sanderson, you've killed my darlin' sister," yelled O'Rourke firing straight at Tully. Tully turned unaware that O'Rourke was even close. The bullet hit Tully in the shoulder. He spun around and fired back. His bullet taking O'Rourke to the ground where Flannery grabbed him around the waist. Despite O'Rourke's wound he helped bundle him into the back of the car.

"It's not over, Sanderson. We killed the English bastard and we'll get you," yelled O'Rourke as the car sped away.

Tully knelt and kissed Briony on the lips. "Goodbye my, Darling."

Quickly he packed all of Carrie's clothes, then his own and drove off towards Belfast. Carrie was still crying and Tully looked back at her but afraid to give her attention. He needed to get her back safely before the IRA caught up with him. As soon as he reached a phone, he rang Pat and was grateful to hear his voice.

"Tully, what the hell happened? I heard O'Rourke escaped."

"Briony is dead, mate, she's dead." His voice was a sob and Pat let him compose himself.

"I shot O'Rourke, Pat but he's not dead. He said it's not over yet."

"It will be for you if you stay here. Where are you?"

He told him, then waited patiently by his car until Pat arrived.

Thirty minutes later Pat picked him up.

"Grab Carrie and get in. Leave the car there."

Pat almost pushed him into the front seat, threw his suitcase in the back and sped off in an instant.

Back in his office, Pat stood by patiently with the army doctor attending Tully's wound. Pat held Carrie in his arms watching the doctor work. Finally placing Tully's arm in a sling the doctor stood back satisfied.

"It's not too bad. It will be sore for a while but it will come good. Keep the wound clean and there shouldn't be any problems."

As soon as the doctor left Pat turned to his friend.

"Better tell me what happened."

He sat grimly as Tully told him how Briony was mortally wounded and in great pain. How she knew she was dying and was afraid what the IRA would do to Tully and Carrie. The pain he felt when she asked him to kill her. The pleading with him to end it for her and her desire for him to take Carrie to safety and to always care for her.

"I wanted to turn the gun on myself after but I had to take care of Carrie."

"You say nothing of this to anyone. Understand, Tully? Carrie needs you now and that's the only thing that is important."

"What now?"

"You're on the next plane out of here. I'll catch up with you in Australia soon. I'm chucking this job in."

As they left the surgery, Tully took his friend's arm.

"See she's buried properly, Pat. I owe her that much."

"I'll do that, mate. How are you going to take care of Carrie?"

"My sister Vera will look after her. I have to earn a living to feed and clothe her."

They shook hands and Tully gathered his baby daughter in his good arm heading out of the door to peace and freedom. Pat gathered his suitcase and followed him to the car. His phone call got them on the first plane out of Belfast.

Tully wasted no time in leaving this country which had on one hand given him so much grief but on the other so much joy in the miracle of his little girl.

He was determined to fulfill his promise to Briony. Carrie was going to have the best life he could give her where he could prove his worth by becoming the most sought after correspondent in Australia.

Chapter Nine

Tully found the flight back easier than expected. The cabin staff was only too pleased to take care of the baby so he could relax as much as his arm would let him.

Twenty six hours later the jet taxied on the tarmac and he was pleased to be home. Australia had never looked so good. It was awkward but with the help of the airline's staff, Tully gathered his luggage and hailed a taxi. No longer having a flat he decided to book into a Motel until he could gather his thoughts together. He removed his sLing and tested his arm. It hurt but he thought he could manage without it. Hell he had to.

Looking after an infant daughter was no picnic even with two arms. Changing nappies and feeding the baby was harder than he thought it was going to be. He took a day or two just resting, then rang Belfast. At last he reached Pat after three tries.

"Any repercussions, Pat?" he asked anxiously.

"A few, mate. We found O'Rourke in hospital and arrested him again. Unfortunately we had to let him go although he's not going far. Seems he's stuck in a wheelchair for the rest of his life. Your bullet struck him in the spine. Our informant was found with his face blown away so we had no evidence again. I reckon your brother -in-law is really pissed off with you."

"Serves the bastard right. Besides, he's no relation of mine. We never had time to get married. I'll let you know where I am. I have to go to see Vera and see if she'll take care of Carrie for me."

"I don't reckon you'll have any worries on that score, mate. She's wanted kids for years hasn't she? Isn't that why her husband split?"

"That and his women. She found him in bed with one of her friends. He never wanted kids and said he wasn't going to adopt some one else's bastard. Compassion and caring are two words that don't come to mind when I think about him."

"She's well rid of him. When do you face her?"

"Tomorrow. Pat ---did you take care of Briony?"

"Yeah, mate. It was a quiet, quick funeral tastefully done. I'll see she has a nice headstone."

"Send me the bill, Pat. You don't know how much I miss her."

"I think I do. Take care of yourself, Tully. I'm chucking this job in and looking for something quieter."

"Sounds wise. See you later."

The next day came soon enough. Tully dressed Carrie in her best outfit wanting to make a good impression on her Aunt Vera. It took him a while to find the right clothes. Does green and pink go together he thought annoyingly as she struggled when he was trying to push arms and legs in the necessary openings? It was a dear taxi fare but he wasn't going to struggle on the train and bus in his condition, especially with a baby to care for.

Vera's house was neat and clean without being ostentatious. The white paint on the three-bedroom weather-board was beginning to look its age. Tully knew she didn't have a lot of money to live on but managed nicely on a part time job and a pension.

Taking a deep breath he pressed the doorbell and prayed today was not her day for golf. Hearing her footsteps in the hall and the heavy wooden door being unlocked brought some relief. Vera's face lit up to see her younger brother.

"Tulston, how lovely to see you."

"Cut it out, Sis, why can't you call me Tully like everyone else? I don't know why mum had to stick me with the family name. You seem to like it, maybe you should have got it being first born."

She laughed stepping out to hug him, almost standing in the carry basket at his feet.

"What's this?" She bent to take a closer look.

"Aunt Vera, meet your niece Carrie."

"What on earth has my baby brother been up to in Ireland? Give her to me. She's a Darling. How old is she? Where's her mother?"

"I guess I have some explaining to do."

"This should be interesting," said Vera cuddling the baby. "Hate the color scheme."

Tully shook his head helplessly. Sitting her down he told her everything leaving nothing out while she held the baby. Vera sat stony-faced listening to the details.

"You poor thing. How awful," she said when at last he had finished. "What are you going to do with Carrie?"

"I'm not sure. Probably put her up for adoption," he lied. "Any other suggestions?"

"You can't be serious. This is your daughter, my niece. You're not going to put her up for adoption. No way."

"I can't earn a living and keep her. I'm a journalist, I travel a lot for Christ sake."

"She is your own flesh and blood. How could you even consider it? There's only one thing to do."

"What's that?" said Tully knowing full well what she was going to say.

"I'll mind her. She's so little and she needs someone who cares about her. You know how much I've always wanted children. I'm the perfect solution."

"You know, that's not a bad idea," he said grinning. "I could send you money and come and see her when I'm home. I'd make sure both of you would never want."

"Tulston you're incorrigible," she said watching his face. "That's what you had in mind all the time wasn't it?"

"I had to hear you say it, Sis. Do we have a deal?"

"We do and I think I'm getting the better part of it."

"Thanks, Sis. I love her so much but she needs a good mother. You'll be the best."

"She'll need clothes, nappies and a hundred other things."

He wrote her out a cheque. "This is almost all I have left at the moment. I'll be applying to work overseas. The trouble spots are where the top money is."

"Then take care, Tulston. The poor mite doesn't need to lose her father too."

"I'll send money when I can. Can you manage in the meantime?"

Bruce Cooke

"Of course I can. I've waited years to be a mother." She smiled happily at her new gain.

"Where are you staying?"

"Haven't found a place yet."

"Go and get your luggage. You can stay with me until you get settled. I imagine you'll be off overseas again anyway."

"Thanks, Sis. Depends on Richard. I have a family to support now."

*　*　*

Tully paused in his story reaching for another coffee. He looked across at his daughter who had tears streaming down her cheeks. She made no effort to wipe them away.

"Oh, Dad, I had no idea Uncle Kevin was lying."

"He wasn't. I was the one who killed her." His voice was filled with sadness. "I can never forget that."

"It was because she begged you. She was in agony and was suffering terribly. She wanted to save our lives. It must be really hard to watch someone you love die slowly. You did the right thing by her."

"It doesn't make it any easier, love. When I see you, I see her. The memories rush back."

"Is that why you kept trying to keep me away from the action?"

"It was a promise I made to your mother. I swore to look after you. I guess I stuffed that up too."

"I'm a big girl now, Dad. Haven't you noticed?"

"I've noticed. It's just hard to realize."

"Maybe things will get better now I know more." Carrie patted his hand.

Tully laughed. "Shit, love, you haven't heard half of it yet."

Carrie looked at the clock on the wall suddenly feeling exhausted.

"Well it's two a.m. I don't think I'm up to anymore tonight. We both need some rest so I'll say goodnight. I'll hear the rest tomorrow."

She leaned across and hugged him, something she hadn't done since she was a little girl. It seemed ages when she broke away. He wanted to hold her forever.

In Ireland he was a young man but now he had hit middle age. Was it a wasted life? Having Carrie told him no but there were other regrets, regrets which would not disappear from his tormented mind.

Tully lay on his bed looking at the overhead fan slowly rotating. The revolving blades above reminded him of the whap, whap, whap of other blades. They not only fanned his body but also fanned his memories of a past maybe best forgotten.

Chapter Ten

Vietnam 1971

Vietnam was oppressively hot and steamy. When he stepped off the plane the humidity hit him in the face like a wet towel. Three American jets screamed overhead and disappeared into the horizon. It was his first reminder he was in a war zone. There was no friendly service from ground crew, it was a matter of grabbing your bag and going after passing through a laughable charade of customs. A quick look at his passport and a thumb indicating the way out.

Richard had said find Craig Cassidy at the Paradise hotel. He was the Tribune's photographer and would show him the ropes. The sweat was beginning to pour from his skin and he'd only been here for five minutes. He hailed a cab and sat back wiping his brow as the taxi weaved its way through the mass of people choking the narrow streets.

The disappointment with his hotel didn't improve things. Certainly not Saigon's top but a cheap place where most journalists used to come and go with the frenzied race to get a top story.

The first thing to strike him about Asia was the smell. Not a bad smell but a sort of pungent, steamy smell where the oppressive heat seemed to mix with the damp vegetation of the jungle. Getting here had not been as easy as he thought it would be.

His editor had kept him at home for over eighteen months; not convinced he could handle Vietnam, especially with the state of his mind after Belfast.

Eventually his persistence won and here he was, ready for action. There was a vacancy and he took it gleefully.

Craig Cassidy would be his working buddy and supply photos with any story Tully sent back. An old hand as far as Vietnam was concerned, Cassidy had been here over twelve months. At least he should be able to fill Tully in on the do's and don'ts of correct wartime journalism.

Tully's shirt was sticking to his back and he could have killed for an ice-cold beer. The streets were full of GI's, most with an Asian girl draped on their arm, all looking for a good time. Asia was a new experience for Tully. The hordes of people, the shops and streets, the market places, even the dress of the people caught his interest. He laughed to himself when he saw a man on a small motor bike carrying his wife and three children weaving his way through the traffic. Bicycles seemed to be a favorite form of travel but then how could the Vietnamese afford the luxury of cars. Most of the vehicles were military and very conspicuous.

Finding the hotel, he was far from impressed. He paid the taxi driver and looked at his new home.

Jesus, I've been in better flea houses than this he thought. It had a French flavor with a balcony around the first floor overlooking the street.

At reception he waited while an overweight Asian man wearing a brightly colored shirt and rather dirty shorts talked on the phone while balancing a huge cigar in his mouth.

It wobbled up and down so much with each word he spoke, Tully thought the action would knock off the ash. The fumes almost choked him. At last the man finished talking and gave Tully his attention.

"I help you, buddy?" The man obviously thought he was American.

"Yeah. I'm want a room for starters and maybe you can tell me where I can find a bloke called Craig Cassidy."

"You Australian?" He gave a rather toothless smile. "I help you, cobber. I have nice room. You want girl?"

"Listen, mate. My name's not cobber. It's Tully Sanderson and I don't want a girl. I want a bloody room. Preferably a room with working air conditioning."

"Maybe you want a girl after. You come see Charlie. I get you a nice clean girl. Very cheap."

Tully rolled his eyes to the ceiling. "Do you know where Cassidy is?"

"Snaps. Him there at bar. Red hair man in crowd."

Tully turned in the direction of the bar where a group of people were drinking and laughing as if they didn't have a care in the world. A few faces were recognizable from news photo services.

There were four of them, each different Tully noted. The Frenchman recognizable by his accent reminded Tully of Santa Claus without bushy eyebrows. His neatly trimmed goatee in character but the baggy shorts he wore looked as though they were supported by spaghetti sticks, a contradiction to his pot-belly. His yellow teeth matched his stained fingers and when he coughed with an abrasive rasp the others leaned back. The square bulge in his top pocket gave evidence as to the cause of his complaint.

The Englishman stood like he had a broomstick stuck up his arse. Working as a butler couldn't have made him more aloof. Even in the humidity he didn't seem to sweat. Being taken for a big game hunter came to mind with his bush hat and khaki shirt with short sleeves. The sharp creases evident on his trousers, which in turn seemed a little stained, unlike the rest of his attire.

The American was easy to pick. A baseball cap with Dodgers across the front, a cigar wafting smoke into the air and a loud voice detecting a New York accent. Probably only thirty but Tully knew his face and reputation of being a first class journalist from photos on the wire service.

The Australian, a red-haired ferret of a man wore a three-day growth of a bright red beard. It clashed horribly with a dirty floral shirt hanging on his body but matched his freckles. An unshaved face. Long straight hair was hanging down over his forehead giving him a larrikin appearance, but the eyes were sharp and clear. Ginger Meggs! He thought of the cartoon character of long ago. The pale skin reminded Tully of his mother's rice pudding.

Tully noted the Pentax camera hanging from his neck. It didn't take much working out to know this was his man.

"Here your key. Room eleven on first floor."

Tully took the key then ambled over to the group of men.

"Craig Cassidy?" Raising his voice he got their attention.

Craig's shock of hair hit Tully again. It was even longer than his first impression, probably because it had been hidden by the small canvas hat he wore. He'd seem similar hats on the golf course. His eyebrows were thick and bushy of the same red hue. Blue eyes sparkled at Tully's voice. White even teeth flashed the friendliest smile imaginable.

Tully knew instantly they could easily become close friends. Pausing mid sentence as he heard his name called, Craig spun in Tully's direction offering his hand all in one fluid movement. Not a drop was spilled from the bottle he was holding.

"Tully Sanderson I presume. I've been expecting you. Welcome to Vietnam."

"Craig?" The Englishman laughed loudly. "Did anyone know Snaps had a proper name? It's really Craig?"

"Ignore this stupid Pommy bastard and the lanky Yank." Snaps grinned at the two men. "They're both useless pricks but Frenchy here's a good mate. It's your shout Frenchy."

The Pom had a charming friendly accent. It seemed like an exclusive men's club with few members, but then journalists respected each other in the dangers of the job they were in. He offered Tully his hand.

"Alex Franklin. The London Sentinel. This lanky Yank as Snaps calls him is Chuck Denver from the Washington News and Pierre Montclair from the Paris Chronicle. I do hope you're a bit more refined than this Australian."

"I sure am, mate. My mother always taught me to be a gentleman and act with decorum. Now which one of you dick heads is going to shout?"

"What will you drink, Tully?" Pierre pronounced it Tooly.

"I suppose an ice cold beer would be out of the question."

"Ze temperature of ze room only," said Pierre. The man at the bar flicked open a bottle and handed it to Tully.

"So you're what they sent to replace Ken Hanson." Snaps took a swig from his bottle and made a horrible expression as if it was poison. "Shit this is awful. It'll never sell."

"Never met him but I guess so. Richard Harding just told me you were a man short. Had enough of the place did he?" Tully sipped his beer.

"I suppose you could put it that way." Franklin's very English voice was quiet and modulated. "Poor chap got himself caught in a barrage. They sent the pieces home in an envelope."

Tully thought they were joking until he saw their faces. Each one had a silent subdued expression. This was one of their ilk and each knew they could be next.

"You're fair dinkum?" he asked.

"Of course. It's a damn dangerous place over here. This your first time in a combat area?" Franklin took another sip from his bottle.

"Apart from a short time in Belfast. They had the odd bomb blast but it was not a war zone, nothing like Vietnam."

"Well, Tully," Chuck drawled. "My advice is to stick close to the soldiers and don't go wandering off on your own. The Viet Cong shoot first and ask who you are later. No-one is safe but you have to work the odds."

"He's right, mate," said Snaps. "You have to learn the ropes quickly here or you don't survive."

"I'll be counting on you for that sort of help."

"My pleasure. Meet me back here at six and I'll show you Saigon after dark. I think you'll find it an interesting place."

"Sounds like it. The first thing Charlie over there asked me was if I wanted a woman."

"There's plenty available. Most are supporting their families. It's the only way some of them survive. The Yanks spend heaps on them."

"What about you?"

"Shit, mate. I'm no virgin. You need something to drive away the horrors of this place. You'll find out."

Tully could see the others nodding in agreement and drank his beer in silence. He hated the place already.

"First thing we have to do is get you some decent clothes and boots. Cotton shirts and army boots are what's needed. Something that will breathe." Snaps was passing on the advice he had received when he arrived.

"Where do I get them?"

"Leave it to me. I know where we can get you army fatigues. Just give me your sizes and they'll be here tomorrow. You sew a press insignia on your sleeve and you're in business."

Tully pulled out a handkerchief and wiped his brow. "Don't they have air conditioning here?" All he could see were two big ceiling fans turning slowly without much effect.

"Do you think this iz, ze Hilton?" Pierre sounded amused. He slapped his thigh and gave a laugh.

"You get used to it, mate," said Snaps. "By the way, don't drink the bloody water."

"This is going to be fun," sighed Tully. "Is it safe to wash in it?"

"Cold showers in every room. Enjoy."

"If that's what's offering I'd better go and try it out. See you around six."

He left them to inspect his room. His air conditioning comprised of a ceiling fan and an open window. It was a double bed, not uncomfortable thought Tully as he sat on it. When he took off his shoe and slapped an insect the size of a matchbox he understood why there was a net over the bed.

If Charlie supplied women it had probably been used for something else besides sleeping. There was a wardrobe of French design but the polish on it had long faded. A small dresser alongside the bed was ample to take his shirts and underwear. A coconut fiber mat was spread across the floor, but only covered the area in front of the bed. The shower was simple. A recess in one corner with a chrome hoop around the top supporting a plastic shower screen. Not in another room, but in full view of the bed. He quickly stripped off his clothes looking for relief under the water.

After a somewhat refreshing shower Tully rested a while and sorted out his belongings, then returned to the bar promptly at six.

"Are we going somewhere classy?" he asked surprised to see Snap's dressed in neatly pressed white trousers and the brightest floral shirt Tully had ever seen. The flowers somehow seemed to scream at his red hair.

"We're off to the Orchid bar. That's where you get good booze, pretty girls and most important, no windows."

"What do you mean no windows?"

"It's semi open air. They have bamboo shutters so if a grenade is thrown at least you won't be cut to ribbons by flying glass."

"Charming," said Tully. "Let's go."

Tully had heard about the horrors of Vietnam but nothing drove the point home more as they walked towards the Orchid Bar. On reaching the American Embassy on their route they noticed a crowd gathering.

"What's going on?" he asked Snaps.

"Probably another demo against the yanks. Let's stroll over and have a look."

"That's what I'm here for," he said shrugging. Anything to break the suffering from the oppressive heat.

Tully could see a flash of orange and heard chanting in Vietnamese, a language he had yet to master.

"He's a Buddhist monk isn't he?"

"Yeah, you can tell from the orange garb they wear."

"So what's he saying?"

"Not sure. Something about the war and the Americans. I haven't learnt their Lingo properly myself yet."

"The crowd seems interested. He's not going to burst out into song is he?"

"I doubt it," said Snaps laughing. Tully looked at the monk who was sitting in the middle of the road rocking backward and forwards in his chant. His bald head glistening in the fading sunlight from the sweat forming over his naked dome. Tully tried to estimate his age. Maybe between twenty and forty.

"Come on," said Snaps. "We're using up good drinking time."

But something told Tully to wait just a moment. He grabbed Snap's arm and pulled him through the crowd. Two American soldiers with rifles held across their chests began pushing the crowd aside trying to clear a path for a car about to leave the Embassy grounds. The monk refused to budge; instead, he pulled a small can from beneath his robes and poured a liquid over himself. Instantly Tully knew what it was. The smell of petrol even penetrated the humid smell of Asia.

"Shit," he said but already Snaps had his camera off his shoulder.

Before they could say another word the monk produced a lighter and gave it a flick, immediately consuming him in a fireball driving everyone back another few paces. Tully couldn't believe it. The man should have been in agony instead of sitting quite still as the flames grew higher. The acrid smell was a forerunner of things to come but it was something Tully would always remember.

Snaps was taking pictures while Tully stood spellbound. They watched until the figure turned into charcoal. A soldier rushing from the Embassy with a fire extinguisher tried to extinguish the flames but it was all too late. By the time he reached the man he was laying on the road like some barbecued carcass.

"Looks like you've got your first story," said Snaps grimly.

"Jesus, what a bloody start. The poor bastard didn't even move."

"It's a shit country and a shit war, mate. Get used to it."

Tully scribbled some notes into his notebook, just a heading he would type up later. Fiery protest ends in death. Jesus, he needed a drink even more now.

*　　*　　*

The Orchid Bar was just as Snaps described. Shutters pulled up to let in the cool evening air and maybe to let out some of the smoke from cigarettes and joints.

Several scantily dressed Asian girls, barely visible through the smoke haze were dancing on a stage in the middle of the room.

The place was filled with Americans, men and some women who were mainly nurses. Music blared and people were talking, drinking and laughing. It was as if there was no war on at all.

As soon as they found a table, a pretty young girl in an almost see through dress walked over smiling her most beguiling smile.

"You like good time, Joe. Me give you good time. Cheap. Only twenty dollar."

"Piss off, love. Maybe later." Snaps moved her on before Tully knew what was happening. "She spotted you for a newcomer straight away. You could have her for ten dollars, no worries."

"Christ, she was no more than sixteen." Tully was horrified.

"That doesn't worry anyone here. Look around."

There were dozens of girls in the building, some sitting at tables talking and drinking, some standing in doorways trying to entice people inside.

Most were clad in cheongsams but a few were wearing very short skirts with a scant strip covering their top half. Nearly all around the age of the one Snaps had just dismissed.

Almost every American who was inside or seated at the curbside tables had at least one girl to absorb their attention and money. He noticed quite a few Australians looking for a piece of the action too.

"Maybe I could do a feature on prostitution, it seems to be alive and well in Saigon." He pointed toward a girl going upstairs with two soldiers.

"No way. You upset the Yanks then you won't get to where the fighting is. We rely on them for a hitch in one of their choppers. Upset them and they might drop you off halfway."

"How do you find out what's going on?"

"General Briggs of the American Infantry holds press conferences every couple of days. They give us bullshit about how well they're doing but lie like hell about their casualties. They only tell us what they want us to write."

"What are the Yankee soldiers like?"

"A mixed bag. Most are real good guys, friendly and courteous. Some are your average arse holes like some of our blokes and a lot are young kids who get stoned when ever the opportunity arises."

"How do you get to where the action is?" Tully knew he had a lot to learn, and to learn it quickly.

"Bribery works best. Most of the journos sit here and just report what the army tells them. The good ones like the three you met find their way to the front and get the facts first hand."

"Is that how my predecessor left us?"

"Yeah. Hanson was like a bloodhound. A great guy and a bloody good journo. He didn't leave a stone unturned to get a story. He just ran into bad luck. How do you want to play it?"

"His way sounds good."

"Shit. I was afraid you would say that." Snaps feigned horror. "One thing. It relieves the boredom."

They spent the rest of the night drinking, talking and getting to know one another. Tully was pleased to have Craig as his photographer. He obviously knew the ropes and his experience would be invaluable. It was the early hours of the morning when they left, Craig purchasing a bottle of bourbon on the way out.

"Haven't you had enough to drink, mate?"

"It's not for me. It's for the chopper pilot. It's part of the bribery I was talking about. We'll go to the base tomorrow and see what's happening."

"The Australian base?"

"Not likely. Some of the Aussies are already leaving. The bloody Yankee base. That's where all the orders come from."

Tully wondered what was wrong with him suggesting the Australian base. It was obvious even to a new comer everything revolved around the Americans.

He'd just follow Snaps until he knew the layout. With his story typed up Tully fell into bed wondering how he was ever going to survive.

Chapter Eleven

The American base was alive with activity when Snaps and Tully arrived next day at six a.m. It was obvious something was on. Twenty helicopters were lined up and troops were already boarding. The whap, whap, whap noise of another half dozen already taken off filled the air.

"There's ours, last one in the row." Snaps pointed to the end chopper just starting its loading. It was distinctive by the large naked woman painted on the front.

"Why that one?"

"Because that's our ride. Come on."

Chewing gum, a fresh-faced young pilot was doing his checklist. Tully thought he might not even have a driver's license.

"Geday, Tex. This is my new sidekick Tully Sanderson. Got room for us today?"

"Hi, Snaps, Tully. I don't know if you want to go on this one. Could be scary."

"We'll take our chances." As always Snaps was good-natured and optimistic.

"Your funeral. Hop in. Usual rules. If wounded have to come back then you're last."

"Agreed, Tex." Snaps pushed Tully in ahead of himself. The chopper already held five other soldiers.

"Our pilot's Harrison Price. He used to be a boxer and fought under the name of Tex Tornado. He's tougher and older than he looks. He's one of the good guys. I always look for him first but there are a couple of others I use."

Nodding toward his fellow passengers Tully could see all were young and two looked extremely nervous. The taller one had his jaw set like concrete, his fingers moving constantly without direction. The other, a black kid was surely no more than eighteen, his mouth in constant motion as he tried to murder the gum being pounded by his teeth. Introducing themselves, Tully and Snaps found them friendly and eager to chat.

"First time?" one asked Tully.

"Yeah, at least in Nam. Why are you sitting on your helmets?"

"Snipers below. Could save you getting your balls shot off," he said grinning broadly.

Tully quickly followed suit much to the amusement of the GI's.

"Does anyone know where we're going?" Tully spoke to a corporal who was nonchalantly reading a magazine as if he were home in an armchair. The only thing missing was the television set.

"Do you give a fuck?"

"It would be nice to know what I'm writing about."

"Search and destroy my friend. There's a village called Thien Tan that's reported to have Viet Cong there. We have to go in and clean them out."

"Any idea how many Viet Cong?"

"Shit, I'm only a corporal. The brass hasn't taken me into their confidence yet. I expect we'll just shoot up a few gooks and come home again."

The GI gave the impression it was a social outing. He had been on these sorties before.

Watching the green of the jungle flash past as the chopper sped on its way, Tully sat quietly not knowing what to expect. Thirty minutes later he could see the village of Thein Tan.

White smoke was spiraling into the air as rockets were fired into the village from the attacking gun ships. It floated upward in a serene motion but there was nothing peaceful about the result of the strikes. Most of the choppers had unloaded their troops when Tully and Snaps arrived. Snaps leapt out quickly with camera ready followed by Tully and the soldiers.

"Keep your bloody head down," shouted Snaps as they ran for cover. Tully could hear bullets whistling over his head as return fire was coming from thick jungle on the other side of the village. After raging for an hour things suddenly went quiet. It seemed the Viet Cong had evaporated into the jungle leaving behind a burning village. The black smoke rising from the fiery ruins of the huts was testimony to the firepower of the Americans.

"Guess its time to go take a look," said Tully but Snaps was already moving. He had used his second roll of film and was busy loading another. Soldiers were laying out bodies. It reminded Tully of the monk back in Saigon. At least twenty dead GI's were on the ground or being placed in body bags. Medics were attending the wounded and didn't give the Australians a second look. Tully could see them desperately feeding plasma into the wounded men's veins.

Racing across the ground toward the village they found a Vietnamese man lying on the ground bleeding badly. He had a terrible wound to his stomach and lay moaning in pain.

"This man needs help," shouted Tully to a soldier running past.

"He's a fucking gook," said the soldier contemptuously.

"But he's wounded," insisted Tully.

The soldier lowered his rifle and fired three bullets into the man. "Not now," he said and turned to run off. Tully couldn't believe what he saw.

"What sort of justice is that?." Tully was furious with the blatant murder.

"Justice? We're not here for justice. We're here to win. Go cry in your beer."

Snaps grabbed his arm and pulled him forward.

They stepped into one of the few huts still standing and Tully almost gagged at the sight. On the floor of the crude construction were two women, one middle aged and the other in her early twenties. The young woman was holding an infant while the other woman had her arms around the body of a young child, a little girl of no more than three. They had all been sprayed with automatic fire and blood was everywhere.

"Shit," said Tully finding his voice at last. "This is the Viet Cong? They're only women and kids. How could they do this?"

"Sickening isn't it." Snaps took more pictures. Bodies lay all over the outside and the GI's walked around checking them for weapons. None were found. As Tully went to walk outside he was almost knocked over by another soldier rushing in, rifle at the ready. He faltered when he saw the bodies of the women and children.

"You guys have done a good job. You must be proud." Tully's voice was bitter and filled with sarcasm.

"Don't yo all judge us," he said with his southern accent. "Ah have two babies about the same age. Ah sure do hate this fucking war."

"They were only innocents. The Viet Cong come into their villages for food then leave. Seems some of you Yanks are trigger happy." Snaps couldn't hide his disgust.

"We yall' only obeying orders," he drawled. "Not many of us are happy about it."

"Yeah. That's what they said at Nuremberg. Get your pictures, Snaps and let's get out of here." Hurrying back across the open ground to the choppers a voice boomed through a hailer.

"Who are those civilians? Bring them here." Tully and Snaps turned toward the voice.

"Shit. It's Bull Rogerson. The meanest son of a bitch in the country."

"Just how mean?" asked Tully.

"Loves the limelight and likes to show whose boss. Be careful, he can get you kicked out of Vietnam."

A soldier came running with his rifle raised. "The colonel wants to see you, sir."

"Sure, mate, lead on." They followed the soldier toward Bull Rogerson.

Tully studied the man as they came closer.

He's a stupid arrogant bastard was Tully's impression.

The colonel looked as though he was dressed for a parade. Clean neat and tidy uniform, the brass buckle on his belt shining like polished gold. A Viet Cong sniper would have a field day thought Tully.

A cigar rammed in one corner of his mouth was smoking like an oily rag. He removed his chromed steel helmet with his right hand and wiped the sweat from his brow with a handkerchief, which magically appeared in his left hand, then he spat on the ground. His hair reminded Tully of the monsoon clouds building up on the horizon, his mood just as dark. The creases on his brow would have frightened Attila the Hun

Despite the contempt he felt Tully forced his lips into a smile.

"Colonel. Let me congratulate you on a fine job. I'm Tully Sanderson of the *Sydney Tribune*. It's a pleasure to meet one of America's renowned fighting men."

The colonel was somewhat confused by the proffer of Tully's hand.

"What the hell are you two motherfuckers doing here?" He wanted to make sure the surrounding troops heard him.

"Sir, we heard there was a mission on and when your name came up we knew it would be a successful run. Would you permit us to take your photo to print with our story? The folk back home love heroes."

Rogerson preened at the comment and straight away his tone changed to one of conciliation.

"Why sure, I guess it would be okay. Just don't get in the way of my men."

"Thanks, colonel. Perhaps if we stand you with the burning buildings behind for good effect." Tully laid on the charm thick as Wimmera mud. Bullshit was one of his specialties.

Rogerson thrust his chest out proudly. Snaps took several photos and smiled gratefully.

"Thanks, colonel. This will be a great shot."

"Arsehole," Tully muttered under his breath as they walked away allowing the colonel to get on with his job.

"Quick thinking, Tully," said Snaps grinning. "You're going to do well out here."

"I'm going to have to develop a strong stomach if we see much more of this slaughter."

"If you think this stinks then your education is about to begin."

The return journey was pretty much subdued. The horror he'd just seen inflicted on the small village was engraved on Tully's mind. He knew the Viet Cong relied on these villages for food and he felt sorry for the people living there.

If they refused the Viet Cong they would most likely be shot and if they helped them, the Americans came in and slaughtered them. It was a no win situation for them.

The next day at the press conference Tully was amazed to hear the GI's had only lost three men at the battle at Thein Tan.

"They must have been bringing back rice," muttered Tully as he recalled the twenty odd bodies he'd seen bagged.

*   *   *

Two months of Vietnam educated Tully. Learning that what was actually happening in this war torn country was a painful lesson. The slaughter of the villages continued from both sides and he was appalled at the savagery inflicted daily. Twice he had been on a patrol with greenhorn marines but quickly left them when he heard some actually playing a radio. He wondered how many were going to survive with such a blasé attitude. The more he was seeing, the more disillusioned he was becoming.

Understanding clearly now, Snaps statement about drinking and using the women to banish the thoughts running through his head made sense.

Finding solace with the girls in the bars but trying to make sure they were not children became normal. He became quite fond of some and was on a name basis with all of them. They always had a cheery greeting for him and he was well known and liked around Saigon.

In between chasing around the countryside after the war, he and Snaps spent most of their nights in the bars trying to banish the horrors they were seeing daily. The weather was still oppressive, making one listless.

Opening another beer, their fourth, Tully's eyes idly perused the crowd, taking in the local scene. Noting even more GI's than usual were in tonight, the young girls were receiving a feast of attention.

The inside tables were all occupied, not that they wanted an inside table. The slight breeze drifting around the outdoor tables was enjoyable.

A young lad of about ten or eleven was trying hard to sell post cards. He went from table to table plying his wares smiling broadly saying "You buy Joe?"

Tully flicked him a coin, which he caught expertly in his free hand.

Grinning broadly he moved on to try his luck further.

Suddenly without raising interest he nonchalantly closed his bag and walked outside leaving the bag under a chair.

"Looks like he's had enough of the hard sell for tonight," Tully commented disinterestedly.

Snaps watched the lad depart and turned back to his drink. It was as if he'd been struck with divine providence. Suddenly he went white, grabbed Tully, upended and dived behind their table.

"Shit," he yelled. "Everybody get down."

Tully had no idea what was happening. The bar erupted in a ball of yellow flame hurling people through the air. Tully was sure his eardrums would burst.

Lifting his head slightly to see where Snaps was, it was almost knocked from his shoulders. Things became out of focus. Snaps seemed to be saying something but it made no sense. He noted how Snap's mouth was going up and down but nothing seemed to be coming out. A blackness enveloping him stopped the stinging pain in his head and then nothing.

*   *   *

Slowly his eyes opened once, flickered and closed again. Feeling a deliciously cool sensation on his forehead he forced them open once more. A soft voice spoke to him from afar.

"How do you feel, soldier?" His eyes flickered again trying to focus.

"Have I died and gone to heaven?" Catching her green eyes he was mesmerized. "You have to be an angel. Right?"

"Sorry, it's not heaven, it's just a hospital ward. You haven't died and you're not likely to. You've got a cut to your forehead, which I've stitched up. It's not too bad but I'm afraid you'll have a scar."

"How long have I been here, nurse?"

"I'm a doctor. Doctor Kate Armitage. Australian Medical Service. One of your mob."

"How did you know I was Australian?"

"I didn't until you opened your mouth. How come you're not with your unit?"

"Because I'm not a soldier, Doc. I'm a correspondent with the Sydney Tribune. Is this an Australian hospital?"

"A bloody reporter. I might have known. No, we all use the American hospital. They've got the top equipment and first class operating facilities. All the wounded soldiers come here."

"Where's Snaps? We were having a quiet drink when the bomb went off. How is my mate?"

"If you mean the red head who brought you in, he doesn't have a scratch. I told him to come back tomorrow. I need your name for the chart?"

"Tully Sanderson."

"Well you can stay the night, Mr Sanderson but you'll have to leave first thing in the morning. We need our beds for wounded soldiers, not for people who sit in bars all day drinking beer and ogling girls." There was a decidedly icy edge to her tone.

"You have such a wonderful bedside manner, Dr Kate. I bet all the patients just love you."

"I'm not here for my good looks or my bedside manner. I'm here to try and help our injured get through a pretty horrendous time. Both American and Australian."

Tully couldn't understand the hostility in her voice. Normally he got a better response from women.

"You're not badly hurt and you're using up a good bed." Her emerald green eyes flashed seemingly to look right through him. She was certainly the prettiest doctor Tully had ever seen. Looking fresh and clean but even in the night air Tully could see the wet stains under her arm. He knew how she felt. All the deodorant in the world didn't stop him from sweating.

"Well, Doctor Kate, seeing you saved my life what if I take you out to dinner at Saigon's finest eatery as a token of gratitude."

The look she gave him dented his confidence. It was as if he had slapped her in the face. "You think this is a bloody holiday resort. Men are coming in here with their arms and legs blown off and you think I should go out to dinner."

Tully was taken aback by her aggressive attitude. "Everyone needs some sort of recreation, Doc or they crack up. Sorry I upset you."

She bit her lip, angry with herself at taking her frustrations out on a patient.

"I'm sorry. It's been a bad day. I apologize for my rudeness."

"Accepted. So when do we go to dinner?"

"Thank you for the invitation but I can't accept. It's against hospital policy and I'm far too busy."

"I don't know how you can turn down my irresistible charm, Doc. There are women willing to pay me to take them to dinner. I admire you're ability to reject such temptation." Grinning like an innocent schoolboy appealed to her and she couldn't help herself. It was the first time she had laughed in weeks.

"Thanks again for the offer." Her tone was a little friendlier. "But I couldn't deny the women of Saigon the pleasure of your company. I'll check you in the morning and if all is well you can leave before lunch time."

"You'll regret your decision. It's like turning down a lottery prize."

Smiling she walked away. The next day a different doctor checked him out and declared him fit. Snaps picked him up and it was back to business.

*   *   *

Life returned to what passed for normal in Nam., continuing hitching rides with Tex on his missions and spending their spare time at a bar, usually the Orchid.

The accolades received for several of their stories didn't impress Tully, however Snaps scored a prize for a particularly compelling photo he managed to get under pretty incredible circumstances at an out-lying village.

Joining a patrol sent in to mop up a village totally destroyed by American bombing, Tully was appalled at what he saw. The ground was now barren and dead cattle were sprawling in a nearby swamp. The bamboo huts totally demolished leaving just a smoking tangle of twisted and broken bamboo.

Dismembered bodies were lying around the ground and Tully was saddened to see women clutching their children and rocking back and forth beside the bodies of their men. It brought back thoughts of Carrie safely in Australia.

The GI's searched them roughly but found no weapons. Gaining some satisfaction, Tully saw a young lieutenant distributing food and medical supplies to the unfortunate group. He had his arm around one of the women trying to comfort her. Snaps was right. Some of them really were good guys.

Moving through the village waiting for the Americans to finish and return to Saigon, Snaps re-loaded his camera and took a few extra shots of the devastation. Leaning back to get a better angle, his leg pressed against the burning ruins of a hut.

"Shit," he said jumping high like some hurt kangaroo. It was too late; his ankle had a large raw burn.

Producing a reasonably clean handkerchief to serve as a makeshift bandage Tully wrapped it gently but as soon as they landed he drove him straight to the hospital. While Snaps was having his wound dressed, Tully found his way to the triage desk.

"Know where I can find Doctor Armitage?" he asked a nurse.

"I just saw her go out through that door." She pointed to her left then ignored him. It seemed everyone was busy here.

Tully walked a few yards down a path. She was sitting alone on a bench seat under a palm offering a little shade. As she raised her head he saw she had been crying. Quickly she wiped her eyes.

"Oh, it's you." Hastily she tried to regain her composure. Tully could see she was embarrassed.

"Had another bad day?"

"I just lost a patient. A young black guy, he was not yet twenty. I thought he'd be all right but he just up and died. This place is so damned frustrating."

"Look, I know it's not policy but I'm not joking this time. You do need to get away from here. Even one night would do you good."

"I'm sorry. I'm not usually like this, and you're right. I need a night off. It's, Mr Sanderson isn't it?"

"Yeah, Tully Sanderson. My offer is still open. How about dinner tonight?"

Blowing her nose loudly she composed herself. It was as if he could see her mind turning over. The stress she was under very apparent. She'd had enough. She wanted to go home. He waited for her answer hoping it would be in the affirmative.

"Why not. This place is getting under my skin. You can pick me up outside the gate at seven. I'll leave the eating place to you."

"Great. See you at seven, Kate."

Tully returned to check on Snaps but had to wait an hour before he was released.

"Well?" asked Tully.

"I'm in agony, mate. The Doc said it will take at least ten stubbies before I'm well again."

"You'll have to do your own drinking tonight, Snaps. I've got a date."

"Oh well. I'll have to see what ten dollars will get me at the Orchid Bar."

Tully grinned. Snaps would never change. He was just like Tully. Booze and women were his hobby too.

The woman waiting at the gate was a very different person from the woman doctor he had left at the hospital. Gone was the uniform replaced by a mufti. It was a mufti like he had not seen in a long time. A softly flowing golden yellow skirt giving great contrast to the shapely tanned legs. Dainty yellow sandals and a black halter neck top.

Her fair hair was soft, shining and hanging loosely around her shoulders, vastly different from when it was pinned up in a ponytail at the hospital. She was totally opposite to Briony in her coloring.

With stifled amusement she watched him.

"I'd suggest you close your mouth, Mr Sanderson. I can assure you the insects here don't taste very nice."

"Sorry, stunning looking women have that effect on me."

"Please. Flattery will get you everywhere. Where are we going?"

"Somewhere relatively safe. I've had enough grenade blasts for a while."

"Suits me. Let's go."

It was one of the better restaurants usually patronized by officers and Kate seemed quite satisfied at his choice. It was a brick building with the eating area on the first floor.

"Very nice. I haven't been here before in fact I haven't been anywhere much since I arrived."

"How long have you been in Vietnam?" Raising his hand he signaled for a waiter and ordered a bottle of wine.

"Twelve months, two weeks, three days and eight hours of sheer hell."

"I can see you like the place too."

"Doesn't everyone?"

"I'm recommending it to the Australian Tourist Bureau."

"You should make a good commission."

"And where do you call home?"

"Melbourne originally. I did my internship in Sydney with the Australian Medical Corp, then volunteered and here I am."

"Sounds like you regret your decision."

"Well I did think I might be able learn different techniques as well as helping our boys. Never for one moment did I envisage this."

"Want to talk about it?" Tully was eager to know more about this woman rapidly capturing his attention.

"Like most twenty six year olds, I thought the world was there for my taking.

From the moment I arrived I've been up to my neck trying to repair the most horrendous injuries one could imagine. Our men haven't had the exposure the Americans have but it sickens me to see young boys suffering the needless injuries inflicted. I'll have a white wine."

Tully filled her glass from the bottle just deposited.

"You should see what's being done out at some of the villages. The poor locals don't seem to have access to hospitals." Tully watched her drink the wine quickly.

"I know what goes on. The commanders have a lot to answer for."

She offered her glass again. Tully filled it immediately.

"I've been out on patrols and seen it first hand. In one village women and children were cut down by automatic fire. Some of them no older than my daughter."

Kate's eyes met his. "You're married?"

"No. When I was working in Belfast, I fell in love with an Irish girl. We had a child but Briony was killed in an unfortunate incident. My daughter Carrie is with my sister in Sydney."

"I'm sorry." She sounded genuinely upset. "Tell me about Belfast, I always wanted to visit the land of my ancestors."

Tully told her about the happy times he had there. Describing the green fields, the rough coastline, and the wonderful Irish people who opened their doors and hearts to you, he had her attention. Kate didn't interrupt him while he was talking.

Describing the little towns and villages Briony had taken him brought back happy memories. Laughing about the time he had seen little donkeys pulling milk carts along narrow country lanes he was pleased when Kate seemed so interested. He made no mention of any of the horrors similar to Vietnam.

"Sounds like you had a good time."

He nodded. "They were enjoyable memories."

They spent a pleasant evening, enjoying a nice meal and a few more drinks. Kate seemed to relax putting the traumas of her job behind her. Tully glanced at his watch casually.

"I'm boring you."

"Of course not. How could I be bored by a Goddess?"

"I see you've kissed the blarney stone while you were there."

"I was going to but I heard the locals peed on it."

She burst out laughing at his comment. He was doing wonders for her.

"I didn't know what time you had to be back."

"No please don't take me back to base yet. I want some more wine. I would really like to get drunk tonight. You know this week I've helped with ten amputations, had five of my fifteen stomach wounds die on me. One of them was a lovely young lad from upper class Boston." She looked bitter again. "He thought I was his mother and held onto my hand and cried. He kept saying, I'm sorry, Mum I've let you down."

Downing another glass of wine in two quick gulps, she then passed it to him for a refill. Tully obliged noting he had only one glass.

"I sent two Australians home this week, one had lost an arm and the other will probably never walk again. I work up to fifteen hours a day."

Down went another half a glass. It seemed to be like water to her. "At the moment I'm pretty pissed off with the army, Vietnam and this whole stupid senseless war."

"I hadn't noticed that."

Filling her glass again he let her talk. Her desperate need to clear her system of her present life style was obvious. He was saddened to hear some of the cases she handled and some of the conditions she worked under. Maybe my chosen profession was a cakewalk by comparison to hers, he thought as she drank some more.

Draining her glass again she reached her hand across the table to touch him. Despite the wine, her eyes were clear and bright, veiled by fair lashes softly tipped with mascara. After the wine she had put away he wondered how she could stand up. Then she shocked him.

"You're a nice guy, Sanderson, please don't think me cheap but I'd really like to get laid and I guess you're nominated."

Tully's mouth fell open; he couldn't believe his ears, it was usually his line.

"I hope you can understand." She had a sad look on her face. "I came out with you simply because I needed sex. You seem like a good bloke and I'll trust you to not tell. I presume you'll manage to comply."

"Let's get this straight. You want me to have sex with you to escape from reality for a while, but want no commitment after."

"Yes." She looked down somewhat embarrassed. "I know women accuse men of using them and I guess this is the reverse. I've never done this before. You don't have to."

"I,--- well I'm lost for words. I must say it was high on my agenda for this evening. What about the hospital policy or is that okay now I'm an ex-patient?"

The sound of her laughter was like a bell tinkling. "I'd forgotten I said that, there is no policy, we just use the line to get out of awkward situations."

Always priding himself on his ability to read female emotions, Tully was astounded. He couldn't fathom this beautiful woman. He had totally believed her lie about policy and had been prepared to step away from the unattainable Doctor Armitage. Now here she was propositioning him. Maybe it was the wine; she'd certainly had more than her share.

"Kate I know what you're feeling. I've felt the same way often and I confess I have used my share of girls at the Orchid Bar. If you're sure it's not just the wine talking then I'd be proud to make love to you."

"Not love, Tully. Just sex."

"My place is not far from here. Shall we go?"

He paid the bill and led her toward his hotel.

Ignoring the smirk Charlie gave him as he entered, Tully led Kate to his room.

"It's not the Hilton but it's adequate. We journos are out more than we're in."

As soon as he closed the door she put her arms around him and kissed him passionately. He knew it was only a need to be wanted by someone, anyone.

"There's no hurry, Kate," he said gently and stroked the side of her face. He could see tears glistening and gently he kissed her eyes, her nose and then her lips. He felt her relax as he dropped his lips to her throat and she stretched her neck higher wanting more.

Tully was determined it would be a night she wouldn't forget in a hurry. He slipped his hand around her waist until he felt the zipper of her skirt, then slowly lowered it until it came loose. It dropped to the floor, the soft fabric forming a golden circle around her ankles. She made no effort to step away. His fingers ran down her back making her give a little shudder.

He noted she had her eyes closed savoring the pleasure. Unhooking the halter of her top, he pushed it down revealing her small firm, perfectly shaped breasts. She stood in just her sandals and panties, totally unabashed.

Lifting her up, he gently lay her on the bed, his fingers expertly running over her body, her neck, her shoulders and down the inside of her arms. The teasing circles he made around her breasts, then sliding his fingers over her firm brown nipples made her sigh. They felt like delicate crystal, which he treated accordingly. Her eyes were fluttering and she was moaning softly, then rolled over allowing him to continue his circling movements across her back and buttocks.

She squirmed and writhed quietly. Quickly he removed his own clothes and lowered himself beside her. He could see the wine was making her drowsy.

"Turn over, Kate." He touched her gently all the while making teasing circles on every inch of her body.

His nibbling and kissing roused her with all his expertise.

Slowly she was spreading her legs making room for his probing fingers. He reached the golden spot and she emitted a tiny scream spreading her legs wider, inviting him into her private sanctuary. She whispered. "Yes, yes," as he eased his manhood into her.

"I'm not a slut Tully, I'm not," she whispered, her eyes closed surrendering to his gentle strokes.

"I know that Kate. You're a woman who needs someone to love her. Just relax and enjoy it."

He moved gently, evenly at a pace readily matched. Pressure built slowly as she enjoyed what was happening. He knew she was divesting herself from the horror she had seen and maybe felt as if she was now in a sanctuary of peace. Digging her nails into his back and softly biting his ear lobe she whispered, "I love you, James."

Tully wondered whom the hell James might be but decided now was not the time to ask. Besides, he was probably dead and gone poor bastard.

She quickened the pace, her breathing coming thick and fast. "Please, James, now, together, James, now." Her body arched and mewed like a kitten until finally shuddering, expelling a breath of air. Sighing she relaxed back on the bed. Tully stayed inside her not moving his body, just his lips kissing her neck and ears softly.

"Thank you," she whispered. "You certainly know how to take a girl's mind off her terrors."

"The night's not over yet." He wrapped his arms around her and held her close. Warm tears wet his neck. Slowly opening the gates of her own private war Kate sobbed and sobbed. Tully was holding her close and making soft soothing noises until finally she fell asleep. Covering her with a sheet, he walked to the drawer and poured himself a whisky from the bottle he kept there.

The sorrow he was feeling for this poor tormented doctor asleep in his bed made him hope, maybe tomorrow things would look better to her. He stared at her sleeping figure, curled up on the mattress without the sheet that had now slipped down. Her form was like a precious piece of art as her chest gently rose and dropped with each breath she took. The moonlight filtered through the window on her body and she brought back other pleasant memories in a land far away and much colder than here. It was the first time since Briony he had ever felt this way about a woman. He quietly slipped in beside her and was asleep almost at once.

Tully woke, reaching across for her but found the other side of the bed empty. Sitting up quickly he wondered if she was in the shower. There was no sound of running water.

On the pillow beside him was a note, which said. "Thank you for giving me back my sanity, Tully, I meant what I said. No commitment. I had a wonderful time, please don't try to contact me again. Thank you."

That's what you think, Kate Armitage, he thought screwing up the note and aiming it at the bin.

Chapter Twelve

Tully let a week lapse before going back to the hospital again. As usual the place was a hive of activity. Ambulances had arrived and the last of the wounded were being unloaded. He knew it was a bad time to come.

"Would it be possible to see Doctor Kate Armitage please?" he asked one of the American nurses. She looked up and gave him her best smile. This guy definitely appealed to her.

"Not unless you've got excellent eyesight. She was transferred to Hue the day before yesterday."

"Did she leave a message for Tully Sanderson?" he asked hopefully.

"Sorry. No message." She shook her head sympathetically. "Maybe I could help. I'm excellent at mending broken hearts."

She was very pretty but Tully resisted the temptation. "Maybe later." He smiled at her. "I'm due to leave on an assignment."

"I'll be here," she said returning his smile. "My name is Elizabeth."

It appeared Kate meant exactly what she said. No commitment, just a passing moment.

Tully knew they'd meet again, he didn't know how or where, he just knew.

Vietnam. 1972

"Have you read this about the My Lai massacre?" Snaps handed Tully the Washington Post. "It sure has upset the people of the USA."

"Yeah, three hundred innocent men women and children are enough to piss anyone off. I bet nothing will be done about it." Tully threw the newspaper down in disgust.

"We have a meeting with Major Macmillan at twelve. Better go."

They were based at Hoa Khue just outside Da Nang the major American airfield. Tully was now one of the most important correspondents in Vietnam. He wasn't afraid to put himself in danger to get a good story. Covering most of the major battles put him in the firing line more than Snaps enjoyed, but he was getting the news as it happened and that made him very valuable. Twice he had been home to see his daughter in a flying visit but each time his boss insisted he return as soon as possible.

Tully wanted to do a story on the daily operations of a typical Australian patrol and knew the dangers entailed.

Australia had already pulled out most of its troops and this might be his last chance. He managed to arrange this meeting and looked forward for permission to accompany the twelve men on their patrol.

Tully and Snaps sat opposite the major in his tent. Tully thought he was the most laid back officer he had ever met. There were no pretensions of self importance here. He'd had a gut full of the place and wanted to go home just like the rest of his men.

"Tully Sanderson, Major. This is Craig Cassidy who answers to Snaps. We both work for the Sydney Tribune. We'd like to print the truth about what's going on in Vietnam and we wondered if we could accompany one of your patrols. The people at home are starved for news of Australians."

"Christ, Tully, why the hell would you want to go on a dangerous mission like this?"

"You don't get many stories sitting in a bar in Saigon Major."

"I've read some of your stories and I approve of what you're writing." He offered them a seat, which they accepted.

"Thanks, Major. We'd like to get Australian troops in the action. Some of the Americans are a bit barbaric as far as the local population is concerned."

"You've been on patrol with the Americans?"

"Yeah, the last time a young kid was smoking a joint and another was playing a transistor radio. We left them and joined another patrol coming back. Neither of us has a death wish."

"Yeah, I know. You understand you'll be required to obey the orders of the sergeant in charge, just as if you were in the army. The safety of the men is the first consideration."

"We know that, Major. We agree with your conditions."

"Then I'll see if I can arrange it. Give us another three months and there won't be any Australian troops still here."

"That's why we want to go with them now. We know most have already left for home."

"Okay. It's your funeral. Report back to me tomorrow and I'll arrange it."

The interview was over and he shook hands.

The next day they met Sergeant Colin Foster.

"So you blokes are coming with us tomorrow," he said after introductions were made.

"We promise we won't get in your way, mate."

"I'll make bloody sure of that," said Foster. "The first sign of trouble you do exactly as I say. I'll tell you now, I don't want bloody journalists fucking up my patrol, especially at this late stage."

"Don't worry, Colin. We're relying on you to look after our arses." Snaps gave him an appealing look.

"And we'll make sure we keep out of your way," added Tully.

Knowing he could do little about it Foster nodded. "It should be a routine patrol. We go into a few villages watching out for trouble. There's usually some people needing attention, mostly women and kids. We do what we can, but sometimes it can be dangerous."

"Don't the Yanks do that?" Tully looked confused.

"Yeah. We run into them sometimes but we both have our areas to cover. Sometimes the locals welcome us but not always. The Viet Cong give them a hard time if they try to help us. No talking unless I say so."

"Roger and out. We'll be ready at five."

"A.M.?" asked Snaps in anticipation. Early rising didn't impress him.

"Shit, whining already," said Foster.

Foster ran a very professional unit. Hardly a word was spoken as they made their way through the thick jungle.

All signals were done by hand and as Tully and Snaps had first hand experience being on patrol in hostile territory, they were quite at home. Apart from the odd birdcalls nothing was heard or seen of the enemy.

The oppressive heat and the steaming humidity of the jungle made each step a laborious task. Some areas were on solid ground but others were boggy where they sank up to their ankles in mud. Both Tully and Snaps were glad of the five-minute breaks Foster called. Tully suspected it was for their sake and not his men but said nothing appreciating the rest periods. Twice Foster led them around booby traps designed to snap up and stab the unfortunate person with a sharpened stake.

It was close to noon when they heard the first shots. The man on point heard a sound from the undergrowth ahead and signaled them to drop. It was just in time as the air was filled with the sound of automatic fire. Tully, Snaps and Foster vied for position behind a fallen log as bullets thudded into the rotting timber. Timber flew from the log and the air was filled with cordite as the Australians fired back. It was returned threefold forcing them to keep their heads down. It was eerie fighting an enemy you couldn't see.

"Anyone hit?" called Foster. Receiving a negative reply he pulled out his map signaling one of his men. Tully strained to see something, but the only thing visible was a blanket of green. Foster lay pointing to a co-ordinate on the map.

"There's a small village about three miles from here. Smithy, you take the others while I attract their fire. I'll meet you there tonight."

"Right, Sarge." Smithy touched Tully's arm. "Let's go."

"What, and leave him behind. Are you crazy?" asked Tully.

"You agreed to obey orders, Sanderson. Now piss off and do as you're told." Foster was in no mood to argue.

"But we can't just leave you. You'll be shot."

"I know what I'm fucking doing. Now go."

Reluctantly Tully followed the patrol into the jungle leaving Foster behind firing his rifle randomly into the jungle. They'd barely gone a hundred yards when Tully turned to Smithy.

"You can go on but I'm going back for him."

"We have our orders. You can't break ranks. Foster is a very experienced soldier."

"We're civilians. Stuff your orders. I'll meet you there with Foster." With that he and Craig returned to the scene.

"Jesus you get me into trouble sometimes." Snaps called as he ran.

"You should have stayed with them." Tully sounded angry.

"And miss out on some good pictures."

When the arrived back Foster was still firing and he turned and pointed his rifle toward their approaching noise, then saw who they were.

"Shit. I knew civilians couldn't be trusted."

"We thought it would be safer sticking with you," Tully cajoled.

"Jesus, you haven't even got weapons. Get ready to run when I throw this." He took a grenade from his belt, pulled the pin and threw it in the general direction of the enemy fire. As it exploded all three ran like hell. They crashed through the thick growth not caring if they were heard at all.

Branches brushed across their bodies scratching any bare skin exposed. The wet undergrowth slapping at their faces was like a wet dish cloth. Both Tully and Snaps screamed for oxygen as they tried to keep up with Foster. It felt as if they were running forever until at last Foster stopped and listened.

"I can't hear them?" Snaps looked from one to the other as he tried to get his breath back.

"No. My guess is they only came upon us by accident. We're safe now. Even the Viet Cong don't run wildly through this jungle."

"What now, Sarge?"

Foster pulled out his map again. "We try to find the village. According to this there's another one about here." He pointed on his map. "We'll head there first, then scout around it to the other one. That way, if they happen to pick up our trail we won't lead them to my men. They should be there before us."

"You're the boss," said Tully happy to be safe.

"I thought you'd forgotten that, Sanderson."

About three o'clock they sighted the village. There were three bamboo huts standing above the ground on stilts. A bullock was munching grass on the other side of a clearing but nothing else moved. Foster froze, his eyes scanning the huts. They knelt down behind some dense foliage as Foster again scanned the huts.

"What's wrong?" asked Snaps nervously.

"There's five bodies under that hut." He pointed toward the first of the three huts on the edge of the village. It was larger than the other two.

"Shit. Viet Cong?"

"I don't think so." Foster knew his enemy. "Stay behind me."

Quietly and quickly they weaved across the open ground and they could distinctly hear a woman screaming and men shouting. Foster looked at Tully frowning.

"Hurry up, Pete. Tie the bitch down," an American voice said loudly.

Tully and Foster carefully peered through the slats of bamboo where five soldiers were standing around a crude table.

Two were holding the arms of a naked girl while another was tying her hands down.

"Me first." The tallest one was laughing as he stood over the young terrified girl. She was around nineteen; her eyes wide with terror knowing what was about to happen.

Her dress lay crumpled on the dirt floor where it had been torn from her body. The other four stood with their trousers open and their penises at the ready waiting their turn.

All were anxious to begin. "Hurry up, Pete, get started. You're not the only one who wants a bit of fun. Shit, I haven't had a girl since forever."

"Tie her legs too," said Pete. "And spread them."

Two of them grabbed her legs forcing them apart as Pete climbed onto the table ready to enter her. Foster kicked open the door pointing his rifle straight at Pete's penis.

"What do you arseholes think you're doing?" he snarled.

Five pairs of eyes turned toward the voice.

"Aussies." Pete was relieved. "We're just about to have a little fun. You're welcome to her after we've had a go."

"It's pricks like you who give your own army a bad name. How would you feel if someone raped your sister or your wife?"

"Shit man, she's only a gook. We'll waste her after. No-one will know."

Tully grabbed one of the American rifles resting against the wall in case there was going to be trouble.

"She's a young girl who's terrified of you bastards. She deserves better respect than you're giving her." Tully was furious.

"Shit guys. We've got some boy-scouts here." Pete laughed trying to ridicule the Australians. "Your guys are not all squeaky clean either."

Foster fired into the floor at Pete's feet. "Zip up your pants and get out of here,---now."

Pete looked at his men and nodded. Tully saw the look and gripped the rifle tightly. The marines zipped up their trousers, then picked up their weapons.

Suddenly one turned and fired a quick shot in Foster's direction. Tully heard the shot whip past their heads.

Without hesitation, Tully fired a burst at them at the same time as Foster. It was over quickly. All five fell to the floor. Silence reigned for several seconds, a complete contrast to the moments before. Tully and Foster glanced at each other, neither speaking but each was thinking of the consequences. The air was acrid with smoke as Foster slowly walked over and checked the bodies. Snaps stood with his mouth open not believing his eyes.

"They're all dead." Foster was satisfied. "Serves the bastards right."

"Shit. Do you blokes realise the trouble we're in." Snaps found his voice at last. He looked stupidly at the bloody bodies lying at obscene angles.

Tully cut the girls bonds and handed her the torn dress as she cowered against the wall holding it modestly across her.

"It's all right, love. You're safe. What's your name?"

She was shaking with tears running down her cheeks. "My name is Soo Ling. Thank you."

"That's your family out there?"

She nodded. "They come, kill all."

Foster's eyes showed disgust as he spat on the floor.

"Take a picture," Tully said to Snaps's amazement.

"Are you bonkers? That would be evidence of what we did."

"No. It would be evidence of a Viet Cong attack on a small village heroically defended by these soldiers. Unfortunately Sergeant Foster got here a bit late but fought off the attackers. That's right isn't it, sergeant?"

"Absolutely." Foster removed their dog tags putting them in his pack.

"Get dressed, Soo Ling. We're getting out of here."

"My baby. I get my baby."

Soo Ling rushed into the small alcove and returned holding an infant, perhaps nine months old.

"You two grab a rifle each from the Yanks," said Foster after placing the dog tags in his pack.

"Jesus, we're journalists, not bloody soldiers," said Snaps.

"You're going to throw your pencils at the Viet Cong when they start firing at you?'

Tully looked at Snaps. "He's right. We'll worry about our journalistic morals after we get out of here. He can't protect all of us on his own."

"Let's go." Foster led them out into the jungle. When they were fifty metres away he halted them.

"Wait here," he said walking back toward the hut. He pulled out a grenade, removed the pin and threw it into the hut. They watched as the hut exploded.

"Why did you do that?" asked Snaps.

"If they're found there'll be no questions about the sort of bullets that cut them down. If anything is said about this I'll ram a grenade up your arse."

Nodding their heads in agreement they followed Foster in the direction of the next village where the rest of the patrol should be waiting.

Chapter Thirteen

As they fought their way through the thick steamy jungle to the rendezvous, Tully was puzzled by Soo Ling's attitude. He had expected her to be sad and subdued but instead she was bright and bubbly. Three times Foster had to tell her to shut up and each time she fell briefly silent only to burst out again minutes later. She had a classical Asian body, slim, narrow waist, and perfect skin. Almond eyes that were deep dark and searching and an effervescent laugh, which echoed through the jungle. Her hair was jet-black and shining, hanging down well below her shoulders. She was one of the most attractive girls Tully had ever seen.

When they were comparatively safe, Tully slipped the rifle on his shoulder and offered to take the baby for a while. She smiled and handed the infant over without a second thought. She walked alongside Tully as they followed Foster.

"Soo Ling. I couldn't help noticing the bodies of your family back there were all middle aged. Was one of them your husband?"

"No husband. Soo Ling not married."

"Then who is the father of your child?"

"Father is Nguyen Huong. He one of dead."

"Then how the hell did you come to be there? Were you raped by this man?"

"Soo Ling's father have many daughters. Nguyen Huong buy me for bullock and two pigs. Soo Ling not cheap. Very expensive."

"You were sold by your father?" Tully couldn't believe his ears.

"Very hard for father with seven daughters. He make good bargain."

"Shit. How old were you when this happened?"

"Soo Ling fifteen. Now nineteen. Nguyen have me like wife. Soo Ling prettier than wife. Have healthy baby now."

And a lifetime of misery, thought Tully as they continued through the jungle. He didn't like her chances of survival.

It was slow going to the next village but Foster knew what he was doing and took no chances. Finally they burst out of the jungle and came across the eleven men waiting for them.

"You took your time. Run into a bit of trouble did you?" said one of the soldiers when he saw Soo Ling.

"Yeah, we stumbled on a village where the Viet Cong had killed some Yanks. We rescued the survivors and made for here." Foster made no further comment.

"Yeah, this bloke saved us all. He's a bloody hero," said Tully. "I'll see he makes the news."

"Forget it," said Foster. "Now line up. We have to get back to base before nightfall."

They continued their journey for another four hours. By the time they broke out of the jungle Tully didn't know if he was relieved or worried.

It was good to get into the open but it made them more vulnerable. They made their way across a rice paddy and down a rough track heading back toward their base.

"Should be back at Hoa Khue in an hour. I want to get there before dark. That's when the Viet Cong take over." Foster seemed more relaxed as the journey became easier.

They were moving closer to distant small arms fire with Soo Ling and Snaps looking anxious. A crump from mortar fire echoed towards them followed by more gunfire sounding closer still.

"You better stay here," said Foster grimly. "That sounds like Viet Cong fire."

"Where you go, I go." Tully intended sticking it out to the end.

"Suit yourself, but keep out of our way." The patrol quickened their pace leaving Soo Ling and Snaps trailing behind. Over a slight rise Tully and the platoon came across the source of the attack. Two army trucks were overturned, one of them burning. There were some bodies on the ground, and three figures crouched down behind the body of the truck.

"Ours or Yanks?" Tully was unsure due to the smoke drifting across the scene.

"Ambulances. See the red cross signs."

Tully hadn't noticed the Red Cross emblem on the side of the burning truck.

"Those blokes are in deep shit." He pointed to the three lying as close to the ground as possible. All had their hands over their heads in a rather vain attempt of some protection.

"They've got no weapons either," said Tully grimly.

"Looks as though the first truck ran over a mine. Work behind Charlie," said Foster to his men. They needed no further bidding and re-acted automatically.

Under the cover of a paddy bank, Tully ran toward the truck.

"Stupid bastard," said Foster watching his progress. He gritted his teeth expecting to be cut down any second but his luck held. The paddy bank hid his progress.

Tully came up almost alongside the truck and shouted to the trapped men.

"Keep down, help is near." Then he ran dodging the hail of bullets suddenly coming in his direction. The zap of the bullets whizzing past his head made him run even faster. He leapt through the air and landed on top of one of the medics who was hugging the dirt. A frightened face turned toward him and he was shocked to see it was a woman.

"Tully," she was just as surprised as him.

"Kate! Bloody hell. Stay down. Our blokes are getting into position."

She had a thin trickle of blood on her forehead and her face was filthy from the sweat and dust but she seemed to be unhurt. She grabbed his neck in a death grip almost choking him. The other two were also women, both nurses and both just as frightened as Kate. Tully motioned them to stay down.

"What are you doing out here?" He could hardly speak for the vice like grip she had on his neck.

"We had a call for some wounded men. They were in the back of the first ambulance."

"I don't think they need your help now. Everything will be all right soon. I promise." He pulled the rifle he had clear and pumped a couple of shots in the general direction of the enemy.

The Viet Cong's total concentration was on the trucks. They knew nothing of the platoon until it was too late. As soon as Foster's men were in position, they opened up with everything they had. There were only eight Viet Cong and they fell immediately. The Australian soldiers made sure they were dead then signaled Tully's little band it was safe to stand.

"Anyone hurt?" Foster inquired.

"No, we're okay. Thank you, sergeant. I'm Doctor Kate Armitage."

"My pleasure, Captain Armitage," he said smiling.

Soo Ling and Snaps appeared and Tully explained to Kate what had happened leaving out the shooting of the Americans. Kate checked the baby, then Soo Ling and declared them both in good health.

Tully led Kate aside. "I was told you were sent to Hue. Why didn't you leave a message?"

"I told you no commitment. I meant it."

"I don't understand you, Kate. We're good for each other."

"We had good sex, Tully. Nothing more."

"Don't tell me you didn't think about me later."

"Maybe I did. But this is not the time or place for relationships."

"I've thought about you all the time. Shit, it's been over twelve months now."

"You don't have to remind me. Anyway my time is almost up in this hell hole."

"You don't have a husband hidden away in Australia do you? I thought maybe that was the reason."

"No husband, no lover, no anyone. I just didn't want to get involved only to have it all taken away again."

"Again?" Tully was puzzled.

"I've seen too much killing since I've been here. I've lost a few friends."

Tully thought she meant more but he let it slide. "Are you still based in Hue?" He was elated now he had found her again.

"No. I'm at the American air base in Da Nang. There's a hospital nearby."

"That's great. I'm based near there now. Please, I'd like to see you again."

"I wish you wouldn't put pressure on me, Tully."

"Bloody hell, Kate, what harm can we come to having dinner like two old friends."

"I must say, Tully, you certainly get an A for obstinacy. Okay. Seeing I'm going home soon, I guess it won't matter much now. I'm due for some R and R starting at the end of the week."

Tully wrote his address on a slip of paper and handed it to her. "Call me before the end of the week or I'll come and tear the hospital down."

She laughed the tinkling laugh that stirred his desires.

"I've been reading your stories, Tully. They're great."

"Thanks. Remember if I don't hear from you I'll have news of our liaison spread over the front page of the *Sydney Tribune*."

"I thought you didn't kiss and tell." Her smile was so dazzling he knew he was losing his heart to this strong willed doctor.

"In your case I'll make an exception. I'll have to help Soo Ling find somewhere to live, then we'll spend some time together."

"She's a very pretty girl and very young."

"Yeah. Poor little bugger. Her father sold her to some farmer for a bullock and two pigs. She was boasting how expensive she was. He already had a wife but wanted something young and pretty."

"That's the way the system works here."

A loud cheer interrupted them as Foster's men got the remaining ambulance up and going. Revving the engine, they put Soo Ling and the baby along with Kate and the nurses in the back. Tully drove while Foster and Snaps rode shotgun, leaving Foster's men to walk back to Da Nang.

After they dropped Kate and her nurses at the hospital, they reported to an American Major and returned the dog tags. Tully helped Foster with his report by coloring the event in favor of the GI's making them almost heroes.

They were thanked for their efforts and Tully promised to write a story of the incident for the Australian papers complete with photos. He assured the major he would send him a copy. It was the best piece of fiction he had ever written.

*   *   *

Tully found a small house for Soo Ling and her baby some distance from the base. He gave her some money and promised he would drop in whenever he could. The only thing on his mind at the moment was Kate.

He and Snaps parted company both heading for a cool shower and a change of clothes at their billet, then met later for an evening meal.

"Some piece that doctor," said Snaps with his mouth full.

"Bloody gorgeous," agreed Tully. "I knew her back in Saigon."

"I can see why you didn't tell me about her. Less competition. Is she the one who sewed up your head?"

"Yeah. We had dinner one night."

"Must have been a memorable dinner. She certainly remembered you."

"She's going home soon. I hope I'll be seeing a bit of her before she goes."

"Lucky dog," Snaps grinned as if he knew what was going on. "Enjoy."

"I intend to." Tully's mind drifted back to their last meeting in Saigon.

Two days later Kate rang. Tully was relieved. He had thought, maybe she might ignore him again.

"I'm on leave for a fortnight and I always try to keep my promises." Her voice sounded light and cheerful. Tully was happy just to hear her voice.

"Then I'll pick you up for dinner tonight."

"I have to come into town anyway so I'll come to your hotel at seven. I haven't had a night out since Saigon. I'm looking forward to it."

"Then I'll see you enjoy it." His heart was pounding when he hung up.

She was there as promised and looked even lovelier than she had in Saigon. Tully took her to his favorite place, again where he knew it would be comparatively safe and Kate was relaxed and enjoying herself, free now from the stress of her job.

"I leave in exactly two months from today. Back home to Oz. I can't believe it."

"Where will they send you?"

"Back to Sydney for a start. Maybe I'll resign my commission and go into general practice. I've had enough of war and destruction."

"Then I'll have to try to get home for a spell too. I haven't seen Carrie for ages."

"Do you miss her?"

"Of course but I have to earn a living to support her. This is the only way I know how."

"You didn't seem like the family man at all when I met you. You care about people, Tully. That's a good attribute."

"I'm a hard nosed, egotistical bastard, Kate. Everyone knows that."

"Not as I see you. Now are you going to buy me a drink or do I have to get my own?"

They enjoyed their evening together and stayed at the restaurant talking and laughing until midnight.

"What time do you have to report in?"

"I told you. I'm on R and R. My time is my own."

"Then you can come back to my hotel for a drink."

"We both know it's not a drink you're meaning. I thought you'd never ask."

Tully smiled at her as he stood up. "Let's go then."

It was just like their first night together. Passion took over from the moment Tully shut the door. Kate almost threw herself at him and they both fell to the bed laughing. He kissed her passionately and found his passion was returned with the same heat. There was no modesty from either, just a need to take each other's bodies and soon both were naked.

"I hope you brought your magic fingers with you?" she laughed as he ran his hands over her smooth skin.

"I'm a bit out of practice but I'll do my best." He probed his tongue in her ear and she gasped.

"Oh yes," she sighed softly. "That's familiar. I've thought about it for months."

"So have I." Her hand covered his mouth.

"No talking, just action."

Tully returned to the job at hand enjoying the feel of her still perfect breasts as she thrust them toward his prevailing mouth.

"I want to feel your tongue all over my body, . . . everywhere," she added lustfully.

Tully willingly co-operated and enjoyed making her whimper at his will. Head back and eyes closed as if in a trance, opening herself to his every touch. Her hands were pressing his head not wanting him to stop as his lips crept lower toward the soft flesh between her thighs.

"God, that's wonderful," she moaned as he continued to play her skillfully. Suddenly she sat bolt upright and smiled as she noted the confused look on his face.

"Any more of that and it will be all over and I don't want it to be over just yet."

He groaned with pleasure as she took him in her mouth, delicately running her tongue up and down his shaft.

"Stop and I'll kill you," he joked and she concentrated on his pleasure. Just when he thought he could stand no more, she changed direction.

Her tongue worked slowly upward provoking, taunting, teasing all across his body. This squirming, wriggling object of delight found its way into his mouth, then his ears. He moaned and purred and writhed with pleasure.

"Kate," he whispered. "You're a very beautiful woman. My feelings for you are over shadowing my life. I think I'm falling in love with you."

Kate's heart was pounding, she really didn't want the complication of falling in love but she was finding it increasingly difficult to deny the attraction this man held for her.

"Let's not get too serious for a while, Tully. We both have lifestyles at the moment that requires our total concentration while we're working. I can't say I'm not having feelings for you too, but lets put them aside for a now, at least while I'm on R and R and then see what happens."

They returned to their lovemaking. He thrilled her with all the little movements she recalled so vividly. They were lost in a world surrounded by delicate pink clouds. Together they drifted across these clouds rising above them, then sinking below. It was so intense Kate thought she would faint. She was barely aware of when he entered her such was her euphoria, all she knew was she never wanted it to stop. With no hope of turning back now, their climax crashed over them like a giant tsunami sweeping all before it.

Later as they lay side by side, Kate's head drowsily resting on Tully's chest, her fingers wove gently through the tangle of damp hair on his chest. She fingered the zodiac medallion nestling among his body hair and lifted her head to examine it. Turning it over she read the inscription. "To Tully with all my love. Briony."

"She was the mother of your daughter?" Her voice was tender, not intrusive on his past.

"Yes, we were very much in love but it was a long time ago and she's gone now. She'll always be in my heart because it's a part of my past I can't forget. I think of her sometimes but not lately. You're the one I think about now."

They fell silent again just lapping up this feeling engulfing them.

"Kate, you have R and R and no pressure on you for a while. Why not stay here and see what works out. We might fall in love or we might drive each other crazy. Then again maybe we'll just screw ourselves silly then move on to new pastures."

"Did anyone ever tell you you're crazy, Tully Sanderson, nice but definitely crazy. I might stay a few days. I'll certainly stay the night then see what tomorrow brings."

Chapter Fourteen

Soo Ling 1972

"Soo Ling, you lazy girl. Why you not work with your sisters? Must all work if want to eat."

Soo Ling's father wrung his hands in despair. Of his seven daughters, Soo Ling was by far the laziest and was always last to take her place in the rice paddy. He wondered what he had done for the God's to curse him with seven daughters and no sons. She was certainly the prettiest, maybe that too was a curse. Her dream was of going to Saigon to find a rich man who would keep her in luxury rather than spend her worthless life as a poor farmer's wife. She felt life was slipping her by.

At nineteen, she looked even younger than Wei Ling, her seventeen-year-old sister but she had more cunning than the entire family put together. Her beauty had already encouraged four proposals of marriage from some of the lovesick men of the district, but she had turned them all down, much to her father's disgust. Her father felt she would be left on the shelf. He couldn't understand her reluctance to accept one of the offers.

Her latest offer was from a man of his own age and her father knew he would be a good catch. This suitor had five bullocks and many pigs, a sign of great wealth. The man's wife had died and he needed a replacement.

It would certainly be an advantage for his daughters to marry well and thus decrease the pressure of keeping his family from starving. Her father respected her decision of not wanting to accept a man she did not love, regardless of how tempting it was. If only she would work like the rest of his daughters then he would have been satisfied.

Soo Ling craved the glamour and excitement of the big city and would have nothing to do with the farmers of the out-laying villages. Such visions were unhealthy, everyone knew of the dangers involved, especially with the Americans here.

He had heard how young girls were giving themselves to these soldiers for money and couldn't understand why. The Americans certainly seemed to have untold wealth but it was no reason for a girl to degrade herself.

His only wish was Soo Ling would soon see sense and marry one of those eligible men valiantly chasing her.

"I not well today father. I have to rest."

"You never well when work to do. You no respect your mother and sisters. They not complain."

"The work in fields hard for back. I stay cook meal."

"You should marry, Soo Ling. Have family, then maybe think of others." He sighed and returned to the paddy leaving his daughter brushing her long black hair. What would become of her when he was too old to support her?

Soo Ling's greatest treasure was a small mirror, which she held aloft studying her features. She practiced expressions of awe, of surprise, of happiness, of seductiveness and any other, which she thought might gain her the approval of some rich man. She was always thinking of ways to get out of the village and get enough money to go to Saigon. There was little work to be had here unless you wanted to sweat your heart out under the blazing sun in a rice paddy. The heat did untold damage to skin and she didn't want to look like her mother did before she was thirty.

Her hopes soared when Nguyen Huong came to her village and spoke with her father.

"Welcome to my house, Nguyen Huong." Soo Ling's father was most respectful to his visitor. "I feel honored you come to my humble home."

"Thank you, Toc Ling. I know you have many daughters. I need girl to look after sick wife. Wife has boy. Six times babies die but now birth made wife sick. Not able to work in fields and mind son. I need girl who help."

"And you come to me?"

"Seven daughters must cost much to feed and clothe. I take one for one year. I give you bullock and pig for her services."

"You not want marry her?" Toc Ling was suspicious.

"Only look after wife and son and cook meals. I pay her 60 Dong, she stay one year."

Soo Ling immediately came to mind. Perhaps having the responsibility of caring for others was just the tonic she needed. When she knew there would be no working in the rice paddy then she might agree.

"Soo Ling," he called. "Come here."

Soo Ling bowed respectfully and sat with the two men. Her father explained Nguyen Huong's mission and she agreed immediately. Money paid after a year would certainly get her to Saigon. It was the chance she'd been waiting for.

"You pay father bullock and two pigs. Soo Ling good worker, not cheap."

Her father sighed at her impertinence but was surprised when Nguyen Huong agreed. He was obviously desperate. Once the bullock and pigs were delivered, Soo Ling left her family to take up her employment. She was pleasantly surprised to find she had a room for herself and was welcomed eagerly by Nguyen's wife. The infant was only four weeks old and would be little trouble. The wife was unable to do any work around the house and was confined to her bed for most of the day. The cooking was no problem as she was well used to cooking at home. Life was pretty easy for a while.

After two months things began to change. The child was beginning to annoy her and the constant attention the wife wanted became an irritant Soo Ling could well do without. She had not seen the slightest sign of money and confronted Nguyen Huong one morning.

"When I see some money for my work?" she demanded.

"I pay when time to leave. Nowhere to spend money here so you not worry."

Reluctantly Soo Ling could see he was right so she continued to do her meager tasks with little more complaint. The wife gradually regained her strength and returned to the fields leaving Soo Ling to take care of the baby.

Their village had seen little of the war raging between the north and the south so when two jets screamed over the village only feet above the huts she was terrified. Twice American soldiers came and searched the huts but left without harming the inhabitants.

The Viet Cong, dressed in their black pajamas came one day demanding rice. Soo Ling thought they would take it all but they left ample for the people to live on. It was a total shock the day the drunken patrol stumbled in. All were tough looking, arrogant, dirty and very drunk. They had become separated from their platoon and were looking for easy pickings.

Nguyen Huong, his wife and three workers rose from their tasks to see who the intruders were. Five Americans burst out of the jungle, guns raised and ready.

"You Americans," said Nguyen Huong. "What you want?"

"You bloody gooks know what we want. How many Viet Cong here?"

"No Viet Cong. We farmers. You want food?"

The American who seemed to be in charge, spat on the ground and wiped his mouth with the back of his hand. "Got any booze slope head."

"No understand. What is booze?"

"Drink you stupid motherfucker. We just used up our last bottle. We need something to take the sting out of this crazy war."

Nguyen Huong understood. "No drink. Only food. You want rice?"

The soldier raised his rifle butt and jabbed it viciously into Nguyen Huong's stomach.

"Don't give me that shit, grandpa. I know you gooks make your own saki. Let's look inside guys."

All five scrambled over Nguyen Huong's fallen body and headed for the group of nearby huts. Soo Ling walked out to see what the commotion was.

"Well guys, lookie lookie, what have we here?"

He stopped in his tracks and his jaw fell open. He looked at the others in the group. They were all grinning evilly. To a woman hungry group of soldiers it was manna from heaven.

"Maybe we could find some other sort of pleasure, Pete," The GI standing next to Pete dug him in the ribs with his elbow. "Sure be a change from fighting our way through this stinking jungle."

"The Captain wouldn't like it," one cautious voice spoke up.

"The Captain ain't here and he won't know anything about it if we waste them after."

"Sure could do with some recreation," said another licking his lips. "Boy, ain't she something?"

"All agreed?" asked Pete.

"We're with you man," they answered in unison. Pete spun around, lifting his gun and shooting Nguyen Huong, his wife and the three workers.

Screaming, Soo Ling and ran back inside the hut, terrified she would be next. One of the soldiers rushed in grabbing her and putting his bayonet to her throat.

Soo Ling stopped struggLing, her eyes filled with terror. The razor sharp end of the bayonet brought a trickle of blood under her chin forcing her to stand perfectly still. She prayed the baby would not wake knowing they would have no hesitation in killing him too.

The remaining four dragged the dead bodies under the hut, then ambled into the bamboo construction to claim their prize.

Soo Ling was pressed against a wall with the bayonet still at her throat, her arms pressed back against the wall, her eyes opened wide with fear. The soldier holding it said nothing but grinned ogling her. She could feel his breath on her face. Trembling, the tears were running down her cheeks. Seeing her up close Pete leered.

"She's a real beauty, boys. Let's have some fun. Strip her."

The one with the bayonet reached down and pulled her flimsy dress from her body in one motion leaving her naked before their eyes.

"Wo-wee. On the bench will do. Find something to tie her with." Pete had already put his rifle against the door and began undoing his zip. Rough hands lifted Soo Ling from the floor slamming her body onto the bench that had been cleared with one brush of an arm. Hemp cords were tied to her wrists, and then her arms were pulled to the bench where they were fastened to the bench legs.

"Tie her legs, and spread them." Pete was drooling. Quickly his instructions were followed and all stepped back to survey their work. The others all slid their zippers down and dropped their trousers eager to get on with the fun.

"Privilege of command," said Pete pointing to his corporal stripes, then climbed onto the bench just as Foster burst in.

* * *

All they knew was that they couldn't get enough of each other. Kate was completely relaxed knowing she was about to leave this God forsaken country.

Slowly she began to realize it wasn't just the sex, she was falling in love and there was nothing she could do about it. It was madness to even think about getting tied up with someone like Tully. He was not really husband material, besides, she would most likely only see him two or three times a year because of his insatiable appetite for news as it happened.

A husband would complicate things more than she needed; all she craved for was the peace and quiet of a general practice. She knew Tully was in love with her. He gave her his complete attention and they spent the days together, mostly in bed, almost as if they were lovers on a honeymoon in some exotic place.

The only reminder of the war was the Airforce jets thundering across the sky and of course the multitude of uniforms flooding the city. Neither of them could remember when the decision for Kate to move in with Tully had been made. Truth being it probably never was, it just sort of happened. The first day they mostly spent in bed, their passion was a flame needing quenching.

Calling at Kate's billet now and then they collected a few of her clothes. They mostly ate in their room and so before long when they looked around they realized Kate was basically living with Tully. It was an arrangement both were happy with and they left it that way. Tully's time with Briony had been loving and gentle. They had both been young. With Kate it was a new adventure every time they made love. Maybe it was something to do with death and destruction outside their private world.

Whatever it was, their passion was like a tempestuous tornado refusing to go away. Kate's two weeks of R and R were over and she was back at work.

Tully somehow managed to always find work near home. She knew he was reluctant to move far from her side in her final days.

She began to wonder what life without Tully would be like. It was going to hurt, hurt badly to be parted from him and she knew he would suffer too.

She wanted to be part of him, needed his love, enjoyed having his arms around her but he was going to be lost from her forever when she left. They were like two comets whose paths had crossed but could not change course.

In what was quite a deliberate decision she abandoned all methods of contraception and willed herself to become pregnant? If it happened then she would have some reminder of him in the years to come.

She didn't want a husband to tie her down but she did want a child, Tully's child. Who knows what the future held? One day he might give up being a foreign correspondent and settle for a normal life in Australia. Imagine his surprise if they ever met again and he found out he had another daughter or perhaps a son. She certainly didn't need his financial help.

After work each night they stayed in their little love nest sometimes not even bothering with an evening meal. If Tully suspected or wondered why her lovemaking was more intense and if possible, more frequent he said nothing. Sometimes as she watched him sleeping she had a tinge of guilt knowing in a way she was out to trap this sweet incorrigible friendly guy who she knew would lay down his life for her.

The news was a surprise to both of them. It came so suddenly even though they were expecting it to happen. When she came one night he could see it in her face.

"What's happened?"

"Looks like I'm going home."

"We both know that."

"I don't mean just me, I mean the whole of the Australian medical corp. All our troops are now gone and we've been pulled out too."

"When?" The realization of their loss was almost overwhelming. He knew she was going but hell, now it was actually happening.

"In three days."

He said nothing and pulled her close, embracing her in his arms. The pressure made her gasp for breath but she didn't want him to release her. It seemed another chapter of his life was over and this was going to hurt as much as his loss of Briony.

The day before she was due to go home she tested herself and found the test positive. Their last night together was the most wonderful night either of them could remember. Both were insatiable one minute soft and gentle the next. Kate was glad she was going home tomorrow. She knew if she stayed, she would end up telling Tully she was pregnant, and she didn't want him to know.

"It doesn't have to be the end. Marry me, Kate," he said as she was packing.

"That's romantic, Tully but why?" Tenderly she reached across to touch his hand.

"You know bloody well why. It's because I love you, in fact I'm crazy about you and I think you love me."

She sat on the edge of the bed among the mass of unpacked clothes.

"You're right. I do but I can't marry you, Tully it would be a disaster. It wouldn't last more than six months. You'd get itchy feet and be off somewhere while I'd be in some hospital or general practice satisfied with the quiet life, because that's all I want after Vietnam."

"It wouldn't be like that. I'd give up being a foreign correspondent. I can go back to being a suburban reporter."

She laughed her tinkley laugh he loved; she was touched by the offer. "In a small country town?"

"Maybe it's just as well you're going home. I heard the communists are making a big push south. Australia is the safest place to be. At least I won't have to worry about you there."

Concern crossed her face. "Are you going to stay and try to cover it?"

"I'll be going back to Saigon for a while. Things are happening down there too. The army wants all civilians out of the area, especially out of Hue."

Two hours later she was packed ready to leave. Tully took her to the airport and watched as others boarded the plane. He was holding Kate back not wanting her to walk up that gangway.

"Then this is good-bye. Kiss me again, Kate. Jesus, it sounds like that Hollywood musical."

"I always said you were crazy"

"Is this going to hurt you as much as it's going to hurt me?"

"You know it will."

"I'm making a promise to you. I'll find you again one day. When this stinking war is over I'll come looking."

"No you won't. There'll be another war in another place and you'll be there. It's in your blood."

"People can change."

"Not Tully Sanderson. You have a child to take care of. She's your first responsibility."

"If I come will you take me?"

"Maybe when your sense of adventure is exhausted. I have my own goal too, Tully."

"I love you, Kate."

"I love you, Tully. Goodbye. Have a good life," she said sadly.

"You too. Maybe we'll meet again one day."

"I doubt it." They hugged tightly, their lips seemingly glued together. Neither wanted to make the first break. The noise of the plane's engines suddenly revved and both turned toward it as if it were the final signal to part. Reluctantly she broke free as her last call was announced. He watched sadly as she boarded a Hercules with dozens of other personal.

He stood staring at the departing plane as it taxied to its starting point and then rose into the air. It was a dot in the sky before he turned away wishing things could be different. The loss was akin to the loss he felt when he lost Briony. At least Kate was still alive; it had to be a plus.

Thoughts about Soo Ling hadn't been in his mind for quite some time, but with Kate gone and now a bit more free time he began to wonder how she was coping. He'd been to see her every now and again to give her money.

Perhaps a visit wouldn't go astray. The communist push had started and he had to think about leaving himself. Maybe he could get her to Saigon too.

Soo Ling knew all about the communist push. It had been common talk amongst the people living around her. Getting out was imperative but the baby was a nuisance she could well do without. She tried to sell it but received no offers. A baby was a definite drawback. Once in Saigon it would be worse, that is if she ever got there. Twice she even tried to give it away but received no takers.

If only she hadn't told Tully it was hers. It had certainly brought the desired result of sympathy at the time and in fact it was the baby who was responsible for Tully finding and paying for the house she lived in, but now it was time to unload it.

It wouldn't take much and no one would know, just hold a pillow over its head and it would be all over in seconds. Provided she put on a suitable show of grief, everyone would have sympathy for her after such a tragic loss. After all, the baby certainly wasn't hers.

Slowly she walked to the baby's crib where it was sleeping. Picking up the pillow she hesitated then brought it down over the child's nose. Pressing gently, she held it over the baby's face and waited. Her problem was about to be solved. Her heart leapt as someone grabbed her arm and pulled the pillow away.

"Soo Ling. What the hell are you doing?" yelled Tully angrily.

She looked shocked and thought quickly after being caught in the act.

"Tully. You not stop me. I kill baby then self. No future, communists come. Better I dead."

It sounded so genuine Tully forgot his anger and pulled her close to him. He could feel the hot tears running down her face. Soo Ling thought she should have been on the stage.

"It will be all right, Soo Ling. It's not as bad as you think."

"Yes," she sobbed. "Communists come, rape Soo Ling. Better I dead."

"I'll try and get you away from here. Where would you like to go?" Tully felt frustrated by the situation.

"Soo Ling like Saigon. Sister there, maybe still alive."

"I'll see what I can do. You must promise not to hurt your baby or yourself. Promise?"

"Promise, Tully. You good man. You help Soo Ling." She paused slightly. "You go Saigon?"

"Yes. We move there next week."

"You go Saigon, Soo Ling go Saigon. I be your woman. I give you good time."

How many times had he heard that from some of the desperate young girls of Vietnam? There were many living openly with Americans and other foreigners alike.

Even officers took them in and, being far from home they lived as man and wife. Of course writing to their wives about such arrangements was taboo and Tully couldn't help wondering what would become of those women and their babies once the men left.

"Thank you for the offer, Soo Ling but that's not necessary. I'll find some way of getting you there without pretending you're my woman."

"You no think Soo Ling pretty?"

"I think you're very beautiful, also very young, but I'd be off working somewhere and you wouldn't see me."

"Soo Ling no care. Soo Ling be good to you."

"I'm sure you would be, I'll see what I can do about getting you to Saigon." He stayed with her until he felt she had calmed down and together they played with the baby as he tried to help her make plans for the future.

Snaps had already made arrangements for them to leave for Saigon. He had been told the last plane was leaving in two days but the earlier they could go the better. Returning to his hotel Tully filled Snaps in on Soo Ling.

Snaps was astounded. "Shit, was she really going to kill the baby, then herself?"

"I got there just in time. God knows what will happen to them if we just ignore her problem. The roads to Saigon will be filled with refugees."

"Go and see some brass. Maybe they'll take her on a plane."

"I doubt it. They won't take civilians, only military personal."

"Bullshit. There's one or two army wives here. Some Yanks have married locals. If they take them then they can take her."

"You think so?"

"Bloody oath. Give it a try."

Snaps had Tully convinced and he made inquiries to the officer in charge of evacuation.

"Sorry, Tully, only army personal and their families."

"Shit, she's only nineteen with a baby. She'll die if she tries to make it on her own."

"Sorry, rules are rules." The officer shook his head sympathetically.

"Stuff your rules," he said savagely, storming out.

Snaps was equally as horrified. "She'll probably die if we leave her."

"Don't you think I know that? We have to leave soon and I can't just desert her."

"Jesus. What a bloody country? What the hell can we do?" Snaps was lost for a solution.

Tully tried every avenue he could think of looking for a logical way out. In the end he said to Snaps, "You go on and I'll try and get her there by road."

"I reckon you have two chances, mate." Snap's tone was cynical.

"I agree it'll be bloody tough but I just can't desert her."

"You're bloody mad but I can see your point. Good luck and hope to see you in Saigon." Snaps packed his precious cameras, then his belongings and headed for the airport.

Tully wasted no time and rushed to Soo Ling's home anxious to make a quick getaway.

"Pack your stuff. We're leaving now."

There wasn't much to pack. A few clothes and some baby things in a carry bag and the baby sitting in a canvas support on Soo Ling's back. Tully took her bag and led the way. The roads were already filled with others all anxious to leave the place before the communists arrived.

"We fly on plane?" asked Soo Ling.

"No. I couldn't get you on one. They only take families of army personal. We're going to have to take the road like everyone else.

Soo Ling was shocked. "Very bad, Tully. Saigon long way. Viet Cong everywhere."

"I know but we haven't any choice."

"Plane take you. You go. Leave Soo Ling." She tried to sound desperate for him to save himself.

"Forget it. Let's go." He bundled up her swag, relieved her of the baby and they made their way into the multitude of people, all heading south. The road was wall to wall people, all walking, and some pushing rickshaws loaded with their few possessions.

An American jet flew low over their heads and people threw themselves to the ground. Tully knew the jet wasn't going to attack, it was just doing a rec. to check them out. The sound of guns echoed from the distant hills, a battle obviously raging somewhere. A sudden shower of rain made things uncomfortable and Tully waited while Soo Ling adjusted a cover over the backpack where Tully carried the baby. The long stream of refugees looked like an ant colony pushing south. The further they went, the more Tully began to think it was a mistake. It would take them at least three weeks to reach Saigon at this rate.

It was the shells exploding no more than a hundred metres away that convinced him. He looked at the sheer terror on Soo Ling's face; her eyes opened wide as the earth erupted from the shell. She clasped Tully's hand in a death grip, the baby screaming from the noise. People including Tully dived for the ditches in the side of the road. He pulled her to the ground and she wound her arms around his neck almost choking him.

There was no point dying on the road to Saigon if there was another way. The decision had to be made. He grabbed her arm and swung her around.

"Where we go?" She was bewildered by his actions.

"Back to Hue."

"No. We gone one day. Communists come. We die. Why we go back?"

"We're getting married. It's the only way."

Soo Ling was amazed. This was the last thing she expected. It was an added bonus falling like a gift from the Gods.

"How that help?"

"The army is taking families of personnel out. It will make you eligible."

"I be good wife. You see, Tully."

Tully sucked in a quick breath. Twice he had asked women he loved to marry him and twice he had been turned down. It was ironic a nineteen year old girl he regarded no more than a responsibility should accept him, but it was the only way to get her out safely.

It was early the next day when they arrived back in Hue. The streets were all but deserted, but he found a Christian mission open and asked the minister to marry them. After some reservations, the man finally agreed and the ceremony was completed very quickly with a promise of fifty American dollars.

"I'll need the marriage certificate," he told the preacher.

"Of course. May God bless your union and keep you both safe."

"Yeah thanks," said Tully impatiently waiting for the certificate to be written out.

"Let's go." He grabbed Soo Ling's arm. "We have a plane to catch." They found an abandoned motor scooter and drove to the airport where people were frantically pushing to board the planes. A few marines stood guard waving them through when he showed his press pass.

The officer in charge eyed Tully dubiously. "I told you the other day, families only, Tully. I'm sorry."

"This is Soo Ling. My wife."

"Yeah, and I'm King Kong."

Tully handed him the certificate. He perused it quickly and handed it back.

"Rather drastic isn't it?"

"Only way to get her out. Will you take us?"

"You got the last three places. Get on board."

Grateful Tully pushed Soo Ling up the steps and settled her on the plane. It seemed forever before the plane moved. The thrust of the engines lifting them into the air was like a lifeline from heaven. Soo Ling held his hand, then her breath. It was the first time she had ever been on a plane.

From the air they scanned the roads below. Refugees seemed to go on forever. Soo Ling squeezed Tully's hand.

"Thank you, Tully. I be good wife. You no be sorry."

"Sure." Now it was done he had time to think about his actions. He wondered if Kate would understand, but then she had made it clear she wouldn't be seeing him again and if it saved Soo Ling's life then it was worth it.

Chapter Fifteen

Grateful to be back in Saigon, Tully immediately rang Snaps at the office.

"Shit, you made it. I didn't really expect to see you again. How did you manage it so quickly? Do you know someone who can work miracles?"

"I took the only solution possible, mate."

"Yeah. What's that?"

"I had to marry Soo Ling. It was the only way to get her out of there."

"You're kidding. Christ. What are you going to do with her now?"

"First up find a place to live. She's my responsibility now." He turned to look at Soo Ling sitting on her knapsack nursing the baby. They both looked so innocent and vulnerable his conscience eased.

"Ring me when you get something," said Snaps. "I'll help you find some furniture."

"Thanks, mate." He stood in the phone box wondering where the hell he was going to find somewhere suitable to live. There were thousands pouring into Saigon, all with the same idea. He rang a few people he knew and but had no luck. Soo Ling was looking around almost tearfully.

"Saigon big, many people, much traffic, Tully, where we live?" Her eyes were wide. She had never seen a big city before and suddenly it was all overwhelming.

"The Paradise Hotel for a start," he said but he knew it would be inadequate for a wife and child. Bundling them all with their few possessions into a passing taxi, he headed for the Paradise Hotel.

Tully could feel all eyes on him as they trudged up the stairs and he was grateful he'd kept his room paid up while he was in Hue. At least it was a starting point. Tully left his new family in his old room and returned to the lobby. Charlie was champing on his half smoked cigar and looking quizzically at Tully

"How come you have woman with baby, cobber? I get you nice girl, no baby."

"That's my family, Charlie, I'm married now."

"No can have baby in room. People no like crying. Sorry you must go now."

"I intended to go, I can't keep them in this flea hole." Tully wanted to ram the cigar down his throat.

"For ten dollar I find you real nice place, cheap too."

Nothings cheap in Vietnam thought Tully as he reached into his pocket and reluctantly paid over the ten dollars, which Charlie pocketed in double quick time.

"You wait." He picked up the phone and had a quick conversation in Vietnamese then handed Tully a piece of paper.

"This my cousin. He rent you house."

"For a small fortune," said Tully cynically.

"Not dear for Australian. You see."

Tully took Soo Ling and the baby to the address written down. He had expected something akin to a slum but was pleasantly surprised. It was a large building and back in the days when the French were masters here it would have been pretty swish. Now it was fairly run down but at least reasonably clean. Charlie's cousin had divided it into separate quarters. The apartment Tully was shown had a kitchen living room area overlooking the river. A crude looking table would suffice but the chairs needed a bit of repair. There was one bedroom with a ceiling fan and an old double bed, a bit of carpet and a shower recess of sorts constructed in one corner. Alongside the bedroom was a small room holding a disgusting looking toilet. Where the sewage went he didn't want to know. A half hour's work would soon clean it up. The rent was surprisingly affordable and so an agreement was made to move in at once. It was not far from the market place but convenient enough to be out of the true slum area of Saigon.

Soo Ling was so happy just to be in Saigon. She would have lived in a tent but having a home and a husband was more than she had dreamed possible.

"Very nice home, Tully," She spun around excitedly swinging the baby in the air. "I cook nice food, be good wife. You see."

"I've got to report to the office, Soo Ling. I'll be back around six. It's not far to the market, I'll give you money for food."

"Soo Ling be ready."

He reported in to the office, which he shared with three or four other reporters from different papers. It was fairly small but they all managed. Co-operation was expected and readily given as everyone was in the same boat.

He read a few messages from his boss, filed them, tidied up a bit and made a few phone calls. Then decided to head home to make sure Soo Ling was settled in their new house.

Unpacking their meager possessions she wandered around the neighborhood familiarizing herself with the area. It didn't take her long to find the market where she bought provisions and prepared him the meal she promised. She was determined to make it a meal he wouldn't forget. Nothing was enough trouble to keep her in Tully's good books, after all, if it wasn't for him she might be now dead. Typical Vietnamese food was prepared, very tasty and very spicy, the smell hitting his nostrils as soon as he entered the room. He ate with relish much to Soo Ling's pleasure. As soon as he finished she jumped up and gathered his dirty plate.

"You like Soo Ling's cooking?"

"It was great, Soo Ling. Thank you, best meal I've had for weeks."

She looked very pleased with his praise and bowed respectfully. The evening was cool and they sat out on the tiny porch-way watching the lights of the city. Light flickered across the water of the river giving it a scenic beauty, vastly different from daylight. Soo Ling faked a yawn and stretched her arms.

"Very late. We go bed. Long day."

He smiled, aware of her acting but conceded she was right. It had been a long day. The baby was already fast asleep. He went to the washbasin to clean his teeth and wash up. When he turned Soo Ling was standing naked by the bed. Tully's eyes scanned her body and couldn't help but admire it.

"Is wedding night. Soo Ling be good for husband."

Shit, thought Tully. I never figured on this angle.

"You go to sleep, Soo Ling. I have to write up some background for tomorrow's story."

He could see the disappointment cross her face.

"You no like Soo Ling. Not want make love?"

"Of course I like you, Soo Ling. You're very beautiful."

"Then we make love. I be good."

"I'm sure you will be. I'm just a little tired," he lied.

"Soo Ling take care of Tully."

"Perhaps tomorrow night."

"I wife, Tully. Wife always ready for husband."

What the hell he thought. It was going to happen anyway so why not now.

"You're right, Soo Ling. You are my wife and we should make love."

She gave a little bow and rushed to him assisting him to take his clothes off. By the time he was naked, she was already on the bed. She was very beautiful and certainly eager to please him, hell he couldn't stay celibate for the rest of his life and besides, they were married so it was quite legal.

When he eventually entered her, she gave a deep-contented sigh. She surprised him with her flair. The rather ancient looking Nguyen Huong must have been a good teacher. Maybe this marriage was not going to be as bad as I thought it would be. Eventually they fell asleep in each other's arms both quite satisfied with their efforts.

*   *   *

It had been three months since they returned to Saigon and life with Soo Ling hadn't been too bad at all.

Tully and Snaps were back into the thick of the war. Sometimes they were away for two or three weeks and when they returned she was always happy to see him, and eager to please him. She saw to it they made up for the nights of passion he had been missing.

Each night she would kneel and place her hands together to thank Buddha for his providence and for Tully who had saved her life. There was much to be grateful for.

When the novelty wore off, Soo Ling found Saigon was not at all as she had expected. Being tied to the house with a baby by herself for weeks on end was not her idea of fun. She had expected to see the bright lights, visit clubs, meet interesting people and enjoy life. Instead she was stuck with a baby that wasn't even hers and life was boring.

When Tully was home things were a bit better. At least they went out occasionally, there was someone to talk to and she certainly enjoyed his lovemaking. He had a talent surprising her. Living in the three- roomed house with her parents and six sisters there had been no privacy at all. She had heard her parents having sex all of her life. She had always thought sex was something just for men as her mother lay silent for the few minutes her father grunted away until he was finished and then rolled over. There were no sounds of pleasure, no laughs or giggles.

Tully on the other hand was caring and considerate and spent a lot of time giving her pleasure. She knew it was her duty but she had to admit it was a pleasurable experience for them both.

She seemed to know instinctively from the first time that Tully entered her what would give him pleasure. He had no idea she was a virgin as he thought of the baby as Nguyen Huong and Soo Lings.

She readily experimented with different techniques and was encouraged by Tully giving her both experience and enjoyment.

It was the one part of living in Saigon she delighted in. When Tully was away she spent the day sitting around, caring for the child she had begun to hate. Occasional walks to the market broke the monotony while she was caught up in the excitement of the hustle and bustle of the bartering.

There were many uniformed men, mostly Americans and they sometimes tried to pick her up. One brash young man offered her fifty American dollars to spend the day with him and she was sorely tempted.

What Tully didn't know wouldn't hurt him but when the man saw she had a child he withdrew the offer. There would be plenty of other takers as far as he was concerned.

On one such mundane morning, Soo Ling left the baby with her neighbor and sauntered along to the market place. She wanted to buy something pretty, indulge herself with the money Tully gave her. She browsed along the row after row of clothes, mostly cheongsams but there were a few racks of the latest American mini-skirts. The smell of cooking filled the air as traders offered their tasty wares. Bartering was taking place between sellers and consumers as Soo Ling worked her way through the crowd.

She was deep in thought when someone grabbed her arm.

Spinning around with eyes blazing, she was ready to fend off pickpockets or muggers. As she raised her hand protecting herself, her younger sister Wei Ling faced her.

"Soo Ling. Where you go? We not find you for long time. How you get to Saigon?"

"Wei. Ling. What you do here? Where father and mother?"

"American bombs come to farm. All burn with napalm. Father say go find work. Mai Ling and Chi Ling marry. Mother get burn, still in hospital. I come Saigon, work in club. Good money, I send little home. How you got here?"

Soo Ling was elated at finding her sister alive and well and living in Saigon. Maybe now life would be better when Tully was away, she would have someone to visit her and go shopping with.

"I live here. You come see my house."

Excitedly Soo Ling dragged her sister off to inspect her house. She chattered happily all the time as they walked a few blocks. Soo Ling was careful to keep any mention of 'her' baby out of the conversation. She hoped her neighbor wouldn't bring the baby back until later. Her sister was surprised to learn of Soo Ling's marriage but pleased her sister had found a good man after hearing how Tully had saved Soo Ling's life twice. It slipped easily into becoming a weekly meeting while Tully was away working although they always met at the market. Soo Ling left the baby with her neighbor and made excuses to not have Wei Ling visit again.

Although Soo Ling had told Tully she had met up with her sister it seemed Wei Ling was never available when Tully was home and asked to meet her.

Soo Ling could not risk them meeting and Tully learning the truth about the baby. That secret had to be kept.

Some weeks later when out shopping, Soo Ling was complaining about only having a small amount of money, compared to what Wei Ling had.

"You should work in club like me," Wei Ling suggested.

"What you do in club to get big money? You sleep with soldiers?"

Wei Ling cast her eyes down demurely. "It not so bad. Boss give pretty clothes and plenty time off. Many soldiers, much music. Is exciting time."

Soo Ling was jealous. "But make love with many soldiers. They hurt you?"

"Most they drunk. Not take long. Close eyes, think they movie star. I pretend and they happy." Wei Ling laughed at her own cleverness.

"Pretend?"

"Is easy. I say you very big Joe. Make sexy noise, ooh, ooh. G.I. pay good. Boss give me half."

Soo Ling couldn't believe her ears. It sounded so simple.

"What this club name?"

"Called Uncle Sam's. You come. I show you."

Wei Ling tugged her arm but Soo Ling didn't need much persuasion. Wei Ling led her down the street to the club, which obviously didn't do much business until nightfall.

There were only a few customers sitting at tables with three or four girls looking utterly bored.

Wei Ling took her sister to the bar where an American was polishing glasses. He was big, bordering on obese. Like a statue of Buddha with long gray hair, almost to his shoulders, thought Soo Ling. Little piggy eyes leered at Soo Ling. He had yellow teeth from his constant smoking and it had to be a week at least since he'd shaved. Soo Ling thought he looked like a hairy monster.

"Who you got there, Wei?" His little eyes studied Soo Ling.

"This sister, Soo Ling."

He nodded as he ogled her body. "Not bad, not bad at all. You Ling girls sure are easy on the eyes. You looking for work, Soo? I'm Chuck Hale. I own this joint."

"Maybe. What work you want Soo Ling do?"

Chuck shot a look at Wei wondering if Soo Ling was crazy. "You don't know what we do here?"

"Wei Ling say she make love with soldiers. You want me do that?"

"Sure. It's easy work and you can make plenty of money if you're any good."

"How much money Soo Ling make?" That part definitely interested her.

"Here's the deal," said Chuck flicking the ash from his joint onto the floor. "You can make as little or as much as you want. The more soldiers you sleep with the more you make. The house charges ten American dollars of which you get five. Ten customers a night will bring you fifty dollars. Multiply that by seven and you have three hundred and fifty dollars a week. I expect you to get the soldiers to drink as much as you can. You ask for whisky and we give you cold tea. Can you dance?"

Soo Ling's brain was spinning. That sort of money was unheard of.

"No can dance."

"It's easy. All you have to do is wiggle your fanny in front of the customers and bob up and down a bit. Wei can show you that. You'll have to take your clothes off. Does that worry you?" He took another drag on his joint. Soo Ling couldn't help but notice the yellow stains spread over his fingers.

"Soo Ling not do that before. You give Soo Ling nice clothes?"

"Sure. Come into the office and let's see what we've got."

Chuck led them both into his office at the back of the bar. He sat down and again perused Soo Ling's body.

"Take off your clothes. I want to see your body."

"Now?" Soo Ling was shocked. She hadn't expected this.

"Show her, Wei. If you can't do it here then there's not much point starting work."

Wei Ling smiled and stripped off her clothes standing naked only in her high heels. Her body matched Soo Lings although she was slightly shorter.

"Is easy, Soo Ling. After one time no trouble."

Soo Ling hesitated for just a moment then quickly removed her clothes. If her sister could do it then so could she.

Chuck stood up and walked around eyeing her critically nodding his approval. He opened a wardrobe filled with dresses and selected a garment.

"Here, try this on," He threw her a brilliant green dress covered in sequins designed to sparkle in any light.

Soo Ling gasped. She had never seen anything so beautiful. After she had slipped into it she twirled around checking herself out in the mirror fixed to the wall. If she had any objections they faded immediately she saw her own reflection.

"Far out," said Chuck licking his lips. "I'll start you on the G.I.s but you're definitely officer material."

"Soo Ling no understand." She frowned at Chuck while she kept swirling around in the beautiful dress. She was reluctant to part with such a beautiful garment.

"You have to learn our technique first so you always make sure you get the cash."

"What is technique?"

Chuck sighed. "I'll pretend to be a customer and Wei will show you. Okay, Wei."

Wei Ling smiled sexily and ambled her naked body up to Chuck pushing against him and playfully pulling his hair. "Hello, soldier boy. You like have fun with Wei Ling?"

"Maybe." Chuck winked at Soo Ling. "How much?"

"Only ten dollar. We have nice time. I very good to you."

She started to undo his shirt.

"Sounds great. Let's go. Okay, now we go up to one of the rooms. Now comes the important part. Go ahead, Wei."

Wei undid Chuck's trousers taking him in her hand. With soft manipulation of her fingers she found an immediate reaction.

"You give ten dollar now and we start."

"Get that, Soo Ling. You always get the money first. Once you've got him up he'll give you anything. Go on, Wei."

"Oh, Chucky you so big. Wei Ling going to love you. Love you all night."

"That'll do. Get the idea? Always tell them how big they are. You've never seen one so big and when they do it to you, you make noises like it's the best one you've ever had."

"Soo Ling act good. Can do that."

"Good. When do you want to start?"

Soo Ling thought about what Tully would think if he found out and of course there was the problem of the brat she was taking care of. Tully was good to be with but he couldn't give her the kind of money offered here. One day he would be gone anyway so a girl had to take care of herself. He'd served his purpose and he had taught her a thing or two about what men liked. She was sure she could get rid of any amorous lover pretty quickly with what came naturally, and what she had learned from Tully.

"Have little problem. When I fix I come back. Okay?"

"That's up to you. Now take off the dress and give it back. You can have it when you start work."

Soo Ling reluctantly removed the dress stroking the fabric lovingly, then put her own clothes back on.

"Sometimes Soo Ling no can work. Soo Ling have husband. When husband away Soo Ling work. Okay, Chuck?"

"Sure, sweetheart. Drop around when you want to start."

The sisters left the bar together. Soo Ling was so excited her feet hardly touched the ground.

"Tully not like you work for Chuck."

"Tully not know. Soo Ling no tell him. Soo Ling make big money. Buy pretty dresses and have fun. That why I come to Saigon."

* * *

By the time Tully took his next trip out to a war zone Soo Ling was ready. She had been busy making plans and when he said he would be away for at least two weeks, she knew it was time.

He and Snaps left early on the appointed day and Soo Ling gathered up the baby with its clothes. It was time to get rid of this chain around her neck. She knew exactly what she was going to do.

With thousands of people flooding into Saigon, the loss of one insignificant baby would never be noticed. She'd thought about dropping it in the canal but couldn't bring herself to drown the poor thing. It had been on one of her shopping trips she'd noticed the Catholic Mission. There had been many orphans playing in the yard and suddenly she had the perfect solution. With the babies clothes placed in a carry bag she made the fifteen-minute trip to the mission.

Timidly she entered the grounds and called to one of two Nuns watching the children. The woman hastened over wondering what the problem was.

"What is it, child? Can I help you?" The sister had a soft voice with a Dutch accent.

"Please. Not know what to do. I walk along lane when I hear cry. This baby in street all alone."

"Goodness me. The poor little mite can't be more than twelve months old. You don't know who it belongs to?"

"Not know. Couldn't leave alone. Bad people get him."

"We have many abandoned babies here. You did the right thing my dear. Please bring him in."

"Found clothes. Maybe belong to him."

The Nun looked suspiciously at Soo Ling. Usually children were just abandoned. A lot of them were half-Vietnamese and half-white. This one was very much Vietnamese.

"Child, are you sure you're not the mother?"

"Not mother. Never had baby. Must go."

She turned and left the now crying child in the arms of the Nun. At least now she was free from this burden. All she had to do was make up some story for Tully when he got back. She was a good actress. She was sure she could manage to be convincing.

When she turned up ready for work Chuck was delighted to see Soo Ling.

"Hi, babe. Come into the office and change."

Soo Ling hurried after him and waited expectantly. He grinned as he opened the cupboard and handed her the green dress. Soo Ling's eyes sparkled when she saw it.

"See, I've kept it especially for you. Strip off and let me see you wearing it again."

Chuck was almost drooling as he watched Soo Ling remove her blue cheongsam and slip the shimmering green creation over her head. She felt like a princess and giggled like a child as she twirled around excitedly waiting for approval.

"Beautiful, babe, beautiful, I think business is about to pick up. Once the punters see you in that getup we'll be packed out every night. Now put these in your bag." He handed her a packet she studied blankly.

"They're rubbers for Christ sake. Hasn't your bloody husband ever used rubbers? Always put one on the John before he does it. It will stop you from getting knocked up and help keep you free of VD."

"No understand?"

"I don't friggin believe this," said Chuck tearing a foil open. He unzipped his fly and dropped out his penis. "Get me up."

Soo Ling expertly took it in her hand and immediately brought a response. When he was erect, he handed her the rubber. "Now roll it on easy like. That's when you moan and talk sweet saying how big they are."

Soo Ling followed his instructions making little cooing noises all the time while rolling the condom into place. When she had finished Chuck pulled her closer. "That's beautiful, sweetheart, now bend over."

Chuck held her hips strongly and entered her from behind thrusting wildly. It only took a few thrusts and he was finished. He removed the used condom and threw it into the wastebasket.

"That's how they work, darlin' and remember, always get the money first."

Soo Ling nodded obediently and followed him out into the bar.

"See the kid sitting by himself, sweetheart, there's your first sucker."

Soo Ling followed his pointing finger to where a young soldier was sitting alone.

"Get to it and make us both some money."

Soo Ling tottered to the table and leaned across the soldier. "Hullo, Joe. Me Soo Ling. You buy me drink?"

The young boy's eyes almost left his face. He had never seen anyone so absolutely gorgeous. Soo Ling could see he was entranced and gave a few wiggles to make her dress sparkle.

He managed to stammer. "Sure, what would you like?"

"Whisky," she said signaling Chuck.

"Yeah, Soo Ling, what'd ya want."

"Joe want buy Soo Ling drink."

"My name is Brent. We'd like two whiskeys please."

Chuck winked at Soo Ling and poured the two drinks. A cold tea for Soo Ling and a whisky for Brent. It only took a few drinks and a bit of encouragement before Soo Ling reached for Brent's hand.

"You like make love to Soo Ling?"

"Would I?" Brent was so excited she wondered if they would make it upstairs.

"Only cost twenty dollar."

"I was told you girls charge ten dollars."

"Other girls, but Soo Ling good. You pay?"

"Sure will, Soo Ling. Where do we go?"

"Upstairs." She kept smiling at him as she led him up the stairs to the first available bedroom. After locking the door she turned to him and slid down his zip. Taking him in her hand she raised her other hand with her palm upwards.

"Is twenty dollar please? Two ten dollar, then we make love."

Brent quickly produced two new ten-dollar notes, which he willingly handed to her, his hand shaking.

Soo Ling took the money and slipped out of her dress carefully folding it onto the chair making sure it was not going to crease. "I help Brent." She slipped her fingers under his belt and flipped the buckle, then slowly lowered his trousers. Brent was already tearing at the buttons on his shirt while Soo Ling was muttering encouraging sounds as she helped him remove the rest of his clothing. She held his throbbing shaft with one hand and tore open a foil with the end clasped between her teeth.

She pushed the eager soldier carefully back onto the bed while she slipped on the condom. Her fingers were gentle and expert in their movements.

"Oh Brent, you big, very big. I no see one so big."

He could hardly contain himself and it was all over in with just a few strokes. Soo Ling didn't even have time to pretend she was enjoying it.

It was the fastest and the easiest way to make money. She had made one hundred dollars the first night. Chuck paid over the fifty he owed her never suspecting she already had fifty tucked away in her bag. Nobody complained about paying extra. She was beautiful and so friendly they were more than willing. Her sister had been right, all she had to do was think of a movie star and pocket their money.

Her only problem was to think up a plausible story about the loss of the baby to tell Tully when he returned. At the rate of tonight's profit she would be a rich woman by then.

Chapter Sixteen

Soo Ling had never dreamed so much money could exist in the world. Tully had been covering the Easter offensive for three weeks and her reputation as the beautiful girl in the green dress had become a legend. Chuck had only kept her on the main floor for a week, then seeing her popularity, transferred her to the exclusive officer's only area upstairs but separated from the usual bedrooms. Here the fee was twenty dollars a time plus tips so Soo Ling was able to ask fifty dollars, which was usually paid willingly although occasionally she took thirty. The volume was not as great as downstairs but the higher fees certainly compensated.

Chuck still paid her five dollars out of the twenty but as Soo Ling pocketed the balance of the fifty dollars plus tips she was making a fortune. Her biggest problem was how to spend it without raising Tully's suspicions. Chuck suspected she was making more than he paid her but let it pass, as she was so popular. He insisted she service him once a week so he decided she was well worth keeping around.

*   *   *

The night Tully returned home, Soo Ling went into her act. It had been carefully rehearsed and Soo Ling was sure she had it perfected. She knew he would be tired and in need of a rest and would be sympathetic without being able to do anything. As Tully opened the door, Soo Ling rushed to him in tears.

"What's wrong, Soo Ling?" It was a complete reversal of the usual greeting he received when he returned home.

"My baby. I lose baby. Him stolen. I never see again."

Tully was shocked. "Calm down and tell me what happened," he held her tightly as she sobbed into his shoulder.

"Soo Ling go to market. Leave baby to buy food. Only one minute, turn around baby gone."

"What? When did this happen? Did you go to the police?"

"Happen next day you gone. Find policeman and tell him. He look, call more police but no find baby. He say impossible. Too many people. Baby gone."

Tully felt helpless. With the thousands of refugees in the city, he knew the police were right. They certainly wouldn't spend much time looking for one child amongst the teeming thousands. There were black marketers and murderers who warranted their attention more than looking for one lost child. After all, there were thousands of street kids roaming the city. Whoever took him would be well gone after three weeks. His heart went out to Soo Ling knowing they were never going to find the child.

"I don't know what to say, Soo Ling, I'm so sorry. He was probably taken by some woman who lost her child in the war."

"You think he have good home, Tully?"

He had no idea but he patted her head to comfort her. "I'm sure he has. We'll keep looking for him but I'm sorry to say, I think he's gone."

Soo Ling continued looking sad all the time Tully was home. As usual the war wouldn't wait and he was off again within the week, sorry to have to leave Soo Ling with the pain she was feeling.

"How long you gone, Tully?" Soo Ling wanted to get her schedule right.

"I know you're lonely, Soo Ling and I'll try to cut it short but I'll probably be away for about three weeks."

"Tully be careful. Soo Ling try no be sad. Sister come and help."

"That's great, Soo Ling. I'd really like to meet her. When I come back we can have her around for dinner."

He was heartened by the fact she had someone with whom she could share her pain.

*   *   *

With Tully safely away on assignment, Soo Ling was back at 'Uncle Sam's' every night, and as usual, was the busiest girl in Chuck's fleet. Jack

Finlay, a marine captain with an aggressive manner was following Soo Ling upstairs. He was a tall, rugged looking Texan about 35 with big shoulders and almost white hair it was so fair. It was cut very short, and being so fair he almost looked bald. He had been out at the front line for months and was ripe and ready for female company.

When he saw Soo Ling in her sparkling green dress he licked his lips. He had five days R and R and he was going to make the most of them. As Soo Ling closed the door she spun around with her hand out.

"You give Soo Ling fifty dollars and we have good time."

"Just a minute little lady. Got any grass?"

Soo Ling knew what he wanted as Chuck always had plenty available for the customers. She pointed to a china jar on the dressing table.

"In there. You give Soo Ling money now."

"Shit, you're sure in a hurry for the dough." He dipped into his pocket and produced the money. "I don't suppose you could give me a hit?" he asked surprising Soo Ling.

"Soo Ling no hit you."

Jack laughed heartily. "Hell, babe. Go down and ask Chucky boy. Tell him I need a hit to get me going."

"Oh-white powder. You want hit with white powder. Many GIs like white powder."

Chuck saw her come down the stairs and knew even Soo Ling couldn't get rid of a John that quick.

"Trouble?" he asked.

"No trouble. Officer want hit."

"Okay. Come into the office and I'll get some."

"White powder like opium?" asked Soo Ling.

"Yeah. It makes them real dreamy like. They'll pay anything for it. Tell him it will cost him another thirty bucks."

Chuck opened his safe to reveal three one-kilogram packets of a white powder and several syringes. He placed a syringe and a plastic spoon in a paper bag and handed it to Soo Ling. As Chuck spooned a small amount of heroin into a plastic bag, he confided to Soo Ling.

"I get it cheap and it brings in a nice profit. So long as we don't advertise we don't get caught. Anything to keep the punters happy and make a buck."

Soo Ling took it from him and added it to the paper bag.

"He eat it?" Soo Ling queried wondering what the spoon was for.

"Just give it to him. He'll know what to do, and get the money first."

Soo Ling nodded and returned to the room where Finlay was waiting.

"Chuck say cost another thirty dollar."

"That's all right, Babe. Here's the dough. Now give me the bag."

He snatched it from Soo Ling's grasp and she watched as he put the powder into the spoon, and mixed it with a little water from the hand basin. He tied his belt around his arm to raise a vein and then jabbed in the syringe. Soo Ling watched amazed as the expression on his face changed to rapture.

"Ever try it, Babe?" he said after he had injected.

"No." Soo Ling was ignorant of the deadly raptures of the narcotic. "My father smoke opium all time."

"This is better than opium my sweet. It makes you feel invincible. Want to try it?"

Soo Ling was not sure, but she was stunned by the change in the man's manner. At first he had been a little aggressive and spoken to her as if she were a street whore. Now he was pleasant and friendly.

"Not hurt Soo Ling?"

"No way. It makes you feel great. Take a shot and we'll make sweet music together."

"Soo Ling take just little bit. No want offend, Jack."

"That's the way, sugar, give me your arm."

She offered her arm and he found a vein, then injected the rest of the heroin. In just a moment the drug began to take effect, and a wonderful dreamy sensation took over her body.

"It's good, Babe, but don't get too used to it. Too much and you become an addict, too pure and you die. Just use it as a recreational hit and you won't get into trouble. Now get that dress off. I want to see what I'm paying for."

Soo Ling complied and was almost unaware of what Jack was doing to her. He took her in every position possible, sometimes roughly and Soo Ling was floating in a haze with no idea where she was or what she was doing. When he was finally finished, he walked out leaving her spread on the bed. Some time later Chuck realized he hadn't seen her around for a while, and came in search of her.

"You stupid bitch, Soo Ling. If you ever use the stuff again you're finished. I don't want any junkies working in my establishment. You hear?" he said shaking her angrily.

His voice seemed to be coming from some distance away but she nodded as he shook her.

"Yes, Chucky. Soo Ling not use again."

"Get your clothes on and go home. You're not much use to me tonight."

Soo Ling dressed in her street clothes and went home. She sort of drifted down the street. Jack Finley was right, it certainly made you feel invincible but it was very dangerous stuff.

The part that interested her most was how quickly the man parted with his money to get hold of the white powder. Maybe there could be more money to be made here.

With the baby out of the way Soo Ling once again let her sister visit the house, and it became a habit they enjoyed after a busy night at 'Uncle Sam's'. They would lay around all morning sipping tea and talking about the family or their customers. There seemed to be much in common these days. They got along much better than when they were working in the fields where Soo Ling tried to get out of any chores her father found for her. Like just two friends enjoying their work and their leisure.

Wei Ling was a spendthrift and used most of her money on self-indulgence and extravagance. She seemed to buy a new dress every second day and wasted a lot on cosmetics, something she really needed little of.

Soo Ling on the other hand was forced to hide her money from Tully, as any extravagance above the unusual amount he gave her would have been noticed. It was burning a hole in her pocket but she hid it away and like scrooge enjoyed counting it when she was alone.

She couldn't believe she had already accumulated fifteen thousand American dollars. Such wealth was unheard of in her village and the peasants would probably have bowed to her and regarded her almost as nobility.

The charade went on for months. Tully and Snaps had been covering an attack on the North Vietnamese army moving closer and closer to Saigon.

The Americans back home were demonstrating to their government about ceasing this useless war and bringing it to an end. Public opinion was beginning to hurt as the casualties grew and President Nixon was feeling the heat. Tully was sick of this damn country and this damn war and wanted to go home.

He was lucky enough to get a lift back a day early and arrived home looking forward to a cool shower and a change of clothes. When he found Wei Ling sitting alone in his lounge he raised his eyebrows.

"Who the hell are you?"

She turned quickly, a smile breaking out on her face. "Me Wei Ling, Soo Ling's sister. You Tully?"

"Of course. She told me you were in Saigon. How is she? Has she improved much?"

"Soo Ling fine. She no been sick."

"I wondered how she was recovering after losing her baby. It's been very hard for her."

Wei Ling looked puzzled. "Soo Ling no have baby. Never had baby."

"You're mistaken, Wei Ling. When I found her in the village she had a baby with her. Old Nguyen Huong used her and made her pregnant."

Wei Ling threw her head back and laughed. "That not Soo Ling's baby. That Nguyen Huong's baby. Soo Ling work and look after sick wife and baby."

"Then that wasn't her family killed in the attack."

"No. Family still alive. Farm burnt by napalm. Father send us away to work and support him."

Tully couldn't believe his ears. How could she have fooled him so easily? He suddenly had visions of her with the pillow over the baby. She was going to kill the child just to get rid of it. God knows what she did with it while he was away. His temper began burning on a long slow fuse.

"And just where is Soo Ling now?"

"She go get food for Tully return, then go to work and pick up pay."

"Pick up what pay?"

"Pay from work. Soo Ling work with me."

"And just where do you work, Wei Ling?"

"Wei Ling work at club, Uncle Sam's. Got good job, make much money. Last week make one hundred dollar."

"What sort of work do you both do at this Uncle Sam's, entertain soldiers?"

"Not so bad. Wei Ling make much money."

I bet thought Tully. "And Soo Ling works there while I'm away?"

She looked down red faced knowing she'd put her foot in it. "Not know. Maybe work in market."

"I think you'd better leave, Wei. When Soo Ling gets home we have something we need to talk about."

"I come later. Okay?"

"Yeah." Tully watched as she smoothed her expensive looking skirt, picked up her expensive looking handbag and left. He wondered what sort of wages his wife and her sister made to enable Wei Ling to buy clothes like that.

He began a search of her room. Hidden under the bed was a shoebox tucked well back behind everything else?

He almost dropped the box when he saw the money, all wrapped in bundles and tied with rubber bands. He sat at the table and counted it.

There was twenty five thousand four hundred American dollars, all in twenty and fifty dollar bills. His breathing was hard and he was so angry. He couldn't believe his eyes.

He had not heard Soo Ling come in until she gasped. He looked up as her wide eyes stared at him, her face deadly pale at what she saw.

"Mind explaining where this came from?" he said casually.

"Tully, you home. We make love now." She began undoing the frogs on her cheongsam. Anything to change the subject.

"The money, Soo Ling. Where did it come from?"

"Money belong to sister. I mind for her. Safe here."

"Really. And where did she get so much money?" He wondered just how much she would lie.

"Wei Ling work very hard for merchant. He pay good but sister not want money at home. Many thieves near her."

"You really are a compulsive liar, Soo Ling. Your sister was just here and let it slip that you had never had a baby. He belonged to some farmer you worked for."

"It true." Her voice became meek. "Without baby, Tully leave Soo Ling in Hue. Soo Ling die there."

"Maybe, maybe not. Did you kill the baby while I was away?"

"Not kill. Take baby to orphanage. Tell Nuns found baby in street. They care for him."

"And you married me knowing this was all a lie."

"Soo Ling like Tully. Happy married to Tully."

"This money doesn't belong to Wei does it?"

"Yes. Wei Ling's money."

"Then I'd better take care of it and put it in the bank for a while seeing it doesn't belong to you."

Her heart raced. She could see her fortune about to disappear. "No. My money, not sisters."

"I thought so. And you earned it working at Uncle Sam's."

Soo Ling could see the game was up. She really didn't need Tully any more so brazenly she admitted it.

"Soo Ling best girl in Saigon. Officers pay big only have Soo Ling. No need Tully now. I take money and go."

"That's the best idea you've come up with. Pack your stuff and go. Remember the communists are going to be in Saigon soon. How will you get your money out then? They'll take it all."

"Soo Ling find way. Chuck take care of Soo Ling. Very valuable to Chuck."

"And who the hell is Chuck?"

"Chuck boss at Uncle Sam's. I go now."

She snatched up her money, packed her things and left.

Tully couldn't believe how easily she had taken him in. Right from the minute he had handed her the torn dress to cover herself. It had been so easy for her. Her beguiling innocence, her wide doe eyes and timid ness with his big heart and Sir Galahad nature had just swallowed him up. When he looked back now he had to admit he probably would have done the same thing in her position. It was a game of survival here, so Soo Ling took her chance and survived. He wanted to hate her but found he couldn't, so he just opened a bottle of whisky and proceeded to get drunk instead.

Chapter Seventeen

As Tully came out of his drunken haze the next morning he began to feel like a prize chump. He thought of how noble he felt saving Soo Ling from smothering the child and killing herself to avoid the ravages of this war. If only he had known it was the baby she was trying to get rid of because of its inconvenience. How long had she been scheming to get him to take her to Saigon? To think how magnanimous he was to marry her to get her away. No sign of shame at being discovered, just a see you later and off. He fell under the shower and let the cold needles of water blast his body.

As he began to feel normal again he smiled to himself. Who the hell was he to judge Soo Ling on her morals? His life and background were far from pure. Good luck to the little bitch, with all that money and her cunning he was sure she would be safe.

As he tramped to the office he could already see movement of panic. Some of the shops were boarding up windows. Not a good sign for the population.

Snaps was incredulous as they sat in the office and Tully related the night's events. "Just shows you can't trust any bastard in this place."

"What are you going to do now?"

"Nothing. I don't care if I never see her again. She's on her own now. We'll be going home soon, this war is coming to an end."

"Yeah. Looks like it could be a merry Xmas. Let's get a drink and toast 1975."

"Great idea," agreed Tully. "Just so long as we don't go to Uncle Sam's."

Snaps wrapped his arm around his friend's shoulder as they headed for the door.

"I'll drink to that."

"By the way," said Tully "the scuttle butt is the Yanks are pulling out early in the New Year."

"Shit, it's all coming to an end isn't it?"

"Seems they're going to give financial support to the South but gradually pull out their troops."

"All of them?"

"All but a few advisors."

"That's where it all started."

"Yeah, the wheel has turned, mate, let's get pissed."

Xmas came and went and Hanoi's resolve to liberate Saigon within two years looked like being a reality much sooner than expected.

Six central provinces fell to the north and their army was heading south at a frightening rate. The Americans had had enough of the endless drain of lives and money and voted to reject any monetary help for south's President Thieu.

The only troops left were the South's army who was holding on desperately. Tully and Snaps continued to monitor the progress of the war but it was becoming obvious the end was near.

Vietnam 1975

Tully was in his office when the news came through.

"Shit, Thieu has resigned and Xuan Loc has fallen. Looks like the end, mate."

"Does this mean we better start thinking about how we're going to get out of here." Snaps was anxious to be on his way.

Tully didn't seem interested in leaving. He saw it as a chance for a scoop.

"I don't think the communists will bother with correspondents. They'll want their victory spread all over the world's papers. I'm staying. If you're game it should get you some great pictures."

"Jesus, Tully, do you ever think about living safely and quietly?" Sometimes Snaps wondered how they had survived for this long.

"Scared?"

"Shit yeah but if you're staying, so am I."

"Thought so. We'd better make some arrangements though. I'll contact the paper."

*   *   *

The push south hadn't worried Soo Ling until early April. When she heard Chuck making plans to close the place then she really became worried. The clientele was dropping alarmingly with the Americans well gone.

Most of the customers were now South Vietnam troops and the odd American advisor. Chuck had once employed over thirty girls when the club was going full steam. Now four were still working and there was only a handful of people around. Most nights they sat idle, barely making twenty dollars. On the night of April 29th, panic hit the city.

Civilians and army were making a frantic effort to reach their Embassy where helicopters were transferring them to an aircraft carrier waiting off the coast.

Chuck had closed the doors and paid off the girls. People stampeding past the building didn't give the once bust club a second glance. Soo Ling and her sister were the only two left and they watched the crowd from the front window.

"What we do Soo Ling, communists come soon maybe kill us."

"Get back to father's before too late. Maybe bus still go or buy motor scooter."

"Have no money, Soo Ling. Not save, always spend."

"You very stupid, Wei Ling. Waste everything."

Soo Ling opened her purse and counted out three thousand dollars for her sister and pushed it into her hand.

"Better get dress like peasant. Go quick."

With tears streaming down her face Wei Ling thanked her sister and hugged her swiftly.

"Good bye, Soo Ling, you good sister. Maybe never see again."

Soo Ling kissed her then pushed her out of the door into the passing stream of refugees and locked it behind her. Now all she had to do was get herself a safe passage away. She was sure Chuck would have some contacts with influence.

Heading for the closed door of Chuck's office, she heard raised voices. Pausing outside she listened to the argument going on inside.

"You said the boat is called The White Duck, wharf six."

"Yes, you no be late."

"You said $2000 you thieving gook." Chuck was agitated and yelling loudly.

"Sorry. Captain say $5000 now. Communists almost here. Must go soon."

"You're sure there's plenty of fuel loaded."

"Sure, Chuck, all ready. You be number six wharf eight o'clock."

"I'll rip your balls off if anything goes wrong."

"No go wrong. Must be ready eight o'clock."

"All right you thieving bastard, now get the fuck out of here. I have to finish packing."

Hearing the back door slam loudly, Soo Ling pushed open the office door a couple of inches and watched as Chuck knelt in front of the safe. He was busy dragging out bundles of notes and small packages of the white powder.

He reached for a valise as Soo Ling opened the door wider and stepped inside. A gun seemed to appear from nowhere as he whirled to face the intruder.

"Christ, Soo Ling, you frightened the shit out of me." He lowered the gun, placed it on the floor beside the safe and continued stacking the valise with the bank notes.

"Chucky take Soo Ling with him?"

"Sorry, Babe, this is a one way trip for old Chucky boy alone."

"Soo Ling die here. You take with you."

"Impossible, Babe. You're on your own. I'm on my way to Australia, now fuck off, I've got a boat and plane to catch and this place is going to go up in flames in just a few minutes." He continued loading the bag with money. Soo Ling's eyes could hardly take in the amount of money lying on the floor.

"Chucky. I be your woman. You have very hot time, you take Soo Ling."

"I told you, sugar, I'm leaving the fucking country. Look, here's the address of a man who'll make you a false passport. You can go to any fucking place in the world if you've got the dough?" He handed her a card.

Soo Ling noticed the address was a sleazy part of Saigon down near the docks.

"Please, Chucky, you take me." Soo Ling's voice was sounding desperate.

Suddenly she dropped her dress and stood naked in front of him. Chuck leered at her beautiful body. Her ivory skin and feminine form always intrigued him. There was no way he was going to take this stupid bitch with him, but one for the road wouldn't be much of a complication.

"Maybe," he said ogling her body. "Show me again how good you can be."

Soo Ling smiled and walked quickly to him. Her expert fingers undid his belt dropping his trousers. One smooth stroke brought him to attention, then she fell to her knees in front of him taking him in her mouth.

He closed his eyes with pleasure and groaned softly. She continued to tease him for several minutes almost bringing him to the brink, then skillfully eased off. Soo Ling smiled sweetly at him, stood up and walked into the bar.

He thought she was going to leave him in this highly erotic state.

"Shit, Soo Ling what's going on?"

"Just get rubber from bar. Back quick."

He eased back into the chair making himself comfortable pleased with her effort but anxious to get on with it. With only a couple of hours to go he had a lot to do. Soo Ling reached under the bar for the condoms where her hand fell to the shortened baseball bat Chuck kept there for drunken soldiers who made trouble.

"You ready, Chucky."

"Ready and waiting, Babe."

"Close eyes. Soo Ling has big surprise."

He smiled laying back in anticipation and closing his eyes as Soo Ling gently touched his throbbing shaft. Before he could draw breath she released her hand and felt for the baseball bat. Her long lean fingers caressed the smooth surface of the wood. Increasing her pressure she lifted it slowly like some great bird soaring skywards on an up-draught into a jet stream. Then brought it down with the speed of a Wedge tailed eagle diving to its prey towards Chick's head. There was a sickening crunch and blood spurted over her. She raised it and brought it down again, then again and again in a frenzied attack until Chuck's head was nothing but a bloody pulp. It was as if she expected him to stand up and attack her for her deed. Dropping the bat beside the body she stood glued to the spot, unable to believe what she had done.

Stepping away from the horror in front of her she fell backwards over the half-filled valise. Falling to the floor she looked quickly to see what had caused her to stumble. The sight of all the money was like a splash of cold water in her face. Regaining her feet she calmly walked to the nearest bathroom and turned on the shower.

As the water trickled down her body, Soo Ling watched it change from bright red, then fade to a soft pink as the blood was watered down.

The crimson pool in the shower recess was diluting, leaving goblets of pink brain matter at her feet before being washed down the drain.

Scrubbing hard removing the blood from her breasts and body, Soo Ling was feeling like she was never going to be clean again. Her splattered face was left until last. The clean fresh water running down her face and through her long black hair was like a sign from the Gods cleansing her of the terrible deed she'd done.

Dressing in her clean top and jeans she returned to the office where she knew there was still work to be done. Blood was still seeping all over the floor from Chuck's battered head and carefully Soo Ling stepped around the enlarging stain.

Inspecting the remaining contents of the opened safe she was amazed at what she saw. Chuck had only removed half of the money. The rest still stacked neatly and tied in rubber bands.

People running by outside and shouting gathered her attention for a few seconds, fear gathering in her face. With a couple of quick scoops she pulled the rest of the money and the small bags of white powder into the bag along with the gun. Bending to check the safe was empty Soo Ling saw four one-kilogram packets of heroin neatly stacked in one corner.

Her eyes widened as she realized just how much money she had. There must have been close to half a million American dollars in the bag plus the value of the heroin. Adding what she herself had, Soo Ling was rich beyond her wildest dreams.

I may as well carry out your last wishes Chucky, she thought as she picked up the Jerry can of petrol Chuck had left ready. Carefully pouring a trail around the room and toward the door Soo Ling was satisfied. She was about to light it when she saw her beautiful green dress draped over a chair. Picking it up lovingly she folded it into the bag on top of the money. Why not she thought, it had been the first thing I got from Chuck, may as well be the last.

"Bye, Chucky boy," she said as she lit a match. The fuel caught quickly and Soo Ling pulled the door behind her as she ran into the street carrying the valise.

By the time she was thirty yards away the place was an inferno. Watching for several seconds she thought about her days in Saigon then quietly joined the crowds all anxious to get to their destinations and avoid the invading army.

It took her thirty minutes to reach the wharf and find the man she hoped was going to make her a passport. It was an old tailor's shop falling down around her ears. The windows were boarded up and paint was hanging from the doorframe where the humid salty air had slowly eaten into it. She banged hard on the door and for a minute thought no one was there. At last the door was opened by a man of about sixty years old.

Soo Ling thought he would fall over stooped in the way he was.

"What you want?"

"Told you could get me passport."

He looked up and down the darkened street and ushered her in.

"Cost five thousand American dollar. Pay first."

"How long to make?" she asked. She knew The White Duck was almost ready to leave.

"All ready, only have to take photo. What country, what name?"

Soo Ling didn't hesitate. "Australia, Soo Ling Sanderson."

"Money?" He held out his hand expectantly. As Soo Ling paid him he took a Polaroid photo and disappeared behind a curtain to finish his handiwork. Fifteen minutes later she was on her way to wharf six.

People were hurrying everywhere all trying to escape and she could hear distant gunfire rumbling across the city behind her. Occasionally the night sky was lit up with exploding shells as the invading army grew closer. In the dim light on wharf six was the White Duck, its engines slowly turning over. A burly man holding a rifle stood guard looking suspiciously at Soo Ling then indicated to her to move on.

"Chuck Hale send me. He no can come but say you take me."

Looking anxiously up and down the wharf the only people he saw were trying to bargain with boat owners for a passage. The White Duck was a thirty footer with powerful engines, the type of craft the rich used for recreation.

"Are you sure Chuck not coming?" he asked.

"Me Soo Ling. Chucky say give money when at sea."

"Let's see the money first." He didn't know whether to believe her or not.

Soo Ling produced the five thousand dollars, then quickly stuffed it back into the bag.

He looked at his watch anxiously. "I guess it's okay," he said helping her aboard. He was as concerned as Soo Ling to leave Saigon before the communists arrived. Soo Ling sat down with relief as the boat eased from the wharf, and turned into the channel leaving Saigon behind.

"We go to plane now."

"Be there in thirty minutes. Money please."

Soo Ling reluctantly handed over the bundle of notes, which the man quickly counted.

"Okay?" she asked.

His reply was just a grunt as he skillfully steered the boat into the darkness down the estuary towards the open sea.

When they reached the village of Nha Be they pulled into the shore.

"You go. Man wait." He pointed to a figure standing on the makeshift jetty.

Soo Ling stepped out of the boat and walked toward the waiting figure. She stopped and turned toward the boat which was already leaving.

"Who the hell are you? Where's Chuck Hale?"

"He come later. He say you to take me."

"Hang on a minute, Darlin', my arrangement was with Chuck, I'm not getting involved with any dames."

"How much Chuck pay? I pay more."

Soo Ling opened the bag and grabbed a bundle of money.

"Okay, Darlin', come up with ten grand and we're on our way."

She counted out the ten thousand and handed it over.

"Hurry, we go now."

"Start running, Darlin', we have three hundred yards to cover through that field, then we're out of here."

Leaving Vietnam was high on his agenda too.

They raced across the fields of stubble which had once been a crop now reduced to slush and struggled for the last few yards through bamboo taller than Soo Ling. Scrambling aboard the small plane, Soo Ling sat in the passenger seat finally catching her breath. She then took time to study her deliverer. He was quite young, very slim and with hair almost as long and as black as her own. He wore a flying jacket with a Canadian insignia

"Where we go?" she asked apprehensively.

"Java, then Australia. Chuck wanted me to drop him at small airfield outside of Darwin. We have to fly low to evade Australian radar. We have about fourteen hours ahead of us so you might as well settle back and take a nap."

"Okay." Soo Ling didn't care how long it took, just as long it was away from Vietnam. There was little conversation from the pilot and nothing to see. It was an uneventful trip and Soo Ling did eventually get some sleep lying down behind the pilot clasping her bag tightly. A quick refuel in Java then back into the air. The pilot handed Soo Ling a bag containing sandwiches, which she ate hungrily. When he frowned she realised she had to share and reluctantly handed it back. Little was said but as the dawn evolved, Soo Ling thought how beautiful it was as it made the sea look like a shining mirror.

As the plane swooped low over the vast brown and dry Australian countryside, Soo Ling's eyes swept the desolation below.

If this was the land Tully came from she wondered why he was always so anxious to return. No green trees, no jungle, just dust and heat. Not a very pleasant environment, nothing like Vietnam.

It was mid morning when they touched down on the dusty deserted airstrip few miles from Darwin. Soo Ling noted a battered utility, was waiting nearby.

"Keys are in the truck. Chuck didn't tell me his plans after Darwin."

As Soo Ling climbed out of the plane, the pilot grabbed her arm.

"Any questions asked, Darlin' and you know nothing. I didn't bring you here and you've never laid eyes on me. You got that?"

"Sure. Soo Ling come on boat. Okay?"

"Right, from now on you're on your own so get your pretty arse off my plane."

Soo Ling watched as the little plane taxied down the runway and flew off into the vivid blue sky. Looking around her she could see nothing but arid land. No people, no nothing. Just a vast expanse of dry desert broken by an odd pathetic looking tree. Sitting in the old car for some time collecting her thoughts she wondering what lay ahead of her in this vast unfriendly looking place. Were there any cities? Were there any people? How could this land produce food to feed them? What was she going to do? Hell she couldn't even drive.

*   *   *

Tully and Snaps were roaming through the streets of Saigon. Snaps already had taken some stunning photos of life in the raw, people fleeing in blind panic, women carrying small children in their arms. People with bundles of their belongings on their shoulders, soldiers running and abandoning their weapons. Complete mayhem.

There was forsaken furniture, animals and clothing everywhere. Children were crying and adults were screaming. It was pandemonium at its best. The sky was now lit up with a red glow from fires to the north. It was like a late sunset thought Tully as they waved their way through the traffic.

Ahead of them was a blazing building where a few people were trying ineffectually to throw a few buckets of water on the flames.

"I didn't hear any shell go off around here." Snaps raised his camera and clicked several times.

"I reckon someone didn't want the commies in so they set fire to it."

A fearful thought struck Tully. He wasn't sure if this was the location of Uncle Sam's and his heart was pounding at the notion Soo Ling may have been in there. He grabbed a member of the bucket brigade.

"This Uncle Sam's Club?"

The man didn't speak English but nodded at the recognition of the name. Tully pulled the nearest person aside.

"You speak English?"

Nodding, the man passed his bucket to a young boy to continue the useless task.

"What happened?" Tully had an eerie feeling in his gut.

"Club burn. All gone."

"What about the girls?"

"All gone."

"You mean dead," Snaps yelled. The old man shrugged his shoulders and moved back to his bucket line.

"Looks like you could be a grieving widower, mate," said Snaps taking a shot of the bucket line

Tully was stunned. "Christ, looks like it. I didn't wish that on her. I was rather fond of her even if she did play me for a chump."

"Nothing you can do now. Come on, let's get out of here."

For a few seconds they stood watching the club collapse in a fiery show of sparks. Tully had a strange feeling of loss. He certainly didn't love Soo Ling and he understood her motives in lying to him, but to end like this was undeserved by anyone. Snaps dragged him by the arm and headed towards the American Embassy but Tully's mind was no longer on his job. Three communist tanks came roaring around a bend and sped by totally oblivious to the man with the cameras recording their progress.

At the Embassy just about everyone was gone and they hung around the final few minutes with Snaps recording the last chopper to leave the area as a tank broke down the guarding gates.

The next day the war was over. Tully scooped some great interviews through an interpreter and sent back his copy to the Tribune.

"You realise we've been here for four bloody years," said Tully as they packed their things.

"Don't remind me. I'll be glad to get out of this bloody place. What are you going to do now, mate?"

"There'll be another war in another place. A bloke has to make a living."

"I've had enough of this. Think I'll go into taking family portraits or something."

"Wish I could but I've got a daughter to take care of."

"At least you're single again. There'll be new women to explore."

"Shit, I hope so. Without them I might as well be dead."

Four days later with their bags full of film and stories, they were on their way home to Oz.

Chapter Eighteen

Sydney 1974.

When Kate flew out of Saigon she was in two minds. Relieved to be leaving this country with its death and destruction but happy she had met Tully and now carried his child. Even now her hands rested on her stomach imagining herself to be six months pregnant.

With an overnight stay in tent accommodation at the hospital, it was an early morning flight in more comfort than the Da-Nang-Saigon trip. The entire medical team was happy and relieved to see the last of Vietnam and some viewed the disappearing coastline in solemn silence until it was gone. The closing chapter of that part of their lives was now behind them but the memories of what they had done and seen would remain forever.

It was a ten hour trip to Sydney and some families were there waiting as doctors and nurses disembarked. No one met Kate for she had not told her only sister of her homecoming. There were things to do before she passed on the news of her pregnancy.

Her tour of duty now completed, Kate resigned her commission. Vietnam held more nightmares for her then anyone deserved. Apart from Tully she was glad to be rid of that terrible place and began to make her plans.

The army, sad to see her leave confirmed her resignation and she was back in civvies within a week. She knew her pregnancy was not yet apparent but she had to confide in someone. Her married sister Susan Farmer was surprised when she turned up on her doorstep.

"Kate! When did you get back? Why didn't you tell us? We would have met you."

"I didn't want a fuss, Sis. I just wanted to slip back quietly and try to forget."

"Pretty awful hey? Come here and give me a hug."

Susan embraced her sister, glad to have her back safe and sound.

"I was shocked when we heard about James. It seems incredible someone could die from a simple thing like appendicitis."

"He was unlucky. The weather closed in and they couldn't get him out in time."

"And only a week after you arrived. It must have been devastating?"

"It was but the carnage I saw in the last three years was also devastating."

Susan nodded. It was easy to see the effects of Vietnam had on her sister.

"Well it's all behind you now. What are your plans?"

"I've resigned my commission and I'm going into private practice."

"Wonderful. At least you'll be safe now. Where are you going to practice?"

"Somewhere nice and quiet. I've got my eye on a little country town called Moruya."

"That's down on the coast."

"Yes. There's something I have to tell you and it's to be a secret."

"Sounds serious. Can't I tell Sam?"

"Only him. He'll know soon enough anyway."

"Okay, what's the secret?"

"I'm pregnant."

"You're what? Who is the father?"

"Someone I fell in love with but won't see again. It was quite deliberate and he doesn't know."

"Why not for God's sake?"

"I have my reasons. I met him in Vietnam when I was feeling lost. He took me to his heart and cared for me. Even asked me to marry him."

"Why didn't you?"

"Because of his lifestyle. It wouldn't have worked."

"You're sure?"

"Maybe one day he might come looking for me, but I told him not to."

"Bad decision. What are you going to tell everyone?"

"In Moruya nobody knows me. I give them the tragic news my husband James Armitage died just after I became pregnant."

"Even if his name was Sutton?"

"They don't know that."

"Are there any other doctors in Moruya?"

"Three, and of course the hospital."

"Can I do anything?" Susan felt helpless but knew her sister well. When she made up her mind nothing would change it.

"Just give me your love and support."

"I guess Stephanie will have a playmate when we come and visit. What do you want me to tell Sam?"

"Just tell him my lover died. Ask him to back me up."

"He will. Good luck, Kate." Again she embraced Kate and hoped her sister's torment was over.

*   *   *

Moruya was the perfect place. Quiet, peaceful and beautiful. When the water in the estuary flowed out under the bridge it left shallow water and large sandbanks. With the incoming tide it was full and a haven for fishermen and small boats. The shopping was adequate, the climate pleasant and the sea air refreshing.

Doctor Squires looked at Kate from across the table of his home. He poured her a cup of tea and handed it to her. Kate noted it would have been his best china. He was surprised an attractive young woman like her would want to live in a small country town. Usually it was hard to get doctors to shift from the city.

Kate took a bite from the biscuit offered. His home was nice, just the sort of place she wanted and his practice seemed well run.

"Now, Doctor Armitage, why would an attractive young woman like yourself want to practice medicine in Moruya?"

"I've been through three years of hell, Doctor Squires. I was a doctor in the army with my husband who died in Vietnam and I'm pregnant. I want to raise my child in a safe healthy place. Moruya seems ideal."

"I'm sorry to hear about your husband. It was a tragic time in a tragic place. You're right, Doctor Armitage, Moruya will be ideal."

"Please call me Kate, Doctor."

"You've come at an opportune time for me, Kate. I'm seventy-two years old and want to retire. If we can come to a suitable arrangement I'd be happy to sell my practice. The house is only a two minute walk to the surgery and should suit."

"Perhaps I could see your books, then we can agree on a price."

"Of course. I'll be sorry to leave the house but I have a daughter in Tasmania who wants me to move there. I think it's time I did."

When the price was agreed upon, Kate felt like a new woman and began a new phase of her life. She missed Tully but his child was going to be some consultation to the loneliness she was enduring.

When she moved in, Kate thought back to what had happened in her life. Her internship with the Australian Medical Corp was more than she hoped for. It was hard but satisfying, in fact she felt she learned more than she would have hoped for. It was also the place where she fell deeply in love for the first time.

His name was James Sutton. When she was asked to assist in a simple operation she felt elated. James was one of the senior surgeons at the base and she was surprised he chose her.

"Thank you, Doctor Armitage," he said as they were removing their rubber gloves.

"Now my next order is a little more personal."

Kate was all ears. The rest of the female staff all raved about the handsome Doctor Sutton and she was no exception.

"What order would that be, Doctor?" She flashed her best smile hoping it didn't sound impertinent.

"More of a request I'm afraid. Would you have dinner with me tonight?"

"Is this a professional request?"

"Strictly personal. Man to woman."

"Then woman to man, I'd be delighted."

One date led to another, then another. They both knew what was happening and before long they were both head over heels in love. It wasn't long before they fell into bed and Kate's heart soared when he asked her to marry him.

Their lovemaking was so intense Kate thought she had met her lifetime mate.

"I have some good news and bad news I'm afraid, Darling," he said reaching into his pocket.

"Love good news, hate bad news. Just tell me the good news."

"The good news is I bought this for you." He handed her the box holding the engagement ring. Kate gave a squeal and threw her arms around his neck. She couldn't wait to try it on. Holding her hand in the air admiring the sparkle from the ring she turned toward him.

"I know you're going to tell me the bad news now."

"The wedding will have to be postponed for a while. I have to go to Vietnam. They need surgeons, as many as they can get and I've been nominated."

"If you think you're going to leave me here all alone for three years, James you need to see a psychiatrist."

"I was hoping you'd say that. I can get you there if you like. It would be excellent experience."

"Then do it. When do you leave?"

"Next week."

"Can I come with you?"

"It will take at least a month before you can go." He noticed the frown on her forehead. "Don't worry, I'll see to it we finish up at the same hospital."

"A month. Perhaps we had better make up for lost time before you leave."

"I knew you were a good Doctor." He gathered her in his arms and led her to his bedroom.

It was actually six weeks before she stepped off the plane in steamy Saigon. James was there to meet her and she rushed into his arms almost knocking him over.

"Welcome to Vietnam," he said responding to her kisses.

"Is it always so hot here?" Already the humidity was getting to her.

"You'll get used to it. There's so much work here you haven't time to worry about the weather."

He was right. Kate found out it was a twelve-hour day with hardly a break. It wasn't just Australian troops she had to attend to. It was American as well.

The army hospital had first class facilities. When it came to equipment the Americans didn't skimp. What she walked into shocked her.

The wounds were horrendous and amputations frightening. She wondered how any of the wounded survived at all and she admired the skills of both the American and Australian surgeons.

It was a week after she arrived. James pushed open the operating door and called to her.

"I've been called out to an emergency, Kate. The chopper is waiting. See you in a couple of hours."

She looked up from wounded man she was attending. "Okay, take care."

She didn't actually see him leave; she just heard the sound of the chopper as it flew overhead. An hour later she tidied up and looked at the sky. The clouds had rolled in and lightening flashed across the horizon.

"Looks like a wet one coming up," said a nurse joining her.

"It always rains at this time of evening," she said, not concerned.

"Yeah, but that seems exceptionally dark." She stared at the oncoming storm.

It was the worst storm Kate had experienced in her short time in Vietnam. The rain came down in a belting torrent, almost like a waterfall. When it was still going two hours later, she became concerned. After four hours, James had still not returned and she went to the communications center.

"Any news on Major Sutton. He should have been back by now."

The operator looked quickly at her. "You haven't heard?"

"Heard what?" A stab of fear crossed her heart.

"The weather has closed in. They can't return until tomorrow."

"But they'll be all right won't they?"

The silent stare alarmed her.

"What, corporal? Tell me."

"Major Sutton has been brought down with appendicitis. He's in trouble."

"Appendicitis? And you mean they can't get him back until tomorrow?"

"No, the medics said his appendix has burst. They have no facilities to operate in the field. They're pinned down by enemy fire."

"But there must be some way? I'll go to him."

"Sorry Captain. Everyone is grounded until the weather clears."

Kate paced the floor all night waiting for the sky to clear. When the chopper finally came back at noon she rushed to James's side. He was deathly white and hardly breathing. An American surgeon brushed her aside and James was taken to the operating room. When he returned, Kate went to his bed. The look the surgeon gave her almost made her faint. At six that evening James died in her arms.

*   *   *

Kate unpacked her clothes from the case lying on the bed. It amazed her how few clothes she actually had. No longer in uniform she decided she needed a new wardrobe to begin her new life in civvies.

The last thing in the case was a picture of James taken before he left for Vietnam. She stared at it for a few seconds, then thought about Tully. James's memory was still with her as it always would be, but the dead were gone and Tully had replaced the love she felt for her deceased fiancée.

It was Tully she thought about now, he was always in her mind. Smiling sadly, she turned the photo face down and put it at the back of the wardrobe. "Sorry, James" she said softly and resumed her unpacking.

As her pregnancy progressed the locals had full sympathy for Doctor Kate who tragically lost her husband before her baby was born. She worked in her garden when time permitted and always had a cheery hello to passing neighbors. When the birth approached Kate was forced to employ a locum until the wondrous day when Jason Armitage arrived in the world. Soon back at work Kate had many offers of childcare so taking care of Jason was not a problem. She found a loving widow to take day care of Jason and Kate was glad to pay her well. By the time Jason was five Kate became the chairman of the hospital charity commission who had long term goal of building a new wing to the hospital. It was going to take years but she was determined to raise the millions needed for the project. Apart from Jason it became the goal of her life to help the good citizens of Moruya.

Chapter Nineteen

Once he'd reported in and given Richard his stories Tully decided it was time to visit Vera and his daughter. He had mixed feelings as he knocked on Vera's door. He'd been breaking his neck to see Carrie again but wondered how she'd react to this stranger who was her father.

"Tulston," cried Vera welcoming him with a hug. "I was beginning to wonder if you were ever going to come home. You look tired."

"Washed out would be a better expression, Sis. Where's my baby? How is she?"

"Probably wondering who this stranger is?Vera stood aside. Tully smiled down at the toddler with her finger in her mouth staring at him.

"Hello, Carrie," he bent to her level. "Come and give your father a kiss." Holding his arms outstretched he waited for her to come forward. She stood shyly not knowing what to do. Picking her up Tully was dismayed to see the frightened look on her face. She reached out for her Aunt Vera who took her from him.

"Don't be frightened, Pet. This is your Daddy. You know Daddy, we look at his photo every night."

Tully accepted the fact it would take a little time for the child to get used to him but he wanted badly to hold her. Once or twice a year was not nearly enough for the child to form a relationship. He could see Briony's face mirrored in the child. After a couple of hours she climbed on his lap as he sat talking to Vera. The smile on his face seemed to be cemented. His sister suppressed a smile as Tully's eyes were glowing with delight.

Gradually the thaw eased and he handed her the presents he had brought. She was intrigued with the doll with the almond shaped eyes and the Vietnamese pajamas. After a couple of days he was chasing her around the house thrilled by her laughter. Vera could see he'd had a bad time in Vietnam. His eyes had a haunted look and he had certainly lost weight.

"I'm so glad you're home again, Tulston. The little one needs more time to get to know you again."

"I can't believe how big she's grown. She looks so much like her mother."

"Then her mother must have been very beautiful. You should get married and settle down and make a family for the child."

"Surprisingly I did ask a girl in Vietnam to marry me. She was an Australian doctor but she turned me down. She preferred the quiet life of a country GP rather than being married to a traveling foreign correspondent."

"I can't say I blame her, you can't really expect a girl to marry someone who's never home. Why don't you give up this foreign correspondent stuff and just do national reporting."

"That's what she said but she knew it was in my blood. I probably wouldn't have made her happy anyway."

Vera shook her head sadly. "You can't lead this life forever. Carrie needs you home."

"I know, Sis. Just a few more years and I'll be well enough off to support her properly."

"You've been more than generous with your maintenance. She hasn't wanted for anything."

"Except a loving father here to care for her." He sighed as he kissed the top of his daughter's head.

"Well it's only you who can solve that problem. How long are you staying this time?"

"Until the boss tells me to go somewhere. I hope it's not too soon. I need some time to get to know my daughter again."

*　　*　　*

Vera Corrigan dipped her fingers into the holy water, crossed herself and knelt in her usual pew to pray. Vera attended Mass three times a week to thank the Lord for His blessings. It was a habit she'd had for years although she hadn't always been thanking the Lord. One time she used to pray for His help. In the eight years she'd been married to the beer drinking, womanizing Fred Corrigan she had often needed to ask the Lord for strength and guidance.

In the beginning things had been good.

Fred was a loving husband who knew Vera's greatest desire was to have children, lots of children and at first it was not for the want of trying.

They tried as often as they could, in fact Vera still blushed as she recalled the time they did it on the train on the way home late one night.

Then for no apparent reason Fred started drinking, not a lot at first but gradually he stayed out later and later. Vera knew there were women too. Once she had asked him about lipstick on his shirt and had been shocked to receive a resounding slap across the face for her trouble. From then she just washed away the lipstick without comment.

In his drunken sprees she often received a sound thrashing so she just lived her life as best as she knew how and went to mass to get comfort from the Lord. When she became a Catholic to marry Fred she promised to love and obey till death do us part so this then was her lot in life.

The day Vera came home and found Fred in their bed with one of her friends was just too much. After a violent argument she ordered him from the house and surprisingly he went. As he sneered his way past her he said he never wanted any sniveling brats anyway, and as she loved the church more than she had ever loved him she could go screw the bloody Lord.

Vera went to mass every day that week and prayed to God to forgive this fallen man, even though she now detested him. She said Lord he knows not what he does. When she opened her door to her brother Tulston and his baby daughter her prayers were answered.

When God took Briony O'Rourke home to His kingdom, destiny shone on Vera Corrigan giving her the honor of being a surrogate mother to this tiny infant. More than sixteen years now she had nurtured her niece and was a happy fulfilled woman.

Although she had loved every minute of being Carrie's only carer she was saddened Tulston had missed her first steps, her first words, and her first day at school. Vera had sent him photos and wrote copious letters in the beginning but with his life style around the globe they didn't always reach him.

He certainly provided for them both. Sometimes Vera wondered did he keep any of his wages for himself so generous was he with his daughter's needs. She was a delight to rear. A sweet tempered child free with her hugs and kisses. For years she called Vera mummy and Vera's heart pounded each time she heard the words.

When she thought Carrie was old enough to understand she'd explained to her that mummy was in heaven and she was daddy's sister, Carrie's aunt.

She didn't think the child understood much about family, but knew it would sort itself out in time, and her father could explain the details when she was older. The little mite had put her arms around Vera's neck and said, "then I'll call you, Mummy Vera."

Vera had been the one attending the Christmas pageant at her kindergarten. Vera was the one who took her to school first day and enrolled her at the Catholic College where she did her secondary education. She often wondered what her brother thought about his daughter attending a Catholic school. He never complained to Vera and she assumed like Vera herself, he knew that was what Briony would have wanted. Now her baby was about to be eighteen and enrolled at university. She was starting on a new branch of her life and Vera was again the one to see her on her way.

*   *   *

Sydney 1988

Carrie was looking anxiously from the window of the train, searching the crowd for Stephanie. She always tried to keep a seat for her friend. Ever since they had met at Uni. they had clicked right from the beginning. When they discovered they both traveled on the same route it had become a daily exercise. With a considerable train ride into the city, the two of them gossiped about fashion, boyfriends or what subjects they had. The journey seemed to fly.

Waving madly Stephanie saw her friend and hurried to the compartment halfway along the carriage.

"Hi, Carrie. Boy, I almost missed the train."

"Hi, Steph. How do you like my new cardigan Aunt Vera bought for me yesterday. Pretty swish hey." Carrie lifted her arms to show off the garment.

"It looks great and that's good because I've had a fantastic idea. It's okay with mum and if your Aunt Vera agrees it will be wonderful."

"Agree to what?" Stephanie's eyes looked as if she'd won the lottery.

"Well, you know how much of our day we spend on this damn journey."

"So. You think we should do a correspondence course and save the time?"

"Carrie, you are crazy." Stephanie laughed at her joke then was serious again. She tapped the ends of her fingers together. "Mum says I can rent a house if you share with me."

Carrie's mouth flew open, she never thought for one moment Mrs. Farmer would allow her little girl to embark on such a thing.

"How come she said me?"

"Because she knows what a sweet, pure, trustworthy girl you are, and I wasn't going to tell her the truth."

Carrie gave her friend a playful slap.

"You didn't tell her about the grass we smoked last week."

"Are you kidding. I'd spend the rest of my life in a cupboard. What do you think?"

Carrie turned it over in her mind. It wasn't such a bad idea. The trip in and out of the city every day took up so much of their study time. The extra hours saved would help with that plus the train fares were a drag on the budget, although her father certainly wasn't stingy.

"Let me talk it over with Aunt Vera tonight. I don't know if she'll agree but it does sound like it might be fun."

"Be sure not to mention the grass." Stephanie laughed again.

Aunt Vera was surprisingly supportive with a few definite provisos. She must come home every second weekend, she must ring at least twice a week, and she must make sure the door has a strong lock and her clothes are always properly washed and ironed. Carrie was amused at the conditions but knew Vera was always worried about her.

The next morning she hung excitedly from the window before the train even reached Stephanie's station. She waved and smiled almost jumping out before Stephanie could board.

"Looks like she said no." Stephanie's eyes sparkled at her antics.

"You great fool, where will we live? What about furniture? How much do you think it will cost? Can you cook?"

Carrie was firing questions so fast Stephanie was almost doubled over laughing.

They spent the next couple of weekends haunting real estate offices and began to become despondent about costs involved in setting up home. Aunt Vera was always helpful and looked in the paper everyday to see if anything suitable was advertised.

Eventually Stephanie's dad somehow tracked down a place which proved to be pretty suitable although the rent was dearer than they had hoped to pay. Talking it over with their families it was decided Sam Farmer would perhaps be able to stretch the budget that little bit further.

Came the big day of the shift and a mini van was hired. Stephanie's dad drove it to Carries as first port of call at where Aunt Vera had donated some crockery. All had been carefully washed and packed. She also parted with a couple of bridge chairs, which only took up space in the backroom, a coffee table and a small chest of drawers.

Carrie helped load her bags and hugged Aunt Vera with a promise to ring her that night and assured her she could visit any time she wished.

Carrie sitting up with Sam Farmer headed back across town to Stephs. Susan Farmer had donated lots of linen, which she said she bought at the op-shop, but quite a lot of it had the feel of new stuff. There were two single beds, a kitchen dresser with a leg missing and a bookcase all from the same op-shop.

The mini-van was loaded and Carrie was put in charge of giving directions, while Stephanie was to follow with her mother to help unload and settle in.

Carrie had the key and opened the door of her new home with a great flourish and invited Sam Farmer to be their first guest.

He laughed along with her as he carried in the bags, before waiting for Susan Farmer to arrive to help with the rest.

On arriving, Steph rushed inside to survey her new place. Carrie could see a young; pimply faced boy of about fourteen disentangling his long legs from the back seat.

"Good heavens, Steph, you haven't found us a flat mate already."

Stephanie wrinkled her nose in disgust. "Don't be stupid, Carrie. That's my cousin Jason. He's come to help. My Auntie Kate lives up in

Moruya, she's a doctor there and Jason is staying with us for the school holidays."

Jason walked up carrying a carton of crockery.

"Where do you want this?" he sort of muttered.

"Jase, this is my friend Carrie, just put the box in the kitchen please."

Jason nodded to Carrie and the back of his neck flushed bright red right up to his ears.

"He's pretty shy," explained Stephanie as Jason walked inside.

"He never mixes much, his father is dead and his mother works horrendous hours. He usually spends the school holidays with us. Auntie Kate is trying to get a new wing on her hospital and he gets left alone a lot. Uncle James was killed in the war, I never knew him. It's a family secret but he was never married to my Aunt Kate. Jason and I have been like brother and sister although he's pretty shy around anyone else.

Just then Susan Farmer came bustling in laden up with goodies.

"Hello, Carrie, isn't this exciting, your first step into independence. Now I've made a tuna casserole for your tea, pop it in the oven about half an hour before you want it, oven on about 350 degrees. There's cake in the blue container and biscuits in the yellow. Tea and coffee in the red plastic bowl and I'll send Jason to the shop for milk."

Carrie and Stephanie clutched one and another in mirth.

"Mum, I thought you just said we are being independent," Stephanie cajoled.

"Sorry, love, I just wanted everything to be nice for you. Now let's get started on some unpacking."

They got their few belongings stowed away and Susan made them their first cup of tea in their new house. They made a toast to their future and raised their assortment of chipped coffee mugs in a salute.

As her parents left, Stephanie tried to disguise the fact a tear was running down her cheek. Her mother sniffed loudly as she hurried to the car waving as they went. They walked around inspecting their little haven both feeling as if they were in heaven.

"Gee, Carrie, I never dreamed mum would let me leave home at eighteen. I love her dearly but she does smother me a bit being an only child. Now we can stay up as late as we like and go out when we feel like it. It's going to be wonderful." Stephanie hugged her knees excitedly. "Freedom from home and all those boys at Uni."

"That's a low priority, Stephanie. Get your degree and then worry about boys."

"I will but we don't have to be hermits do we?"

"I guess not. As long as we get our assignments done and in on time I suppose we can have a little fun."

Steph placed a book on the coffee table. "What are you going to do after Uni?"

"I'm going to become a journalist. I thought I told you that."

"Like your father?"

"Not like my father. He's almost a stranger to me."

"But he's pretty famous. Isn't it exciting having a famous father?"

"I'd rather have had a father who was home once in a while."

"I'm going to be a schoolteacher, then I might be able to do exchange teaching in England or somewhere like that."

"Let's get our degrees first, Stephanie, then we can think about foreign ports."

"A girl can wish can't she?"

Chapter Twenty

Australia 1975

Soo Ling had never driven a car before. After the pilot had flown off into the blue sky, she studied the dashboard in wonderment. She'd been in taxis and sort of watched what they did, surely it couldn't be too difficult. Turning the key the car gave a lurch and stopped. Her little feet jumped from pedal to pedal as she thought she had noticed the men doing. The next effort proved slightly better managing to jump along a few yards. Eventually she found neutral, kept the engine going and crawled to the roadway in first gear. With no idea about gears Soo Ling just kept steering.

There was no other traffic on the quiet back road so she inched her way into Darwin at ten miles an hour. It was probably just as well that she didn't know how to change gears. She made the trip all the way in first gear not risking the car to stall. Any faster and she would never have been able to stop. The dirt track led to a bitumen road and she followed the sign that read Darwin. After twenty minutes she could see the town in the distant. Only one car passed her going in the opposite direction and Soo Ling was glad it was not busy Saigon.

As it was, she just sort of ran into some shrubbery and as the town was in the near distance she left the car there and walked. Her first priority would be getting Australian currency, but was sure presenting $500,000 American dollars at the bank was not a good idea. Removing $1000 from her hoard she nervously entered the bank to join the short queue of people. When it was her turn she placed her thousand dollars on the counter.

"Please. Could have Australian money?"

The teller looked at her, then the money. "That's a lot of money, how would you like it?"

"Must go to Sydney, meet husband."

"I see. Do you have any identification?" He was a little suspicious and expected Soo Ling to tell him to mind his own business. Not many young girls entered the bank with one thousand American dollars.

Soo Ling handed over the fake passport. This was the first test and she held her breath. He looked at it, then her.

"You're married to an Australian?"

"Yes. We marry two years. I Australian now."

"Of course. Congratulations. What denominations do you want your money in, Mrs. Sanderson?"

"Don't know. Just give please."

The teller counted out the money in fifty and twenty dollar bills.

"Must go Sydney now. Where airport please?"

The teller gave her instructions and watched her leave. She could guess what he was thinking. Poor bugger. Must have got out just in time. Certainly pretty. Just as well she was married to an Australian or she might never been able to leave.

Soo Ling knew she could not board the plane with the gun in her luggage so she strolled casually around town looking for a place to dispose of it. Before long she found herself at the harbor side. Walking along the pier she passed some fishermen engrossed in their hooks and bait, sitting on their creels talking animatedly while sipping a beer from a bottle each held. They took no notice of the pretty little Asian woman walking by. Sitting on the edge of the pier, she glanced around furtively and took the gun, wiping it clean before dropping it into the deep water. After it had sunk she sat for a minute or two so as not to raise any glances, then stood and sauntered back the way she had come, smiling sweetly at the two old men as she passed.

It only took her a few minutes to find the airport and purchase a ticket to Sydney, but then had a frustrating three hours to wait for her flight. It was dark when she arrived and the lights of Sydney sparkled like jewels against the dark sky. The only baggage she had was the knapsack with the money and heroin in it, covered by the green dress and a few cosmetics. No way was that leaving her sight and she clutched it to her all the way, refusing when the flight attendant offered to stow it overhead.

A taxi trip into the city was uneventful, then to the nearest motel to shelter for the night. Making herself coffee the next morning she then paid her bill and went to shop for some western clothes. The hustle and bustle of the busy place amazed her.

It was nothing like Saigon. Cars and buses traveled fast along the narrow streets. There were not as many people but they were all hurrying faster than they did back home.

The harbor was busy with ferries going back and forth. People seemed to rush everywhere. The size of the bridge and the volume of traffic on it astounded her.

Several buskers at Circular Quay plied their trade and the plaintive strains of the hit song Blowing in the Wind saddened her. She ate lunch on an empty park bench pondering her next move. Perhaps she should go into one of the big banks and take a safety deposit box for the money and the heroin, then find somewhere to live.

Finding a bank was easy and soon the safety deposit box was rented. Soo Ling felt a bit like an alien on a strange planet. She began to wonder if maybe she hadn't been too hasty in coming to Australia. The people seemed strange, the food had no flavor, she had no friends and was very frightened at night, although now she had her money and heroin safely tucked away in the bank she felt better.

Maybe she should have gone to Korea instead or somewhere she felt more comfortable among other Asians if not Vietnamese. She watched as two little Asian children ran playing on the grass and listened to their laughter. They looked happy and contented. It was a few minutes before she realized they were Vietnamese children and she looked around as she heard a woman calling them.

They had Vietnamese names and eagerly Soo Ling jumped to her feet and walked toward them. She spoke to the little girl in Vietnamese and the children ran to their mother.

Soo Ling approached the woman and spoke apologetically. It was such a relief to hear a familiar language and ask a few questions about this strange new country.

Soo Ling learned the family had been in Australia three years and were running a food store in a place called Cabramatta.

"You new in Sydney?" the woman asked.

"Yes. All alone. Know no one."

"Many Vietnamese people here. You want me to show you where?"

Soo Ling nodded, grateful to speak with someone from home.

"You come with us. I take you to Cabramatta. You meet many people. You have money?"

"Not much," said Soo Ling coyly.

"No matter. We help you find room and job. Man in restaurant need help. You come." She gathered her picnic basket and called her children, then set off for home.

Soo Ling accompanied them to Cabramatta where they found her a cheap room to rent and a job. The room was very basic, one of five rented out to other Vietnamese but Soo Ling found it comfortable for her needs. When she was more familiar with the area she could always find something better. Although she didn't need to work it would help in familiarizing herself with the surroundings and the people.

Working such long hours in the restaurant didn't please her but she needed to find her way in this new place and make sure she was not found out as an illegal immigrant before she looked for an outlet for her heroin.

Grateful to be safe, she went shopping and bought herself some items in thanks for her deliverance. That night she lit a candle and burnt incense. Soo Ling dressed herself in the green dress and knelt where she had arranged a small statue of Buddha placed alongside a small prayer flag and prayed.

I respect the teachings of Buddha,

May all beings be filled with joy and peace,

Let no one deceive another,

Let no one out of anger or resentment wish suffering on anyone at all,

I vow to practice mind, breathing and smiling looking deeply into things,

I vow to offer joy to my husband who saved my life,

I vow to relieve the grief I caused to his trust,

May the Buddha support my effort.

After three months she was quite happy with her new life, although still not one to work hard, she knew it was not for much longer as she was constantly learning more and more about the drug trade.

Daily she noticed the way the pushers hung around corners and customers approached them. Soo Ling had seen the exchange between them knowing each one had certain territory. This type of trade really didn't interest her; she had bigger things in mind but wanted all the facts first.

One young pusher near her rooming house interested her with his friendliness, always greeting the elders respectfully and playfully talking to the children. Eventually Soo Ling approached him one morning.

"If I have heroin, who I sell to?"

"I'm sorry, this is my corner." The man was polite but firm.

He was quite open about his work. He looked about twenty, very slim with pock marked skin and several tattoos on his hands. There was no trace of an accent; he was either born here or had been here since he was very young,

"No want to sell on street. Who I must see?"

"If you don't want to sell on the street, you must have a fair amount."

"Have one kilogram pure grade."

"Wow! You're talking about a $500000 street value. Can you give me a sample? Maybe I know someone who can help. If I can help I'll expect $1000 commission."

"I bring one gram tomorrow. You bring man to buy?"

"Can you bring it tomorrow at noon? Just sit on the bench and wait."

Soo Ling nodded. If it was worth five hundred thousand on the street then her profit would be at least half of that."

Next day at the appointed time Soo Ling sat as instructed. It was a pleasant day but grey clouds were gathering. People were going about their business. A Chinese man already seated there kept his face averted. He was throwing bread to the pigeons who were fighting each other for the tit bits. He spoke softly looking straight ahead.

"Are you the girl with something for sale?"

"Yes," said Soo Ling keeping her eyes down playing along with his game.

"Put the sample in my newspaper. I'll be here same time tomorrow."

Soo Ling placed the small plastic envelope with a gram of pure heroin into the opened newspaper. He stood and left without a backward glance. That night Soo Ling hardly slept. If this deal worked out she would be very rich. The American dollars in her safety deposit box would need to be converted. If they paid in Australian dollars there would be no rush, as she would have working capital available. The American dollars could be changed gradually without raising suspicion.

Soo Ling went in search of the young man who had set up the deal. If all went well she would like to show her appreciation to him for his trouble. He really interested her, maybe it was because she missed her family and he reminded her of her days back home. Afternoon trade was a bit slow, probably due to the steady rain that had begun with little warning. He was sitting in the corner deli having a late lunch. The shop was crowded with people sheltering from the drizzle, the windows fogged up by the crowd's breath. Soo Ling didn't notice him at first.

Pushing her way to the counter she ordered a cappuccino and a muffin, then looked for a space to sit down.

There was one seat at the window table and as she worked her way over, she almost tipped her drink down the front of the young man she had been searching for. He smiled broadly as he recognized her and found a chair to drag up beside him.

"You met the man I sent?"

Soo Ling nodded. "I gave him sample. Said to come back tomorrow."

"Great. Don't forget my commission if the deal goes through."

"Soo Ling not forget. What is you name?"

"Timothy Ng. I've lived here for seventeen years. We came when I was five. You're new to Sydney?"

"Yes. Escape from Saigon. Husband still in Vietnam. He Australian."

"Then he must be worried about you."

"Not worry. We no longer live together. You live near?"

He told her yes and she was surprised to find he lived two blocks away in a basement apartment. They had an instant rapport and chattered like old friends.

He told her about his first years in Australia, how his parents had fled Vietnam when he was only five. His mother never settled here as she had left two older children behind so she had returned to Vietnam when Timothy was ten. His father had remarried and gone to Queensland so he had pretty much looked after himself for years. He fell into drug pushing before he left school and now had quite a good income. Soo Ling learned the man who was interested in buying her goods was a Mr Wang from Kowloon. Very rich, he had a big hold on the drug trade in this area. It was well known he was a fair man to deal with so long as you did the right thing by him. Cross him and people were known to never be heard of again. They sat talking for ages while the rain continually fell and the crowd continued to fill the little deli's capacity. Soo Ling had to force herself to leave in order to get to the restaurant in time to start her shift. She agreed to meet Timothy again tomorrow after her deal with Mr. Wang had gone through.

Next day she waited on the same bench at noon. This time a middle aged very well dressed Chinese man arrived.

"You man who buy from me?"

"My name is Mr Wang and you are?"

"Me Soo Ling."

"Well, Soo Ling, maybe we can do business. I believe you have 1kg. pure."

"Yes."

"We'll pay you $200000. Australian."

Soo Ling laughed. "You think because I woman I not know about heroin."

"How much did you have in mind?"

"$400000."

"That's too much my, dear. We will go to $300000."

"$3500000 and we have deal."

He realized he was not dealing with an amateur here. "Okay but if the goods are not pure my dear you will finish up in the harbor feeding the sharks."

"You bring money tomorrow, I take you to heroin."

He nodded agreeably and walked away quickly. Soo Ling slept well that night once again giving her thanks to Buddha.

Mr. Wang was already waiting with his briefcase when Soo Ling arrived at the appointed time.

"Good morning my, dear, do you have the goods with you?"

"I get if money okay."

"Then I bow to your request, the next move is yours."

Soo Ling allowed him to accompany her to the bank where she requested entrée to her safety deposit box.

The Chinese gentleman was obviously familiar with the etiquette of safety deposit box procedure and stood politely back in the small antechamber while Soo Ling accessed her box privately. Removing one of her bags of heroin, she slipped the box back into place and walked the few steps to Mr. Wang.

Fingering the parcel lovingly he slipped the seal and dipped one gold ringed finger in and tasted his purchase. Satisfied it was pure he passed across the briefcase to enable Soo Ling to count her earnings. With both parties happy with the transaction Mr. Wang shook hands with Soo Ling, a gesture not often offered to women in his world.

"I pray we shall both have good joss. Perhaps we can do business again one day. Goodbye my, dear."

Making sure there were no bank staff in viewing range, Soo Ling returned to her safety box where she tenderly stacked the new pile of money safely beside her existing fortune. At the last minute she removed $1000 for Timothy's commission. Patting the three remaining packets of white powder she smiled inwardly and thanked the mighty Buddha and Tully Sanderson for the good joss she was experiencing and asked it might continue.

*   *   *

Stephanie's range of escapades had always amused Carrie but she had to admit the one suggesting they share a house together was nothing short of brilliant. They were having the time of their lives. It was so good to be responsible for their own decisions do their own cooking and washing. It brought a maturity both reveled in. They still kept close contact with their families and the freedom of being independent was not as daunting as she had first thought it would be.

The first time Tully came to visit toward the end of the first year, Carrie thought Stephanie would pee her pants with excitement just meeting the well-known journalist.

Tully was at his charming best and brought them a huge indoor palm as a housewarming gift. Stephanie beamed as if he had given her the crown jewels. Carrie was stunned by the thought of him suddenly raised to movie star status by Stephanie who was equally stunned Carrie wasn't excited by his visit.

"He's so handsome, Carrie, and charming. You're so lucky having a father like him."

"He drinks too much and I've heard he's a womanizer. He's hardly ever been home all my life. I've only seen him two or three times a year. I'd swap fathers with you in a second."

"I can't really blame him for womanizing, after all, he had no woman waiting at home and he's very attractive," said Stephanie. 'I'd go to bed with him myself if he asked me."

"Stephanie! This is my father you're talking about."

"Just joking but he is a spunk isn't he?"

"Depends on the definition, anyway we won't see him for at least another six months."

"I'll look forward to it."

Halfway through their second year they discovered sex. A law student named Greg Slater smote Stephanie. He had been sitting next to her during lectures most of the semester, and then out of the blue he invited her for coffee. Before long they were considered an item.

Steph. always felt a tinge of guilt going out without Carrie who always assured her she had study to do. It was the end of term dance and Stephanie insisted Greg find a friend for Carrie. The night of the dance he arrived with his roommate, Warren Kincaid who was studying Veterinary science.

Carrie quite liked him although she felt like she was talking to the top of his head when speaking to him. To please her friend she kept her opinions to herself. They had a very enjoyable night and went back to the girl's place for coffee afterwards. It was arranged to go on a picnic the next day.

Warren was the one with the car, an orange Volkswagen.

His father was a doctor and Warren received a bigger allowance than the others so he was the only one able to afford the running costs of a car. They packed their picnic basket with the carefully prepared sandwiches, drinks and fruit into the boot and headed to Rose Bay for the day. It was a sunny, mild sort of day, definitely better than the previous few and hopefully they might even get to wade along the edge of the water.

There were a few people around sharing their picnic area but they had a thoroughly enjoyable time and Carrie found Warren to be a great companion feeling very relaxed in his company. Stephanie and Greg lay on the blanket soaking up the feeble rays of sun while Carrie and Warren wandered along the shore scrambling over rocks and watching the little crabs and other creatures caught in the many rock pools. Stephanie and Greg were cuddling and kissing on the rug when the other two returned so Carrie suggested rock climbing a bit longer to give the lovers some privacy.

That night as the girls lay companionably on the lounge divan Stephanie confided she thought she was falling in love. Carrie was thrilled for her friend as she really liked Greg and thought they made an ideal couple.

"Wouldn't it be great if you and Warren fell in love and we could have a double wedding."

"I think you might be jumping the gun a little, Steph." Carrie really didn't think Warren would turn out to be the love of her life.

"Carrie, would you think I was cheap if I told you Greg wants to go to bed with me?"

"Good grief, Steph. I think that's between the two of you. If you feel its right then do it?"

"Have you ever done it?"

"No. The Nuns always taught us it was a sin, so I've never been game."

"I wonder what it's like?"

"It's been going on for years so it must be okay."

They both rolled around laughing at that.

"Susan Watson who was in my form in high school tried it in year 10. She said it hurt at first."

"If you do decide to do it make sure Greg has some protection, you don't want to end up pregnant."

"My God, how would I ever tell mum and dad, they'd kill me? Perhaps I could sneak up to Moruya and get Auntie Kate to give me an abortion."

Carrie gave her friend a playful slap. "You really are shameful, Stephanie Farmer. If Aunt Vera knew I was living with a house mate with such loose morals she'd make me move back home."

The four of them became known as 'the four mouseketeers' as they went everywhere together and were always leaning on one another laughing or lolling on the lawns studying. That's if they weren't racing around in the 'orange terror', as Warren's little Volkswagen had become known.

Toward the end of October Stephanie seemed withdrawn and Carrie couldn't understand what was wrong.

It was very out of character and Carrie was worried about her. After dinner one night when they were alone studying she couldn't stand it any longer.

"Steph. Please tell me what's worrying you. I've never known you to be so quiet."

"Sorry, Carrie, it's nothing you've done. It's Greg; he's really putting the pressure on me to go to bed. I want to but I'm still a bit scared."

"Have you told this to Greg?"

"Yes. He's very understanding and he's already bought condoms cos. he knows that's my big worry."

"Well my friend, if he has the goods and you both want it I reckon you should go for it before the rubber perishes."

"You really are incorrigible but thanks, when you put it that way it sounds like a good idea. I'd better set up a romantic evening and see what happens."

"Hey, why not this Friday. Warren is taking me to the movies. The grand is showing Gone with the Wind again and would you believe, he hasn't seen it. We won't be home for hours so you can seduce Mr Slater at your leisure"

"Oh, Carrie, what a great idea, thanks, I'll get a chicken and cook a roast and what about you making your wine trifle. That should really seal it."

Warren was only too happy to take Carrie for a Chinese meal before the movie. He knew what Greg had in mind for the evening so agreed with Carrie they would stay away.

It was a very long movie and Carrie cried as she had done the previous four times she had seen it. Warren held her hand to comfort her and on the walk back to the car put his arm protectively around her.

"It was a great movie and I'm glad I waited to see it until I had you to take me."

"Thanks, Warren, that's a lovely thing to say. I'm glad you enjoyed it."

Halfway home he stopped the car on the edge of Hyde Park.

"Do you think we should stay longer? Maybe the seducing isn't finished yet."

"Gosh, I never thought of that. Perhaps we should just sit here and listen to the radio for a while."

Warren turned the radio to the all night station where they were having a phone in for lovers program. Every song they played had a romantic theme and before she knew what was happening, Warren had taken her in his arms and kissed her tenderly. She responded with a fervor that surprised both of them.

Before either could size up the situation and think sensibly, they were in the back seat and removing each other's lower clothing with a speed unheard of in a Volkswagen. Warren entered her as gently as he could in the confined space and it was over in the space of minutes.

They lay locked together in embarrassment.

Finally Warren stammered. "My God, what have we done?"

"Don't worry, Warren, it's as much my fault as yours."

"We didn't even wait to buy protection, what if you get pregnant."

"Well I guess we'll just have to do a lot of praying for the rest of the month."

Dragging her clothes on almost as quickly as he had dragged them off she said. "Let's get out of here, I'm sure we can go home now."

Warren dropped her at the front door and drove off in a cloud of dust. Stephanie was still up when Carrie walked in. Almost throwing herself at her friend she twirled her round and round.

"Oh, Carrie, it was wonderful, you couldn't believe how wonderful Greg is. He was so loving and considerate. I love him so much, I'm sure it was the wine trifle. I'm so happy; you can't believe how great sex is. I can't wait for you to try it."

"I have."

Stephanie stopped dead in her tracks.

"You what? When? you sneaky thing, you never told me."

"I haven't had a chance, it just happened now in Hyde Park."

"Wow, isn't that great, we both lost our virginity on the same night. Does this mean you and Warren are an item?"

"No, Steph. I just made the greatest mistake of my life. I don't think of Warren like that. We're like brother and sister; we've never had those sort of feelings for each other. We just enjoy being together and doing goofy things. How am I ever going to face him tomorrow?"

She flopped down on the divan holding her head in her hands. "I feel so foolish, I think Warren feels the same way. He drove off as if the Devil himself was after him."

"Really, Carrie, I'm sure it isn't that bad. Maybe you'll find you both really love one another after all."

"No way. We're good friends and that's all. Anyway, enough of me tell me about your night. I gather it was successful."

Stephanie chatted on and on relaying every detail about the meal and how tender Greg was toward her. Carrie was happy for her friend and kept a smile forced on her lips. There was no way she could burst Stephanie's bubble by telling her Warren had not used a condom. Next morning the phone woke Carrie from her fitful sleep. It was Warren.

"Hi."

"Hi." She waited but there was a decidedly long pause.

"How are you?"

"Fine, how are you?"

"Look, I don't know how to say this."

"Then don't. I know what you're thinking. We made a mistake so let's put it behind us and forget it."

"Can we do that?"

"Sure we can if we agree never to mention it again."

"That sounds great, but what if…?"

"Well let's both pray and hope. I'll keep you posted."

"Okay. Want to all go to the footy today?"

"I think we both have too much study thanks anyway."

"All right, we really need to study too, exams are not too far away. How about we bring a pizza over for lunch tomorrow?"

"That's a great idea, see you then."

When the boys walked in the next day there was a minute where Carrie and Warren felt awkward, then suddenly they slipped back to the way it was before the sex experiment and life resumed its 'four mouseketeer' status again.

* * *

The final exams came and went and Carrie sat back confident she had done as well as she could.

"Finished," she said with a satisfied smile on her face.

"And now a new life begins." Stephanie was as satisfied as Carrie was. "Let's get Greg and Warren to take us to one of the clubs to celebrate. They've got years to their finals but they'll be happy to celebrate with us."

They booked a table for the Saturday night and when they arrived at the club, Stephanie waved to two people already seated.

"Who are they?" asked Carrie as they approached.

"You remember my cousin Jason, he's just done his first year and he rang to tell me so I invited him too."

This couldn't be the pimply-faced boy from three years ago. He was tall, fair, broad shouldered and athletic looking. He was also rather good-looking. No longer a shy little boy.

"Hi, Jason, you remember Carrie don't you. This is Greg Slater and Warren Kincaid."

Jason smiled warmly at them, shook hands with the boys and then introduced Teena, a small attractive dark hair girl who was engrossed with some exotic cocktail.

The evening went well and everyone mixed sociably. Greg and Stephanie had danced every dance. It seemed they just wanted to be in each other's arms. Carrie was worn out and she sat with Jason while Warren whisked Teena across the dance floor.

"You've certainly changed, Jason. I hardly recognized you. You were only young when I first met you and---"

"I was a useless dork," he flashed his white even teeth in a dazzling smile.

"I was going to say shy but I can see that's changed."

"Yes, thankfully I grew up a bit. You four all get along together, did you meet at Uni.?"

"Yes, Greg is doing law and Warren is going to be a Vet. What's Teena studying? She's very pretty. Are you two serious?"

His white teeth flashed as he laughed. "Let's just say we help each other out when we have to study anatomy. My best subject at the moment."

"She looks like she enjoys it too. I gather you're doing medicine."

"Yeah. I want to be a surgeon like my father."

"I heard your father died before you were born."

"He did. He died in Vietnam."

"I'm sorry. How did he die or would you rather not talk about it?'

"It's okay, you won't believe it but he died of a burst appendix. Just after he arrived he was at some remote post and his appendix burst. They couldn't get him back because the weather closed in and he died of blood poisoning."

"How bizarre for a doctor. Your mother meet him in Vietnam?"

"No. She met him while she was an intern with the army. He went to Vietnam and she volunteered to be with him. He was dead a month after she got there."

"How awful. Were they married long?"

His green eyes danced with amusement. "I hate to tell you this but I'm a bastard----literally, that is they were never married. His surname was Sutton but mine is Armitage."

Carrie burst out laughing. "Would you believe I'm a bastard too in the literal sense. My mother died in Ireland just after I was born. Dad never talks about her. Looks like we're both in the same boat."

He held his arm to his face in mock horror. "How can we ever face the world?"

Carrie laughed at his humor. "You've grown into a very nice person, Jason. I'm glad we met again."

"Me too. What are your plans now?"

"I haven't told Stephanie yet but I've got an interview for a job as a journalist with my father's paper."

"I hear he's quite famous isn't he?"

"Sort of. Stephanie tells me your mother is trying to raise money for a new wing at her local hospital."

"She's been doing that for years. She's a great doctor and the world's best mum. You must meet her one day."

"I'd like that." The music finished and the others returned to the table. More drinks were ordered and everyone was talking and laughing. Carrie had no further chance to learn more of Jason's life.

Exam results came out a month later and both Carrie and Stephanie where rapt.

"We passed, we passed," screamed Stephanie dancing around the room.

"Three years of hard work over. Now we can let our hair down."

"I thought we did that a long time ago."

Carrie thought that rather droll, one try of both sex and grass was the extent of her sinfulness in their decadent lives. Both were failures best put behind her.

Graduation night was a disappointment for Carrie. She looked hopefully down the auditorium for her father hoping he would be there for the proudest night of her life.

Vera was there of course but the only message she received from Tully was a card which read, somewhere in Bosnia, wish I could be there. Congratulations.

Stephanie was still excited the next day. "Mum rang and she wants to have a barbecue on Sunday as a celebration. You'll come won't you?"

"What, miss out on a free feed? Of course I'll be there."

"Bring any friends you want, especially Aunt Vera."

"We'll be there with all guns firing."

Sunday was a beautiful day, not a cloud in the sky, no wind and best of all no flies. Sam Farmer's back lawn was the perfect place and Carrie was astonished at the number of people present. Stephanie's mum Susan welcomed her and Aunt Vera, and Susan and Vera were soon lost in conversation leaving Carrie to mingle. She was surprised to see Jason, this time without Teena and he greeted her like a long lost friend.

Jason handed her a drink and the delicious smell of the cooking meat, expertly handled by Stephanie's father, swept across the lawn making Carrie hungry.

A striking looking woman walked towards them and slipped her arm around Jason's waist. She was tall, fair and had the greenest eyes Carrie had ever seen.

"There you are, Darling. I thought you'd left."

"Hi, Mum." He turned to face her. "Have you met Stephanie's housemate?

"No I haven't," she said offering her hand.

"Meet Carrie Sanderson."

"Pleased to meet you, Doctor Armitage, I've heard a lot about you." As she offered her hand she thought there was a strange reflection in Jason's mother's beautiful eyes. Was it jealousy, did she think she had a rival for her son's affections?

"Please, call me Kate, Carrie. I'd never heard Jason mention you, have you known him long?"

"Actually he helped us move into our house years ago and I'd not seen him again until last week."

"I see. Congratulations on your results. What are you going to do now?"

"Well I hope to be a journalist."

"Carrie Sanderson, you wouldn't be related to Tully Sanderson would you?"

"Guilty. Do you know him?"

"I used to read his stories when I was in Vietnam. Some of them were very good." All of a sudden she seemed interested in Tully Sanderson.

"Well he does have a way with words."

"Is he well?" Kate asked suddenly.

"He's a strange person my dad. He always seems bright, but then seems to drop into a depression for no apparent reason. Probably due to the wars he's seen. Apart from that he keeps good health."

"He never married?" It was an unexpected question from someone she had only met.

"He says who would have him. Thinks he'd be a disaster as a husband. Someone told him that once and he believed it."

Kate sipped her drink contemplating Carrie's words.

"And you're going into journalism too?"

"Yes. I start work at the Sydney Tribune next week."

"Then good luck, Carrie. It's very nice to have met you."

She walked away to mingle with the crowd.

"She's rather beautiful, Jason. How come she hasn't married?"

"Says' she hasn't time for men. Too busy with her practice and charity work. I think a husband would do her the world of good sometimes. Shall we get some food?"

Carrie nodded, the smell tingled her nostrils. She spent a few more hours there enjoying the family life and being with her dear Aunt Vera again.

Soaking up the sun she had more than her share of food and drink. When they left Susan insisted they take half of the leftovers with them for tomorrow. It had been a wonderful day and she fell into bed that night happy and exhausted.

Chapter Twenty One

Carrie had worked at the Tribune for twelve months, the most exciting twelve months of her life. When Tully first heard she'd been employed, part of him was pleased but part was unsure. He felt Carrie had traded on his name to get the job, which she had, but he had the good grace to wish her luck in her chosen career. It had been an interesting twelve months and Carrie had been eager to learn as much as she could. She quickly showed the persistence of her father in hunting down stories and her stoicism impressed her editor.

When she approached Richard Harding with her proposition she thought he would turn purple.

"I know I'm young, Richard but how about letting me go overseas as your foreign correspondent like dad did."

"You must be kidding."

"I'm deadly serious. I want to see something of the world and be an even better journalist than my father."

"There's good money to be earned here, Carrie, better you stay at home."

"But there's not the experience. You gave my father his chance when he was even younger than I am."

"That's true. I see you've also inherited his nagging ability, besides you're a girl."

"This is not a sexist paper is it? You'd keep me here because I'm female?"

"You know better than that."

"Then let me do it. Please, Richard, you know I can."

Harding sat back and stared at her. Tully had been giving him a hard time for years. Always arguing, always wanting to do it differently and it seemed his daughter was just the same. He had to admit having the country's ace reporter on staff hadn't hindered the circulation at all. Of course it had cost him plenty to hold Tully, but he was certainly worth it.

In the twenty odd years he had worked for him, he had brought in some terrific stories for which the paper had won many awards. He'd been to almost every point of conflict on the globe. Maybe his daughter was made of the same stuff. He had a perverse thought, revenge for the hard time Tully had given him over the years.

He could see Tully's face when he heard the news. No he wouldn't tell him, he'd just leave it as a surprise. He liked Tully immensely but it was a gesture he couldn't let pass.

"Tell you what, Carrie. I'll send you to Bosnia with certain conditions."

"Great, Richard. I'll do anything."

"You haven't heard the conditions yet."

She waited expectantly.

"The conditions are you work side by side with your father, but follow his instructions. Where he goes you go unless of course it's not safe. I'll inform him I'm sending a young reporter who needs to learn the ropes and he has to baby sit you as he covers the war. That way you'll have our most experienced reporter with you and he may not take the risks he normally does."

"That's it?" Carrie was a little dubious about working with her father. She knew he'd be far from pleased when she turned up in Bosnia.

"That's it. Agreed?"

"When do I leave?"

"Next week. Tidy up anything you're working on, make sure your passport is valid and I'll make the arrangements about the plane."

Carrie jumped up to leave.

"Carrie. It's dangerous over there, not like Australia. Please be careful and don't take unnecessary risks."

"I don't have a death wish like dad. Don't worry and thanks, boss."

As she left he wondered if he'd done the right thing. Nevertheless if she wanted to be a top journalist she had to learn the hard way, just as her father had.

*　　*　　*

Kate watched her son lovingly as he pushed his food around the plate. It was obvious his mind was on other things.

"Girl trouble?" She tried to keep the inquisitive tone from her voice.

"What?"

"I said have you got girl trouble. You've been playing with your food for ten minutes. Remember you only have an hour before you go back to begin your third year."

"Not girl trouble, Mum. It's something else."

"Care to let me in on the secret?"

He didn't know how to break it gently. She had always been so supportive.

"I'm not going back, at least not now."

"What do you mean not going back? It's always been your dream to become a surgeon."

"It still is but I've deferred my course for a year."

"Why for goodness sake?"

"Look, Mum, once I complete my course I've still got years ahead before I become a surgeon. I'll be thirty something by then. Life will have passed me by and I'll miss out on a chance to see the world."

"You can still travel once you become qualified." Kate was horrified; this was not the son she knew.

"Mum, I want to see it while I'm young. If I don't go now I'll probably marry, have two or three kids and be tied down for the rest of my life. You went to Vietnam didn't you?"

"That was work, not sight seeing. I don't want to hold you back, Jason. I just want you to be happy."

"I don't like disappointing you, Mum but it's something I feel I have to do now."

"I'm not going to be able to talk you out of it am I?" Kate knew her son had his father's determination and once he made up his mind that was it.

"I'll only be away a year. It will fly."

"What part of the world do you want to go to?" She knew the apron strings couldn't stay tied forever.

"I thought I'd back-pack across Europe and learn a bit about the world. I can pick up work here and there so you won't have to support me totally."

"Try England first. At least I'll know you're safe."

"I thought I'd spend a month in London, then head for Europe, how does that sound?"

"Like you've already booked. When do you leave?"

"I fly out with QANTAS next week."

"Then I'll have to take you shopping. You can't go gallivanting around Europe without warm clothing."

Jason saw the tears running down her face and hugged her tightly.

"I'll be fine, Mum, you'll see."

"I know you will but I'll miss you terribly."

"Me too."

A week later Kate watched as he flew off to his date with destiny. She prayed he would come back to her safe and sound.

*　　*　　*

Soo Ling was present the day Timothy was arrested. Her first deal with Mr. Wang had been three months ago and things were going well for her.

After Wang had paid her for her heroin, she quit her job as it had served its purpose. Now she had some money she didn't want to put up with the long hard hours at the restaurant.

The rooming house was still her home, mainly because it was convenient. Each day she spent the morning taking some American dollars in amounts up to $1000 to different banks to exchange for Australian dollars. There were many Vietnamese living here now, all bringing money with them, so all she had to do was keep the amount viable.

With the money from Wang plus what she changed she had no financial worries and still had three kilograms of pure heroin to trade.

Most days she took lunch to share with Timothy. They sat on the nearby bench to eat so if any of his customers were looking for him he was on hand. He was Soo Ling's only friend and his company was all she needed. She found herself more and more attracted to him and rather wondered why he had never asked her to his bed.

The day of the arrest was no different. Soo Ling sat waiting for him and watching the way he was with his customers and everyone else. He had a natural talent for attracting people.

A street sweeper moved down the street towards them as Timothy waved across to her signifying he wouldn't be long. A well-dressed Caucasian girl parked her car and approached Timothy. Soo Ling wondered what such a person was doing in this part of town. It was unusual seeing a white person here, let alone one so well dressed. Soo Ling thought when the white powder controlled the mind, all walks of people would go to any lengths to buy it.

The man beside Soo Ling put down his paper and nonchalantly strolled across the road. The Caucasian girl removed something from her Louis Vuition handbag and then shook hands with Timothy, an act to hide the transaction.

Suddenly Timothy was on the ground with the street sweeper straddling him while the newspaper reader was clamping handcuffs on him. The well-dressed lady customer was reading him his rights.

Soo Ling went to rush to his aid but a quick eye gesture from Timothy sent her in the opposite direction just as they bundled him into the car and sped away.

It was some hours later when Soo Ling gathered enough courage to go to the police station where she was able to bail Timothy for $1000. He grinned at her as they left the police station and she wondered how he could be so cheerful.

"Thanks for getting me out, Soo Ling. I better get back to work, I've missed enough time."

"You want to risk arrest again?"

"Listen to you, your English is getting better. Keep it up and you'll sound like a native. I have to work or I'll starve. It's no problem; I've been arrested before. They just fine me and then I have to work harder to pay the fine."

"How much they fine you?"

"Last time it was three thousand dollars. Maybe they might put me in jail for a while but that doesn't matter."

"Timothy, why not you work for me? I have money now and I need to put it to use. I not know about business so you be manager."

"Hey, Soo Ling, that's a great idea, what sort of business do you mean?"

"That where I need your help. What would you suggest and where you suggest we look for something?"

"Well you could buy a restaurant, after all you have some experience there. If you really want my advice I would buy a massage parlor."

"Soo Ling no can do massage."

"Most massage parlors are just fronts for brothels. They make a bundle, sex is worth a fortune."

"How we know where to buy this brothel?"

"Perhaps we should talk to Mr. Wang, he knows everything and everyone about business deals. He won't be happy to lose me from his organization but if he gets some profit from your deal it might keep him sweet."

"Sweet! What is sweet?"

Timothy laughed at Soo Ling's naivete; she still has a long way to go with her education. "Wang is the head of the local Triad. He is happy when he makes a profit."

Mr. Wang put them in touch with an agent who looked for suitable real estate for them.

He didn't like to lose Timothy but knew he was still available to him through Soo Ling and her business. He had a soft spot for Soo Ling so he was quite comfortable in helping her set up; besides, he didn't see her as a business rival.

Timothy was the best investment Soo Ling ever made. He handled the negotiations with the estate agent and hired a lawyer to check all papers before allowing Soo Ling to sign anything.

He took her to meet interior decorators and together they selected an exquisite range of furnishings to turn their brothel into a thing of beauty and taste.

He helped Soo Ling interview girls and made sure they all knew the rules about honesty and cleanliness. Their motto was, you be fair to us and we'll be fair to you. They all understood the Triad and knew what they could expect if they tried to cheat Soo Ling.

Timothy hired the best security service in town to make sure the premises were well protected.

"Once it becomes known you own a business then every thief in town thinks it's his duty to try to rob you."

She paid him a wage way above anything he could have earned on the streets and so far he was proving to be worth every cent.

Soo Ling insisted Timothy make a room available for himself on the top floor so he could live on hand and have somewhere to go with his private friends if he should care to. She hoped she would be the first private visitor he invited home.

Opening day was drawing near and Timothy called at Soo Ling's rooming house to take her for a last minute inspection.

"Close your eyes," he said then led her the last few yards. He helped her up the two front steps. "Now you can open them."

Her eyes opened wide in delight when she saw the small shiny brass plaque he had had made together with a tastefully designed doorbell. The dainty print announced "Madam Soo."

"Timothy, you great person. I lucky I know you."

Together they inspected her investment room by room. The staff was not beginning until tomorrow and Soo Ling was pleased they were alone as she had plans of seducing her friend and being the first person to anoint her business. They toured the building happy with everything that had been done. If it all ran as smoothly as they hoped, the money would soon be rolling in.

Opening the door to his private room Timothy ushered Soo Ling inside. He was like a child with a new toy.

"I haven't spent much money on my room, Soo Ling, I'm on my own and will be working most of the time so I don't need much."

She slipped off her shoes and felt the beige Ax Minster carpet under her feet, the duck egg blue walls held several Monet prints. The curtains were darker blue velvet and there was just a bed, a chest of drawers and a small table with one chair.

"It very nice."

Soo Ling closed the door behind her and slowly walked towards him.

"Why we no be first customers."

She reached her hand towards him and he stepped back quickly, his mouth falling open.

"Soo Ling, I'm flattered you think about me that way, I really am but I'm sorry, I thought you knew I'm gay."

Soo Ling stopped as if she had walked into a brick wall. Her mouth dropped open, then closed and opened again. No words came out and she turned and fled down the stairs.

Timothy left her alone for a few minutes, he could see she needed to compose herself. Finally he walked to where she was sitting in the lounge room. He could see her eyes were moist with tears.

"Are you all right, Soo Ling?"

"Soo Ling good." She brushed a hand quickly across her tear-streaked cheeks.

"I sorry I make fool of self."

"Don't be silly, let's forget what happened."

"Is okay, now I know you not want to use my girls and no pay money."

They laughed good-naturedly and Timothy assured her he was a definite asset.

Right from opening night the business was a great success. Soo Ling's experience at Chucks gave her an insight to what the customers wanted and she provided it all.

She had Timothy to see the girls did not come to any harm and he proved on more than one occasion his martial art skills were more than enough for any troublemakers. She was a good friend and boss to her girls and they forever seemed to be vying for her praise all anxious to be her favorite. While most of the girls were Asian, there were also others giving the establishment a cosmopolitan touch whereby attracting men of all walks of life.

She went from strength to strength and her bank accounts built up steadily.

Occasionally Mr. Wang called in, always declining Soo Ling's offer of a girl on the house. He just had a couple of drinks, graciously thanked Soo Ling and left. Nothing missed his eyes.

Towards the end of the year, Mr. Wang approached Soo Ling about another purchase of heroin. He had lost a shipment to customs and needed supplies in a hurry. Soo Ling knew she could charge him more than the $500,000 they had agreed on last time as prices had soared over the year, but she wanted to keep Wang on her side. This time Mr. Wang brought the money to Madam Soo's and the transaction was completed in Timothy's small office.

After Wang had left and the money was stashed in the wall safe, Timothy asked Soo Ling what she intended to do with her wealth.

"What you think, I buy new restaurant or another brothel. How you like I have a chain of places."

"I think that's a sensible plan Soo Ling. Madam Soo in every suburb. It would also be wise to invest some of it in the share market. I know a broker who will find you some blue chip shares."

"You make appointment, we go and spend some money. I want to give you $20000 bonus for hard work. You buy shares too yes?"

On the afternoon of the following day Soo Ling and Timothy sat in the office of Watson and Hamilton, stock broking agents. Jeffery Watson was a fatherly gentleman who went out of his way to instruct them on the ways of the stock market. They were only too happy to be guided by him and accepted his advice willingly.

He also suggested Soo Ling put some of her assets in the name of a family member both for tax reasons as well as a possible take over bid. Soo Ling momentarily considered her family but then realized they would never comprehend such vast amounts of money.

Timothy suggested a silent partner to which she agreed and arranged to have 49% of her business put in the name of her husband Tully Sanderson. All profits would go to her with the partner having no voting rights to over ride her. If she died then Tully would inherit it all but she didn't care if that happened. She felt she owed him that much. It amused her to think of a respected journalist like Tully having his name involved in drugs and prostitution. After all, she prayed each night offering thanks to Tully Sanderson for giving her this new life.

Before the week was out her solicitor had drawn up the papers and she had signed. Anyone who tried to take over would now find it exceedingly difficult.

By the end of 1980 Soo Ling estimated her worth was over $5,000,000.

*   *   *

Sarajevo 1992

The NATO jet taxied to a halt and Carrie stepped onto the tarmac. Through the quickly failing light she could see three armored personnel carriers with the UN insignia painted on the sides. Armed men wearing blue helmets stood idly by watching the new arrivals. It appeared even

UN soldiers were not safe albeit in daylight hours at the airport. She noted some buildings carried the scars of isolated shells exploding and the pilot had told her more than once shells had landed on the runways preventing planes from landing or taking off.

She asked directions to her hotel after checking the address on the slip of paper Richard had given her. Another typically cheap place for Journos to stay while they reported the day's events.

"A word of warning, Miss," the tall officer with the clipped English accent said.

"Keep out of sniper alley. He won't care if you're press or some poor Sarajevo citizen; you're just another target. Three or four people have been killed today and that's a good day."

Finally arriving at the hotel she asked the desk clerk for Tully Sanderson. Looking at her cynically, he told her room 103.

"I believe you have a room for me," she said signing his book.

"You're his wife?" He looked at her signature. "Is he in for a surprise," he said as she walked away.

Carrie deposited her luggage in her room. It was simply furnished with a single bed and dresser but at least it had a toilet that worked. She freshened up before going to Tully's room to let him know she was here. Was he going to be more than surprised when he found out who his new sidekick was? His door was ajar and as she could hear voices she walked straight in. Then she was shocked. Through the open bedroom door she could see Tully's naked buttocks going up and down between the thighs of a naked woman who had her legs wound tightly around him.

"Oh, Tully, Tully," the woman moaned as she came to her climax. She gave a little scream matched by Tully's audible sigh as he collapsed over her.

"Tully." The woman could see Carrie over his shoulder.

"What?" Christ, he hoped she didn't want to start again.

"Behind you."

He clutched the sheet and half turned around. His face went white when he saw Carrie.

"Jesus Christ. What are you doing here?" He snatched up a robe from the bed and wrapped it around himself; not caring the woman was still stark naked. She buried herself among the bedding and grabbed the discarded sheet to cover her own naked body.

"Carrie." He walked toward her. "This is Celeste. She's a reporter for the Paris Chronicle. Celeste, this is my daughter Carrie."

"Your daughter." The woman looked even more embarrassed. "I didn't know you were married."

"I'm not but it's a long story. Leave us alone will you, pet. I've got some questions I need to ask my daughter."

She gathered her clothes and made a hasty retreat leaving them alone.

"So have I." Carrie scowled at Celeste's departing back.

When they were alone, they both started together, then Carrie stopped letting him get his questions in first. She watched as he struggled into his trousers.

"What the hell are you doing here?"

"I'm your new sidekick. Didn't Richard tell you?"

"The bastard. All he told me was a cub reporter was coming and to teach him the ropes. No mention of a name."

"He said you'd be surprised."

"Well you can just turn around and go home again. This is a bloody dangerous place and I don't want you here."

"I'm here to learn and I'm not going home, by the way who was that whore?"

"She's not a whore. She's a French reporter who needed a little company. We're both grown people you know. You're not still a virgin are you?"

Carrie blushed knowing if she answered that she would get into an argument with him.

"All right, our sex lives are private but I'm here to stay whether you like it or not."

"You're the last person I expected to see. If you're here to work then you get no favors from me. You do exactly what I tell you."

"That was the deal with Richard. If you can manage to get the rest of your clothes back on you can show me around."

"What's your room number, I'll call you when I've showered."

Half an hour later he knocked loudly on her door.

"Let's go. The first place will be Snipers Alley. Never go there unless it's absolutely necessary. Understand?" He had a scowl on his face and had raised his voice with the last few words.

"Okay, I hear you."

For the rest of the day her father gave her a tour of a city under siege with special emphasis on the street exposed to the sniper fire from the surrounding hills.

"The Serbs are no more than eight hundred meters up there." He pointed to the slopes above the city. Carrie gazed up into the hills surrounding the city.

"If the shells start, find shelter anywhere you can. The UN is giving a press release at three. I'll show you where tomorrow."

They had a quick bite to eat but little was said between them. It was plain Tully was far from pleased she was here. The next day he took her to the meeting place.

Several journalists attended the meeting, which was pretty boring with the same questions being asked and the same evasive answers given.

"Do they ever give any straight answers here?" she asked.

"They only tell you what they want you to hear, that's why not many go to the press release. We prefer to go out and find the truth ourselves."

"Mind filling me in?"

"Jesus, why did I pay all that money for your education? I'm not a bloody history teacher?"

Carrie flushed. She had to admit she knew little about the war. "I've been concentrating on domestic issues back home. I've only read your stories."

"Christ, I'll say this once, then do your own research."

"Thanks." Carrie bit back her anger.

"When Tito died in 1980 the shit started. This country is made up of six republics, Serbia, Croatia, Slovenia, Bosnia, Hercengovina Montenegro and Macedonia. You've got the Serbs and Montenegrins who are Orthodox Christians. Then you've got the Croats who are Roman Catholic and the Bosnia Muslims.

"It's a bloody multiethnic state with no particular group forming a majority. The Serbs are the largest with 36%. Then strongman socialist Slobodan Milosevic took over."

"Then what happened?"

"Slovenia and Croatia wanted to go their own way. Some were oriented to Bosnian Muslims, some to Bosnian Serbs. The Yugoslav People's army took over the Serbian army, halted delivery of weapons and confiscated all weapons held by Slovenia and Croatia. Croatia and Bosnia decided to go their own way but the problem was there were Serbs living in the republics who didn't like that at all."

"So the Socialist Federated Republic of Yugoslavia decided to stop the breakaways," added Carrie.

"Now you've got it. The SFRY purchased a large quantity of weapons from the USSR and transferred them to the illegal Serbian militias in Croatia and Bosnia. When Croatia and Slovenia declared their independence last year, the Yugoslavia People's army called JNA attacked the next day."

"Didn't they fight back?"

"No heavy weapons. It was like throwing stones at artillery. They destroyed a number of villages and put places like Sarajevo under siege. Then the UN imposed an embargo on weapons leaving the Serbs in the box seat. The poor innocents in the towns and villages were caught up in the whole bloody mess. The Serbs began what they called ethnic cleansing."

"Shades of Adolf Hitler." Carrie's understanding was increasing.

"Yeah. Some of the poor Muslims have never seen the inside of a mosque. Some are about as religious as me and can't understand what's going on. They're Muslims because their great grand parents were Muslims but they're suffering because of that."

"And the UN stands back and watches?"

"All political. The UN countries couldn't agree on the best day to go swimming. It's a bloody mess."

"So what do we do?"

"Report my, sweet. Nothing else and remember, you do what I tell you."

"You're the boss."

"And don't you ever forget it," said Tully aggressively.

Carrie sighed. It was not going to be easy working with her father.

Chapter Twenty Two

London was everything Jason had expected it to be. The excitement, the vitality of a big city made his heart beat stronger. This is what he came to see. A culture foreign to him, a place reeking with history. Names of places mentioned only in history books.

Booking into a cheap backpacker's hotel he spent a full week just taking in the sights. The changing of the guard, the Tower of London, St Paul's Cathedral, the river Thames and all the other historical places he had read about. Finding work in a pub he spent a month then began to travel around the countryside of England, Scotland and Wales. Trudy was a Canadian girl doing the same thing. Meeting in Edinburgh and again in Wales they hit it off straight away. After a quiet lunch together Trudy presented Jason with an idea.

"How about we travel together for a while, Jason? We seem to be heading in the same direction. We could share food and rooms which would make things a lot cheaper for us both."

Jason looked at her and could see Trudy was not much younger than he was, and although he couldn't call her beautiful, she was pretty enough and had a great personality. He found her company refreshing and stimulating. Obvious she was well educated, as she seemed very knowledgeable about history and the world.

It wasn't a hard decision to make and together they enjoyed a close friendship as they traveled around Europe. Jason's Sir Galahad approach made him feel it wasn't safe for a young girl to travel around foreign countries alone. The dangers of rape or assault were all too apparent so he was pleased to accompany her. Like a dutiful son he rang his mother at least once a fortnight and they enjoyed the sound of each other's voice. Kate wanted to know where he'd been, what he'd seen, the people he'd met and everything else, just to hear his voice. Telling her about Trudy, she seemed pleased he had a companion in his travels.

"Do you have any family, Jason?" asked Trudy one day.

"Just mum. She's a doctor, my dad's dead."

"That's too bad. My parents are divorced. Dad runs a bank in Quebec and Mum is still looking for her fourth husband." Trudy laughed as though multiple marriage was the expected norm. When they were in Germany she asked him for a loan. He exchanged a $100 traveler cheque at Stuttgart and lent her the equivalent of $50.

Stuttgart's back packer hostel was full so they hiked the few miles to EssLinger where there was a small backpacker hostel. Most of the rooms were taken but as they had shared before it didn't worry either of them. During the night Trudy climbed into his bed awakening him.

"I wanted to thank you for the money. We've been together long enough now, Jason, let's enjoy ourselves a bit."

"Fine by me but I haven't any condoms."

"I come from a long line of boy-scouts. We're always prepared. " She handed him a foil.

Sex or the lack of it hadn't worried him but if the opportunity arose he had no intentions of being a monk. She surprised him with her aggression and innovative ideas and when finally they were ready for sleep, he cast his mind back to Teena and wondered if she and Trudy had had the same sexual instructor.

Sometime through the night he heard her moving around but assumed she was going down the hallway to the toilet. He turned over and went back to sleep muttering don't get cold out there Trudy.

Reaching for her in the morning he found the bed empty. He noticed her clothes were no longer dumped on the floor and her backpack was missing.

Panic hit him making him grab his trousers, fumbling for his wallet only to find it devoid of all cash and travelers cheques. At least she left his cards and passport. There was a note tucked inside saying "Sorry" and he threw it down in disgust. How easily he'd been fooled. What the hell was he going to do now? He'd used up most of the money he'd earned in London. He always kept about $10 in his shoe, he called it his just in case money.

It was enough to pay for the room and coffee with a bread roll. He didn't want to ring his mother and worry her, besides, that would feel as if he was still tied to her apron. Work was the only answer; he would have to try his luck and hoped they spoke English.

There was a queue of young people lined up at the employment agency, a big percentage were backpackers trying to supplement their meager incomes. Taking a number he waited until they called 'number 27'.

The fair-haired Aryan man sitting in a little cubicle, his desk covered with papers and books gestured for him to sit down. Beside him was a heap of maps and files and his name painted in black letters on a small wooden block read 'Heinrich Wagner.'

"What sort of work are you after?" His pen was poised ready above an application form. He appeared anxious to get the interview over as quickly as possible.

"Anything will do. I'm broke and I only want a short term job to get some money."

"I'm afraid there are many others all wanting the same thing. What sort of work did you do in Australia?"

"I was at University but deferred it to see the world."

"Ah. And what course did you do?" The man felt he was getting somewhere at last.

"The first three years of medicine. I'll go back to it when I get home."

Chewing the end of his pen, the interviewer appeared to be thinking hard.

"You know there is little work around here and competition is fierce. I could possibly get you a job for three months; it's a little dangerous? You have the qualifications, in fact you'd be an asset."

"Hmm. Three months is a little longer than I wanted. What sort of work is it?"

"An ambulance driver for the United Nations. Bosnia is desperate for help and with three years of medicine behind you I think you would be useful."

"Isn't there a shooting war going on in Bosnia. Just how dangerous is it?"

"Very dangerous for the civilians, but not very for the United Nation forces. They're purely observers."

Jason was considering his predicament. It could prove to be exciting seeing what was actually going on in the world. Of course his mother wouldn't like it but she'd been through similar conflicts. He decided to take a chance.

"Okay. When do I leave?"

"We have a small bus leaving tomorrow. There are about 10 people going to a variety of jobs. We need to see your passport and then you must fill in these forms." Wagner handed Jason the forms and a pen.

Soo Ling. 1987.

It had been twelve years since she'd left the shores of her homeland. The darkened room she was reminiscing in matched the somber memories racing through her mind. Most nights she gave homage to Buddha and thanks to her husband who delivered her from certain death in her home country. The birthday card given to her by Timothy made her realize just how much she missed her family. Soo Ling looked at the pile of letters returned to her from Vietnam. On several occasions she had tried to contact them without success. All her letters had been returned stating the address could not be found. Not even a picture to look at but they were forever in her mind. Cabramatta had become almost a second Saigon with a continuous stream of refugees joining family and friends already settled in Australia.

Her green dress was worn proudly every year on this day as she sat thinking over her past. Her figure was still slim.

Her beauty had not faded, as she had feared it would back in the days when she worked out in her father's fields. Tully's image forced itself into her brain and she sometimes wondered what he was doing today. His stories in the paper were read with interest and she often contemplated what he would say if he knew she was living in Cabramatta. Shocked, there could be no other reaction.

The chance he had given her of a new life always made her grateful for at times she felt a stab of guilt for using him in the way she had. She'd kept well clear of men since coming to this new land. Apart from the one attempt with Timothy she now felt men were only useful for supplying an endless stream of dollars to her massage parlors. There was also the added bonus of the heroin they bought.

The two kilograms of it still in her safety deposit box was not needed for sale, as her income was more than adequate. She kept it for an emergency fund for the bad times. Now it was looking as though the bad times might be here. She prayed Timothy would come out of this all right.

Her relationship with him had not changed. He had been her most valuable asset since the day she had first met him. He was loyal, honest, a great friend and confident. He had been her personal bodyguard for years now. After they opened their second Madam Soo establishment he suggested it was more than time she bought herself a little house on the waterfront.

As usual he organized things with the agent, lawyer and decorator. Again he insisted she have the latest in security systems, this one having surveillance cameras in every room. Soo Ling didn't want such an elaborate affair but Timothy insisted on the cameras saying she was worth a fortune and still lived alone. He wanted to be sure she and the tasteful range of antiques she had amassed were well protected.

Soo Ling had employed a young Australian man as manager of her second establishment. He was the brother of one of her girls so she did not bother to get Timothy to check out his background.

He was polite and pleasant to the customers and seemed to revere Soo Ling. She often had a late supper with him and then he escorted her safely home. Soo Ling lowered her guard this night inviting him for a nightcap.

Hardly across the doorstep, he produced a razor threatening to slash her pretty face unless she showed him where the safe was. A slim, apparently helpless girl would be no threat and he needed cash to support his habit. He suspected Soo Ling kept large sums of money in her safe, which would allow him to live the life he wanted, probably in another state.

Soo Ling was petrified. His eyes were glazed and staring blankly. It was plain to see he was using heroin, how come she hadn't noticed it before? Stalling for time she talked soothingly to him trying to distract him but he was becoming more and more agitated.

"All right. I'll get you the money, please don't cut me."

Nervously she turned her back on him while she slid aside a Dobell painting revealing a wall safe. Expertly her fingers worked the numbers while she talked constantly hoping he was not too close. The door clicked as the last of the numbers dropped and she reached inside pulling out a bundle of bank notes. Soo Ling threw them at his feet, bank notes floating everywhere. With desperation his eyes averted to the scattered money. As he stooped to gather in some of the money she had time to find the small silver automatic pistol Timothy had bought her.

With one quick movement Soo Ling turned and fired, the bullet catching him in the chest. He crashed heavily to the floor, the look of surprise on his face. Sinking into the nearest chair she poured herself a brandy before dialing Timothy on his mobile phone.

"I need you here at once."

"What's happened?"

"I tell you when you arrive."

He was there inside ten minutes. Quickly and quietly, without questions he set about cleaning up the mess and disposing of the body. There was no explanation asked for or given and the next day a body was found floating in the harbor. Newspaper reports suggested a Triad payback and after a few days there was never a mention made of the event. Never again was anyone employed at Madam Soo's without a scrutiny rivaling ASIO being carried.

The telephone woke her one Thursday morning a lot earlier than she liked to be disturbed. It was Jeffery Watson her stockbroker. He suggested she and Timothy come straight to his office, he needed to talk to them urgently.

If Soo Ling felt angry at being woken early it was nothing to how she felt when Watson told her the stock market had crashed and the value of her now $10,000,000 worth of shares had decreased remarkably.

Her fortune had plunged to less than 30% of her original stake. They discussed the possible outcome and Watson said if it was he and he had spare capital he would buy, not sell. If she could survive for a year or so then when the good times returned she stood to make a lot of money.

Timothy drove her home but seemed to be in deep thought.

"You are troubled, Timothy?"

"I've been thinking about what you can do. I think you should sell another kg of heroin. It will give you working cash to buy more shares."

"Mr. Wang would take it if I offered it to him."

"No. I think we should sell it ourselves. I know how to cut it and we can raise $1.8 million without the worry of a middle man."

"Mr. Wang would be very angry. Not want to cause trouble."

"Once it's sold there is nothing he can do about it."

"Only cut my throat."

"If he complains, offer him some compensation. It would save him face and give him a profit without working for it."

"You think we can do that?"

"Yes. He's only interested in making money."

"Okay. I get heroin tomorrow."

Although the whole country was in recession, Soo Ling had never considered it affected her as most nights her houses were all running to capacity, and she had money in the bank.

The stock market crash came as such a shock she was willing to undertake any transaction to see her through this crisis. It was only the lure of $1.8million that buoyed her spirits, but deep down she knew Wang would be angry for excluding him.

He had the lion's share of the drug trade and that was how he wanted it to stay.

Timothy knew the dealers and how they worked the system and knew he would have no trouble distributing the cut heroin. Everything was going so well, Soo Ling paid Timothy a $50000 bonus.

Wang still made his occasional visits to the original Madam Soo's but he had never been invited to Soo Ling's house, therefore it was entirely surprising to find him ringing her doorbell one Sunday morning.

"Good morning, Soo Ling. May I come in?"

"Certainly, Mr. Wang, how nice to see you."

Her knees were shaking as she stood aside and allowed him to enter. When the formalities of offering tea and asking after his family were completed, she asked how she could help him.

"I am very disappointed in you, Soo Ling."

"I'm afraid I don't understand what you mean."

"I helped you get started in business when you first came to this country and I trusted you, Soo Ling."

"You can always trust me old friend." Keeping her eyes averted she prayed he could not see her hands trembling as she pressed them tightly together under cover of the table.

"I have many soldiers in my army and I hear reports of new supplies of white powder being offered for sale."

"I have heard no such reports."

"Please, Soo Ling, afford me the courtesy of not insulting me."

"Excuse please." Her years of practicing to lose her accent slipped away and she spoke like a newly arrived immigrant.

"I will not lose so much face in front of my people. I wish $200,000 compensation."

"Most sorry, Mr. Wang. Forgive please." Her mind was working overtime. That would still give her a profit of over $1,600,000 above the usual price if it sold well. She drew a deep breath and regained her composure.

"I apologize for my indiscretion. I lost a lot of money and needed more than I dared ask you for. If we can work this out then I trust things can be righted between us. I have no wish to cause you to lose face."

"I was sure that was how you would see it."

"At the moment I can't afford the full amount in one payment. If you are agreeable I can give you $50,000 and a monthly payment until the debt is settled."

"It would please me if you would make it known you made a wrong decision and make sure I am seen not to be at fault."

"Of course. Would it be convenient to meet with me at 2 p.m. tomorrow and I shall give you the first payment?"

"I think that will be most satisfactory. Shall we say the first day of each month for further installments?" He rose to his feet and she bowed slightly.

"Soo Ling, if you try to sell heroin in my area again I'm afraid you may find yourself in deep water, if you get my meaning."

"I understand, Mr. Wang." Soo Ling was more than happy to be let off so easily.

Carrie's first few days in Bosnia left her exhausted. An early morning flight from Australia. Eighteen hours in the air, then a confrontation with her father, followed by a tour of the city. After a fairly sound sleep, she was amazed at the change in her father. Yesterday he had been the surly boss; today he was a friendly helpful work colleague.

"Good morning, time to start seeing what you're made of," he said over breakfast. "I want you to go to the UN news conference and make a report. If it's good enough then you can send it home with your name on it."

Carrie nearly fainted with shock. "You're trusting me to do it by myself?"

"You're a bloody professional aren't you?"

"Of course but I didn't think you thought so."

"Haven't got much choice have I? You were sent over here to learn so learn."

Carrie grabbed up her bag. "Thanks, Dad, I appreciate this."

"Don't call me Dad, I'm Tully at work and keep out of the way of snipers."

Carrie left her half-eaten breakfast and almost ran to the UN conference center. Children on the street were playing in burnt out car bodies littering the road. When she was a kid they played hopscotch and chasing, she wondered if this was normal and whatever sort of a life these children were going to have. One little boy about six with a leg missing and a crutch support was watching sadly from the background as the others played. She felt like going over and hugging him trying to bring some joy into his young life.

The meeting had just started when she arrived, and she listened as a UN spokesperson gave a report on the current position of a fragile cease-fire and the position of UN troops observing it. Then another on the violation of a cease-fire being carried out in Maglaj. She decided to detour around Sarajevo and talk to the ordinary people. Some were willing to talk to this foreigner but others scowled and continued walking.

Learning of the personal losses, the horror and starvation experienced by everyone, Carrie began to get a feel for the population. The ones suffering most were the children and old people, for often they could do little to ward off the degradation of starvation. She wrote up her story and sent it off as soon as she returned, then proceeded to write another report on what she'd seen. The human interest was something, which touched her deeply.

Tully never appeared until after six and he made no comment about his day.

"How did it go?" he asked later that night.

"Fine. I sent off the official report then wrote a story of my own about what's happening to the people. Where have you been all day?"

"Had to look up an old school friend out at Dvor."

Carrie thought no more of it until the next day at the news conference when she heard of severe shelling on the village of Dvor. He was sending her to these mundane meetings while he claimed all the glory out where the action was.

It kept happening for weeks until she finally cornered him about it.

"I thought the conditions were you do as I tell you, not question my authority. Where I say, you go. Understand?"

"You bastard." She turned and stomped away aware of his eyes following her.

Tully Sanderson may be her boss but she was not going to let him make her the flunky while he chased the glory. She wasn't his daughter for nothing.

Chapter Twenty Three

For five weeks Carrie kept attending the news conferences while Tully slipped away to the hotspots. What made Carrie even angrier was that often she was sent to do Tully's bidding while he was entertaining Celeste in his room.

Tully was upstairs making passionate love with Celeste when a reporter from the London Sentinel came looking for him. He was tall and well groomed with a beautiful English accent. Probably around Tully's age.

"Seen Tully Sanderson?" he asked Carrie, as she was about to walk outside.

"Why?" Carrie didn't bother to tell him what Tully was up to. If he was too busy to attend to work then that was his problem.

"I'm Alex Franklin. Tully and I are friends from Vietnam. He said to let him know when the next UN chopper was leaving for Busovaca."

"Something happening there?" she asked, her interest roused.

"There's another breach of the cease-fire. The Serbs are bombarding the town. Tully said to let him know when the next chopper is leaving with the UN observers."

"Great. He said he can't make it, too busy and for me to go. I've been waiting for the word."

"Then you'd better hurry. They're leaving from the UN compound in fifteen minutes."

"I'm on my way." Carrie hurried to her room, changed into heavy gear, grabbed a warm coat and rushed to the UN compound.

"Carrie Sanderson, Sydney Tribune." She flashed her press pass.

"Where's Tully?" The UN captain asked as she climbed into the Sea King.

"Caught up in something he can't leave. He told me to fill in for him." She had to shout above the noise of the rotating blades of the chopper.

"It could be dangerous."

"I've been on trips like this before." She wished he'd take off before Tully arrived.

"Okay," he replied and she breathed a sigh of relief as the Sea King rose into the air.

"What are you expected to do when you get there?" she asked as they made their way toward the village.

"View the breach. We're only there as observers. The Serbs have been pounding the village for four hours and the Security Council is real pissed off at them. Make sure you stay with the UN troops and don't go wandering off. We can't protect you if you do."

Carrie watched the treetops whiz by as the Chopper rushed to the besieged town where the Serbs kept up a constant barrage from the nearby mountains. The sky was a deep grey and snow covered the village and surrounding land.

Ugly black marks showed clearly where shells had been falling. The chopper let all passengers off and waited for the old shift to enter, then took to the sky again as they ran toward the UN bunker.

From their vantage, Carrie could see all before them. There were two bodies lying on the road outside a wrecked house and people were crouched behind a low stone wall. From here they looked like women and children but she couldn't be sure as light snow was falling, giving almost a Xmas scene amongst the rubble which was once a proud village.

"Can't you do anything?" Carrie was frightened for the people sheltering.

"Not unless they fire on us. Then we can call in an air strike but the Serbs are not that stupid. Even if we did it would take at least four hours before permission was given." A Coldstream guard in captain's uniform grimly surveyed the scene. He was just as angry as Carrie but red tape prevented him from doing anything.

Carrie timed the shell bursts; they were falling every two minutes. How could anyone make any sort of rescue? She felt helpless. A little girl about 7 or 8 suddenly emerged from nowhere walking down the middle of the road crying loudly, obviously hurt and frightened. Carrie's heart was pounding.

A shell hit the road barely one hundred meters away and without hesitation, Carrie opened the door and ran from the concrete bunker to the child. Hands tried to stop her but she was too quick, and the soldiers could only watch what was about to happen. Two minutes felt like ten seconds as she ran, oblivious to the calls from the UN personal.

Scooping the child in her arms she ran towards the nearest wrecked building for protection.

The next shell hit the road exactly where the child had been standing and Carrie hugged her protectively as earth and rubble fell around them. The shrapnel made a horrible whack as it hit the bricks and rubble above her head.

A woman yelling frantically appeared from nowhere and grabbed the child from Carrie.

"Thank you, thank you, you save my Nadja." She and the child ran through the rubble leaving Carrie alone in the shelled out building.

A hail of machine gun bullets thudded into the damaged walls of the building and Carrie changed her mind about making a dash for it. She would have to stay put until dark and hope a direct hit didn't put an end to her brief career.

Tully and Celeste finally emerged from his room and headed for the bar.

"What would you like, love?"

"A rest after such an energetic afternoon, Tully. You're insatiable."

"Beats reading a book. Gin and Tonic?"

He ordered two drinks and they sat back sipping the cold beverage thirstily. Alex Franklin from the London Sentinel joined them. Tully had run into him several times since leaving Vietnam

"Your new reporter is a good looking lass, Tully?"

"What?" Tully had no idea what he was on about.

"Your partner, she's good looking. She said you were too busy to go on the chopper so she filled in for you."

"Carrie went on a UN chopper?"

"To Busovaca. You told me to let you know when it was leaving."

Tully's face went white. He'd been so preoccupied with Celeste he'd forgotten all about it. "Jesus." He headed out the door calling over his shoulder. "See you later, Celeste."

The dash to the UN chopper port was done in quick time. He had to find out what was going on, almost shouting at the pilot when he caught up with him.

"You took my partner out to Busovaca."

"Yeah, she's real pretty, lucky you."

"When are they due back?"

"I brought the chopper back straight away. There's a new shift due to go at six."

"I'm coming with you. I have to get the stupid kid back."

"Okay if we have room. Make yourself some coffee and hang around a while. I'll give you a call around five."

Tully checked his watch, shit, it was still four hours away. There was nothing he could do but wait. He'd spent plenty of time waiting before but this time it was a nightmare. His promise to Briony to look after their daughter was looking decidedly shaky. The hours seemed to drag. It was as if the clock on the wall was permanently stuck. After his sixth cup of coffee the pilot signaled him and he joined the crew on the way to relieve the last lot of observers.

*   *   *

After two weeks in Sarajevo Jason felt like he was living in a nightmare. How on earth could he have let himself get into this? The hardest part of driving an ambulance was leaving the vehicle to pick up wounded or dead civilians.

Each time he expected a bullet to hit him and in fact one had bounced off the road near his foot once, as he struggled to lift an old woman into the back. That taught him a lesson to always use the ambulance as a protective shield.

His worst experience so far was arriving at a shooting to find the victim was a young girl. Barely out of primary school this little girl had been playing with her friends when she ran into the open to fetch her ball. She was shot in the chest and was now a crumpled heap in the middle of the road. No one was game to run out and gather her up. She lay moaning as her blood oozed out onto the road.

Jason drove straight into the line of fire with only his ambulance for shelter as he gathered her up. He tried to stem the flow of blood but could see she wasn't going to make it. The bullet had gone straight through her tiny body and her breathing sounded as if it was going through a meat mincer. It was a lung shot and blood was trickling from her mouth and running down her chin. He barely got her back to the hospital before she died. He was so angry and frustrated at this useless war that he kicked the side of his vehicle in protest.

Back in Stuttgart Wagner had made no mention of the hazards to be faced daily, nor had he mentioned the long hours he would need to work due to the lack of volunteers to relive him. Thank God two months had gone and he was looking forward to the end of this nightmare.

He had to admit his medical skills had been invaluable. Many patients would have died if he hadn't been there and knew a little to help but there were others, like the young girl who had no hope. With only a few weeks left to the end of his contract he was looking forward to leaving this horrible place behind.

When he was ordered to the country town of Asdjica to pick up a wounded UN observer, he was pleased to be able to get away from the daily dose of death for a while. Now he understood his mother's frustration in Vietnam. She rarely talked about it but when she did he had seen the torment in her eyes.

*　　*　　*

Tully went with the observers when they changed shifts. There was a mad scramble to find the safety of the bunker. The door was thrown open by the waiting observers and the new shift piled in. He climbed into the bunker with his eyes on full alert, searching for his daughter. Unable to see her he grabbed the arm of a young captain.

"My partner, a girl, have you seen her?"

"If you mean the reporter, she defied my orders to rescue a young girl. At the moment she's in that building over there."

Tully followed his pointing finger, every instinct telling him to rush to her aid.

"Steady on old chap. Shells are falling every two minutes. It will be dark in half an hour, you may be able to reach her then."

"I can reach her now."

"No. There's a machine gun firing at anything moving. That's why she's sheltering."

Tully knew he was right. "How long are you going to wait?"

"Sorry, but we're supposed to be back before dark. As it is we're not going to make it. If you're planning to rescue your friend you'll have to wait here until tomorrow's shift."

"It's snowing. She'll freeze to death."

"She had a thick coat on, she'll be cold but she should survive the weather."

Tully was resigned to the fact that there was nothing he could do. He watched as the change of shift took place and felt useless as the chopper left them behind. The sky worried him, as the dark clouds seemed to be getting darker.

He waited over an hour and just as he could stand it no longer a shell landed directly on the building where Carrie was sheltering. Watching in horror, he saw the roof collapse and snow and rubble was thrown high into the air.

"Carrie," he shouted and broke from the safety of the bunker. A bevy of arm's tried to hold him but he pulled free and sprinted to the almost demolished building.

Machine gun bullets raised a trail in the snow but miraculously he avoided them and dived into the rubble. His breathing formed condensed droplets in the cold air as he searched frantically for his child. Bricks and rubble were thrown indiscriminately aside as he searched in vain for her. He scrambled amongst the ruin for what seemed an eternity until his hand felt her coat. Following the cloth into an opening he could feel her body huddled against a fallen chimney.

Frantically he pulled her free searching her for any apparent wounds. Her face was covered in blood from a head wound bleeding profusely.

Fearing she was dead he fumbled for a pulse and was relieved to hear her groan mournfully. Tenderly he wiped her face with his handkerchief and almost cried with relief when she opened her eyes.

"Thank, God," he said holding her close.

She winced with pain.

"Carrie. Do you know where you are? Are you all right."

"My leg. I think it's broken, Dad."

Tully had been so worried about the blood; he had failed to check her for breaks.

"Why did you come here," he cried angrily. "You have no business being here."

"I'm a reporter. Just like you. You couldn't fob me off forever." The building began to spin as she fought to stay awake.

"And look where it got you."

"There was a little girl. I had to get to her." Carrie fought to clear her head.

"You're as stupid as your mother. That's exactly how she died."

"You never told me anything about her."

"Maybe I will one day," He looked around for something to use for a splint. "I'm going to have to carry you back to the bunker. It will probably hurt like hell but there's no other choice."

"If I scream just ignore me."

He gathered her in his arms, then lay her over his shoulder in a fireman's lift.

"The shells land every two minutes," Carrie gasped trying to stifle her scream.

"I know." As soon as the next shell landed he took off as fast as his legs could carry them both. Carrie gave a piercing scream but he kept on until he reached the bunker.

The snow was getting heavier; the wind was almost blowing it sideways, which helped shield him from the snipers above the town. At least the machine gunner could no longer see them.

"Have to get the chopper in," he said when she was safely on the bunker floor.

"I don't think so. Not in this weather." The officer in charge shook his head.

"She's got a broken leg and probable concussion. I have to get her out of here." Tully's voice was rising in desperation.

"Well I don't hold much hope." The officer tried not to sound totally negative.

"All I can do is try," he said switching on his radio. When Sarajevo answered he explained the position.

"It's an Australian journalist, one ---" He looked to Tully for an answer.

"Carrie Sanderson, she's my daughter.

"I'm sorry. No hope in this weather. All planes are grounded," came back the reply.

"She has a serious head wound."

"Just a minute." There was a long pause and the operator came back on. "There's a UN ambulance on its way to Asdjica to pick up one of our observers suffering a slight wound. I can't order anyone into that area, all I can do is ask."

"Please," said Tully. He couldn't just let Carrie die.

The message was transferred to the ambulance and Jason received it as they arrived in Adsjica. By this time the blizzard had taken hold and it was hard to see your hand in front of your face. His partner shook his head knowing the danger they faced.

"It's impossible to get there," said Jason.

"It's only a request, not an order. Seems some Australian journalist has got herself blown up. She'll just have to take her chances."

The thought of some girl, Australian or not, lying injured and without help pricked his conscience. He gave his partner an appealing look. "It's only about 20 kilometers."

"Might as well be 120 in this weather and in the dark. Think of the danger, we could get blown off the road."

"You stay here and look after this one and I'll try to get through."

"I always knew Australians were mad. Suit yourself."

Jason radioed back. "I'm going to try to get through. Who is it I'm I looking for?"

"A Carrie Sanderson. Good luck."

Jason could not believe it. Could it be his Cousin Stephanie's friend? It had to be. She was a journalist and quite adventurous. He hadn't seen her since the barbecue after she and Stephanie graduated.

"If everything goes well I'll be there in about two hours." He switched the radio off and began the trip into the blizzard.

The message the ambulance was coming was relayed back to the bunker. Tully was so relieved he sat holding his daughter's hand so tightly he almost cut off her circulation.

Chapter Twenty Four

Jason had never experienced weather like it. The snowing was bad enough but having the ambulance lights dimmed giving minimum light for safety made him feel he was driving blind. For an hour he struggled to hold the vehicle on the small winding road but he felt, at least the weather would keep the Serbs lying low thus giving him a chance to get there unobserved.

The howling of the blizzard made it impossible to hear anything outside, and he was more than thankful at least the heater was working. A flash of light caused him to quickly turn off his headlights. Just ahead he could see the huge outline of a tank and veered off the narrow track just in time. Slowly the tank rumbled past barely ten metres away. It was obvious the driver was having the same difficulty in seeing where he was going.

The snow was becoming deeper with each minute and he began to despair he was ever going to get there. The wipers were working flat out but with little effect. Checking his map he estimated there was still five kilometers to go and the snow seemed to be getting heavier, if that was possible.

To his left there was a faint glow which, as he got closer turned out to be a burning building. His arms were aching from the drag of holding the car on the road. He could feel his concentration slipping so he started singing at the top of his voice.

Can't be far now he thought, what's that bit of color moving there. He had to stop the ambulance and step outside to see what it was, then almost cried with relief when he discovered it was the UN flag fluttering strongly above the bunker.

Switching off the engine and lights, he grabbed his medical bag and pulled his parka hood down over his ears. Wading as if through deep water he reached the bunker and pounded on the door. A rush of light and warmth greeted him as he was virtually dragged over the threshold.

"Hi, ambulance service, where's the patient?"

"Over here." Tully jumped up and grabbed him by the arm almost knocking him over.

Carrie was lying still and deathly white; her leg was obviously giving her pain. Her eyes were closed and Jason felt for her pulse. Carrie stirred slightly and moaned.

"Carrie, can you hear me?" Jason's voice was firm but gentle. Her eyes opened and she blinked in the light.

"Jason!" she managed to stammer. He sent a pencil light into her eyes looking for trouble.

"I thought you said journalism was an easy profession," he replied feeling her brow.

"You know her?" Tully was amazed.

"Dad, this is Jason, Stephanie's cousin." Carrie managed a weak smile.

"Stephanie?"

"The girl I board with, you remember."

"Oh yeah. Hello, Jason, it's nice to see a friendly face."

"Nice to meet you, Mr. Sanderson. Sorry it's under these circumstances." Jason attended to Carrie inspecting her leg.

"It's certainly broken," he said. "Pull her trousers down nice and easy. I'll have to put it into a splint."

Carefully Tully eased her trousers down and watched as Jason applied an inflatable splint to hold her leg securely. He checked her eyes again with the pencil torch and shook his head.

"I'm a bit worried about the head wound. It could be a fractured skull. We should get her back to hospital."

"That's what I reckon." Tully was somewhat relieved by Jason's enthusiasm for getting her back for proper medical attention.

"It would be better if you waited until the weather cleared." The UN captain thought it was madness to even try moving her.

"I really don't want to take the risk leaving it. She could suffer a brain hemorrhage and die. Help me get her into the ambulance please, Mr. Sanderson."

"The name's Tully, son." Tully leapt to his feet and helped lift Carrie onto a stretcher. They opened the door and together fought the few steps to the ambulance through the driving snow. The ice was built up over the windscreen.

"Good luck," the captain called after them. "We'll let them know you're coming."

Tully nodded and leapt into the driver's seat.

"I'll drive, you look after her."

"Okay but be bloody careful. I passed a tank on the way here."

Tully eased the ambulance into gear and took off in the direction of Asdjica.

They drove for a while in silence. Tully's promise to Briony to take care of his daughter pounding in his head. He felt he had failed miserably. Never being there as she grew up, missing all those special events so precious, now being responsible for her injuries by spending the afternoon in bed with Celeste. If he hadn't been thinking about his own gratification, then she wouldn't be lying there on the stretcher as he drove slowly through this blasted blizzard. He wondered what else could go wrong.

Opening the window slightly to allow air in to clear the windscreen he was met with an icy blast. Shutting it quickly he did his best to clear the fogging glass with his arm. It was like driving into a brilliant white nightmare surrounded on all sides by a dark gloom. His rear vision mirror gave him a glimpse of Jason attending to Carrie.

"How is she?"

"Her breathing is normal but she's unconscious. Pulse is okay but I'll be happier when she gets some hospital attention."

"Thanks for coming for her. I owe you one." Tully wrestled with the steering wheel.

"When I heard her name, I couldn't believe it was the same Carrie Sanderson. What's the odds of meeting up with her on a battlefield in bloody Bosnia?"

"Journalist's can be found anywhere. You say you're a cousin of Stephanie Farmer. Have you known Carrie long?"

"It's about 8, maybe 9 years since we first met. I helped them shift into their house, then we met a couple of times at Uni. We spent the day together at a family barbecue when they graduated."

"Nice girl your cousin. I met her once or twice just after they moved in together."

"Yeah. I've lived on and off with her for years. Mum was always pretty busy so I always spent the school holidays at Steph's."

"Must be nice to have a close family."

"I'm an only child but Steph. has been like a sister. We get on well."

"Have you always been an ambulance driver?" This tall young man interested Tully.

"No, only two months. I've done three years of a medical degree. Thought I'd see the world before I settled down and became a doctor. Now I'm beginning to wonder."

"Lucky for Carrie you did."

They lapsed into silence again as Tully concentrated on the road ahead. The sharp bend loomed in front of him before he could adjust and the ambulance went straight into a deep snowdrift and came to a sudden halt. Jason was thrown forward but fortunately Carrie had been tied down tightly before they left.

"Shit." Tully punched the steering wheel in anger. "Are you all right?"

"I'm fine but it looks like we're stuck pretty solidly."

Tully forced open the door and was met by an unimaginable blast of cold air. The wheels of the ambulance were buried up to the axles.

"What do you think?" asked Jason jumping out to inspect the damage.

"Do these things have a bloody shovel?"

"Everything but. If we jack up the wheel we can drag some branches under it to give us some traction."

"Might work," agreed Tully. "You jack it up while I find some timber."

Jason removed the jack while Tully wandered off in search of something to put under the wheels. The wind was screaming in his ears and he shuddered pulling his coat tightly around him. He pulled some branches from a tree and dragged them back toward the ambulance. A piercing scream shattered the air over the storm as the jack collapsed and Jason's hand was trapped under the tire.

"Jesus." Tully rushed to help him.

"Get it off," yelled Jason, his face contorted with pain. The intense cold had snapped the metal causing the jack to fail. Tully knew he had no hope of lifting the ambulance without a jack so he rammed the heavy branch alongside Jason's trapped hand.

"Brace yourself son, I'll try and move it a couple of inches."

The thick tree branch took the weight of the ambulance as Tully revved the engine and reversed onto the timber giving Jason an inch or two to quickly withdraw his injured hand as the tire rose onto the branch.

The wheel spun and slipped back again but thankfully Jason was free. Jumping from the ambulance, Tully ran to help him to his feet.

"Shit, it's crushed. I can hardly move it."

"Get inside out of this cold and we'll look at it."

Tully helped him into the back where he found some scissors to cut off his glove. Tully could see the hand was clearly broken.

"Can you move your fingers?"

"Barely." Jason tried to flex his injured fingers. Tully noticed a slight movement but also noticed the pain expressed on Jason's face.

He dabbed a bit of antiseptic on and wrapped Jason's hand as gently as he could.

"There's only one thing to do. I'll have to try and go on foot. Asjidca can't be far away."

"Probably four or five kms. You can't walk far in this. All you'll do is die in the snow. We'd be better to stay here until the blizzard blows itself out. Then you can try and make it."

"What about Carrie?"

"There's nothing we can do now. Just keep her warm until you can get help."

Tully knew he was right. There was no sense in him being frozen to death outside, and then Carrie and Jason freezing here without help. They'd wait the storm out and he'd try in the morning.

All three huddled together sharing the blankets and body warmth as the wind howled so loudly that they could hardly hear each other. After a while they gave up and tried to sleep. Tully and Jason each lost in their thoughts while Carrie lay blissfully unconscious. The first rays of the morning light were met by the wind suddenly dying.

"Listen," said Tully shaking Jason awake.

"What? I can't hear anything."

"Exactly. The blizzard is gone. I'm going for help."

Tully checked Carrie's pulse as she slept, then re-bandaged Jason's hand, which was almost black with the bruising. He covered them both with blankets and promised to be as quick as he could.

"Asdjica should be eight kilometer's down the road. If I go over the mountain I can cut about four ks off the trip."

"Don't worry about Carrie, I'll look after her. Be careful and don't get lost. If you don't make it then we're all dead."

"I'll make it," said Tully grimly. "Just take care of my daughter."

Jason handed him some emergency rations, then watched as he dug his way out. Snow had piled up around the metal body of the car almost entombing them and the only way out was through the driver's window, then to scramble out into the snow. Tully felt a satisfaction that the ambulance would be well camouflaged if any Serbs came by.

The first hour was a nightmare. Every step he took swallowed his leg into the snow. It was as if some great suction cup was pulling him down. After only a hundred metres he was almost exhausted. He was glad he'd never been a smoker for he needed every bit of oxygen his lungs could absorb.

Almost reaching the peak of the hill he heard voices approaching. Throwing himself over an embankment he slid down about sixty metres.

Reaching for any vegetation to halt his fall he was disappointed but he suddenly stopped behind a snowdrift.

Above him ten Serb soldiers passed, and Tully said a prayer thanking them for their loud conversation or he would have walked straight into them.

He scrambled back to the trail and continued on until forced to rest from hunger and exhaustion. Sitting in the snow against a tree trunk, he chewed on some of the tasteless rations Jason had given him. Something cold and hard was pushing into his neck and he turned to see a rifle pointed at his head. The man was hardly visible in heavy snow covered trousers. A coat buttoned up to the neck with a thick scarf across his face, and a Russian style hat sitting on his head, he was pressing the rifle into Tully. He looked like Attila the Hun with ice encrusted across his heavy eyebrows and moustache, his clothes a mantle of white. The scowl he had matched anything Tully could come up with. Behind him was a wooden sled loaded with wood.

"Serb?" he muttered angrily in Croatian.

"No Serb. Australian journalist," said Tully.

"No Serb? He seemed to have limited vocabulary.

"UN. Doctor need help."

"UN? You UN?"

"Yeah mate, UN," agreed Tully.

"Come." He signaled with his arm.

"Where to?" asked Tully.

"My house. Warm and I give food."

"I can't. I have a doctor and an injured woman who need help. Can you help us?"

"Where doctor and woman?"

"Back that way about three kilometers. I passed some Serbs on the way here."

"I kill Serbs."

"There were ten of them. Will you help me?"

"Come, we go."

He tipped the wood from the sled and followed Tully back in the direction he had come. They struggled on for yet another eternity to the ambulance where Tully was thankful to find both Carrie and Jason still alive.

"Put woman on sled." The man picked up Carrie as if she was a butterfly and gently placed her on the sled. Tully wrapped her in all the blankets from the ambulance and tied her down.

"We go." The Croatian and Tully both pulled the sled with Jason following up behind.

The big man, taking most of the weight made the torturous journey easier. Knowing his way and being used to the snow, he went faster than Tully would have liked but it only served to make Tully more determined to keep up. The only sign of a house in the valley below was the spiraling thread of smoke from the chimney; everything else was a sea of white. A woman who appeared to be the man's wife welcomed them.

"My wife Arina. I am Nedzad. Get soup woman, these people need help."

She bustled over Carrie as they carried her inside insisting they put her close to the stove. She poured four bowls of steaming hot soup.

Having sent most of his rations with Tully, Jason was famished and was sure the soup was nectar from the Gods. They spooned it down greedily and soon began to get some feeling in their bones.

"How's the hand?" Tully was concerned about Jason's plight.

"Not good. It's broken for sure. I think that's the end of my career as a surgeon."

"I'm sorry, son. It may recover enough after it heals. You can still do medicine. You may have to choose an area other than surgery."

"Yeah, I guess I'll be limited to a GP, that's not so bad. My mother has done okay." He tried hard to hide the disappointment in his voice. "We still have to get Carrie back to Sarajevo. Any ideas?"

"Maybe Nedzad can help us." He turned to their rescuer to ask his advice.

"Many Serbs around. Asdjica is a short distance away. I can get help in one hour."

"There's a UN observation post on the left of the town." Jason pointed it out on the map. "If you go there they might help."

"I know it. Stay here out of sight. I come soon." He closed the door disappearing into the white haze.

Tully and Jason both slept with exhaustion and it was Arina's frantic calls waking them. Three men were scouting the place, leaping from one place of shelter to another.

"UN?" asked Jason.

"Shit. Bloody Serbs. Pass me the rifle."

Arina passed the rifle to Tully. "They kill us if they come here." Her voice shook with fear.

"In a pigs ear," said Tully angrily. "They probably want some shelter from this bloody weather." He hadn't brought Carrie this far only to lose her now. He lifted the rifle, slipped the bolt on the door and opened it a few inches, then fired several rounds through the open door shutting it quickly.

The three Serbs dived for cover and fired a few shots back in return. The occupants of the house dived to the floor; Jason throwing himself over Carrie as bullets passed through the window breaking the glass.

Tully pumped more shots at them with no result. He was keeping them at bay but he knew they had AK 47s. They were powerful weapons, and compared to them he felt like he had a popgun. A splinter of wood from the window frame left a rather deep cut to Tully's cheek.

"Jesus, I'm getting too old for this," he said savagely as he wiped away the blood.

Tully's ammunition was getting low and he was worried; wanting to conserve it in case they rushed the place. A prolonged burst raked the house and Tully guessed two were rushing the place while the third kept him busy.

More shots this time with a higher pitch and he saw two fall to the ground. The third tried to run but fell under a hail of shots as Tully looked warily toward his rescuers. Five UN soldiers were checking the bodies as Nedzad ran to the house.

"Everyone all right?' he asked hurrying to his wife.

"We are now thanks to you," said Tully relieved to see the UN soldiers.

A Dutch soldier surveyed the room. "Mr. Sanderson. I'm glad to see you're safe. We had a message from Busovaca saying you were on your way. For a while we thought you were gone."

"Yeah thanks. Can we get my daughter to hospital?"

"The storm has broken so a chopper can be sent. I radioed for one when Nedzad told us your needs. Come, we must get to the bunker."

Jason thanked Nedzad for his help and handed him the bag containing the emergency rations.

"I'm sorry but it's all I have. We'll try to get some rations back for you. If you go to the UN bunker next week I promise there will be food for you."

"I have three Serb rifles now. I ready if they come again."

Nedzad and Arina wished them a safe return; they shook their hands and thanked them for the promise of food. Outside the sky was clear, all signs of the blizzard were gone and they were back inside the UN bunker within the hour where the chopper was waiting nearby. Carrie and Jason were stowed on board and when Tully stepped up to enter the pilot restrained him.

"Sorry Mr. Sanderson. Not enough room. You'll have to wait until the next one comes in."

"When will that be?"

"Later today."

"Take care of her, Jason, I'll come straight to the hospital," he said stepping away from the Sea King.

"See you back in Sarajevo, sir." Jason waved his good hand as the door was closed and the chopper lifted into the air.

I have to give up this life style, thought Tully watching the sky until the Sea King became a dot in the distance.

Chapter Twenty Five

When Tully finally arrived back in Sarajevo he went straight to the hospital. There was no thought about stories or reports, the only thing he cared about was the welfare of his daughter. He was lucky enough to get a ride in one of the UN vehicles, the driver dropping him outside the door. Without hesitation, he leapt out and went bounding up the steps into the hospital. With instructions on where to find her, he burst into the ward only to be told to conduct himself in an orderly manner or expect to be thrown out.

The staff was used to distraught parents of friends rushing to love ones so they gave him a little leeway. When he saw her laying in her bed his heart thudded in his chest with fear. He was somewhat relieved when a passing nurse said she was resting comfortably. She looked just like Briony, smooth skin, dark hair, just as beautiful but no blood streaming down her face and no body ripped open by bullets. Her head held a clean bandage and her leg was encased in plaster but the bonus was, she was alive.

Tully's nostrils tingled. The antiseptic smell of hospitals always repulsed him, but he was determined not to leave Carrie's bedside till she woke. Fondly he watched as she slept, her color had returned and she was breathing evenly.

Tully grabbed the doctor hurrying by.

"How is she, doc?"

It was obvious he was irritated and had work to do but he stopped and spoke.

"We need to keep her here for a few days because of the head wound. No fractured skull, just severe concussion. Her leg is in plaster and will be fine in time. Can't stay as I have patients to see."

"Thanks," said Tully but already he was moving away.

Looking at her, the past came back hauntingly. Her likeness to Briony was remarkable, but of course with a little extra maturity as she was older than her mother had been at her death. He could see the beautiful, innocent, naïve face that had held him spellbound all those years ago. Sometimes it seemed like yesterday when they had walked the streets of London, hand in hand sharing their love for their brief time of happiness.

The dreadful day when he lost her was indelibly marked on his conscience. Her eyes pleading for him to end it for her, the hope he would take care of their daughter, the heart rending sob he felt as he had pulled the trigger giving her the peace she craved. It was all too painful to recall for any length of time.

It was as bad again in Vietnam, the brutal gut wrenching war that effected so many.

His new found love with Kate had given him some hope for the future, but that too was snatched from him when she left for judicious reasons. She'd always been in his thoughts; even when he had been with other women, and it was the one part of his life he wished hadn't died. Thoughts of her often frequented his dreams, and at times he had pondered about throwing in the life of a journalist to go in search of her.

He figured he was jinxed when it came to one-woman relationships, and it was not fair to Kate to come along and wreck her life just as he had wrecked Briony's and Carrie's.

Then there was the tragic Soo Ling. He had saved her from a fate inflicted on many young girls in that horrible place, then for her to die in the flames of the club on the last night in Saigon. True he had never loved her but she was his wife and he did have a fondness for her. He never blamed her for anything she'd done. Her lot in life was not what he would have wanted for any woman, certainly not his daughter.

Carrie would probably hate him even more for having her sent home while he stayed with the action, but he needed to know she was safe.

He was sick of the whole bloody thing and looking at Carries inert body with the tranquil face resting on the white pillow, he decided to throw in the towel.

Enough was enough. He would write one last report showing Jason to be the hero he was. He would always be grateful to Jason for his role in saving Carrie.

His last story would tell of Jason Farmer, an Australian hero who risked his life and limb to save a young Australian journalist from certain death from the guns of the Bosnia Serbs. In doing so he likely forfeited all chances of becoming a surgeon when he severely injured his hand during the rescue.

Carrie's doctor told him she would not wake for hours yet, so he decided he may as well take a break from the distasteful odor and seek out Jason for a few personal details to finish up the article.

Jason was busy packing when Tully arrived.

"They kicking you out already?' he said good naturedly.

Struggling to close the case one handed, Jason looked up and smiled. "Yeah, I only have another two weeks to complete my contract but I'm not much use to them with a busted hand, so they're sending me home. Good news about Carrie."

"Thanks to you. I'm getting her sent home too. She's going to be really pissed off but at least she'll be safe."

"Well it's the only decision open for her, she'll be at least three months getting over the broken leg. I suppose you'll be going back to the war."

"No way. I've had enough of wars to last me a lifetime."

"Going back to national reporting?"

"Giving it up altogether. Pulling the plug, retiring completely."

"What will you do?" Jason was surprised. Famous reporters didn't do that.

"Retire. Drink booze and chase women. I want to do one last story, then I'm out of here. I just need a few details about you and that's it."

"Me! Why me?"

"You're the story I'm going to send back. The great Australian hero."

"Bullshit, Tully. I don't want you to write anything about me."

"I gather ambulance drivers are a dime a dozen over here."

"Christ, are you kidding. I had to work double shifts to cover the shortfall."

"With a bit of luck then this story might attract a few to give it a go."

Jason absorbed his words slowly. "Maybe---what do you want to know?"

Tully grinned, opened his notebook and sat on the bed. "Full name Jason Farmer aged 22, born in…?"

"You got the age right but it's Jason Armitage, not Farmer."

Tully's pen stopped in mid sentence. "Did you say Jason Armitage? I thought you were a Farmer."

"No. Farmer is my Aunt's married name. She's my mother's sister. My mother's name is Armitage. She was never married and if you call me a bastard I'll thump you." He grinned as he said it. "I happen to know Carrie is a bastard too? It was a joke between us. She told me her mother died in Ireland just after she was born."

"What was your mother's first name Jason?" Tully felt his limbs go numb.

"Kate. She's a doctor."

"And your father?"

"His name was James Sutton. He died in Vietnam while they were serving there."

"Your mother was in Vietnam? I was there. What part was she in?" Tully's heart was racing.

"As far as I know, mostly Saigon, then Hue and the American airforce base at Da Nang. Seems she got pregnant there just before she came home."

"I was at Hue for a while." Tully had a cold sweat running down his spine.

"It's strange you should say that. Mum told Carrie she read your stories while she was there. She said you were a great correspondent and admired them greatly."

"And how did your father die?" Tully's hand was shaking. He'd been shocked before but never like this.

"He actually died from a burst appendix. He was caught behind the lines in bad weather and they couldn't get him back in time. It's almost funny isn't it?"

"There was nothing funny about Vietnam. Where do you call home now, Jason, Sydney?"

"No. We live in a little country town called Moruya. Do you know it?"

"Near Bateman's Bay isn't it?"

"That's the place. Mum wanted peace and quiet after Vietnam. She fitted in perfectly and has a good practice there. She's head of the charity committee to raise money for a new wing on the hospital. Been doing it for years. Matter of fact at present she's organizing a gala charity auction. Last time we spoke she was very excited about articles she'd acquired, especially Greg Norman's favorite putter."

"She never married?" Tully kept probing.

"No. I guess she never got over Dad. She's happy just the way things are. Actually it would do her the world of good to get married. I worry about her sometimes."

"She sounds like a nice lady."

"She is and she's a very special mum. I thought you said this story was about me?"

"Sorry," said Tully coming back to earth. "Tell me all about yourself, your likes and dislikes. Where you went to school, which University you're at, all the interesting parts."

Jason related details of his life and Tully listened avidly. He wanted to learn about everything this impressive young man had done. This young man who was his son. His heart leapt inside his chest; he wanted to touch him, to tell him. He fought to restrain himself and remain calm. He had to keep this on a professional level for Kate's sake. She'd lived the lie for twenty- two years and if she'd wanted him to know then she would have told him. When he was finished he put away his pen.

"Do you mind if I keep in touch, Jason. I owe you a lot."

"You owe me nothing and sure, I don't mind. In fact I'd quite like it."

He began to leave, then paused. "Jason. You said your mother thinks I'm an all right reporter and famous person and that she's having a celebrity auction for charity."

"Yeah."

Removing the zodiac medallion from his neck he handed it to Jason.

"Give her this to sell. It might bring a few dollars." He knew she would guess that if he'd met Jason he would soon work out who Jason's father was.

Jason turned it over and read the inscription. "She wouldn't accept this. It has to have sentimental value. It was obviously given with a great deal of love."

"It was but those days are gone. If she doesn't want it then she can post it back to me. Just look at it as a donation from a grateful father."

Jason shrugged and put it in his pocket. "Good luck, Tully. Thanks for everything, I hope we'll meet up one day."

Again he offered his hand to Tully. He had a strong grip and Tully again had an irresistible urge to hug him, but he kept back and smiled.

"You can bet on it. See you, mate."

"Yeah, give my regards to Carrie. I'll catch up to her when I get back home."

He waved and smiled as he walked out of Tully's life. Kate's face was reflected all over him and Tully wondered why he hadn't noticed it before. His heart felt a little heavy as he walked away from his son and back to his daughter.

Checking on Carrie he found her still dead to the world. The duty nurse again assured him it would be a while yet so he found a quiet corner where he could get his story onto paper.

He praised Jason's deeds and the UN for their part in the war and assistance they gave Carrie. He kept all mention of himself out of the events, then together with his resignation; he faxed it to Australia.

Richard Harding granted his suggestion or rather his demand Carrie be brought back to Australia, and he took the news to her personally. Pat Scanlon had been right, he certainly knew how to stuff his life up but now he'd had enough. He'd finish his tour of Bosnia in the next month and retired from journalism forever. He wasn't rich but certainly comfortable. He'd find something to do, maybe write a book or some articles, which would bring in a small income, it didn't matter but he knew he had to give up this life of war and horror.

Carrie was awake when he returned.

"How are you feeling? The doctor said you will be up and around in a few days."

"I feel fine but this leg is going to be a nuisance for a while. I won't be able to do any field work, I'll just have to do UN reports until I get the plaster off."

"You won't have to worry about any of that."

"What's that supposed to mean?"

Tully took a deep breath knowing he had to face the music. "I spoke to Richard. I asked him to bring you home until your leg is healed. You go back early next week."

"You what?" Carries eyes widened in anger. "I'm not going."

"Yes you are. Richard agreed that for your health and safety and for the good of the paper it would be best if you went home. If you don't agree then you're out of a job."

"But I've got a story to write about what happened. The world should know what's going on."

"Actually I've already sent off the story of the breach by the Serbs and of your rescue by Jason. It made the front page today."

"You bastard." She exploded. "You send me on every mundane task you can find, then get a scoop printed at my expense. When I tread on your territory you want to send me home out of the way.

"It's all arranged. You leave next week."

"That's it as far as I'm concerned," Carrie shouted. "I hate you and I never want to see you again. Now get out of here."

"Carrie, you don't understand," he said pleading with her.

"I understand all right. Now go before I call for some help."

He left feeling worse than ever. He'd stuffed up again but at least she would be safe for a while. The day she left he was there to see her off but she just ignored him, refusing to even acknowledge his presence. He stood nervously waiting for some sign that he was forgiven. All he could see was the scorn in her eyes as she turned her back and hobbled towards the plane with her crutches. His heart was heavy as the plane raced down the runway and into the sky.

Two children, both estranged from him, one by choice and one by ignorance. Surely, he thought, somewhere, sometime I must have broken a dozen mirrors.

Carrie found a window seat trying to make herself comfortable. She thought he looked a pathetic figure standing alone as the plane taxied to the runway. That was it. He was out of her life forever. Maybe now she could put her life together without the complications of Tully Sanderson.

Chapter Twenty Six

Sydney 1996

Sydney University's auditorium was filled with graduates and Jason Armitage sat nervously on the stage with the class of 96. He felt self conscious in his flowing robes and mortarboard as he scanned the sea of faces below him. There must have been over four hundred people there, all friends and relatives of the graduating doctors who had completed their University training and were now ready to take up an internship at some of the hospitals around the state. He was actually the third last of a long list called up to receive that precious piece of paper, but while he waited he only had eyes for the two women sitting in the front row.

Proudly Kate applauded as his name was called and she turned excitedly to Carrie who sat beside her joining her in her applause. It had been over three years since they had returned to Australia from Bosnia, and while Carrie had been recuperating from her broken leg, Jason had headed straight back to complete his course in medicine.

Carrie thought about her return to Australia. It wasn't hard to find Jason and she was happy to see he took an interest in her recovery from the broken leg. Steph. was also glad to see her back safe and sound but was distressed to see her hobble up the path of their house.

"Look at you. What have you been up to in Bosnia?"

"You wouldn't believe. I met Jason there and he saved my life."

"I heard from Mum he was an ambulance driver over there. Seems he hurt his hand and they sent him back."

"You better make a cup of tea and I'll tell you all about it."

Stephanie sat silently as Carrie related her adventure in Bosnia. She understood the conflict between Carrie and her father but said nothing about it.

"You need a holiday. I know just the place."

"Where?" Carrie had to admit, a week or two away would do her the world of good.

Stephanie walked to the phone and dialed a number. She waited and then smiled.

"Jason, guess who I have back?"

"Carrie. She's home?"

"Yes, and needs a good rest. Any suggestions?"

"A few weeks in Moruya is what the doctor ordered."

"You're not a doctor yet."

"I will be in a year or two. I'm going back to Uni. Put her on."

Steph handed Carrie the phone. "It's your hero."

"Hi, stranger, good to see you're back. I've told Mum all about you and you're coming down here to rest up. She remembers you from that barbecue way back and insists she meet you again."

"I don't want to impose, Jason."

"You won't be imposing. It's a great place and she's anxious to meet you again. I'll come and get you tomorrow. No arguments, just look at it as doctor's orders."

"Thanks, Jason. I'd like to meet your Mum again too."

It was the most pleasant time Carrie could remember in years. Kate made her more than welcome and before long they became close friends. Instead of the two weeks Carrie had planned, it developed into two months until she felt it was time to get back to work. She was actually sorry she had to leave, but Kate insisted she keep in touch whenever she could. It became a habit for her to go to Moruya at least once a month whenever she was home.

Richard began to send her to exciting places around the world and she rewarded his confidence in her by bringing back top stories. Her reputation was growing every day and she had to admit, the money was good too. At the end of two years, she liked the beach area so much she bought a small holiday shack in Bateman's Bay, which gave her a haven to retreat to when she needed rest.

Her friendship with Jason and Kate developed so strongly, she regarded them on the same plane as Stephanie. Life was good except for her father who had almost disappeared from the face of the earth.

Kate was surprised at the bitterness Carrie had toward Tully when she heard Carrie's account of events. Between her visits to places of news around the world, she and Jason kept in close contact, almost as if there was some bond between them. Kate said it wasn't unusual for this bond between two people who had spent such a horrendous time together, but she kept quiet about them being related.

Carrie had built up a reputation as a reporter who got things done. She'd been to many hot spots including the Gulf and Israel. While Tully had disappeared from the scene, she had taken over the mantle of the tribune's ace reporter. Occasionally she heard from Pat who told her Tully had dropped in once or twice. She remembered he had seen her no more than five times in three years. It seemed he was drunk many times and was living in a dingy apartment somewhere in Bondi. She had no idea how he earned a living.

Sitting in the auditorium waiting for Jason's award, Kate showed Carrie her father's zodiac medallion causing her gasp.

"He never takes the thing off. He must have been really grateful for Jason's help."

"It was obviously given by your mother and meant a great deal to him. I've had it ever since Jason came back. I couldn't bring myself to sell it and I really can't keep it. Perhaps you could return it." She offered it to Carrie who shook her head stubbornly

"I rarely see him now, we've grown apart. Not that we were ever close. Through my life when I wanted his love and companionship, all I got was presents. It was never presents I wanted."

"You must have been shocked when he resigned, it was the last thing I would have expected from him."

"I was surprised. I told him I hated him and didn't want to see him again, but I never expected that."

"It's ironical isn't it? He almost disappears from the face of the earth and you slipped into the role of being the famous journalist."

"I don't think I'll ever reached his heights, but I have seen a few of the world's hot spots since he's been gone."

"More than any girl should have been exposed to," said Kate squeezing her hand. "How long since you've seen him?"

"Once in a while he surfaces and comes to see me when I'm back, but there's always tension there. We sit in a strained silence for a while, and then he gives me a peck on the cheek and leaves. Neither of us seem to be able to break the ice and open up to each other."

"You should, Carrie, you really should. He's the only parent you have and I'm sure he loves you."

"Pat Scanlon sometimes rings and tells me he's been drinking and feeling sorry for himself, but when I see him he puts on this brave face and tells me he's all right. I know it's bluff but he's a hard man to get close to. He lives in a one-bedroom apartment in Bondi. I think Pat is the only friend he has."

Kate took her hand and placed the medallion firmly in her palm closing Carrie's fingers over it.

"I insist you keep it yourself. It was a gift from your mother to him and it was given with love. It could be the only thing you ever have of your mother's."

"It is," said Carrie sadly. "I don't even know what she looked like. Thanks, Kate." Carrie fastened it around her neck just as Jason's name was called.

Jason joined them after the ceremony proudly waving his certificate.

"Do I call you doctor Armitage now?" Carrie was pleased and proud of his accomplishment.

"Only if you come to see me for a consultation. Thanks for coming, Carrie, it's nice to see you again."

"It's the least I can do for the man who saved my life." She looked around playfully. "No Teena?"

"She finished a year ahead of me remember. She's just a friend and she's working in Newcastle. Now let's go somewhere and celebrate."

He put an arm around each of the women and escorted them through the crowd and out of the auditorium. None of them noticed Tully standing in the background watching his family. Kate was just as beautiful as ever, so was his daughter and he had great pride in his son. He had never felt so lonely and decided tonight was a night to go out and get drunk.

Tully often tried to drown his sorrows and Pat Scanlon was very worried about his mental state; he could see the first signs of self-destruction.

Depression could become a serious thing and he tried to keep in close contact with Tully, inviting him to Goulburn where he now presided in his role of Inspector. When they were together Tully seemed his old happy self, laughing and joking with Pat but when he sat alone on the patio, Pat noticed he just sat and stared into space.

He usually stayed less than a week, then went back to Sydney with some excuse he was working on a special assignment. Of course Pat knew it was a lie but short of arresting him, he couldn't do much about it.

It was a few weeks later when Tully went to a club to break the monotony of his empty apartment. As his cab pulled up a young girl waiting impatiently outside, kept looking at her watch.

"Stand you up did he?" said Tully as he passed by. He threw his best smile and the girl snapped at this stranger.

"All men are bastards," she said stamping her foot.

"Care to have a drink with a real bastard. It might teach him a lesson."

She was barely twenty-five and made Tully feel like an old man. She was really angry at her date and so jumped at the invitation.

"Why not. I've been standing here for an hour. This is the last time he's doing this to me."

"The name's Tully," he said offering her his arm.

"I'm Jane. Pleased to meet you, Tully." She took his arm and they entered the club together. Tully bought some drinks and conversation came easily. He hadn't been with anyone for nearly twelve months now, and it was nice having female company for a change. They danced, had a meal, and danced some more. Jane relaxed after a few drinks and seemed to forget about her date. They were laughing like old friends when a young man approached and grabbed Jane's arm.

"Who's the old guy," he said glaring at Tully."

"A gentleman who was kind enough to buy me dinner after I waited for over an hour for you. We're through, Steve, now leave please."

"You must be desperate if you're going to screw this middle aged codger. Come on, let's go."

"I said we're through now leave us alone."

Tully stood up. "You heard the lady." He was at least four inches taller than Steve who backed off.

"You'll be back, Jane."

"Sorry about that," said Jane. "He thinks he's God's gift to women but he's a nasty little bastard really. I'm well rid of him."

"I think so too. Can I escort you home?'

"Thanks, Tully I'd like that, let's have one more dance first."

When the evening finally came to an end Tully paid the bill and escorted Jane outside. He didn't even see the first blow come from behind as Steve and two friends attacked him. He fell to the ground and a boot thudded into his ribs. The last thing he remembered was Jane screaming. He woke in the hospital with Pat's concerned face staring at him.

"Shit you look awful," said Pat relieved he was awake.

"I'm still better looking than you." Talking was an effort, he felt like his rib was going through his chest. "What hit me?"

"Three thugs. You really shouldn't pick up girls with friends like that."

"Did you get them?"

"They were well gone before the police got there. Jane gave their names so we'll follow it up. You look like being in here for a few days."

"Nothing better to do," he managed to say. "Might be some good looking nurses here."

"I've never been that lucky, but you might. Now you're awake I have to get back. Look after yourself, mate. Come down and spend time with us when you feel better."

"Yeah, thanks, Pat." He sank into a fitful sleep; happy to let the painkillers take control. Next morning Carrie came and picked him up.

*   *   *

He woke to the sound of the waves rushing onto the sand. Wind was gusting and trees were arching wildly. He had no idea where he was. Every part of him ached and he could hardly breathe from the pain in his ribs. He stared at the ceiling fan and for some reason thought of Vietnam. Slowly it came back to him. He was at Carrie's beach shack. She had collected him from the hospital yesterday. He remembered she had a gun, then they had a long talk about her mother. Shit what else had they talked about?

Had he told her about Kate and Jason? Why had he talked so much, it must have been the drugs the doctor gave him? He sat up slowly and gradually his mind began to focus. He had only talked about Belfast, he remembered now. She had said it was late and they had gone to bed. The rest was in his head, he had just been thinking, thinking deeply.

Now he wondered how much more he should tell her. He slipped a robe over his pajamas and walked toward the smell of coffee and toast.

He could see Carrie's attitude toward him had changed. No longer was there the tension in the air and he found breakfast on the table waiting for him. Looking around the kitchen he noted a clean tablecloth, canisters neatly arranged on a clean bench, Christ, the exact opposite to his place.

"Feeling better," she asked watching as he ate.

"Heaps. I'm sorry I unloaded the story of your mother on you last night, but you said it was time you knew the truth."

"Overtime I think, I'm glad you did, but it's changed my thinking. I see now I've been pretty awful towards you over the years and I'm sorry. I've always blamed you for everything."

"You had good cause. I've been a rotten father, I know that." Tully drank his coffee, strong and black. He studied his daughter, she was still the spitting image of her mother, even had her mannerisms. The likeness was uncanny.

"Dad, why did you give up journalism?"

He remained silent for a few seconds thinking back to the wasted years he'd missed when his daughter was growing up. He'd made excuses about earning a living to keep her, but he knew it was the rush of adrenaline racing through his blood making him do it. Now it was like salt water on an open wound. He no longer wanted it.

"I'd had a belly full of the horror over the years. When I nearly lost you in Bosnia I thought my pledge to your mother had been violated. I just don't want to do it anymore."

"But it's all you know."

He was touched. It was the first time Carrie had ever shown real concern for him.

"It's over now, Carrie. I still have other secrets you don't know about."

"Should I know about them?" She could see he was still tortured.

"Depends. Let's have some breakfast first."

They finished breakfast and Tully showered and dressed while Carrie cleared the table. She was sitting on the verandah wrapped in a blanket when he emerged.

"Here, Dad, you have the blanket, the wind is very chilly. I'm going to shower and get some warm clothes."

He was grateful for the extra time to gather his thoughts. How much should he tell her? He had always been worried something might develop between Jason and Carrie. He knew they were close so it was only right they knew they were siblings. He hoped he wouldn't lose his new found respect Carrie had for him.

When she returned she was carrying a tray with two mugs and a jug of hot chocolate.

"Not much else to do in this wind except drink warm beverages." She handed him a mug and curled upon the deck chair beside him.

"Now, Dad, shall we get onto chapter two?"

Tully laughed. "That's not a bad idea. Maybe I'll put it in the book and you can read it for yourself."

"I'm sorry. I don't intend to wait that long. I've waited all my life for the first half, now continue please."

"Let me ask you first. How do you feel about Jason Armitage?"

"We've always been good friends. Even back when I first met him and he was a nerd we got on well. I've met his mother lots of times, she's lovely in fact I stayed with her when I came back from Bosnia. I regard her as a close friend now."

"You stayed with Kate? Where, ---at Moyura?"

"Yes, she gave me this." Carrie reached inside her jumper for the zodiac medallion, which she wore constantly. "She said you gave it to her to sell for charity. It was my mothers and you can't have it back."

"I don't want it back, I'm glad you have it."

"How did you know she lived in Moruya?"

"Jason told me when we were in Bosnia. You know, I saw you at his graduation."

"You were there?" Carrie was dumbfounded.

"It was an important night for Jason. I wanted to share in it because he saved your life."

Tully sipped his hot chocolate, his eyes never leaving her face.

"I don't understand why you felt you should go to his graduation, why you gave Kate this medallion. It's not gold so it's not very valuable."

He took another sip before answering. "I wanted to send her a message."

"What sort of a message?"

"Answer my question first, are you involved with Jason?"

"I admit there's some sort of bond between us but nothing's happened if that's what you mean. You forget I'm a few years older than Jason."

"His mother is a few years older than me too."

"What's that supposed to mean?"

"I didn't want to tell you this but I must have your word it won't go further than this room."

"What won't?"

"First the promise. You say nothing unless you have my permission."

"Okay, if it's that important."

"It will be a hard promise to keep. I mean it, Carrie. I want your word as a daughter and as a journalist. It will be hard to take."

"Harder than the news about my mother?"

"Yes."

"My God you're serious aren't you?" Carrie could see the torture behind his eyes.

"Yes. No promise, no truth."

"All right, I promise." Carrie sat back breathlessly.

"I'm only telling you this because of your association with Jason." Tully was scared she would throw him out again.

"Are you going to tell me or not?"

"Carrie, if you never want to see me again I just want you to know I love you more than anything."

"I love you too now for Christ sake tell me."

"Jason is your half brother."

The color drained from her face as she struggled to comprehend his words. "That's impossible. His father was a surgeon who died in Vietnam."

"James Sutton died in Vietnam all right but just after Kate arrived. She was there three years and we met in Saigon and again in Da Nang where we fell in love. I asked her to marry me but she turned me down, wisely I might add. She didn't want a husband who was away from home most of the time. I didn't know about Jason until Bosnia where I put two and two together. That's why I sent Kate the medallion."

"My God, that's why she kept asking about you. I thought she was just being friendly."

"She knew who Briony was and gave the medallion back to you."

"And Jason doesn't know?"

"No, and you mustn't tell him. It would kill Kate."

"And it's not killing you?"

"Maybe but I don't want to hurt Kate again. If he's to know then she'll have be the one to tell him."

"You're telling me this because you thought I'd jump into bed with Jason?"

He nodded. "Think of the bloody mess if that happened."

"It won't. I love Jason but not that way. He treats me like a sister."

"And so he should. Are you angry with me?"

"No. I'm glad you told me. Maybe one day he'll know. How do you feel about Kate?"

Tully looked down. "I've loved her for years but it was doomed a long time ago."

"Maybe it doesn't have to be. Things are different now."

"There's more."

"I was afraid you'd say that."

"I haven't told you about Soo Ling."

"Soo Ling? Don't tell me I've got a Chinese sister too?"

"She was my wife. I married her in Vietnam."

Carrie had to sit down. She poured herself more chocolate then stared at him.

"I can see this is going to be a long day. You'd better start now."

He could see she wasn't angry, just interested to learn the last of his secrets so she let him get it all off his chest.

The whole of Vietnam, of Kate, of Soo Ling and of her death in the fire. The morning had become afternoon when he finished. He waited for her to say something but she had tears in her eyes. At last she went to him and wrapped her arms around him.

"My God, I can't believe this has happened to my own father. You've had a miserable time haven't you?"

"My intentions were always good but I seem to have a talent to stuff up everything I do."

"Not any more, Dad. We're going to start again. Looks like I've found a brother and a new father."

"Does this mean you're not going to shoot me now?"

"I can see why you didn't care if I did. The gun is going into the ocean never to be found again. I'm going to take care of you here until you're better, then we'll work things out."

"I'm better now," he said hugging her. They spent the next week catching up on each other's lives and lost emotions; emotions they had both thought would never eventuate.

Chapter Twenty Seven

A week at Bateman's Bay developed into a month and heralded a new beginning between Carrie and her father. It had been a long time since Tully had felt so needed and he relished this time with his daughter. Just spending these days with her was a decision formed in heaven. They realized how much they had missed never having spoken at such lengths before. Now able to share their feelings, Tully suddenly felt it was good to be alive again. By the time he returned to Sydney his ribs no longer troubled him and his facial bruising had disappeared.

Now with a new purpose in his life he began writing again, not much but little by little his confidence was returned. At least until he heard the fateful knock on his door.

*   *   *

When Soo Ling read the newspaper report about the Federal Police intercepting a large shipment of heroin entering Australia, she knew instinctively she would be hearing from Wang. He knew she had one last kilogram of pure stuff, which she kept aside in case she ever needed quick cash.

With his supplies confiscated he would be anxious to appease his regular customers. To refuse to sell to him would cause tension between them, and Soo Ling had no such desire to lose this fragile tolerance Wang offered her. She knew she had been lucky as a woman to be allowed to gain such a foothold in Wang's territory.

The value of her heroin would have doubled overnight due to supply and demand and she wanted at least $1million for herself. The fact Wang knew her stuff was top quality was a bargaining lever for her. Timothy was worried for her safety and worried again about Wang's Triad methods if things weren't to his liking.

"He will most likely cheat you, Soo Ling."

"I am not naïve enough to doubt that. I will be very wary, you have no need to worry."

"I think perhaps you should suggest he comes to your house to conduct the deal, then I can keep an eye on things from the surveillance monitors."

Soo Ling's affection for Timothy and his concern for her brought tender warmth to her body.

"I shall be more comfortable knowing you are here to protect me."

It was late at night as she was preparing for bed when the expected call came.

"Hello."

"Hello. Soo Ling, this is Horace Wang. I'm sorry to call so late."

"Don't be sorry, it is never too late to talk to an old friend." Steadying her hand she waited for his request.

"You will have read the papers I'm sure, Soo Ling and most probably know I would be forced to ask for your help."

Soo Ling suppressed a smile as she had a vision of how Wang must be feeling being forced to conduct urgent business with a woman, and try to save face with his important regular customers.

"Indeed. I have been anticipating your call and as usual I am happy to do business with you, although I must say right from the outset the price is higher."

Soo Ling could feel bad joss flowing down the phone line and knew Wang would be struggling to compose himself.

"It is unfortunate but I'm sure we can reach an agreement."

"There is no compromise to be reached. My price is $1 million."

An audible gasp reached her ear and the blood pounded in her veins. She knew Wang's capabilities if things upset him seriously.

"It is most inopportune but I am afraid I must leave tomorrow for overseas to try to invest in a new area of trade, but with your approval I shall send my first warrior to work out the deal. You can tell me a suitable time in which to meet for mutual covenant."

Negotiations were discussed and a time of 10 p.m the next evening was settled on.

Timothy spent half the morning checking and re-checking all cameras and angles in the house. They worked out where she should stand and sit to offer the best view for Timothy to be sure all was going well. Neither of them could put their mind to their work that day, so they stayed home checking to make sure nothing could go wrong.

They ate an early dinner and played a half-hearted game of Mahjong. As the time drew near, Timothy removed the silver pistol from the safe and handed it to Soo Ling.

"That won't be necessary, besides, you know I hate guns."

"Please, Soo Ling, humor me and just slip it into your pocket."

Cheongsams weren't designed to disguise the bulk of a pistol, even a small one so Soo Ling slipped upstairs to change into jeans and loose top so she could hide the offending article. With the pistol tucked into the top of her jeans and covered by her blouse it was not visible. She turned around in front of the mirror to double check. Satisfied she looked up as the doorbell sounded. Knowing Timothy was there she didn't hurry as it was still half an hour till the meeting was due to get under way.

Carefully smoothing her clothes she gave an idle glance to the surveillance monitor, and was astounded to see Wang's number one warrior with two of his henchmen already in the entrance hall. Timothy appeared to be arguing with them and right before her eyes she saw the one standing behind him withdraw an ice pick from his boot and ram it upwards through Timothy's neck into his brain. Soo Ling vomited onto the floor in shock. Waves of fear and nausea swept over her. Never in her wildest dreams had she thought Horace Wang would try to kill her. She knew she should run but was rooted to the floor unable to move a muscle. Footsteps were pounding up the stairs and somehow her fingers found the silver pistol, which she aimed shakily toward the door.

The first henchman crossed the landing and Soo Ling fired. The Gods were guiding her bullet and it struck straight and true through his heart.

By the time she stilled her hand and readied herself, the second henchman was already facing her and they fired simultaneously.

Soo Ling's bullet missed but his struck her in the chest and she sank slowly to her knees staring at the spread of blood seeping across her blouse and jeans.

More pounding footsteps and Soo Ling braced herself for another assault. There were sounds of a struggle but her brain wouldn't focus, instead a police uniform reached toward her and lifted her onto the bed. Her head was swimming; she did not understand what was happening. A grey haired man in a navy suit was leaning over her. All she knew was this pain stabbing into her chest.

"Can you hear me, Soo Ling? Soo Ling, stay with me, the ambulance is on its way. Don't you go and die on me now."

The grey head leant close and tucked a pillow under her head. He was pulling on a pair of rubber gloves and Soo Ling wondered if he was washing the dishes.

"Soo Ling," he called again as he grabbed a towel and pressed it into her wound. Slowly she seemed to emerge from the fog of shock and terror.

"Who are you? What happened?"

"My name is Inspector Tom Jordan of the New South Wales Narcotic Bureau. We've been following Horace Wang and his little band for weeks now and have had a tap on his phone. We knew of his arrangement here tonight and had your house staked out all day. I'm sorry to tell you, Timothy Ng has sustained a fatal wound downstairs. The ambulance has been sent for, it shouldn't be long."

"No time for ambulance. Please could you send for my husband Tully Sanderson? He lives in Bondi, 26 Edward Street I think. Hurry please."

Inspector Jordan dispatched one of his men to fetch Tully while he tried to hold the towel in Soo Ling's wound, which was still pouring blood faster than he could mop it up.

"Please, could you pass me a pen and paper."

Soo Ling forced herself into a semi-sitting position, which caused a gush of blood to spurt across the bed and floor. Inspector Jordan handed her his notebook and pen and she struggled to scribble a few lines of untidy scrawl.

"Please, you sign."

She pushed the notebook back to Jordan as the wail of sirens pulled up outside.

The Inspector glanced at the note. It was a simple will leaving all her assets to her husband. Her solicitor's name and address were also added. He added his signature as a witness then gave Soo Ling his full attention.

The medic hurried up the stairs and immediately set about tending to Soo Ling. By the time they plugged the wound and applied a temporary bandage, which was already soaked in blood, Tully arrived with the junior officer.

Noisily the policeman thumped on Tully's door. Inside, Tully was spread across the sofa half asleep as he watched a movie he had already seen twice. If he could be bothered, he'd get up and change the TV dial but it was easier to just laze where he was. The constant thumping on his door spurred him into action. He switched off the TV calling loudly.

"I'm coming, don't knock the bloody door down."

The sight of the uniformed cop sent his mind reeling.

"Mr. Sanderson?"

"Yeah, my daughter. Is something wrong with my daughter?"

"Could you come with me please, Mr. Sanderson?"

"Where is she? What's happened to her?" Tully was frantic, he was sure Carrie had been injured or worse.

"I'm afraid I was just told to bring you to an address in Vaucluse. Could you hurry please, sir, I was told it was urgent."

Tully slammed the door without bothering to check if he had his keys. His heart was pounding as he climbed into the police car and they sped, siren blazing, lights flashing straight up the middle of Southhead Road.

"Christ. If this is just Pat Scanlon's way of getting me to a party I'll kill the bastard."

Skillfully the young policeman wove his way to Vaucluse and screeched to a stop outside a neat, double story terrace house where two police cars and an ambulance were gathered across the road. Interested neighbors stood or leaned outside houses up and down both sides of the narrow street. Tully raced across the doorstep calling Carrie's name as he ran. A policeman stationed inside the front door indicated upstairs and Tully bounded up two at a time still calling Carrie's name. A middle aged grey hair man in a navy suit met him at the top of the stairs and raised a hand in a gesture for Tully to stop.

"Carrie, where's Carrie?"

"Are you Mr. Tully Sanderson?"

"Yes, what's happened here?" Tully tried to see past the sentinel to where he could see paramedics leaning across a person on the bed. There was blood on the floor and across the bedding. He tried to push his way into the room.

"It's not your daughter, Mr. Sanderson. Could you answer a few questions please? Do you know a Vietnamese national called Soo Ling?"

Tully's eyes widened. "Soo Ling was my wife, she died in a fire in Saigon years ago."

"I'm afraid your wife is lying on that bed, sir with a bullet wound in her chest. I'm sorry to tell you it doesn't look good."

Tully felt weak in the knees and looked straight into the room with disbelief.

"It's not possible, I saw her die ---or rather I saw the fire and was sure she had died. How long has she been in Australia? What's she doing here?"

"If you wait a minute, Mr. Sanderson, the paramedics may let you talk to her soon."

Tully danced from foot to foot anxiously waiting for permission to see Soo Ling, when finally he saw the medics packing up their gear. Jordan stood aside allowing him to enter. One looked him in the eye and shook his head indicating there was no hope. Taking a deep breath Tully sat on the edge of the bed and held one of Soo Ling's tiny cold hands.

"Soo Ling, can you hear me? It's Tully."

Her eyes fluttered and opened slightly. "Tully? Tully, is it really you?"

"Shh, I'm here, you rest now."

"I need to tell you something's. I have made my will for you. There is safe behind Dobell painting. The combination is written in a red book in the drawer next to bed. One number every six pages so nobody know. Also have safety box in Commonwealth bank in Oxford Street. Key in same draw. Thank you, Tully for giving me new life years ago. I pray for you all time. Many times I wish I could talk to you since I come here. I come on illegal passport but I have marriage paper so they think I all right. I make good business here."

Her voice was getting fainter and she struggled to breathe.

"You stay please until I die."

"Don't talk like that, you'll go to hospital and you'll get well."

"No, Tully. I ask medic, he say no hope."

She gave a small cough as she tried to force a smile. "Okay, I not die yet. Really wish I could die in Vietnam. Could you please take ashes home to bury with family."

"Of course I will, Soo Ling. Do you have any family left in your village?"

"Not know if anyone live. Never get answer back when I write. Not visit there." Her breath was laboring and she was growing weaker. He stroked her brow soothingly.

"Please, Tully, put green dress on body for burial service. Always look pretty in green dress."

Tears welled in Tully's eyes and trickled down his cheeks. She was still pretty. Poor little bugger, what a way to go. She reached out with one hand to wipe away his tears.

"No cry, Tully." Her hand fell to the bed and her head rolled to one side. She was gone. He buried his head against her and let the tears run. He felt sorry he had not known she was here in Australia. Maybe he could have helped her settle and find a good job, after all, she was his wife? Not even forty and she was dead.

Inspector Jordan gave him some time alone with Soo Ling and allowed him to compose himself. When he emerged from the room Jordan said he wished to have a few words with him. Perhaps downstairs would be better.

He stepped around the body of the man Soo Ling had shot. At the bottom of the stairs was another body covered with a sheet. Tully had not even noticed it on his rush to get inside.

"Who's that?"

"His name was Timothy Ng, he worked for your wife."

"Worked? What sort of work did she do?"

"Sit down please, Mr. Sanderson and I'll tell you as much as I can."

For the next half-hour Jordan told him what he knew of Soo Ling and her association with Horace Wang who was their main target. It seemed Wang had skipped the country and his Triad warriors had done all the damage here tonight. Whether or not it was on Wang's orders or just their own undertaking was unclear as yet. They had found a suitcase with $1 million beside Ng's body and according to phone taps the police had, the money was to buy heroin, but as yet they had not found any.

Jordan hesitated before going on. "I know you're a reporter but do you intend to file a story about tonight's events?"

"I'm retired now but if it's okay by you, I'll see an accurate report goes to print."

"I was hoping you'd say that. Don't mention the money. We think if Wang reads about it, it may force him into coming back for his money, then we'll be able to nab him."

Tully was told there was nothing more he could do tonight and perhaps he might like to get a start on his story. He knew he was being dismissed and was pleased to leave the murder site to the professionals.

He stepped out into the fresh night air as the state coroner and forensic people arrived then hailed a passing cab, glad to be away from the scene.

Giving the cab driver Carrie's address, he lay back in the seat and closed his eyes. Soo Ling's laughing face and silky black hair danced across his mind. He could hear her screaming the first day he saved her from the rape. He heard her crying as she explained how she had given the baby away. He saw flames engulfing the club where he thought she had died. He felt the warm blood soaking through the bandages as she bled to death before his eyes just one hour ago.

Jesus how come some poor buggers never seem to get a chance in life?

"Fourteen dollars eighty cents, mate." The cab driver's voice brought him back and he realized they were outside Carrie's place. He paid the fare and dragged his weary body to the door.

"Dad!" Her face lit up as she answered his knock.

"Hi, love. Can I come in? Sorry it's so late."

Carrie stood aside and he stumbled across the doorstep.

"Are you all right, Dad? Have you been drinking?"

"That's a good idea. Do you have any whisky?"

Carrie followed her father into the tiny lounge area and reached for a bottle of Grants. She walked to the kitchen for a couple of glasses, poured them both two fingers and sat beside him.

"Do you want to tell me what's wrong?"

He downed his drink in one gulp and reached for the bottle.

"Get your pad and pencil, I'm going to give you the story of the week."

Chapter Twenty Eight

Exhausted by the night's events Tully slept on Carrie's divan bed covered with a pink fluffy blanket. Carrie had listened to his tale with eyes and mouth opened in amazement. She let him sleep as she sat at her computer punching in her story. There was only an hour or so till the presses started rolling, so if she hurried it might just make the front page.

She couldn't believe Tully's wife; her own stepmother had been living just a few suburbs away for years and not a word from her. Swiftly her fingers flew over the keys until she was satisfied all the details given to her were accurately recorded. Finished at last, she pressed the appropriate buttons to send her story on its way to head office where the type setter would soon be flat out getting it ready to print after approval by the editor.

Switching off the computer and the lights, she fell into bed hoping to grab a couple of hours before Tully woke ready to go to the bank.

She had promised she would go with him to go through Soo Ling's safety deposit box and then see if they could make arrangements about a burial service, and the eventual transportation of her ashes home.

Sleep came the instant she hit the pillow, but unlike Tully who slept soundly helped along by several slugs of Grant's smooth blend, Carrie sleep was haunted by visions of a green sparkling dress being engulfed in flames. Her father was beating out the flames, Carrie was being shot and blood was seeping down her front with voices calling her.

"Carrie! Carrie wake up, you're having a bad dream."

Her father was bending over her and lifting her in his arms. She clung to him desperately.

"Oh, Dad, thank, God it was only a dream."

She was drenched in perspiration and shaking with fear. He soothed her gently and sat with her until she went back to sleep. In the morning she woke to the smell of bacon, toast and fresh coffee. Tully was standing by the bed with two mugs of steaming coffee. He sat on edge of the bed.

"Here, love, drink this then have a nice hot shower while I get the eggs ready."

Together they sipped their coffee and she was grateful there was no mention of her nightmare. Now in the cold light of day she felt foolish but it had all seemed so real. She shuddered and jumped out of bed heading for the shower.

Walking through to the kitchen with her wet hair wrapped in a towel and a white toweling gown draped over her body still tingling from the needles of hot water, she sank into a chair and hungrily devoured a plate of scrambled eggs and bacon.

Tully poured more coffee and headed for the shower himself.

"I won't be long, don't want to use up all of your hot water."

She finished breakfast, dried her hair and still he was showering. When he finally opened the bathroom door, she just finished dressing

"Glad you didn't take long."

"Well I had a few things I wanted to think about and time got away."

They left the house and climbed into Carrie's little blue car and headed for the Oxford Street branch of the Commonwealth Bank. At the traffic lights a young boy was selling copies of the Sydney Tribune. "Sydney Madam killed in drug war," he shouted.

Tully wound down the window and waved the boy over. Handing him a dollar coin he grabbed the paper just as the lights turned green and Carrie sped away.

"Hey, I didn't get my change."

"Bad luck, think how pleased the kid will be. A whole twenty cents tip."

Head down he studied Carrie's story all the way into town.

"Good story, love, you captured the essence of what I was trying to portray."

Occasionally she heard him say. "Yeah, true, bloody oath, this is good."

She laughed to herself thinking I guess it's meant to be praise.

Finding a parking spot in Oxford Street was usually impossible; so Carrie took the first spot they found vacant and walked the fifty meters around the corner.

Tully presented himself at the counter and showed his key with the necessary number. They were taken downstairs where a staff member put a key in one lock while Tully did the same. Together they turned the keys and when they heard the click the teller left them alone.

Tully removed the long box and they both walked a few steps to a private area where there was a row of cubicles each with a small table and two chairs. Seated each side of the table their eyes met above the box and Tully said quietly. "Are we ready?"

Carrie nodded and he slowly lifted the lid as if expecting a dancing cobra to emerge. Carrie gasped and Tully swung the lid fully open revealing piles of neatly stacked one hundred-dollar bills.

"Shit-bloody hell." They just stared neither knowing what to say.

Carrie whispered as if frightened they would be overheard. "Do you think it's real. There must be close to a million dollars here."

Tully reached in and grabbed one bundle. He counted a few bills and did a rough guesstimate. "Well certainly half a million anyway. Shit, look at those bonds and share certificates. There's bloody million's in them too. Christ, love, I think we're seriously rich."

They read a few of the share certificates, enough for them to realize they were all in blue chip shares and companies. In the corner were two black velvet boxes. Carrie lifted the smaller one and flicked it open. A flash of light greeted her, and nestled on the soft black material was at least two dozen unset diamonds of various sizes.

With her mouth open she passed it across to Tully and reached for the other one. This time her surprise was not as sudden as a flash of diamonds greeted her again, but these were set in bracelets, rings and neck lets.

Lovingly she removed a pink argyle bracelet with perfectly matched diamonds set in yellow gold. There must have been thirty baguettes. It was the most beautiful thing Carrie had ever seen.

She dropped it over her wrist.

"That looks nice, you can have it if you want."

She dropped it back into the velvet box as if it burnt her fingers.

"Dad, I couldn't. It's too beautiful."

"Don't be stupid. If it's mine legally then I can give it to you. Mind you I don't think I would wear it to work. Richard might think you didn't need a pay packet if you turned up in that."

They played with the new found wealth for a while, then carefully packed it all just as they found it, locked it away and then left the bank. The walk to the car was in silence; both still too stunned to talk. The ringing of Tully's mobile phone interrupted their thoughts.

"Yeah, yeah, yeah, okay, fine, yeah," then he hung up.

"That was a pretty one-sided conversation," Carrie remarked as she hunted in her bag for her keys.

"It was Inspector Jordan, he wants to meet me at Soo Ling's house in Vaucluse. Have you got time to come with me?"

"Are you kidding? Let's go."

They drove straight to Soo Ling's house, which Tully really hadn't noticed much last night. Now in daylight he saw it was a very nice place indeed. Small front garden kept tendered. Pink and white standard roses along the front fence. Masses of impatiens in pink, white and mauve were under the bay window and a silver birch tree was gracefully adorning the corner space.

Touches of green were pushing through the lovingly tendered soil and looked like a cluster of daffodils about to push their way into the world.

Inside the plush the carpet was pale cream pure wool, the furnishings pale and tasteful. There was lots of pink, Soo Ling obviously liked pink but it was beautifully toned in several shades both pale and dark. The walls held some beautiful paintings, all originals. Tully could see a Dobel, a Constable and a Turner in this room alone and he was sure the one in the entrance hall was a Picasso.

"Good morning, Mr. Sanderson. Thanks for meeting me. We have a few things to sort out."

"Inspector Jordan. This is my daughter Carrie and please call me Tully."

Jordan nodded his agreement. "Likewise Tom, now let's sit down and discuss a few details. You said you didn't know your wife was in Australia, for that matter, even alive."

"That's right, Tom. The day Saigon fell, the club where she worked was an inferno and burnt down to the ground. I was passing by and one of the men fighting the fire told me all the girls were gone. I guess I assumed he meant dead, so I left the place thinking she had died."

"Well we know she came here on a false passport in 1975 and as you can see by the house, she has done rather well for herself."

Tully laughed heartily. "You know last night I was feeling sorry for her and thinking that if I'd known she was here I might have been able to get her a job. Bloody hell, she could have bought and sold me."

"Sure looks like it, it seems she owns quite a bit of property. Now our problem is, we had Wang's phone tapped and we heard him make arrangements to come here and buy pure heroin. We haven't found it yet and didn't want to smash the place up if we didn't have to. Seeing you own it now, can we have your permission to search for the safe?"

"I think I can help. Soo Ling told me there was a safe behind one of the paintings just before she died. You can certainly have my permission to search the place for anything."

Tom Jordan gave his men the signal to go ahead and search making sure they caused no damage and to refer to him or the new owner if they had any queries. Tully and Carrie tried to keep out of the way and checked out the small back yard leading to the waterfront. Both were impressed by the view. The harbor looked magnificent with the bridge and opera house in full view. Ferries and all sorts of watercraft were moving across the blue waters. Tully had to admit; he hadn't seen any harbor in the world that could match Sydney's. Pink and white roses were again prominent but as the hot sun was not suitable for impatiens, the plants facing the sun were pink, white and mauve petunias.

Upstairs the main bedroom was roped off with a police ribbon as the forensic team was still chasing any trace of evidence. There was still evidence of the blood spilled when Soo Ling shot one of her assailants.

Tom Jordan called Tully. "We've found a small wall safe behind the Dobel painting and we need you to be here when we open it."

"I think I can help. Soo Ling said the combination is on every sixth page of a little red book in a drawer."

The book was found and they watched as a policeman spun the numbers. "Bingo," he said as the safe opened. Right in full view was a packet of a white substance, which brought a long low whistle from the officer searching. Carefully he removed the package and called to Jordan who slit the end open and dipped the tip of his penknife into the powder and tasted it.

"Wow! That's the true blue variety. Worth about 2 million on the streets by the time it was cut."

Carrie and Tully exchanged glances with raised eyebrows. Tom inspected the safe for more heroin but found only papers.

"No more drugs so the rest is personal. It's none of our business and I guess it' yours now."

The back of the safe seemed to be just papers and some jewelry so the search was wound down and the police departed. Tully and Carrie were allowed to stay a bit and tidy up provided they didn't go upstairs into the bedroom.

With the house to themselves they hurried to the safe to fully check out the rest of the contents. Title deeds of several properties in the best part of town along with three restaurants at Cabramatta, another box of assorted jewelry with emeralds and sapphires inter-set with diamonds, a few share certificates. By the date it seemed they had only been purchased last week and right at the back was a long black box.

Being black and in a deep safe it was hardly visible and when opened, Tully was very pleased Jordan and his men had gone. There was a pile of new hundred dollar bills which at a guess was at least three or four hundred thousand dollars.

"I swear if I live to be a hundred, I'll never be able to find something to do with all this stuff. She must have been worth bloody millions."

After a week or so the police withdrew from the house and declared the case closed unless Wang came back to Australia and gave cause to have it re-opened.

Tully was able to claim Soo Ling's body and he arranged a service and cremation for her. Looking at her body one last time dressed in her green dress, he felt a sadness overcoming him. He and Tom Jordan were the only one's present as Carrie was away on an assignment.

Tully purchased a beautiful jade urn to hold Soo Ling's ashes and stow them in the wall safe until he could arrange to go to Vietnam and deliver them to her village.

He decided he would have a few days down in Goulburn with Pat and his family. They did some trout fishing, a fair amount of drinking and had a good relaxing time.

Pat was very pleased at the change in his friend and glad Carrie was at last a proper part of his life. Tully went back to Sydney a happy and relaxed man and hastily made arrangements to go to Vietnam for a few days. He had no desire to spend long there; he'd had his share of that place.

The steamy weather hadn't changed but the countryside had after the napalm and Agent Orange devastation of that horrible time. Hiring a car he drove to Soo Ling's village where he could find no trace of any of Soo Ling's family. He left the urn at the temple with a Buddhist priest who promised faithfully to put her ashes with her fathers who he remembered well and knew where he was buried. Tully gave him a check for half a million dong for use in the village and for a family headstone or whatever the equivalent was in Vietnam.

Tully wanted it known the money came from Soo Ling who had fled the country and made her fortune in Australia. The priest couldn't thank him enough. Tully was thankful that part of his life was all behind him. The girl who he had saved in the jungle had now given him a new perspective on life and he intended to make good use of the money.

Back in Australia Tully set about selling off some of his newly acquired property. He spent long periods with Soo Ling's solicitor and now had a full resume of Soo Ling's business properties. He had no desire to own a chain of brothels and was sure he could put the money to better use. The solicitor arranged a quick sale finding eager buyers without problems. He signed Soo Ling's house over to Carrie. She had not been there the night of the murder and she had never met Soo Ling so she had no compunction about living there. To say she was quite delighted with her new home was an under-statement.

Vera refused to leave her home so Tully insisted she go on an overseas trip with some friend to wherever she wanted to go. While she was away he had the house painted inside and out, then purchased quite a bit of new furniture being careful to consult Carrie about what she was sure Vera would never want to part with, and what she wouldn't mind what was replaced. He had her poor shabby garden landscaped and planned in such a way she had little maintenance to bother with.

A gardener was employed to call weekly and send the account to Tully. She could wander around and weed a bit, or leave it to the gardener, whatever took her fancy. He also deposited $200000 in Vera's bank account.

When Tully and Carrie collected her from her trip and returned to the house she cried.

She kept going from one room to the other repeating "Oh, Tully, what can I say. I don't deserve it." Tully thought it was at least some reward for taking such good care of his daughter for all those years.

"Now, Dad, it's time you did something for yourself, don't you want a nice house or a car? After all, it is your money."

"Matter of fact I've just ordered a new Volvo in bright yellow and now I'm going after something I've wanted for a long time."

"And pray tell. It wouldn't have anything to do with someone of the female persuasion who lives in the country would it?"

"Can't a man have any secrets around you. Now don't go saying anything but yes, I have been making some inquiries about Kate. I've sent a generous donation to her charity for a start."

"How generous?"

"One million dollars."

"That's generous. Just how much are you worth altogether?"

"About thirty four million. I reckon I might have to buy her affection."

Carrie gasped. "When do you plan leaving on this excursion?"

"Tomorrow. I may as well tell you, I've also looked into buying the Moruya and District Times. The old guy who owns it has just had heart surgery and I might be able to talk him into retiring. If ever you want to work for me I might take you on."

"If I know you, you'd start me at the bottom sweeping floors. Go and find Kate for heavens sake and don't let her get away this time."

"Thanks, love. I'll give you a ring in a day or two."

Tully mused over his intentions. Would Kate still be interested after all this time?

What would she say about him knowing the truth about Jason?

There was only one way to find out and he wasn't going to let this chance slip by.

Chapter Twenty Nine

Tully was impressed with his first look at the Moruya and District Times office. A dark green, heavy-duty commercial carpet newly laid by the spongy feel. Soft green walls and a great old lead light window. The front window plate was large and obviously new, the paper logo blazed across the center. Printed neatly in one corner was small blade lettering announcing Forrester and Son? Est. 1925. Inside was light and airy with a homely feel. An air conditioner cooled the warm afternoon and the work areas through the glass screen had modern looking printers and computers.

The front desk was polished lovingly and had a small bowl of red carnations on the corner. An elderly woman was manning the desk and greeting people arriving to do business with Forrester and Son.

Tully studied the walls adorned with an array of photos of the changing face of Forrester's over the years, and several awards the small country paper had won.

"Good morning." The woman looked up from her work.

"May I help you, sir?"

"I'd like to see Mr. Forrester please." Tully noticed a scowl appearing on her face.

"Mr. Forrester only works three days a week. Do you have an appointment?"

"No. I didn't think I needed one."

"Perhaps you could see our junior executive Mr. Roberts.

"No. It's Joe Forrester I want to see. Perhaps if you rang. It's very important."

"And you are?"

"Sanderson. Tully Sanderson."

"The foreign correspondent?"

"Ex-foreign correspondent I'm afraid." Tully flashed his best smile.

She reached for the intercom and pressed the top button. "Mr. Forrester, there's a gentleman here to see you. His name is Tully Sanderson."

"Tully Sanderson? Send him in." An excited voice blared back at them.

She smiled politely and pointed to a door on her left. "Through there, Mr. Sanderson."

Tully followed her directions, knocking and entering. The elderly man sitting behind the desk slowly rose to his feet.

"Joe Forrester. Extremely pleased to meet the famous Tully Sanderson."

He offered his hand and quickly resumed his seat. "Excuse me not coming to meet you, Mr. Sanderson but I've not been well."

A triple by-pass and he says not well thought Tully taking a seat in front of a large well-worn desk.

"Now, what can a paper like mine do for a reporter like you, son?"

"I'd like to talk business, sir if that's all right?"

Joe Forrester blinked in surprise. "You're not after a job are you? I'm afraid we couldn't run to your type of salary."

"No, it's not a job exactly. I understand you haven't been well if you'll forgive me for being personal."

"Has Mavis been talking again? I keep telling her not to mention my operation."

"Mavis?"

"My wife. She's the dragon at the front desk. Won't let anyone see me if she thinks it might stress me."

"I think she's only looking after your health, Joe, but actually it wasn't Mavis who told me."

"I suppose she means well but I've worked here since I was ten. My grandfather started the paper after the war, and then my father had it. I took over when he died."

"How many on your staff, Joe?"

"About thirty, not big but it keeps people employed."

"How much do you think its worth, Joe?"

Joe threw his head back and laughed. "Why, are you thinking of making an offer?"

"Actually yes."

Joe shot straight up in his chair. "Now why would a hot shot reporter like you want to buy a small quiet country newspaper like mine?"

"That's exactly why, Joe. It's small and quiet. I've had enough chasing news around the world, never sleeping in the same bed for a week, on and off planes. I want to retire and this looks a nice place to do it."

"Moruya is certainly quiet if that's the sort of life you're after. But really, Tully, I can't imagine you would want to live here."

"Why don't you bring Mavis in and listen to what I have to say."

Joe reached for the intercom and pressed for Mavis. "Could you come in here for a minute, dear. Get Jenny to mind the desk."

Mavis bustled in anxious to see what her husband was up to.

"Tully here wants to buy the paper. What do you think?"

Mavis looked startled then smiled broadly. "I know how you feel about your baby, Joe but it is time you slowed down. Maybe we could think about it. Is it a good offer?"

"We haven't got that far yet. I'm not sure if I want to part with it. My grandfather started it, remember. It's a good paper even if we do only put it out three days a week."

"I know it's a big decision, Joe. Perhaps we could hear the rest of Mr. Sanderson's offer."

"Tully, the Forrester name has always been a big part of the community. I have staff who have been with us for years. They have mortgages and school fees, I wouldn't want them all out of work."

"I promise you nobody will lose their jobs in fact we may even create some new ones in time."

"Well some of the locals mightn't take too kindly of a stranger coming in and taking over."

"What about if I didn't take over totally, just 80% and you stay on as partner. You could keep your name over the door and still get ink on your fingers whenever you felt like it."

Mavis looked at Joe and her pudgy hands fluttered to her face.

"Oh, Joe, that sounds wonderful. What do you think?"

"I think I'm interested dear, what else are you offering, Tully?"

"How about ten million to see you over the hard times, Joe."

Mavis gasped loudly and Joe jumped up and clasped Tully's hand.

"You've got yourself a country newspaper, son, welcome aboard."

"Glad to come aboard, Joe. I have to go back to Sydney and sort out a few things. I'd like it if you kept it quiet for a while. We can tell the staff when it's all signed and sealed. I'm sure they'll agree that with my experience and reputation we shouldn't have any trouble maintaining your excellent standard."

They shook hands and Mavis invited him to stay the night and have dinner with them, but Tully wasn't ready yet to risk bumping into Kate so he declined.

"What are you going to do now you're retiring, Mavis?"

"First I'm going to book an overseas trip and buy a new wardrobe to take with me. I could use a few more dresses and a couple of pair of shoes."

Joe shook his head amused at his wife's reaction, but deep down he was pleased as she was. For years he had dreamed of visiting Rome and walking through the Coliseum and going to the ruins of Pompeii. Now at last he had the chance to go.

Tully returned to Sydney and put his solicitor on the job of sorting out the details involved with owning a newspaper. Carrie was away interstate at a tragic bridge collapse so at least he didn't have to explain anything to her just yet.

*   *   *

Kate Armitage just sat and stared at the letter. One million dollars. Who on earth would donate one million dollars to Moruya? Maybe it was some farmer from the outer district, who had his life saved, or one of his family saved at her hospital at some time and now they were rich and wanted to share?

Or maybe someone had won the lottery, or perhaps it was from the Mafia? Who cares where it came from, it was hers and in her hospital account. This and the money already accumulated made it all possible. She thought that last million would take at least five years to raise. As soon as the news came through she was in touch with the architects about the plans for the new wing. Already the committee was having meetings to decide just which area would be used for which department. Kate was ecstatic. She had rung Jason and told him and he was thrilled for her.

His suggested it was from a secret lover. She laughed as he said that but after she had hung up her mind did flash to Tully. She'd read in the paper about some Sydney drug madam murdered and there was one brief line saying she had once been married to Tully Sanderson. Maybe? No that's stupid.

For a week she sort of glided around as if in a trance. Now the constant fund raising, things she had always devoted her time to could slow down a bit. Hospitals always needed money but the main pressure was off for a while.

It was about a month later when she received a phone call from old Joe Forrester at the local newspaper inviting her to call next Tuesday at 2pm. Maybe Joe was her benefactor. She knew he had not long had major surgery. Anyway tomorrow was Tuesday so perchance she would learn then.

Tuesday morning started out raining and Kate hoped Joe Forrester wouldn't want to go out to photograph the new site, as now it was a mud heap.

By afternoon the sun was out and most of the puddles had dried up. Kate promptly arrived at 2 p.m and was shown into Joe's office by the young office girl.

Kate wondered where Mavis was; she had manned the front desk for as long as Kate could remember. Joe welcomed her warmly and made a bit of small talk about plans for the new wing. A buzz on the intercom caused Joe to jump up excitedly.

"Kate, I'm sure you will be more than pleased to meet my guest. He's the one who made all this possible for you."

He headed for the door as Kate's head spun toward the entrance.

"Come in, come in."

Joe was in the way and she couldn't see anyone. Who was this person who got Joe so excited? Joe stepped back to allow his guest to enter. Kate half stood, then quickly sat down again before her knees gave way under her. There he was, in the flesh after all those years. Still handsome, still smiling, still causing her heart to thump.

"Hello, Kate. Nice to see you again."

Her mouth went dry and no words came out, just a sort of squeak.

"What was that?" He was making fun of her, her cheeks flamed. He stepped closer and gave her a bear hug. Suddenly she found her voice.

"Tully, how good to see you again. However did you find your way to Moruya."

"Just followed my instincts and my heart, Kate."

She wasn't sure just what that was supposed to mean, but fortunately Joe Forrester's voice was booming on about the very generous gift and six months building plan and new staffing opportunities. His words were all running together and Kate thought she would faint.

She wanted to run outside but she wanted to run to Tully more. She wanted them all to stop talking and let her think. As if he could read her mind Tully suddenly said,

"I think Kate's had enough for now, Joe, why don't we let her go and we can meet her at the hospital tomorrow for some photos at the new site."

"Good idea, Tully." Joe opened the door and before she could protest, she found herself outside the office with Jenny opening the street door and saying goodbye Doctor Armitage. She drove home in a daze. What sort of a fool must he think she was? She had barely uttered two words that made sense. God, for years she had dreamed, planned what she would say if ever she met him again and now she hadn't even thanked him for the generous gift. Did he say he would be there tomorrow? Why didn't I listen? Why did I freeze up? God I wish today had never happened. Well as my old mum said, no use crying over spilt milk. She would do better tomorrow if he were there.

The cup of strong tea she made herself was relaxing and she sat on the back patio while she drank it. Then a hot bath and a soak in it for ages.

At last she felt as if she had cleared today out of her system and threw on an old tee shirt over a pair of jeans. A vigorous brush of her hair made it shine like silk, and then she let it hang loosely around her shoulders.

Opening the freezer door, she stood trying to decide what to do about dinner. The doorbell sounded its one long buzz. Closing the freezer door she padded barefoot toward the front of the house. Her wooden door was open with just the wire door closed, for no one here locked their doors, hardly ever shut them.

There he was again, Tully Sanderson, her Tully Sanderson here in Moruya, here in her house. She pushed the wire door open and he stepped inside.

Neither spoke, their eyes locked and together they took one step and were in each other's arms. Their kiss was long and hard. He buried his face in her hair breathing deeply.

"You smell so good," he muttered with a mouthful of hair. Her mouth found his again and again. It was a long hungry kiss washing away the wasted years.

"I never stopped loving you, Tully." She stroked his hair, his face, and his neck. They kissed again less hungry now; the desperation was being satisfied.

He drew back and looked deeply into her soul.

"Why did you never tell me about Jason?"

It was not an accusation, just a statement.

"I knew you had your wars to fight, your places to go. I knew one day you'd come back to me but I didn't think it would take quite this long."

She led him to the kitchen where they sat talking and talking, each telling of their lives and what they had accomplished, where they had been. Kate scrambled some eggs while Tully kept talking. It was just as if they had never been apart.

They stacked the dishes on the sink and as naturally as if they did it every night, they headed for the bedroom. It was only when they stepped inside Tully suddenly stopped and turned to Kate.

"Are you sure this is what you want, Kate?"

"Tully, for years I've mentally rehearsed this minute. If you change your mind now I'll not be responsible for my actions."

Slowly they undressed each other and gently made love. There was no need for haste and fervor they had been through those years ago.

Now it was just tender caring love and wonderful sex. Kate had always said their bodies were designed to go together, they fitted like a pair of gloves. The extra five kilograms Tully was carrying no longer bothered him and it seemed Kate didn't even notice them. Each had their share of grey at their temples but their love was true and deep, and cosmetic beauty was far from their minds. The night was one of meaning sharing and re-discovery and at last they slept together, their arms entwined. As the morning sun rose slowly over the treetops, the parrots and kookaburras started up their morning anthem. Tully almost leapt from the bed as the cacophony got under way. Kate stretched and laughed.

"That's the local alarm clock."

"Shit, does it go on every day?"

"We don't even notice it but if you lie here and listen it really is beautiful."

"Well I wish you had warned me. Sydney has digital alarms we set for a required time. I suppose I'll have to learn to wake to the birds now."

"Are you trying to suggest you might stay a while?"

"Longer than a while my, love, you are sleeping with the new owner of the Moruya and District Times. I'm soon to be local. What do you think of that?"

She wrapped herself around him and covered his face with kisses. "That's the best piece of news I've had in ages, apart from the million dollar news I got a while back. That was very generous, Tully, you have no idea what it will mean to the community. Why don't I thank you properly?"

She rubbed her body seductively against him and he responded eagerly.

"Don't start something you may not be able to finish."

"We have all day don't we?"

Later as they sat eating a leisurely breakfast, she asked him about Soo Ling. Holding back nothing he related the story from the day in Vietnam right up until her murder. Kate was saddened someone so young had faced such misery and horror in such a short space of life.

"Kate, about the million dollars for your hospital."

"I don't like the sound of that, do you want it back now you've had your wicked way with me?"

"I would really like it if you could see your way clear to have a drug rehab center incorporated in the building and name it after Soo Ling."

"Tully, that's a wonderful idea, of course I will."

Back in Sydney to sort out a bit of financial business, Tully made a phone call to Carrie.

"Hi, stranger, how would you like a weekend away with your poor old man."

"Old you might be, Dad, but poor, certainly not. Where do you want to take me?"

"Kate has asked Jason up for the weekend. She's hoping to get a chance to tell him about his parentage. She would really like it if we could both be there. I'll pick you up at lunch time Friday if you can get away."

"Sounds good to me. I'd really love to catch up with Jason again and am dying to see your investment there."

Carrie talked almost all the way to Moruya. She had been overseas covering Wimbledon. It was not her usual field but at the last minute someone had broken their ankle and she asked Richard for a chance to do something different.

Tully had booked them into the local motel, as he wanted to give Kate some time alone with Jason. They were all to go for lunch the next day. Kate looked stunning in an apricot slack-suit with bronze sandals and a wide matching belt. Her hair was up in a sort of bunch with an ornate clasp holding it in place. Carrie was thrilled to see her again and Tully seemed nervous at the prospect of seeing his son once more. He looked around expectantly.

"He's not here yet. He rang last night and told me he was bringing a surprise. He keeps telling me I need a micro-wave oven so I think he might have bought me one."

They all helped to set up the barbecue area and prepared a couple of salads. Tully marinated the steak and was all ready just waiting for Jason. His red sports car whizzed up the drive and ground to a halt almost at the front door.

"Out the back, Darling," called Kate through the open door. They heard footsteps through the house and Jason stepped onto the back patio firmly holding the hand of a shy looking fair-haired girl with glasses.

"Hi, Mum. This is Lauren. She just agreed to be my wife."

Kate almost dropped the glass she was holding.

"Darling, how wonderful."

She ran to embrace her son and her new daughter in law to be. Suddenly Jason realized Carrie was sitting on the step.

"Carrie, I didn't know you were here, and, Tully too. What a surprise."

Introductions and hugs were required all round and everyone seemed to be talking at the same time. Tully looked happily at his family thinking how his luck had changed.

He lit the barbecue and cooked the meat leaving the others babbling away. Jason approached him with a can of beer.

"Looks like wedding talk over there, think I'll join you for a while. Here, have a cold one. What brings you up here, did Carrie drag you out for some fresh air? Pretty place isn't it?"

"Firstly thanks for the drink and to answer one of your questions, I'm up here because I've bought the local paper and I'll be living here now, and yes, it is a very pretty place. Not nearly as pretty as your mother, which brings me to another subject. I've asked her to marry me, I hope its okay with you."

Jason offered his hand to Tully and shook it vigorously. "How the hell did this all happen? I couldn't be more pleased. Hey, Mum, does this mean we can have a double wedding."

Happily Kate spun to face the two men in her life.

"I'm glad you approve, Darling. I never told you I knew Tully back when we were in Vietnam. We were rather friendly then so this is just a renewal."

Jason raised his drink in salute. "Let's drink to our future, what a day of surprises this is."

Kate put her arm affectionately around her son and led him inside.

"Can I talk to you privately for a minute?"

"Sure, Mum. What's wrong?"

Kate bit her lip before speaking. "This is going to be a shock to you Jason but the time has come to explain something to you."

"I've had a few shocks in my time. I guess today is a day for shocks."

"It's just that…"

"Relax, Mum. I think Tully's a terrific bloke if that's what's worrying you."

"I'm glad you feel that way because there's some news I haven't told you. Sadly I've been holding back from the time you were born."

Jason frowned. "Is it bad news?"

"It's about your father."

"He died before I was born. That's old news."

"He didn't actually. In fact he's alive and well."

Jason was stunned. "Are you trying to tell me that James Sutton wasn't my father?"

"It happened a long time ago. I was desperately in love and he restored my sanity. We had a stormy love affair. We couldn't get enough of each other. It was just before I left Vietnam, three years after James died."

"And the bastard just let you bring me up alone?"

"No. I didn't tell him. He asked me to marry him but I declined."

"Why for Christ sake?"

"Because his lifestyle was entirely different to mine? He wouldn't have been at home while I was raising you. I didn't want an absent husband."

"He was army?" Jason was anxious to learn his father's true identity "No."

Suddenly the penny dropped. "Shit, you mean Tully?"

Kate nodded, her eyes filling with tears.

"Please don't be angry with me, Jason. And don't be angry at Tully. He didn't know until you met in Bosnia."

Jason turned and walked to the door leaving Kate standing alone.

Tully busied himself with the steaks and Carrie kept Lauren engaged in conversation, as they knew what Kate was about to do. With the meat cooked and moved to the side of the hot plate to keep warm and the salad bowls placed in readiness, Carrie, Lauren and Tully were sipping drinks in silence waiting for the return of Kate and Jason.

Tully's mind was racing, would his son punch him? Had he lost all respect for him? Would he ever come to terms with the shattering news his mother had just delivered to him? Slowly he walked to Tully and stood in front of him.

"Shit, you might have told me back in Bosnia."

Tully's mouth went dry, he tried to speak. Carrie rose to her feet ready to defend her father's actions.

"We could have been doing this years ago, Dad." Jason threw his arms around his father in a flood of warmth. Tully could see Kate, tears running freely down her cheeks. He hugged his son, his own eyes moist and damp.

"Where's the champagne. This calls for a toast," said Carrie fetching glasses all round. She was elated with Jason's attitude. He'd been a pillar of strength to her and she so wanted him to like Tully.

"How come you knew, Carrie? Why did you never tell me?"

"It wasn't my secret to tell, brother dear."

"Lauren, are you sure you still want to marry me now we're finding all these skeletons in the cupboard?"

"I'm sure, Jason, and besides, it gives me a sister-in-law and hopefully a bridesmaid."

Carrie was delighted in that suggestion. She filled each glass with champagne and raised hers to toast.

"Here's to a new future. I've found a brother and a new stepmother. I think we all deserve a little happiness from now on."

Epilogue

It was hard to believe it was nearly their first wedding anniversary. Tully had never been happier and fingering the delicate gold necklace he had bought Kate for the occasion gave him great pleasure. He slipped it into the safe in his office and locked the doors of his newspaper. Turning to survey his little kingdom as he switched out the lights he thought what a good investment made here. The paper had gone ahead with him at the helm and with Joe there to guide him in the ways of the locals for the first few months he had been readily accepted, and as Kate's husband, welcomed into the community.

The Soo Ling drug rehab ward was doing good work and they often had people sent down from Sydney to take advantage of the facility. Kate was always hopeful one day Jason would work with her at her hospital but he had his life in Sydney and was happy at St Luke's private where he was a senior medical officer. Lauren had told Kate when they started a family, she would like to move to the country so Kate secretly kept her fingers crossed that it wouldn't be too long.

Kate's charity work kept her busy but she did do a couple of days a week at the clinic.

She still kept her folder of clippings of Tully's stories right from when she had returned from Vietnam. Tully had been dumbstruck when he learned how closely she had followed his career. Nowadays, most of the clippings she added were from Carrie's stories. There was a wonderful full page article just last week from Iraq but Kate knew how much Tully worried about his daughter as Kate did too with her away chasing news. She certainly was her father's daughter.

She had come home late last year to attend Vera's surprise sixtieth birthday party Tully had put on for his older sister and had promised her father she would think about giving up the foreign side of corresponding. Tully kept offering her work here at a comparable salary so who knows, one day they may be all living together at Moruya.

Tully started the motor of his yellow Volvo and headed toward home. He really had a lot to be thankful for these days. He mused over his life and wondered how things would have been if Briony had lived, would they still be in Belfast, and what about the time Carrie had tried to shoot him, accidentally or not on behalf of her Uncle Kevin. Thank God she hadn't. Suddenly he had this perverse idea. First thing tomorrow he would send Kevin O'Rourke a get well card. He wouldn't sign it; he would simply say 'The Sun Has Set.'

Tully sped through the night chuckling at his own sense of humor.

The End

Printed in the United States
by Baker & Taylor Publisher Services